DEMON OF [THE AIR]

'The adventure proves gripping and always surprising, and uses its historical background to perfection. A most rewarding read' *Guardian*

'The tale makes for a neat twist on the historical detective story and is packed full with details of an Aztec world at its height. A formidable debut' *Good Book Guide*

'Fascinatingly complex and unusual, providing intriguing insights into a coherent and brutal society; the language, food, customs and family. I loved the black humour' Conn Iggulden

'An exciting murder mystery mixed with a mordant sense of humour, *Demon of the Air* is one of the few novels to vividly recreate and clearly describe the glorious but bloodsoaked culture of the Aztec empire . . . A marvellous read' Paul Doherty

'The storyline is intriguing, with sufficient wit and humour to balance the bloodthirsty descriptions of torture and brutality that were the norm in Aztec society . . . The writing is excellent, and given the unusual setting and the intriguing "whodunnit" component of the story, I suspect the wily slave Yaotl will join the ranks of Brother Cadfael and Marcus Falco as another favourite historical sleuth' Bernard Knight

About the author

Simon Levack trained as a solicitor and still works in the legal profession. He lives in east London with his wife and son. *Demon of the Air* is his first novel, and won the Crime Writers' Association's prestigious Debut Dagger Award. The sequel, *Shadow of the Lords*, will be published by Simon & Schuster in 2005.

Visit www.simonlevack.com

DEMON
OF THE AIR

SIMON LEVACK

POCKET
BOOKS

LONDON • SYDNEY • NEW YORK • TORONTO

First published in Great Britain by Simon & Schuster UK Ltd, 2004
This edition first published by Pocket Books, 2005
An imprint of Simon & Schuster UK
A Viacom Company

Copyright © Simon Levack, 2004

The right of Simon Levack to be identified as the author of this work has
been asserted by him in accordance with sections 77 and 78 of the
Copyright, Designs and Patents Act, 1988.

Extracts from Bernadino de Sahagun, *The Florentine Codex, A General History of the Things of New Spain*, translated and edited by Arthur J. O. Anderson and Charles E. Dibble, are reproduced by kind permission of the University of Utah Press and the School of American Research.

Extracts from *Fifteen Poets of the Aztec World* by Miguel Leon-Portilla are reproduced by kind permission of the publishers, University of Oklahoma Press.

Extracts from *The Conquest of New Spain* by Bernal Diaz del Castillo, translated by J. M. Cohen, are reproduced by kind permission of the publishers, Penguin Books Ltd.

1 3 5 7 9 10 8 6 4 2

Simon & Schuster UK Ltd
Africa House
64–78 Kingsway
London WC2B 6AH

www.simonsays.co.uk

Simon & Schuster Australia
Sydney

A CIP catalogue record for this book
is available from the British Library

ISBN 0 7434 6814 7

Typeset by M Rules
Printed and bound in Great Britain by
Cox & Wyman Ltd, Reading, Berkshire

For Sarah and Isaac, with love

Acknowledgements

My heartfelt thanks to Lisanne Radice, Jane Gregory and Broo Doherty for their support, guidance and seemingly inexhaustible patience throughout the process of writing this book. It goes without saying that I could not have done it without you!

Also deserving of acknowledgement are the authors and translators whose work I have plundered in my efforts to bring the world of ancient Mexico to life. It would be impossible to list all of them, but there are two works in particular that I must mention. The first is Arthur Anderson's and Charles Dibble's translation of the Florentine Codex, Fray Bernardino de Sahagún's wonderful encyclopaedia of all things Aztec, one volume or another of which has been at my elbow for most of the last two years. The second is Inga Clendinnen's *Aztecs: an Interpretation*. When I first picked this book up a decade or more ago, I had no idea where it would lead me, and it continues to inspire, surprise and occasionally provoke me to this day.

Most of all I must thank my wife, Sarah, for putting up with me during all the years when I was writing for no apparent reward, for her ingenious suggestions and unstinting criticisms, and for only once referring to my novel as 'that bloody book!'

The murderer is cruel, a dog at heart – a dog indeed. He is a hater of people, a trouble-maker, a killer, a spy, a tempter. Daring, he is rash, brutal, disorderly. He bears false witness; he accuses people; he hates, slanders, calumniates, libels them. He strikes, he charges at them; he kills, he leaves his mark on them. He is a demon of the air – a demon. He sheds blood.

The Florentine Codex, Book X

Author's Note

With such wonderful sights to gaze on we did not know what to say, or if this was real that we saw before our eyes. On the land side there were great cities, and on the lake many more. The lake was crowded with canoes. At intervals along the causeway there were many bridges, and before us was the great city of Mexico.

Bernal Diaz del Castillo,
The Conquest of New Spain

On 8 November 1519 the Conquistadors, led by Hernan Cortés, entered the Aztec capital, Mexico-Tenochtitlan. They were astonished by what they saw, these first Europeans to set eyes on the greatest city of the New World. Their astonishment can only have grown in the succeeding days and months, fuelled by the sight of the whitewashed houses, the gardens, the temples, the palaces, the markets and above all the sheer numbers of people milling around them. The twin cities of Tenochtitlan and Tlatelolco alone were home to more men and women than the Spaniards would ever have seen in one place, and daily perhaps as many more would have poured onto the island the cities stood on, either by canoe across the surface of its surrounding lake or on foot via the causeways linking it to the shore, bringing tribute or produce or goods to trade in its markets.

The Conquistadors would have been still more amazed if they had appreciated that the vast metropolis before them had been founded less than two hundred years before by a wandering tribe of despised barbarians, and that the mighty empire whose heart it was had existed for less than a century. The Aztecs did not live in some ancient, decadent, ossified society: theirs was a young, vigorous state, still expanding and seeking new conquests, and it would have carried on growing but for the irruption of Cortés and his men.

Within two years of that day in 1519 – on 13 August 1521, to be exact – it was all over. Nearly all the magnificent buildings that had so impressed the Spaniards were reduced to rubble, and in the struggle to possess them many of their inhabitants had perished – of European diseases such as smallpox, to which native Americans had no immunity, of hunger or thirst as the invaders besieged their city and cut off its water, or of Toledo steel.

But this novel is not about the conquest. It is about the conquered: the extraordinary people we call the Aztecs, whose own name for themselves was the Mexica, or Mexicans. It is a modest attempt to bring their city back to life in all its beauty and brutality: from the poetry and flowers and exquisite feather-work they adored to the human blood they believed they had to shed to pay their debt to the gods.

It opens nearly two years before Cortés's arrival, in the winter of 1517, the year the Aztecs called Twelve House. This was the year when a Spanish expedition first made contact with the Mayans in the Yucatán peninsula, and rumours of pale-skinned men with beards began to trouble the dreams of Montezuma, the Emperor of Mexico.

THE AZTEC EMPIRE

THE POSITION OF THE AZTEC EMPIRE

U.S.A.

MEXICO

Gulf of Mexico

TOTONACS

OTOMIES

VALLEY OF MEXICO

TARASCAN EMPIRE

CHICHIMECS

TLAXCALTECS

MAZAHUAS

MATLATZINCAS

Texcala

TLAPANECS

CUITLATECS

YOPI

MIXTECS

ZAPOTECS

Xicallanco

MAYANS

Xoconochco

TOTONACS

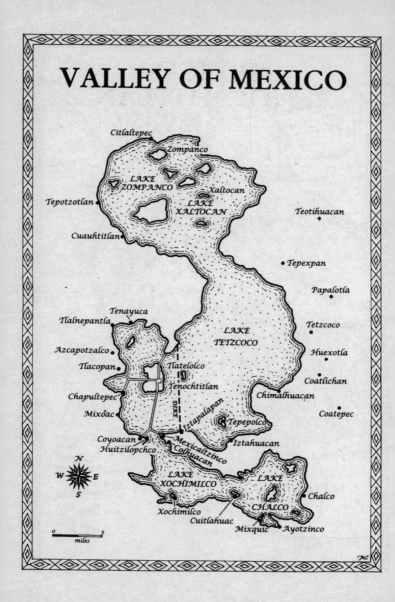

VALLEY OF MEXICO

Citlaltepec

Zompanco

LAKE
ZOMPANCO

Xaltocan

LAKE
XALTOCAN

Tepotzotlan

Teotihuacan

Cuauhtitlan

Tepexpan

Papalotla

Tenayuca

Tlalnepantla

Tetzcoco

LAKE
TETZCOCO

Azcapotzalco

Huexotla

Tlacopan

Tlatelolco

Tenochtitlan

Coatlichan

Chapultepec

Chimalhuacan

Mixôac

Coatepec

Iztapalapan

Tepepolco

Coyoacan
Huitzilopchco

Mexicaltzinco

Iztahuacan

Cohuacan

LAKE
XOCHIMILCO

LAKE
CHALCO

N
W   E
S

Chalco

Xochimilco

CHALCO

Cuitlahuac

Mixquic

Ayotzinco

0   5
miles

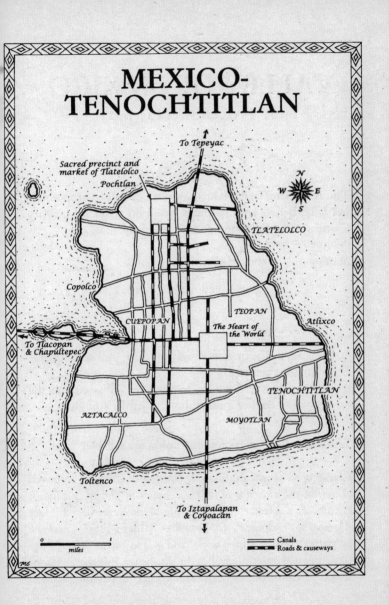

MEXICO-
TENOCHTITLAN

To Tepeyac

Sacred precinct and
market of Tlatelolco

Pochtlan

N
W   E
S

TLATELOLCO

Copolco

TEOPAN

CUEPOPAN

The Heart of
the World

Atlixco

To Tlacopan
& Chapultepec

TENOCHTITLAN

AZTACALCO

MOYOTLAN

Toltenco

To Iztapalapan
& Coyoacan

0   1
miles

Canals
Roads & causeways

A Note on Nahuatl

The Aztec language, Nahuatl, is not difficult to pronounce, but is burdened with spellings based on sixteenth-century Castilian. The following note should help:

Spelling	Pronunciation
c	c as in 'Cecil' before e or i; k before a or o
ch	sh
x	sh
hu, uh	w
qu	k as in 'kettle' before e or i; 'qu' as in 'quack' before a
tl	as in English, but where '-tl' occurs at the end of a word the 'l' is hardly sounded.

The stress always falls on the penultimate syllable.

I have used as few Nahuatl words as possible and favoured clarity at the expense of strict accuracy in choosing English equivalents. Hence, for example, I have rendered *Huey Tlatoani* as 'Emperor', *Cihuacoatl* as 'Chief Minister', *calpolli* as 'parish', *octli* as 'sacred wine' and *maquahuitl* as 'sword', and have been similarly cavalier in choosing English replacements for most of the frequently recurring personal names.

In referring to the Emperor at the time when this story is set I have used the most familiar form of his name, Montezuma, although Motecuhzoma would be more accurate. To avoid confusion I have called the people of Mexico-Tenochtitlan 'Aztecs' rather than 'Mexicans'.

The name of the principal character in the novel, Yaotl, is pronounced 'YAH-ot'.

The Aztec Calendar

The Aztecs lived in a world governed by religion and magic, and their rituals and auguries were in turn ordered by the calendar.

The solar year, which began in our February, was divided into eighteen twenty-day periods (often called 'months'). Each month had its own religious observances associated with it; often these involved sacrifices, some of them human, to one or more of the many Aztec gods. At the end of the year were five 'Useless Days' that were considered profoundly unlucky.

Parallel to this ran a divinatory calendar of 260 days divided into twenty groups of thirteen days (sometimes called 'weeks'). The first day in the 'week' would bear the number 1 and one of twenty names – Reed, Jaguar, Eagle, Vulture and so on. The second day would bear the number 2 and the next name in the sequence. On the fourteenth day the number would revert to 1 but the sequence of names continued seamlessly, with each combination of names and numbers repeating itself every 260 days.

A year was named after the day in the divinatory calendar on which it began. For mathematical reasons these days could bear only one of four names – Reed, Flint Knife, House and Rabbit – combined with a number from 1 to 13. This produced a cycle of fifty-two years at the beginning and end of which the solar and divinatory calendars coincided. The Aztecs called this period a 'Bundle of Years'.

Every day in a Bundle of Years was the product of a unique combination of year, month and date in the divinatory calendar, and so had, for the Aztecs, its own individual character and religious and magical significance.

The date on which this book opens is 9 December 1517; in other words, Thirteen Grass in the week beginning One Flower, the twentieth and last day of the Month of the Raising of Banners, in the year Twelve House.

THIRTEEN GRASS

1

Blood lay in layers on the steps near the summit of the Great Pyramid, the afternoon's flowing over the morning's, the fresh over the dry. My bare foot struck it with a wet slap and came up again with a sound like thin cotton tearing.

Two temples crowned the Pyramid: Huitzilopochtli's, the war-god's, on the right, and Tlaloc's, the rain-god's, on the left.

This evening the blood seeping down the steps belonged to the war-god. It was the annual Festival of the Raising of Banners, when a treat awaited the Fire Priest and his flint knife: something more than the usual shuffling lines of anonymous captives. Today, the merchants, the long-distance traders known as Pochteca, presented their gifts to the god: strong, beautiful dancers, the pick of the slaves in the market, selected, pampered and trained for months to make their last day on Earth a flawless masterpiece.

'You've seen more sacrifices than I have, Yaotl. Did you ever see one go like this before?' The man climbing beside me had a gruff voice made gruffer by the effort of lugging a heavy burden up the side of the Pyramid. He was called Momaimati, and he had the solid, useful look that went with his name, which meant One Skilled with his Hands or, as I thought of him, 'Handy'.

We were so near the top of the pyramid that we had to stop and wait while, just above our heads, the priests ended a man's time on earth and scattered his blood to the four Directions. The rich merchant who had paid for the victim and escorted him all the way to the sacrificial stone looked on like a proud father at a wedding.

I knew a hundred ways to die. I had seen maimed, glazed-eyed prisoners of war stumbling insensibly to their fate and captured nobles clinging to their dignity to the end, and even a few mad creatures dancing up the steps crying out brave nonsense about the sweetness of the Flowery Death. No two were ever the same.

'No,' I admitted, 'I never did.'

Behind us a little party trudged up the steps: the next victim and his sponsor, a timid-looking merchant got up in the finery of a seasoned warrior, with his much more fero-cious-looking wife on his arm. Their sacrifice was on his feet, though, and apart from his shaven head and the deathly pallor of his skin might have been any slave or retainer run-ning an errand.

I looked ruefully down at our own offering. I was cradling a dead man's head in the crook of my arm so that it would not flop about so obviously. The bloody mush at his temple would be harder to hide than the broken neck, I thought, but I doubted the priests would be fooled either way.

The only escort this one would have on his last journey would be Handy and I: a common man and a slave. The affable young man who had sponsored him had disappeared, along with the rest of his entourage, scattering as quickly as frightened birds when their carefully prepared, expensive victim had run amok. We had dragged the body halfway back up the pyramid from where we had found it, broken by its fall, only to find the rest of our party vanished like mist over the lake and ourselves left with nothing to offer the war-god and his bloodthirsty minions except a human sacrifice who was already dead.

A novice signalled to us from the top of the steps.

'I'll let you do the talking,' Handy grunted, as he picked up the corpse's feet.

'Let's try and keep him upright,' I hissed. 'Maybe they won't notice.'

Smells assailed my nostrils and it was hard to say which of them was the worst. The priests had not bathed for months and gave off a miasma of blood and stale sweat that not even the sweet resinous odour of the temple fires could mask, but what was truly appalling was the stench of putrefying offal that hung in the air around them: the smell of decaying human hearts, torn out of the breasts of sacrificial victims, cast, still beating, into the Eagle Vessel, and left there to rot. I could all too easily imagine my own among them. Slaves, unless they had been bought for the purpose, were not usually killed, but when the priests saw what we had brought them, I was afraid they might be angry enough to make an exception.

Handy and I each got an arm under the sacrifice's shoulders and heaved him forward. Apart from his feet dragging on the stones between us and his head lolling on each of our shoulders in turn, I told myself, he looked convincingly alive.

'What's the matter with him?' demanded the novice who had signalled to us.

'Passed out,' I said. 'They do that, don't they? It's the sacred wine they make them drink.'

'He's not passed out. He's dead,' the novice stated flatly.

'Dead?' Handy had decided to play dumb.

'It looks to me,' said one of the older priests, 'like he fell down the steps trying to make a run for it. I wondered what all the fuss was about down there.'

'Perhaps he slipped.' I was running out of excuses.

'So he ran away. How can we offer up a creature like this to the war-god?'

There were six priests up here, grouped around the altar in front of the temple. Five of them wore short ceremonial capes and feathered head-fans hung with pasted paper pendants, and had their cheeks painted with red ochre. Among them was the Fire Priest, whose rôle in the proceedings was all too obvious from the enormous, bloody, glistening flint knife he bore.

It was not the knife which made me nervous, however, but the sight of the sixth priest, the one the others kept looking at for their cue, a man resplendent in a flowing cloak of blue-green quetzal feathers and a towering, shimmering quetzal feather headdress, with a turquoise rod through his nose and an obsidian mirror on his chest. When this man glared at Handy and me, the bars on his cheeks and the star design painted around his eyes rippled menacingly. He was in charge today and he was not happy. As the representative of Peynal, the war-god's lieutenant, he had just run a circuit of the city, from the sacred precinct all the way up to Tlatelolco and back again, killing several sacrificial victims on the way, and this after an eighty-day fast. Had he not been hungry, exhausted and very irritable he would not have been human, and if a man in Peynal's position felt slighted then events could quickly turn nasty.

'The war-god,' he growled, 'needs his nourishment.'

I swallowed. Needing inspiration, I looked across to the temple of Tlaloc.

I thought I saw a movement in its shadow.

Without sparing the time to think I called out: 'Hey, you! What are you laughing at?'

Seven heads snapped round to follow my glance. Only the dead man kept his eyes on the floor.

For long moments nothing happened. The summit of the Pyramid, so far above the bustle of the city, was as silent as a mountain top. We were not a people given to raising our voices and my calling out seemed to have shocked the air into stillness. Then, just as seven pairs of eyes began turning back towards me and questions began to form on seven pairs of lips, a man stepped out of the shadows.

His gaunt face was stained black with soot, black blood stuck to his temples and he wore a black cloak: a priest of the rain-god, Tlaloc.

He stared at us, his eyes narrowed in an expression that I might have taken for curiosity if I had not noticed a barely perceptible movement at the corners of his mouth.

He was indeed laughing at us.

I stared back at him, savouring the sight and letting it register with the blood-soaked men around me. The rain-god's priest looked away and pointed towards us, and soon he was joined by another, also laughing and gesturing.

As innocently as I could, I asked: 'Who are they, then?'

A priest of Huitzilopochtli answered me without taking his eyes off his neighbours. 'They're nothing. Ignore them.'

'Why do you think they're laughing?' I persisted.

The two priests of Tlaloc were clowning around, one of them rolling his head about in an imitation of a man with a broken neck while the other made mock stabbing motions towards his chest.

'Because they don't know any better,' growled the Fire Priest.

'They love seeing us made fools of,' said the novice who

had first called us forward. 'One of the biggest days of the year, a queue of rich merchants waiting on the steps, the Emperor and everyone down there in the sacred precinct, watching – and we're dithering over a stiff!'

Two of his elders started speaking at once. One raised an arm, probably to make a point rather than do violence to anyone, but Peynal stepped sharply round the altar to restrain him. One of the men from the neighbouring temple had fallen over and was slapping the stuccoed floor in a display of exaggerated mirth.

One of the war-god's priests snapped. Shaking a fist at the rain-god's temple, he roared, 'Shut up, you!' in a voice they could have heard on the far shore of the lake.

His colleagues stared at him.

The embarrassed silence was broken by a cough, just a little too loud to be called respectful. There was a procession on the steps behind us, and every member of it, one way or another, was impatient for his moment of glory. I heard a female voice remark in an audible whisper that if these idiots did not get a move on there was not going to be much of a feast. There would scarcely be time to get their slave's remains back home to Tlatelolco, let alone cook him, and no way was she eating him raw.

Peynal scowled, distorting the bars and stars on his face still further. He was sweating. A moment longer and his paint would start to run. His mouth twitched dangerously.

'He didn't try to run away,' I protested desperately. 'He slipped. It was an accident. It was our fault. We are clumsy and stupid. He was too strong for us, truly worthy of the god.'

The priests looked unconvinced. They seemed more interested in their neighbours' antics.

'Those bastards are laughing at us. One of these days . . .'

'Please,' I begged, 'we've brought the war-god an offer-ing. It's not much but it's all we have. He will have his fill of hearts this evening. Can't you accept this one, even if it isn't beating?'

Peynal seemed to come to a decision. He gestured sharply at the Fire Priest. 'Get on with it and get them out of here!'

Then everything happened very fast.

The priests pulled the corpse from our grasp and a moment later had it stretched over the sacrificial stone with one holding each arm and leg and the chest arching towards the sky. The Fire Priest stood over it for a moment, his lips moving swiftly through the words of a hymn. He bran-dished his blade high over his head and brought it down with both hands.

It crunched into the chest and the whole body bucked in the hands of the other priests as if in a death throe. They were used to the real thing, though – to men who fought for life to the end or whose bodies fought on for them afterwards – and they clung on while the knife rose and fell again.

There was no fountain of blood when the heart came out, just an inert lump of raw meat that the Fire Priest tossed disdainfully into the Eagle Vessel without sparing it a glance.

They dragged the body off the stone by its feet. They took it to the edge of the steps – the great, broad flight that we had toiled up – and threw it away with an easy swing born of years of practice before turning silently back in our direction.

The silence endured.

The six priests stared at Handy and me. Peynal's eyes were narrow with disgust. The Fire Priest shook his flint knife absently, to flick some of the blood off it, and I felt some of the warm fluid splash my face and run slowly down my cheek.

I was suddenly aware of the space between the priests and us. Now that the dead man's cored body had been cast so contemptuously aside, there was nothing in that space but the rapidly chilling evening air and the ugly angular blood-stained hump of the sacrificial stone.

Handy and I looked at each other uncertainly.

Peynal shot a brief, contemptuous glance at the steps his acolytes had thrown the body down, before turning back to us.

'You're going the same way he did,' he spat.

Without looking at each other, Handy and I both took a step backwards. I found myself on the very edge of the temple platform with a void beneath my heels. A squawk of alarm from behind me reminded me that there were people waiting on the top stair.

One of the priests started towards me. He stopped to look uncertainly back at Peynal, and that gave Handy and me our chance.

The big commoner darted sideways and leapt down the pyramid steps. I followed him, my feet slithering on fresh blood, until I found myself staggering at the very top of the World's most terrifying staircase. The vast expanse of the sacred precinct we called the Heart of the World wheeled sickeningly below me, and when I looked up the setting Sun's bloody glare swamped my vision.

I hurled myself blindly down the face of the pyramid.

2

Handy and I ran from the Fire Priest's flint knife as fast as we could, alternately bounding down the steep narrow steps and sliding through the slick of blood that covered them.

We caught up with the remains of our sacrifice where they had come to rest, two-thirds of the way down. We were too tired and badly winded to run any further by then, and our panic was beginning to subside. In its place came anger and resentment and as there was no one else about we took them out on the corpse, shoving and kicking it the rest of the way to the base of the Great Pyramid, where the butchers were waiting for it.

As the bodies came bumping down to the bottom of the steps they were promptly hauled to one side and dismembered by burly men wielding knives of flint and obsidian. At times like this, when there were so many victims, the butchers had to work rapidly to keep up with the priests at the Pyramid's summit. They hacked off the head, to be flayed and mounted on the skull rack. They took a little more care over the left arm, stretching it out and severing it as neatly as they could, as it was going to the palace to feed the Emperor and his guests. They discarded the trunk, as a man's entrails and offal were thought fit only for the beasts in the Emperor's zoo. The remaining limbs were placed in a neat pile, ready for the victim's owner to come and take them home, where they would be cooked up into a stew with maize and beans and eaten at a ritual banquet.

Handy and I expected to find the affable young man there, among the crowd of people waiting to collect their offerings, but there was no sign of him.

'Have you seen Ocotl, the merchant?' I asked one of the butchers.

'Are these his, then?' Blood dripped from the man's fingers as he gestured towards a pair of legs and an arm lying next to him. 'You'd better take them quick, before they get mixed up with someone else's!'

'No, you don't understand, I'm looking for . . .'

Behind me, a series of soft thumps announced the next victim's arrival at the foot of the stairway. I stepped aside hastily as the butcher made as if to push me out of the way. 'Look, take your meat and bugger off, will you? Some of us have work to do!'

I caught Handy's eye and between us we carried the severed limbs to a quieter spot at the edge of the crowd. We waited for the merchant there, but still he failed to appear.

'The young fool will have to go without his supper,' Handy observed eventually. 'Not that there was much eating on this one anyway.'

We both looked dispassionately at the arm and legs.

It was hard to associate them with the living, breathing person we had seen die just a little while earlier, but I knew that was part of the process, the victim's dismemberment, the final step in his obliteration as a human being.

Not for the first time that day, it occurred to me that there was something not quite right about our offering. His arms and legs looked too skinny to be a dancer's, and the skin, exposed now, with most of the chalk dust that had been used to give it a corpse-like pallor knocked or rubbed off, was covered in wounds of all kinds: scratches, punctures, bruises, and a few marks that looked like burns.

'It doesn't look very appetizing,' I mumbled non-committally. Not all the marks could have been made by the fall, I realised, and some must be a few days old at least, as they looked half healed. How could that be, I wondered, when I knew the merchants insisted on physical perfection when they selected their victims?

'Never acquired the taste, myself,' Handy said. 'I know it's only polite to have a mouthful, if someone from your parish brings home a captive, but give me a slice of turkey or dog any day.' He turned his back on the severed limbs and started rummaging in a cloth bag he had brought with him. 'I could do with something to eat now, though. Tell you what. I've a tortilla left over from lunch. We'll split it, and you can tell me what that was all about.'

I glanced doubtfully up at the Pyramid. The blue and red of the temples at its summit still gleamed vividly in the sunshine, but the line of shadow creeping up the bloodstained steps told me it was not long before nightfall.

'Just a bite, maybe. I have to get back. Can't keep my master waiting.'

We left the merchant's offering where it lay, for want of any better idea of what to do with it. I gave the pathetic pile of flesh a last look as we walked across the Heart of the World towards the marketplace, but nobody came to collect it, even though I lingered as long as I decently could, still wondering about those strange marks.

We sat beside the canal that bordered the marketplace and munched on our round, flat bread.

'I only know what I was told,' I said, 'which isn't much. Go to the merchant's house, join the procession, make sure the sacrifice goes according to plan. My master wanted me there because I know how these things are done. I guess he owed the young man's family a favour. Do you suppose he expected this to happen?'

Handy curled his lip. 'How should I know?' He glanced over his shoulder at a corner of the now deserted market-place where bearers and day-labourers could be found squatting at daybreak, plying for hire. 'They took me on as an escort the day before yesterday. They needed an extra pair of hands, in case the offering got frisky. Muscle, you know.' Flesh flowed suggestively under the brown skin of his arms, making me glance wistfully at the bony claws holding my food. 'Not much to do in the fields today, so I came here. Too many mouths to feed to be sitting around idle at home. Some young lad came up to me and told me I'd do.'

I had found Ocotl and Handy that morning at daybreak, waiting by the short, stumpy pyramid of the parish temple in Pochtlan, one of the merchants' parishes in Tlatelolco, the northern part of the city.

Ocotl sported an amber lip-plug, green shell-shaped ear pendants and a netted cape, and carried his feather fan and feathered staves with the assurance of a veteran warrior. He was tall for an Aztec, although it was hard to tell what he looked like beneath all his finery; and he had the cheerful, cocksure manner of the young. His name meant a pine torch, or, figuratively, a Shining Light, one who led an exemplary life.

Handy wore what had once been his best clothes – an embroidered breechcloth with trailing ends, a little frayed at the edges, and a two-captive warrior's orange cloak that had lost much of its colour.

There were two servants, too, whose sole charge was the

heap of fine-looking cloaks that Shining Light had brought along in case he needed them for his slave's ransom. He needed these because his offering's last journey to the war-god's temple was not going to be a straightforward one. While the priest dressed as Peynal ran his exhausting circuit of the city, all the offerings due to be presented by the merchants would be conducted first to the parish temple at Coatlan, where a crowd of warrior captives would be waiting in ritual ambush.

The ambush was a curious part of the day's proceedings, whose meaning I had never really understood, unless it was simply to teach the merchants that everything worth having had to be fought for, notwithstanding that they had already paid forty cloaks for it at the slave market. The warrior captives – men who were themselves due to die before sunset – would do their best to take the merchants' offerings away from them, and the doomed slaves were expected to defend themselves with shields and obsidian-studded swords. It was a real fight, fuelled on both sides by sacred wine and the courage of despair, and if a warrior captive managed to get a slave he would kill him unless the slave's owner paid a ransom to the warrior's captor. The ransom was always paid, since otherwise the merchant would have nothing to offer the war-god, and all his expensive preparations would have gone to waste.

One look at the slave himself convinced me that his owner must have little notion of the value of money.

He was not an impressive sight. He had been made to keep vigil at the temple all night and then plied with drink. His hair had gone at midnight and the fine clothes he had been given the night before had been taken away at dawn, when his face had been washed and his skin covered with chalk to give it a deathly pallor. Now he looked twitchy and

febrile, starting even at the gentle voice of the woman who
attended him, his bather, as she whispered soothing words
into his ear. There was not even a suggestion of the dancer
he must once have been in his spindly arms and legs and
even though the chalk hid the marks on his skin he had one
obvious physical blemish. His ears stuck out of his head at a
ludicrous angle, like wings.

There was no time for talking as we took our places in
the procession but I watched the sacrifice closely. He shuffled along, making no response to the constant chatter of the
old woman walking beside him, with his eyes fixed on the
road ahead.

At Coatlan, he mutely accepted a shield and an obsidian-
studded sword when they were pressed into his hands but
made no use of them. That was not altogether surprising:
sometimes the sacred wine made the victims fight like
wounded jaguars, but you never could tell what they would
do in advance. What struck me, as Handy and I led him
back to his master with our ears still full of the warrior captives' jeers, was the young merchant's indifference to losing
his ransom. There had been enough cloth there to keep me
in some style for two years.

Peynal's arrival at the head of a crowd of panting follow-
ers stopped the fight and began the victims' final journey to
the foot of the Great Pyramid, where the Emperor sat before
a great crowd to watch the war-god receive his due.

Our slave acted his part with the others as they ran or
staggered four times around the Pyramid's base before lining
up meekly at the bottom of the steps. He watched in silence
while Peynal ran to the top, and the sacrificial papers and the
paper, cloth and feather image of the Fire-Serpent were
brought down and burned. He said nothing as Peynal
descended once more to show the war-god's image to the

victims before leading them to their deaths at the summit of
the Pyramid.

It was only on the way up that things began to go awry.

Shining Light, the victim and his bather mounted the
steps side by side, with Handy and me behind them. I could
not take my eyes off those absurd ears. The bather had fallen
silent at last, but the merchant kept up a cheerful banter.

'Not long now. How I envy you! The Flowery Death! To
dance attendance on the Sun and be reborn as a hummingbird, a butterfly! I spend my days scratching around like a
turkey after corn, and when I die I will go to the Land of the
Dead like every other wretched soul, but you . . .'

'Can't see him shouldering the Sun's palanquin, myself,'
Handy mumbled. 'You could count to twenty on his backbone. It would help if he held his head up, but he looks all
in to me. I thought the merchants were choosier . . . Look
out! There he goes!'

The slave fooled us. Instead of running down the steps,
and so blundering straight into us, or simply racing up them,
where there was no escape and one of us would have caught
him almost immediately, he broke sideways to dart across the
broad face of the Pyramid. He had gone ten paces before
Handy and I were after him.

The young merchant kept climbing, seemingly enjoying
his moment so much that he failed to notice that his offering had escaped. The bather just stood and stared after her
charge.

'Come back here, you . . .!' Handy roared as he dashed
after the sacrifice.

We raced along the narrow steps with a hopping gait,
each foot on a different level, and if the gods have a sense of
humour then some at least must have been laughing. It took
an agonizingly long time for our quarry to run out of space

and find himself looking out over the steep side of the
Pyramid from between two of the stone banner-holders that
lined the stairway.

I knew he was going to jump.

'Listen to me, all of you!' he cried, as though the whole
vast teeming city spread out beneath him could hear. 'It's the
boat — the big boat! Look for the big boat!'

'Wait!' I said, desperately. What could I say to a man
who was about to die, no matter what he or I might do? I
tried to make out his expression, but against the background
of the evening sky and the lake shining like gold in the
sunset he was just a shadow with large ears.

'You mustn't jump. You're destined for the war-god — you
heard your master, you're going to join the morning Sun . . .'

The Bathed Slave turned back towards me then, twisting
and stepping backwards at the same time, so that he was
poised on the edge of the steps.

'It's a lie,' he said quietly. 'Bathed Slaves go to the Land of
the Dead, like everyone else.'

When he smiled his teeth showed white among the shadows of his face.

'Just tell the old man,' he said.

I dived for his feet, almost going over myself as I crashed
onto the stones where he had been — but he had taken his
last step and was lying, broken, far below me.

3

I sometimes forget how much has happened since the days when the priests used to sacrifice to the gods at the summit of the Great Pyramid. No doubt the old ways now seem strange and barbaric, and people wonder what it was all about, and why so many like Shining Light's slave had to die under the Fire Priest's flint knife.

This is what we were taught.

The World had been destroyed four times: once by ravening jaguars, once by the wind, once by a rain of fire and once by a flood. In each disaster the people had perished or been transformed beyond recognition, and so after the flood, at the beginning of the present age, the gods had to populate the Earth anew.

After the last catastrophe they sent one of their number, Quetzalcoatl, the Feathered Serpent, down into Hell to gather up the bones of the dead. This he did, despite the Lord of the Dead's best efforts to stop him, but even after he had retrieved the bones and given them to the goddess Cihuacoatl to be ground up into powder, there was still no life in them. He had to slit his member and add his own blood to the powder to make it into a paste from which the first man and woman could be moulded, and all the other gods then had to do likewise. The gods gave their blood to give us life, and our debt to them could only be repaid with blood.

What is more, we believed that without the daily tribute of human hearts, the Sun would not move through the sky. This part of the story went like this: after men and women had been created, the World was still in darkness, and so the gods gathered to recreate the Sun. They built a great pyre, which burned for four days. Then they called on a splendid, richly adorned god named Tecuhciztecatl to leap into the fire to be burned and reborn as the Sun. However, the fire was too hot, and while this magnificent god hesitated, shrinking from the fierce flames, the despised, wizened, pimply and disgusting god Nanahuatzin leapt past him into the inferno. As Nanahuatzin's flesh blistered and split in the fire, shame overcame the splendid god's fear and he jumped onto the pyre as well. Thus Nanahuatzin was reborn as the Sun and Tecuhciztecatl as the Moon. At first each was as bright as the other, but the other gods threw a rabbit in the Moon's face to dim his light, and we still see the rabbit's shape on the Moon's face to this day.

So now the Sun and the Moon had been born, but they would not rise. They merely sat on the horizon, wobbling uncertainly from side to side, until the remaining gods sacrificed themselves to give them the energy they needed to move through the sky. Quetzalcoatl cut the other gods' hearts out one by one, throwing them into the fire before at last leaping into it himself. Then the first day began, thanks to the self-sacrifice of the gods, and we believed that we had to follow their example, for the day the gods were denied their feast of human hearts and blood was the day the World would end.

But we were like gods ourselves! No Aztec, not even the Emperor, believed himself to be a god, but surely we and the gods were partners in the never-ending struggle to sustain the Sun in his progress through the sky. Why else had the gods elevated our city over all its rivals, to be the greatest in the World? Why else were our armies sent forth, but to gather captives for sacrifice – for the Flowery Death, as we called it? Why else did we join in the gods' feasting, eating the flesh of those who died on the killing stone even while the gods were consuming their hearts?

Hence it was not our own breasts which were torn open to satisfy the gods. We gave our own blood freely enough, and all Aztecs took part in this, piercing our earlobes with cactus spines whenever we were called upon to repay a little of what we owed. Our priests used to go further, slitting their tongues and penises with obsidian knives and drawing ropes through them, and presenting the bloodied ropes as a mark of their devotion. But the most precious offering of all, the gift of hearts that made the Sun rise, came mostly from captive enemy warriors and slaves bought for the purpose.

Enemy warriors were the most prized victims and the greater a man's prowess in battle the more the gods would savour his heart when they tasted it. The Aztec warrior who captured a distinguished opponent and presented him to be sacrificed could expect great rewards: lavish gifts from the Emperor's hand, for instance, the right to wear cotton and sandals in the city and have his hair arranged in a certain style, the right to eat at the Emperor's palace and get drunk on sacred wine. Above all he would have what all Aztecs craved: fame and the chance to vaunt himself in front of his fellows.

Some slaves, however, were almost as valuable as captured warriors. These were the Bathed Slaves, purchased at great expense and pampered and groomed and bathed until they were a credit to their masters and a worthy gift for the god they were to die for. It was a great honour to be allowed to present one of these slaves. It meant shouldering some of the burden of the debt we all owed to the gods. It meant being allowed to play at being a mighty warrior for a day.

No group within the city competed more fiercely than the merchants for the privilege of presenting a Bathed Slave. No matter how wealthy he was, the merchant's demeanour was habitually modest, marked by a cloak of coarse maguey fibre cloth instead of cotton, long, loose hair like a commoner's and bare feet instead of sandals. In a city where wealth earned through trade, rather than as a reward for great deeds on the battlefield, was viewed with a mixture of envy and contempt, this assumed humility was only prudent. Once in a while, however, a few selected merchants were allowed to dress up as warriors and present expensive slaves for sacrifice as if they had personally dragged them home from the wars. Such an occasion was the war-god Huitzilopochtli's great festival of the Raising of Banners.

I knew what elaborate preparations the young man who had presented our offering would have made for this festival. He would have gone to Azcapotzalco, the town on the mainland that boasted the World's greatest slave market, where he would have picked his man out from among the strongest and most beautiful the dealers had to offer. There, he would have found him displayed in the finest cotton and the softest leather sandals, with his lower lip pierced by an amber shaft and amber pendants hanging from his ears, all of which finery the dealer would strip off him the moment a sale was completed. The slave would have been put through his paces. The merchant would have squeezed his muscles, looked into his eyes and mouth, inspected his body for bruises, scars and wens, and watched him dance to the beat of a two-toned drum. A good dancer was worth a

fortune, and our young merchant may have had to part
with thirty or forty of the large capes we used for money to
secure him.

Then he would have led his slave home, barefoot now
and dressed in common rough maguey fibre instead of
cotton, and shut him in a wooden cage.

I sometimes wondered what made so many of these
Bathed Slaves go unprotesting to their deaths. No doubt
some really believed our poets when they sang of the sweetness of a Flowery Death, and looked forward to joining the
dead warriors who escorted the Sun towards his zenith and
were afterwards reborn on earth as hummingbirds or butterflies. Others probably just resigned themselves, but I
suspected that for many, caught up in the ritual of preparation for the festival, whatever they may have been and done
in their previous lives – all the decisions and mistakes and
accidents that had led to their being paraded before prospec-
tive buyers in the market – it must all have seemed remote
and strange, and the Fire Priest's flint knife the only thing of
substance that remained.

The Bathed Slave was given a fine new cotton cape and
breechcloth, along with a long curved labret, pointed quetzal feathers to put in his ears, rattles made of ocelot skin and
seashell for his ankles and strips of gold, turquoise, coral and
obsidian to bind in his hair. He was given tobacco tubes and
flowers and good food. Then he was made to dance.

For four nights he danced to the sound of drums, gliding
sinuously through the steps of the Snake Dance before the
admiring gazes of the young merchant's family and invited
guests. On the third night he was given more clothes and
adornments: a long, feather-bordered jacket, coloured blue,
black and red and decorated with skulls and bones, a feather
headdress, dyed turquoise with white pendants, obsidian

sandals, brightly painted wooden earplugs, falcon wings made of paper. These were sacred, and the man who put them on must have felt himself changed, a step further down the road towards his own death and transfiguration.

On that third night, also, he met his companions on that road – the escorts hired to stop him running away at the last minute, the priest who would supervise his vigil during his last night on Earth and his bather, the grotesquely motherly old woman who would tenderly wash his face, cosset him and speak soothingly to him and be with him constantly, up to the moment of his death.

On the fourth night he was taken to the merchant's parish temple. He was made to drink sacred wine, laced with sacred mushrooms – what we called obsidian wine. Drunk, he staggered through one last dance until midnight.

Then they cut off his hair.

How you wore your hair mattered in Mexico. Along with your clothes, it was the measure of who you were and what you had done. Tangled hair, matted with sacrificial blood, was the mark of a priest. Commoners and merchants wore their hair long and loose. An unbloodied youth, who had yet to take a captive in war, had a big tuft of hair on the back of his head, which was shaved – all but for a single lock on the right side – when he took part in his first capture; and the last lock was taken when he took his first enemy warrior unaided. After that his hairstyle revealed his achievements in war, and a stranger could tell you what a man had done just by looking at the top of his head. A tonsure meant he had never taken a captive unaided while a mass of hair piled on top of his head in the style we called 'stone pillar' meant he had taken at least two. Our mightiest and most feared warriors, the Shorn Ones, wore their hair in a stiff crest on one side only.

To cut off a mature man's hair was not simply to humiliate him. It was to deny him any status at all. The moment the Bathed Slave's hair was taken, he ceased to exist. From that moment, he was already dead.

4

In the West, the souls of mothers who had died in childbirth were bearing the Sun down into the Land of the
Dead.

'Time to go.' Handy tucked the uneaten portion of his
food away in his lunch bag. 'Always save a bit for the children,' he explained.

I stared into the darkening water at our feet, watching the
reflected light from the temple fires above us as it broke up
and put itself back together in the wake of a passing canoe.

'Wonder why he did it?' I mused.

He yawned. 'Nothing to lose, I suppose. Maybe he
thought he might as well save himself a climb.' He got up,
letting his cloak fall over his knees. 'Don't know what all that
crap was about a big boat, though. What's that got to do
with anything? And what was that about Bathed Slaves
going to the Land of the Dead – is that right?'

'It is. They don't join the morning Sun's retinue like captured warriors. Mind you,' I added thoughtfully, 'we don't
tell them that, naturally. I wonder how he knew?'

'And I wonder who the old man is we were supposed to
tell.'

'I don't know. Still, I wasn't talking about the slave. I
meant that young merchant, Shining Light. The last thing
the merchants' chiefs would have wanted to see representing

them in front of the Emperor and everybody is a scrawny creature like that slave he bought. Having to watch him jump off the side of the Pyramid will have provoked them beyond endurance.' Gestures like that were not appreciated in Mexico, where even those appointed to die were expected to play their part in the ritual drama of our festivals, in return for the honour of a Flowery Death. It was shameful to cheat the gods of their due, as Shining Light's slave had done. 'That young man must know how much trouble he's in now. He'll be lucky if he can ever show his face in the city again. What made him choose that slave? It doesn't make sense.'

'Well, that's a good thing about only hiring yourself out by the day,' Handy said, pointedly. 'I won't have to worry about it in the morning.'

'I know.' I stood up with a sigh, just as the distant mournful warbling of a conch-shell trumpet signalled sunset. 'I don't really care either, I just want to know how I'm going to explain this to my master.'

How *was* I going to explain this to my master? I rehearsed the scene as I headed home, imagining myself stumbling through my account of the day's events as I squatted respectfully in front of the old man and waited for his gathering incredulity and wrath to break over me like a storm.

Slaves in Mexico had many rights, for we were sacred to Tezcatlipoca, the Smoking Mirror, a capricious god who laughed at men and delighted in the sort of reversal of fortune that servitude represented. We could have possessions of our own – our own money, even our own slaves. We could marry and have children who would not be our masters' chattels. We could not be ill-treated. A slave could not even be sold unless he had given his master cause to be rid of him, and even then only after his third offence. He could not be killed, unless he was one of that special class, the Bathed Slaves destined from the first to dance and die at the festivals. This was the law.

My master, however, was Lord Tlilpotonqui, He Who Is Feathered in Black. He was the *Cihuacoatl*, High Priest of the goddess called Snake Woman, and incidentally the Chief Priest, Chief Justice and Chief Minister of the Aztecs. Old Black Feathers was the most powerful man in the World, save only for the Emperor himself, and if he was not exactly above the law, still, from where he stood, he could at least look it in the eye. What if he thought I should have foreseen what had happened to Shining Light's offering? He would do nothing himself, of course, but he might look the other way while Huitztic, his sadistic monster of a steward, vented his own rage on me on his master's behalf.

As Handy had reminded me, I had seen a lot of sacrifices. I had seen many of them at close quarters, and I knew every step in the ritual that should have led to the death of Shining Light's slave under the Fire Priest's knife, because I had once been a priest myself.

The temple and the Priest House had been my world from early childhood, from the day my father, swollen with pride at his son's acceptance into the harsh school we called the House of Tears, had handed me over to sinister, black-robed strangers.

We called the Priest House the House of Tears with good reason: I wept when I saw my father leave me, and when soot was rubbed into my face and my ears were cut to make my blood splash onto the face of the idol, and I wept many times afterwards, during the ritual blood-lettings, the fasts, the vigils, the endless rote-learning of hymns and the Book of Days, the beatings meted out for the slightest delict. Over the years, however, I became hardened to it: I learned to do without food and sleep and not to mind that my hair was matted and lousy and my skin permanently caked with dried sweat and dried blood. I learned to love the priest's world, because it was where I belonged, and because even the fiercest of warriors, seeing my soot-blackened, blood-streaked face coming towards him on a narrow street or canal path, would stand aside for me. The tears I shed on my first day were no more bitter than those I cried years later, when it was all taken away from me and I was cast roughly back out into the world.

Now I had many reasons not to want to dwell on that time, but as I approached the Chief Minister's residence, I thought about all the sacrifices I had seen as a priest, all the varied ways in which we had sent men, women and some-times children to the gods, and realised that Handy had been right: I never had seen a sacrifice go the way today's had. It was not just how the man had died or his strange, prophetic-sounding words as he prepared to jump. There had been something unreal in the way both he and his master had behaved throughout the day – from the slave's first appear-ance as a wasted, spindly-limbed freak to the merchant's disappearance – which made me think that each of them had been acting a part. But I could not see any way in which I could have foretold what finally happened.

So my master had nothing to reproach me with. I kept telling myself this as I scurried fretfully through the few streets leading from the Heart of the World to his house. I was muttering it under my breath, hoping to convince myself that the Chief Minister might see it the same way, when I turned into the narrow path bordering the canal that ran by his house and bounced off a large man hurrying in the opposite direction.

'Out of the way, you clumsy . . .!'

'Sorry,' I began, before another voice, one that I knew only too well, interrupted both of us.

'Yaotl! There you are, you termite! We've been looking all over the city for you!'

Disbelief and a renewed sense of life's unfairness made me groan. I looked again at the large man, noting the wicked-looking cudgel in his paws, and at his fellows, who looked as if they had been hewn from identical lumps of granite, and finally at the man in their midst, the owner of the familiar voice, only slightly smaller and no less fearsome than his escort.

He wore a yellow cloak with a red border, flowing about his calves as only the best cotton could, and tubular plugs in his ears. White ribbons caught and bound his hair firmly at the nape of his neck. His body was stained with soot, like a priest's. Yellow sandals with oversized straps adorned his feet. His appearance would have told anyone what he was: a distinguished warrior whose achievements had been rewarded by high office. An attentive and knowledgeable observer would have known that he was one of the Constables, the men who kept the peace in the city by braining, strangling, stoning or cutting to pieces those whom the judges had condemned. He might have been able to name the man's office – *Atenpanecatl*, Guardian of the Waterfront. He would certainly have known that this official's escort, with their stone-pillar hairstyles and their blue-and-white cloaks, were seasoned veterans who would be only too happy to use their cudgels at their leader's whim.

I needed no observer to tell me any of that, however. I would have known it without seeing the cloak or the ornaments or the bodyguards. As much as I might wish to, I could scarcely fail to recognize my own brother.

'Mamiztli,' I responded as coolly as I could, with his bodyguards glaring down at me and no doubt wondering whether they were supposed to bow three times before me or bash me over the head. 'This is a rare honour. Since when have the Constables handed their messages to the Chief Minister's slave in person?'

My brother's name suited him. It meant 'Mountain Lion', and no mountain lion ever gave the deer lying trembling between his feet as fierce a glare as the one he turned on me. I returned his look evenly.

'More honour than you think, brother,' Lion assured me. 'It's not Lord Feathered in Black we've come for. It's you.'

'It will have to wait.' I glanced warily up at his escort and tried to keep the tremor out of my voice. 'I can't keep the Chief Minister hanging about, you know that.'

'Oh yes you can. It is not I that wants to see you.'

'Then who . . .?' But I knew the answer, and the knowledge was like a cold claw suddenly twisting my entrails. What man's summons could take precedence over the Chief Minister's?

'Why, the Emperor, of course. Congratulations, brother! You've succeeded in attracting the attention of Lord Montezuma!'

5

M y brother set a brisk pace as he led us back towards the vast sprawling complex on the south side of the Heart of the World that was our Emperor's palace. He did not so much as glance over his shoulder in answer to my questions. He had the air of someone who viewed the errand he had been sent on with distaste and wanted it over with as soon as possible, and in the meantime was determined to pretend the shabby creature his bodyguards were hustling along in his wake was nothing to do with him.

I should not be surprised, I reflected morosely. I was only too aware of the contrast between Lion's appearance and mine. What would this splendidly adorned warrior, all sleek muscle and taut sinew, have seen when he set eyes on me? A nondescript man, neither tall nor sturdily built, with an ordinary, straight-nosed, high-cheekboned Aztec face, partly hidden by a mass of dark hair with a little grey in it at the sides. There would have been nothing there to make someone of my brother's standing look twice, had we not been related.

But I knew his contempt for me ran deeper than a wish not to be seen with a skinny slave in a worn and blood-stained cloak.

Lion and I grew up in Toltenco, at the edge of the rushes at the southern limit of the city. Our house had two rooms and a little walled yard, almost filled by a dome-shaped bath house. The walls were daubed with mud and whitewashed until they gleamed, and roofed over with thatch so old you could no longer see it for moss. We were commoners: my family's womenfolk made paper for a living. It was not very good paper. My mother was never able to get the best bark, since there were hardly any wild fig trees left in the valley and we could not afford to buy it from further afield, and for all the effort she and my sisters put into beating it out, she was able to make only the sort of cheap, coarse stuff that got burned in people's hearths as an offering.

For all that, both my eldest brother and I had seemed destined for great things. He was the great warrior in the making, ferocious, strong, brave and fast, certain to drag home many illustrious captives, provided he did not meet a Flowery Death first. I had none of his gifts, although I was smart and had a tongue nimble enough to talk us out of trouble as quickly as my brother's bravado and hot temper got us into it.

However, I had one other advantage that, from the outset, set me apart from all of my brothers: my birthday. I was born on One Death, in the year Nine Reed. It was a day so auspicious that I was pledged to the service of the gods almost from birth, since in those days the priests could still accept commoners. How my father could afford to feast the Head Priest well enough to persuade him to let me into the Priest House was something I never knew, because he would never tell me just what it had cost him, although he used to hint at it often enough to show how bitterly he resented it. It must have been one of his proudest days when, seven years later, wearing an old, frayed maguey fibre mantle, made by cutting one of my grandfather's cloaks in half, and a breechcloth that I had only just learned to tie myself, I went to live among the richly adorned sons of the nobility in the House of Tears.

Twenty years after that the priests expelled me, and I was home again.

My family took me in out of duty, but never forgave me for their disappointment, or the shame I had brought upon them, or the wealth they had squandered on my education. There was some kindness at home, but there were insults too, and petty humiliations and cold silences, and when I was not being berated with my failure as a son and my ineptitude with a canoe paddle or a digging stick, I was wallowing in self-pity and self-reproach.

Small wonder that I soon fled from my parents' house into the secret, soft-edged world of the sellers and drinkers of illicit sacred wine.

My mother sent me to the market to sell her wares. She never saw the proceeds.

Even in a city where drink was the preserve of a few – priests, four-captive warriors and the very old – and where being found drunk could cost you your life, there were many places where your troubles could be dissolved in exchange for a few cocoa beans: innocuous-looking stalls in the local markets, nondescript houses by narrow canals, secret spaces among the tall rushes at the edges of the lake. At one of these places a man I had known slightly pressed a gourd into my hands, and when we had emptied it I returned the favour. I did not go home that night.

For a while I lived in the marshes at the lake's edge, scraping scum off the surface of the water for local dealers who made it into cakes for sale in the market. As often as not they paid me in kind, with the roughest sacred wine I ever tasted. I kept myself going that way for a while, ignoring the great city, whose effluent I spent my days wading in, so long as it ignored me. We might have gone on like that for ever if I had not been caught raving in the streets, out of my head on the dregs of a cast-off gourd.

I was arrested for the crime of being found drunk in public, and for a former priest there could normally be only one penalty for that: to be publicly executed by the Constables in the Heart of the World.

I lived only because my brother interceded with the judges. He persuaded them that, although I had once been a priest, I was still a commoner, and so should be punished only as a commoner. A noble or a serving priest would have been cudgelled to death. My brother spared me that, but not my humiliation: the Emperor's ritual admonition before a great crowd of my fellow Aztecs, followed by the shaving of my head.

Lion insisted on inflicting the lesser punishment on me himself, and carried out the sentence with evident relish. The strong arms that hauled me up by the hair and then cut it all away were his and it felt at the time as if he would have taken my scalp too if he had been allowed to.

At the time, I would rather have died. Any Aztec would. I never forgave my brother for saving my life, any more than he and the rest of my family forgave me for blighting theirs. When I sold myself into slavery, I thought I was turning my back on them once and for all.

Even with night about to fall, the Palace's entrance and the space around it were choked with people. The lord of a foreign city on a state visit, bedecked with feathers, jade and gold, had to mingle with the litigant whose argument with his parish over a land grant had found its way into the court of appeal, with the seasoned warrior claiming his right to be fed at the Palace and with the special envoy whose voluminous ceremonial jacket entangled his neighbours' elbows. They made a colourful crowd, shuffling slowly, mostly silently, towards the entrance, to be admitted or dismissed as the stewards saw fit.

Ignoring them all, my brother strode directly towards the great stair that led up to the Emperor's apartments. The crowd parted before us, putting a safe distance between themselves and our escort's cudgels.

My brother's and the escort's sandals clattered across the stuccoed patio. A few guards stood about, as stiff as statues, swords at the ready for any uninvited visitors. I imagined they would loosen up a little when my brother and I were called in, and they and his bodyguards could swap war stories and all be old soldiers together.

'Is this going to take long?' Suddenly looming over the fear of what my master would do to me for being late was the prospect of meeting the Emperor. Even to look at his face was said to entail death for a commoner. What could I possibly have done, that he should want to interrogate me in person? 'Why don't we come back in the morning? Look, I'm in no fit state to be seen, I'm still all over blood from the sacrifice . . .'

'Shut up,' growled Lion, before disappearing into an antechamber. He came back a moment later, barefoot and lacking his earplugs, his fine cloak swapped for a plain one just too short to cover his knees.

'And you always used to complain you had nothing to wear.' Nerves made me spiteful.

'You know perfectly well I'm not allowed to appear before the Emperor in a fine cloak. If I'd had time to go home instead of trailing around looking for you all evening, I wouldn't have had to borrow this thing.'

A steward called us forward. As we shuffled towards the

room where the Emperor was waiting for us, he hissed urgently: 'Don't forget, you make three obeisances. You don't speak unless he speaks to you first. If he makes a joke, laugh! You'll know because he'll be laughing too. Keep your eyes on the ground and your arse off it. When he's finished with you, you leave walking backwards. Turn your back on him and you're dead!'

6

A few years ago I met a man who had served in the Palace in Montezuma's time. His task had been to move the screen that the Emperor had placed in front of him at mealtimes, so that no one could watch him eating, and this meant he had been in Montezuma's presence almost every day.

I asked him whether he remembered what the Emperor had looked like. The question seemed to puzzle him.

'I don't know what he looked like,' he said eventually. 'I never dared to look.'

I had seen Montezuma from a distance. The first time had been his coronation, when he was borne about the city on an eagle-and-jaguar throne perched precariously on a litter. With no particular part to play in the ceremonies I had been in the crowd, watching the feathers of his towering headdress swaying as the bearers set him down at the foot of the Great Pyramid, and listening to my fellow spectators betting on whether the whole unstable arrangement would collapse and tip him unceremoniously out onto the ground.

I had seen him much more closely the last time. It had been in the plaza before his Palace, in the Heart of the World, when I had heard his ritual homily to the people about the dangers of drinking sacred wine, before he turned to the miserable specimens huddled in front of him and signalled to the Constables to administer the penalty for public drunkenness. As the cudgels began to fall and the heads of my fellow prisoners cracked sickeningly under their first blows, I had even dared to look at his face, believing I had nothing to lose.

I knew better than many, therefore, how our Emperor looked – a middle-aged man of middle height, slightly built but well muscled, with a neat beard and a penetrating gaze that you would remember if you met it and survived.

I dared not risk so much as a glance at him now, but if I had I would have been disappointed, as Montezuma was nowhere to be seen.

Besides my brother, I saw five men in the room. They were all standing and all dressed in plain cloaks, like commoners come to present a petition. I knew none of their faces but I guessed that they included the Council of Four, the Emperor's chief advisers. These men gloried in such titles as Keeper of the House of Darts, Keeper of the House of Darkness, Man Cutter and Raining Blood. They stood two on each side of a large wooden screen bearing pictures of the gods Quetzalcoatl and Tezcatlipoca picked out in gold. At right angles to it stood another richly decorated screen, and from the crackling and the wisps of smoke coming from behind it I guessed this concealed a hearth. A medley of delicious cooking smells, few of which I recognized, hung in the air.

The fifth man, who stood apart from the others, next to one of the screens and a little in front of it, would be the Emperor's interpreter, for it pleased Montezuma to speak to his subjects through an intermediary. That meant, I realized, that the Emperor himself was hidden in the angle between the two screens. He must be eating: no doubt he had felt like a light supper after presiding over the festival.

I was taking all this in when my brother suddenly threw himself on his knees and cried: 'O Lord! My Lord! O Great Lord!'

Hastily I did the same, while the Council and the interpreter looked on impassively.

In answer came a mumbling from behind the screen, followed by the interpreter's harsh, high-pitched cry.

'Is the Chief Minister's slave here?'

Unsure whether this meant I had been spoken to, I appealed silently to the Council. One of them nodded at me.

'My Lord, I am Yaotl.'

'You know the Cuauhcalco Prison.'

It was a statement, not a question, and in its uncompromising certainty was as penetrating as an obsidian-bladed spear. Montezuma had not forgotten that moment in the Heart of the World when my name had been called and my brother had hauled me upright by my hair, to show me off to the silent, expectant crowd before carrying out my sentence. It was not the pain of the obsidian razor scouring my scalp that his words recalled, though, nor the ripping sound my hair made as it came away. It was the cage they had kept me in beforehand, a wooden box too small to stand up in, and the smell of putrefaction from the whimpering skeleton in the prison cell next to mine, a man who by Montezuma's order had been given a little less to eat each day until he wasted away and died.

'Yes, my Lord.' The bile in my throat reduced my voice to a hoarse whisper. The Emperor could have found no better way of reminding me that he held my life in his hands and could take it from me whenever he chose.

'Then tell me why we should not have you sent straight back there.'

'My Lord!' I cried, alarm momentarily overcoming eti-
quette. 'I've done nothing wrong!'

'Have you not?' The Emperor's tone was impossible to
read, but there was no denying the sneer in the interpreter's
voice. 'Then how do you account for what happened this
evening?'

He could only mean the sacrifice that had gone wrong.
'My . . . my master, Lord Feathered in Black, the Chief
Minister,' I stammered, 'he . . . he ordered me to help at the
sacrifice of a merchant's Bathed Slave. I didn't know what
was going to happen – my Lord, how could I?'

'Because your master knew!' the interpreter spat back as
quickly as if he had known the Emperor's reply before it was
uttered.

'But I don't even know why I was there! I will eat earth!'
I touched the ground with my fingers and put them to my
lips. It was our favourite way of showing sincerity, a sacred
oath that meant that, having taken earth in your mouth,
you would be returned to the earth, your ashes buried in it,
if you were not speaking the truth.

For a moment I felt more alone than at any time in my
life. I turned desperately to my brother, but he had eyes
only for the floor, and the four Councillors kept theirs
focused resolutely on the middle distance in front of them.
When rescue came it was in the most unlikely form: a voice
from behind the screen – soft and lisping, but undeniably
meant to be heard – the voice of the Emperor himself.

*'Who can teach me about this? For this I, alone, try to do away
with my suffering.'*

I knew the words, for I had had to commit them to
memory once. They were from a poem by Montezuma's
father, Emperor Axayacatl. They had expressed the old man's
bewilderment and pain at the destruction of his army by the

Tarascans, in a war the Aztecs had fought and lost when I was a baby. Why had his son chosen to quote them now?

'So tell me, slave,' that deceptively soft voice added, 'tell me what you do know.'

There was no hiding his eagerness. The fact that he had chosen to speak betrayed it. I imagined him leaning forward over his dish of turkey, snails, water-fly eggs, stewed human meat or whatever, staring at the screen as if he could see through it, in his anxiety to hear me as I stumbled through my account. When I got to the point where Shining Light's victim spoke, telling us to look out for a big boat, something like a sigh broke from him: the sort of sound you make when you have recognized something that was there all along.

There was a long silence after I had finished. Then the Emperor spoke again, quietly still, but for us all to hear.

'These are disturbing times. We hear of omens, of portents: fire streaming through the sky, temples burning, the lake boiling and flooding on a day without wind. We hear rumours from the East, from our outpost at Xicallanco on the coast of the endless Divine Sea: rumours about men with pale skins and hair on their faces. We hear stories from the land of the Mayans. They tell of strangers from islands on the Divine Sea, of dreadful things that have happened there – how pale-skinned men with beards came and all the people died or fled or were made slaves. We have seen pictures of pyramids on the sea, borne on huge canoes.' He lowered his voice almost to a whisper. 'And now the whole city hears a Bathed Slave raving about a big boat before throwing himself off the Great Pyramid. Does all this mean the peril – whatever it is – is coming from the Divine Sea?'

He fell silent. Naturally everybody else did too, including me, although I had the feeling that he wanted someone to

answer him. The words of Axayacatl's poem came back to
me. What was our Emperor afraid of – the sort of terrible
defeat that had befallen his father, all those years ago? Defeat
at whose hands, though: the mysterious pale, bearded
strangers he had spoken of, the men from beyond the shores
of the Divine Sea?

Plainly Montezuma had long feared that a dreadful fate
was going to overtake his city. Now something as simple as
a few words about a big boat, spoken by a crazy man about
to die, had pitched him into a void of unknowing terror
which no word from me or anyone else in that room could
fill.

When he spoke again, it was on a surprising note of
anger.

'Soon there will be strangers among us – that much we
know from the omens. But will they be gods, or men dis-
guised as gods? How would you answer that, slave?'

I stared at the screen, avoiding the eyes of the dignitaries
standing above me while I struggled to come up with an
answer. Visions of what happened to people who disappointed the Emperor drove everything else from my head. I
had to say something but for a moment all I could think of
was that prison. Then I saw the prison's darkness and,
swirling around in it, the shapes my half-starved, exhausted
mind had peopled it with when it surrounded me: sinister,
threatening shapes that might be men or animals or
demons . . .

Desperate, I blurted out the first word that came into my
head, a word for the men and women whose home was
darkness.

'Sorcerers!'

Sorcerers: men and women who went abroad at night,
changed into jaguars, coyotes or weasels. Men and women

with the power to cure the sick or paralyse and pillage a
whole household, as the mood took them. Men and women
who could travel to the next World and bring its secrets back
with them. 'My Lord, if I needed to know who those
strangers were, I would need a sorcerer to tell me.'

For a long time there was silence from behind the screen.
Then I heard something else: something that sounded like
the ghost of a wry chuckle.

Was the Emperor laughing? He seemed to be, although
nobody else was joining in; and it was the interpreter who
replied.

'That was wisely answered. We consulted sorcerers. His
Lordship, the Keeper of the House of Darkness, will explain
what became of them.'

Out of the corner of my eye I saw one of the four
Councillors give a start and risk a quick scowl at the screen
before condescending to look at me.

'Lord Montezuma sent for sorcerers to interpret the
omens he spoke of,' he said mechanically. 'He had them
brought from their homes and questioned them personally.
When they failed to give him the answers he wanted, they
were imprisoned.'

'They were imprisoned,' Montezuma's interpreter added,
'in a place you know very well.'

'My Lord, please!' I begged. I was shivering, because
there was only one place the Emperor could be referring to.
'Tell me what you want me to do.'

'Find them,' came the short reply.

'Find . . .?' I gasped, as I realized what the command
meant. Nobody escaped from the Cuauhcalco Prison: either
you were let out or you died there. 'But . . .'

The interpreter ground on relentlessly. 'Your master,
slave, is Chief Justice and Chief Minister. When the sorcerers

disappeared we commanded him to look for them. He sent men after them, but did not find them. He took extreme measures — ill-advised measures, perhaps, because they are still at large. We find this hard to understand.' He let the Emperor's words hang in the air for a moment before continuing. 'Granted that these men were sorcerers, did they turn themselves into birds, bewitch their guards, or use some other form of magic to escape? Where are they?

'Your master has not been able to account for what happened. Perhaps these men did fly away on the night air. We might believe that — but when we see a man presented as a Bathed Slave who is plainly no such thing and hear him utter prophetic words and learn that our Chief Minister ordered his own man to be present when he died, we start to wonder.'

'My Lord — you can't mean that Shining Light's offering . . .?'

The words died in my throat as the Emperor spoke again — this time to me alone.

'You are spoken of most highly, slave. I know that your life has been troubled, but we can only accept whatever fate it amuses the gods to send us. Now I need a man of discretion and good sense. I know there are things I have not been told — things that men I should have been able to trust have kept from me.' Montezuma paused significantly. 'Too many of those around me think only of themselves. The sort of man I need will remember his duty to me — Quetzalcoatl's heir, the servant on Earth of Tezcatlipoca.'

The silence that followed was full of memories of a dark, damp, noisome, cramped place, the agony of an empty belly, the despair of knowing you might never stand upright or see the Sun again.

'Now tell me you are the man I need, Yaotl.' The voice

behind the screen had become so soft it was almost inaudible.

'Yes, my Lord.'

I could say nothing else now. If the Emperor had told me he needed a man who could produce live rabbits out of his anus, I would have been that man.

I barely heard the interpreter's words as he gave me my instructions. I did not need them. It was plain what I was being told to do: find the sorcerers who had vanished from Montezuma's impregnable prison, although my own master, the Chief Minister, had failed to locate them; and find out if there was any connection between them and the man I had seen die this evening.

'Bring those men to us, slave – not your master, or anyone else!'

In short Montezuma wanted me for his spy in his Chief Minister's household; and if my master had secrets he was determined to keep from the Emperor, then so much the worse for me.

The interpreter's final words were like one more twist in the cord I could already feel tightening around my neck. 'You will begin your search tomorrow,' he informed me loftily, 'at the Cuauhcalco Prison.'

7

My brother's guard made as if to fall in as we left the Emperor's apartments, but he dismissed them with a gesture, and we crossed the patio alone, silent apart from the flapping of his sandal straps and the padding of my bare feet in his wake. He spoke to me only when we had got out onto the open plaza and I had turned to leave.

'We need to talk, Yaotl.'

Stars were starting to come out overhead. 'My time isn't my own,' I pointed out. 'I'm late already. When my master can spare me . . .'

He snapped at me, in a strained voice: 'This is the Emperor's business! Do you think I'm wasting my time with you for the sake of my health?' Then he added, more mildly: 'I have to show you something. So you know how important finding these sorcerers is to the Emperor.'

'I already know! He as good as told me I'd find myself in a stew with maize and beans if I don't find them — that's important enough for me!'

Lion was already trotting briskly across the plaza. After a quick, nervous glance at the heavens I set off after him.

'Where are you going?'

'The palace of Axayacatl.'

The palace that had been built for Montezuma's late father was on the far side of the Heart of the World. It was now used to store weapons and valuables, and so although dark and silent was heavily guarded.

The warriors at the entrance took one look at my brother and let us through with barely a nod. He seized a torch and plunged into the maze of echoing corridors that was the deserted complex's interior.

'Look, I told you, my time isn't my own. The Emperor won't thank you if I can't serve him because my master's had me beaten to death for keeping him waiting . . .'

Ignoring my protests, my brother turned one last corner and stopped. Anchoring the torch in a niche in the wall, he turned to me and gestured silently at something lying by his feet.

We were in a small, bare room. The flickering torchlight lit up no details except for the thing Lion had evidently brought me here to see: a large wooden box in the middle of the floor.

'What's this?' I asked suspiciously.

'Open it.'

The lid was heavier than those of the wicker chests I was used to. At first sight there was not much underneath it: a few old pieces of cloth and one or two other things I did not recognize.

'Clothes?' I said. 'What, the Emperor wants me to do his laundry as well?'

'Pick it up,' he said sourly. 'Touch it. Then you'll see.'

At the top of the heap was something like a woman's blouse, but with long sleeves and an opening in the front like the jackets that priests and imperial envoys wore on special occasions. It had been white, with a simple but unfamiliar pattern embroidered on it, although even in the torchlight I could see it was now badly discoloured. It was not the design or the pattern, though, that made me catch my breath. The cloth had a texture like nothing I had ever felt: it slipped through my fingers, slithering between them so smoothly I thought I would drop it, but when I dared to tug at it I realized it was also stronger than any cloth I had handled.

'What do you think?'

'This is better than cotton.' Awed, I replaced it reverentially and let the lid of the box fall shut. 'Better than cotton!'

'This box was washed up on the eastern shore of the Divine Sea, a few years ago. Montezuma gave most of the things in it away to the kings of Tetzcoco and Tlacopan, but he kept these.'

I forced my mind back to the conversation with Montezuma, while my fingers tingled with the memory of how that cloth had felt. 'The Emperor mentioned strangers from islands on the Divine Sea, pale men with beards – did they have things like this?' I was beginning to see what had so disturbed the Emperor. There was something unearthly about this material.

'Yes – and other things besides. Look.' The lid of the box opened again with a creak, shatteringly loud in the silent, empty space around us, and Lion pulled something out of it. It was long and narrow and glinted in the torchlight.

'A weapon,' he breathed. As he held it up I saw that it was like a sword, except that the blade, instead of being a flat shaft of fire-hardened wood with obsidian slivers set in its edges, was a single piece of metal, a little like silver but duller and somehow more solid looking.

'This is harder than bronze,' my brother said. 'You remember what the Tarascans did to our army, a few years ago, with their bronze swords and spear-points? Imagine what our warriors could achieve, armed with this metal instead of wood, flint and obsidian!'

'And what our merchants would do in their wake, with cloth like that to trade,' I added, gesturing at the open box. 'Is that what the Emperor thinks?'

'He thinks whoever possesses things like this must be like a god,' my brother said soberly, lowering the sword but not replacing it, 'and you do not trifle with gods. According to the reports I've heard, the strangers came across the Divine Sea in canoes the size of palaces, and they fought the Mayans with swords like this one, and a weapon that made a sound like thunder and produced fire and smoke and threw stones hard enough to kill.'

A tremor had crept into his voice. Lion had always been devout, even for an Aztec, and this talk of gods was making him nervous.

'I gathered that he had the missing sorcerers rounded up,' I said, 'so they could tell him who these strangers were and what to do about them.'

'It's more than that. Montezuma thinks one of these pale-faced strangers might be Quetzalcoatl, come back to reclaim his kingdom!'

Now I saw the real source of the Emperor's anxiety to have the sorcerers back, and the fear I had detected in him even through his wooden screens.

Many bundles of years before, all the lands that were now in Montezuma's realm had been ruled by the Toltecs. They had been a marvellous race, and all the fine things we Aztecs had, the arts of painting and poetry and feather-work and casting precious metals, had been learned from them. Their blood ran in the veins of our rulers, even though their last king, Quetzalcoatl – a man who bore the same name as our god, the Feathered Serpent – had ended his reign fleeing into exile in the East, across the Divine Sea towards the land of the Mayans. It had always been rumoured that he might return, however, to claim his kingdom back from his descendant, the Emperor of Mexico.

If that was what Montezuma believed, then he was not just concerned to find out what some unknown savages from across the sea were up to. He was terrified that his ancestor was going to come to him, call him to account for his reign, and destroy him if he was found wanting. What he had wanted the sorcerers to tell him was nothing less than his own fate.

'Now, do you see?' my brother went on. 'Montezuma thinks his very life is at stake. He was jittery enough before, which is why he had the sorcerers thrown in the prison. That was nothing compared to the state he's in now it seems they were able to fly out of their cages!' He spoke with feeling, and I wondered how afraid he was for his own position, knowing what the Emperor was capable of. 'If it turns out they were able to use magic to escape . . .'

'I'm not so sure,' I said thoughtfully. 'There are men who can turn themselves into birds or animals at will, of course there are, but they're pretty rare. Most sorcerers are fakes. They just use a lot of cheap tricks to fool gullible people. You know that way of curing a sick man by sucking a stone out of his body? Chances are the curer's got a stone in his mouth ready and he bites his cheek so it's all bloody when the patient sees it. Most magic's done that way. So maybe these men flew away, but until I see feathers lying around on the floor of the prison, I'd sooner believe they got out on their feet.'

'But how? And where did they go?'

'If I could answer that . . .' I paused, remembering that the moment I could answer his questions was the moment my troubles would really begin. 'I have to get out of this, somehow,' I added, half to myself.

My brother stared at me as if I had just sprouted a third ear. 'What do you mean, "get out of this"?'

'Don't be simple, Lion.' I tried to keep the exasperation out of my voice. 'What if the Emperor's right and old Black Feathers knows more about these sorcerers than he's letting on – what then? If I were to find anything out, which I won't, do you think he's just going to let me go running to the Palace? He'd have me impaled first! I'm a dead man whatever happens!'

'So just do your duty,' my brother said coldly.

'Bollocks! I'm a slave – I've no duty to anyone, unless they've paid for it.'

The metal sword shook and flashed in the torchlight as Lion fought with his temper. 'You selfish worm!' he cried. 'Who cares about your miserable life? How do you think it's been for your father, your brothers, watching what's become of you? How do you think it's been, trying to make a career, trying to practise a craft, trying to keep up a reputation, when all people keep saying to you is, "Oh, yes, I know you, you had that brother, the drunkard – how did he escape getting his head broken, anyway?"'

'I might have known you'd bring that up . . .'

'You've done your best to drag the family name through the dust over the years – one thing after another. Now, just when you have a chance to repair some of the damage, all you can think of is how to make it even worse . . .'

'Next you'll be telling me I owe you my life.'

'You do.'

My retort died in my throat, because he was right. A sudden recollection of the pain and the crowd's laughter made my eyes sting and I turned sharply away, to hide my anguish.

The warning came too late. I heard the weapon's faint

whistle as it swung through the air in the very instant the blow fell.

He hit me with the flat of the sword, catching me between my shoulders with a force that sent me staggering to my knees. As I fell I half twisted around to see him launch himself towards me, the gleaming blade held aloft and a feral snarl on his lips.

'Remember this game, brother?' he cried.

I remembered: and suddenly we were little boys again, playing at being warriors, with sticks for weapons, and I had been knocked down, as usual, and my big brother was about to seize my hair in the tear-jerking grip that on a real battlefield would make me his captive.

'This is my beloved son!' His gloating cry completed the warrior's ritual as he reached for me with his empty hand.

But I remembered the game better than he did, it seemed, including the way I had played it all those years before. As his fingertips brushed my hair I snapped my head around and sank my teeth into the base of his thumb.

He howled in pain and outrage. He tried to pull away but I held on like a stoat with a rabbit. I watched the sword twitching as he fought to control himself, to stop himself cleaving my neck in two with it, and then he threw the precious thing hard into the far corner of the room to free his remaining hand.

He bent towards me, aiming to pinch my nose and make me relinquish my grip, and I drove my fist into his side, just under his ribcage, as hard as I could.

As he fell I rolled quickly away, opening my mouth and spitting his blood on the floor.

For a moment we both lay on our sides, panting and glaring impotently at each other.

A distant shout and the sound of running feet told us that

someone had heard us. We got up, still watching each other warily.

'Your point, brother?' I gasped, as bemused-looking warriors trooped into the room behind me.

'My point, brother,' Lion growled, as he went for the sword, 'is that you don't have any friends. Get the Emperor what he wants and maybe he will protect you — but don't expect me to look after your worthless hide this time!'

8

My master's house was as imposing as you would expect a lord's to be, a miniature version of Montezuma's palace: two storeys of smooth whitewashed stone decorated with curling friezes and a broad stairway at the front leading to a patio and the great man's apartments on the roof. I had no intention of setting foot on the stairway: I used to spread my sleeping mat on the ground floor at the back and that was where I was headed. There was just a chance that my master had not sent for me yet and my lateness would not be noticed.

'Where do you think you're going, Yaotl?'

I cursed under my breath. The voice that brought me up short belonged to a dark figure lurking in the shadows at the foot of the stairs: Huitztic, my master's steward.

'Home to bed,' I replied, hoping his question had no purpose and that I might be able to get away before he thought of one.

'Not so fast! His Lordship wants to see you. He's up there.' He jerked his head towards the stairway before adding ominously: 'He's been waiting.'

I loathed Huitztic. He was a typical three-captive warrior, a strutting bully who had done just enough in the field to convince himself he was the Emperor's right-hand man and nowhere near enough really to make anything of it. His sort

usually ended up with meaningless jobs as messengers or
overseers in the houses of the great, where they might just
have the brains to realize how futile their lives had become
and to take it out on their underlings and the household
slaves. He reminded me of the oafs who had taught in the
House of Youth that my brothers had attended, another
favoured career for cast-off warriors, whose bumptious self-
importance all too often rubbed off on their charges. The
difference was that Huitztic was cruel as well as overbearing.
His name meant a sharp object, so naturally I just thought of
him as 'Prick'.

'I am, as ever, at his Lordship's command,' I said, as I
started up the stairs. Sarcasm was safe with the steward: he
was too stupid to recognize it.

'But you're too late.' He sneered. 'He's got someone with
him now.' Before I could ask who, he had turned on his
heel, smirking, leaving me with one foot poised on the
bottom-most step, unsure whether to go on up or not.

I could not see past the top step onto the patio, but I
could picture the scene. Old Black Feathers would be sitting
in a high-backed wicker chair under his late father's favourite
magnolia tree, gripping his knees with thin, liver-spotted
hands, with his visitor squatting respectfully in front of him.
I climbed the stairs cautiously. If I kept my head beneath the
level of the top step, I thought, I should be able to hear them
without being seen.

The first voice I heard was my master's. He sounded
weary.

'That's all he said? "Watch out for the big boat." Nothing
else?'

'That's all I was told.' The visitor's voice was a surprise: it
was a very young man's, barely broken, with a distinctive
accent, and I knew it from somewhere. I was still trying to

place it as he went on. 'He shouted it from the side of the Great Pyramid for all the city to hear and then jumped. Then your slave and that other man . . .'

'Yes, yes,' my master interrupted. 'No doubt when my slave deigns to put in an appearance I will hear a full report from him. In the meantime, what does Shining Light want from me? Did anyone tell you that?'

During the short pause that followed I realized who the visitor was: Quimatini, the son of Ayauhcocolli, a man my master sometimes did business with and who used his son as a messenger. I had never met Ayauhcocolli, but I had seen the boy when he had come to the house: a well-built, lithe youth who looked as though he merited a name that meant 'Nimble'. The first time we had met he had glared at me as if he wished me dead. I suspected that my master's dealings with the lad's father were not wholly legal. This would explain his familiar manner towards my master: he spoke more firmly than I would have done, and had not once addressed the Chief Minister as 'My Lord'.

'I don't know. He doesn't confide in me, or in my father.' The youth giggled suddenly. 'Except when he's run out of money and is trying to persuade us to take his bets on credit, that is!'

'I'll have my slave disembowelled!' old Black Feathers raged. 'How could he just stand by and let Shining Light make a fool of me – and so publicly as well? You realize what that young merchant's done, don't you? He's made it impossible for me to move against him without making a spectacle of myself! What do I do now – watch those men being killed, one by one, until Shining Light chooses to tell me what he wants?'

The youth did not answer. I dared not break the silence by breathing but my mind was racing. It sounded as if my master knew a lot more than I did about the Bathed Slave, and the young merchant had some hold over him on account of it. Was the Emperor right? Were the men my master had mentioned the missing sorcerers, and had the Bathed Slave been one of them? It would explain how he had known he was destined for the Land of the Dead: a sorcerer might well have learned that much.

Old Black Feathers let out a long sigh. 'You may as well go, Nimble. But if that young man says anything to you or your father, I want to know straight away – you understand?'

'Of course,' replied the boy smoothly.

'Off you go, then.' I tensed, ready for the lad to appear and for my cue to go and face my master's displeasure. I had a moment longer to wait, though.

'What about tomorrow?' the youth asked.

'Tomorrow? Oh, the ball game. Do you know, I'd forgotten all about it.' A flicker of the old eagerness and energy stirred in the Chief Minister's voice. 'What odds is your father offering?'

'Three to one against the team from Huexotla.'

My master snorted. 'Sometimes your father's a fool to himself!' There was silence while he considered the proposition. 'Of course, I'll have to back the Emperor's team, publicly,' he announced at last, 'but I'll have twenty large capes on Huexotla. Tomorrow is going to be a better day!'

It was as much as I could do not to gasp audibly. Almost everyone who had the wealth to spare gambled on the ball game at one time or another; and so did some who did not have it to spare and whose pastime ended up costing them their liberty. But bets were required to be placed openly, the stakes displayed by the side of the ball court for the players and the spectators to see. Surreptitious arrangements such as the one my master had just made were strictly illegal.

I barely saw the boy as he passed me on the stairway, although I heard the sharp hiss of his indrawn breath – the sound made by an especially venomous snake – as he noticed me. All I could think about, as I mounted the rest of the steps up to His Lordship's patio, was my master's casual, barely considered gamble.

Twenty large capes! I had sold myself into slavery for that amount!

I found old Black Feathers as I had pictured him, sitting in a bearskin-covered wicker seat under the magnolia tree in the middle of the patio.

He was dressed for a feast or a formal dance. A gorgeous cotton cloak, ornamented with the faces of eagles and bordered with eyes, floated over his knees and fell to his ankles. A gold labret fashioned like a pelican hung from his lower lip and a double spray of bright plumes, red, blue, yellow and green, towered above his head. Even in the dark of the evening, with his back bent forward with age and a rabbit's-fur mantle slung over his shoulders for warmth, he was magnificent.

He was also furious. Even if I had not heard what he had said to the boy, I could have told as much by the soft tapping of a jewelled sandal on the stuccoed floor. I wondered how long he had been waiting for me before the boy had turned up. I wished he had sat indoors, enjoying a cup of chocolate or the attentions of his favourite concubine, rather than out here, feeling the gathering chill seeping into his bones.

'My Lord.' I made my obeisance, throwing myself abjectly on the floor.

'Yaotl. You're late. Where have you been?'

The Chief Minister was capable of rages that could make Mount Popocatepetl at its most violent seem tame, but I knew he was never to be feared more than when refined, controlled anger lowered his voice to an intimate whisper.

'I'm sorry. I fell asleep, after the sacrifice . . .'

'You're lying. You've been to see the Emperor.'

I stared fixedly at the floor, thankful that at least I did not have to meet my master's eyes.

'That brother of yours was here.' My master's deceptively gentle voice hardened. His own father had been Guardian of the Waterfront in his youth, and old Black Feathers often bemoaned the fact that a man of Lion's humble birth should be allowed to hold the rank. 'Everyone knows what a toady he is. He was obviously running some errand for Montezuma. Do you think I'm so stupid I can't work out what you've been up to?'

'I couldn't help it!' I protested. There was no point in denying that I had been with the Emperor but at all costs I must not let my master know what I had been ordered to do. 'He sent for me to give him my account of the sacrifice – there was no way I could refuse!'

'Oh, the sacrifice!' he said as if he had forgotten all about it. 'And tell me, slave, are you going to favour me with your account as well? Or do I have to make do with getting it second-hand from some passer-by?' He was no longer whispering.

'My Lord, I came as soon as I could . . .'

'After all, I could ask anyone, couldn't I? The whole city heard what that Bathed Slave said and saw how he died. "Watch out for the big boat." That's it, isn't it?' Now he was shouting. Age had not weakened his voice. 'Anyone could tell me how my fool of a slave let him go – if they could only stop laughing long enough, that is!'

'My Lord, I'm truly sorry, we couldn't hold him.' I cast about frantically for something that would mollify him. 'But he did say something else, before he went – and no one else heard it.'

'What?' Something creaked – either his bones or his seat's wicker frame – as my master leaned forward urgently. 'What else did he say?'

I told him. I had no idea what the words might mean to him. 'He said: "Tell the old man."'

He stiffened visibly. Watching discreetly through lowered eyes, I saw his face darken to the shade of the sky above us. For a moment I thought he was going to be taken ill. Then he slumped in his chair.

'What do you suppose he meant?'

'My Lord, I've no idea. Unless . . .' I could just see one of his knuckles in the corner of my vision, and the answer was there, in the tautness of his skin over the swollen joint. The merchant's slave's last words had been a message for my master.

'Unless he meant you, my Lord.'

'Me?' he asked sharply. 'Why should he have meant me?'

'I . . .' I hesitated. It was all too easy to guess why: because Montezuma and my brother had been right. The man who had died this evening had been one of the Emperor's escaped sorcerers and my master had been behind it all. 'I don't know,' I added wretchedly.

It must be more complicated than that, I realized. Whatever my master's involvement may have been in the sorcerers' disappearance, it could not explain how one of them had come to throw himself off the Great Pyramid, or account for the anger and distress old Black Feathers felt on account of his death. Whatever plans my master may or may not have made for the sorcerers, something had clearly happened to frustrate them.

'Where do you think the merchant got his victim from?' my master demanded.

'The market at Azcapotzalco?'

'Don't be stupid! You know perfectly well he was never anywhere near a slave market!'

'Then . . . my Lord, you do know where he came from!'

'Know?' Old Black Feathers' sudden laughter was a dry, mirthless cackle. 'Of course I know! How Shining Light got hold of him is another matter – I wish I knew that! That young man used him to make a fool out of me, you know. No doubt it suited him to have the man raving like a lunatic just before he died, with my own slave in attendance to make sure every word was passed on to me. No doubt he thinks he'll get away with it, keeping them all from me, just to make sure I keep dancing to his tune, but he won't.'

'You mean the merchant has the sorcerers?' Simple astonishment made me blurt the words out even as I realized they were a mistake.

I was still prostrated before my master, with my hands stretched out flat on the floor in front of me. Suddenly something was squeezing each of them: the rough sole of a sandal. I heard a creak as my master leaned forward in his chair, and felt his breath on the back of my neck as he bent down to speak once again in that deadly whisper.

'I may be old, but I can still break every finger in both your hands before you can even scream – and that's before I give you to my steward to play with. You understand that, don't you?'

'Yes,' I gasped.

'Now I know Montezuma didn't summon you just so that you could tell him about a botched sacrifice. He told you about the sorcerers and ordered you to spy on me. What else did he say to you? Don't lie or leave anything out. You know what I will do to you if you do.'

I found myself stumbling through the events of the

evening since I had met my brother, as helpless as a man staggering through a nightmare, with the thought of frail bones cracking driving me on like a demon at my back.

As I neared the end of the tale I felt the pressure on my hands relax. I flexed my fingers automatically. Long moments of silence passed before I summoned the courage to look up.

My master had raised his head to look at the branches spreading above him. They were bare now, stripped by frost.

'My father's tree.' He sighed. Abruptly his manner had changed: it became abstracted, almost wistful, as his fingers began caressing a naked branch. 'All I ever wanted was something that wasn't his: some renown of my own. See this tree? My father, Lord Tlacaelel, planted it before I was born – the best part of two bundles of years ago. It will still be growing here when I'm dead.' Suddenly he seized a twig, twisted it violently until it snapped off, and hurled it out of sight into a corner of the patio. The rest of the tree shook and rattled. 'And they will still talk about him then, won't they? The great Tlacaelel! The man four emperors looked up to, the Chief Minister who turned down the throne because he was king enough already! What do you suppose they'll say about his son?'

I was too afraid to answer. The question was not really addressed to me anyway.

'I dance attendance on my young cousin, Montezuma, and amuse myself sitting in the court of appeal trying to work out which of two depositions amounts to the bigger pack of lies, or deciding which parish's turn it is to muck out the zoo. But I should be happy with that, shouldn't I? Because I'm the great Tlacaelel's son, and that should be enough for anybody!' He sighed. 'I suppose it will have to be enough for me, now.'

'My Lord – I don't understand. Even if Shining Light's offering was one of the sorcerers, what was he to you? Why does it involve your father?'

'Can't you see, Yaotl? It's because of my father that the Emperor is afraid of me! Montezuma acts as if the gods themselves installed him on the throne, but they didn't – the chiefs elected him, just as they elected every Emperor before him. But he knows his throne is rightfully mine!'

The almost wheedling note in the Chief Minister's voice did not fool me. He had no need to justify himself to his own slave: what he was saying now was addressed to the Emperor's spy.

I listened resignedly to a story I knew very well. When the aged Tlacaelel had declined the throne in favour of Montezuma's uncle, Emperor Tizoc, he had stipulated that his own sons should inherit it on Tizoc's death. By the end of Tizoc's short reign, however, Tlacaelel himself had died, and his wishes were no longer of any account. The throne was given to Montezuma's surviving uncle, Ahuitzotl, and on Ahuitzotl's death old Black Feathers was again passed over – this time in favour of Montezuma himself.

'Maybe Montezuma thinks he's going to be poisoned, like Tizoc,' my master grumbled. 'Maybe he thinks I had his sorcerers spirited out of the prison, to weaken him, or to cast some sort of spell on him, to sicken his heart with magic. Or maybe he doesn't – maybe he told me to look for them because he knew they could not be found, to humiliate me.'

'My Lord – he told me to look for them. I have to go to the Cuauhcalco Prison. What do I do if he asks about my progress? I can't tell him you've told me not to obey him – he'll have us both strangled!'

'Then you'd better do as he says. Whatever my cousin may have told you, I don't have those men. No matter: the

Emperor will get them back – but through me, and in my own good time, so that he knows I can't be trifled with. And that young merchant is going to be made to regret what he has done!'

My master leaned towards me then, planting his trembling bony hands on his knees.

'You will find the sorcerers, Yaotl, and bring them to me – to me personally, do you understand? To me and no one else – not even the Emperor! And before you get any clever ideas about running to Montezuma the moment you set eyes on them, just listen to this.

'I know Montezuma will have told you that when you catch up with the sorcerers you're to take them straight to him because he'll have you strangled if you don't. So hear me now, slave: if I learn you've been anywhere near the Emperor before those men are safely in my hands, I'll have you flayed alive!'

9

I spent much of the night prowling around my master's courtyard, listening to the sounds made by a city stirring in its sleep: the conch-shell trumpet wailing at midnight, a distant answering call from a priest patrolling the city's bounds, the cry of some creature disturbed on the lake. From time to time the lads from one of the Houses of Youth would break into song, so that the sound would carry across the water and convince our neighbours that we Aztecs never slept.

Then the stars started to disappear, one by one, and the first drops of the winter rain began to fall around me. I went indoors, treading softly to avoid disturbing my room's other occupant, and huddled on my sleeping mat with my cloak wrapped around me.

My mind would not rest. It kept revisiting the evening's events.

I lay on to my back and stared up at the ceiling. Somewhere above it were the Chief Minister's sleeping quarters. 'What's this all about?' I muttered. 'Are you just trying to show you're cleverer than the Emperor?'

'If you can't sleep,' grumbled a voice out of the darkness, 'then you can come here and turn me over before I get fucking bedsores.'

Talking to myself, I had woken my room-mate up.

Patiyoh was his name – or rather, it was the name he had been known by for as long as I had dwelled in my master's household. I was sure it was old Black Feathers' idea of a joke, for it meant 'costly'. He had once been a useful slave, but he had been crippled by a stroke years before, and now all he did was lie on his sleeping mat, consuming his master's food and doing no work in return. He was safe enough as long as he gave his master no cause for complaint, since by law a slave could not be disposed of unless he had been formally admonished on three occasions before witnesses. A few of his fellow slaves, including me, kept him alive by small kindnesses, such as changing his soiled breechcloth from time to time and carrying him out into a secluded corner of the courtyard when the weather was good. The others did it because they knew they might one day find themselves in Costly's position. I had my own reasons to feel indebted to the old man.

Seizing him by his bony shoulders and rolling him on his side took little effort. As I crawled back onto my own sleeping mat, however, I learned I was not going to get away that lightly.

'So, what's the old bugger done to you now?'

'Never mind,' I mumbled. 'Go back to sleep.'

'I can't,' he said petulantly, 'not since you woke me up. Now the floor under this mat is as hard as stone, and it's not as if I can toss and turn until I get to sleep, so you'll just have to keep talking to me, won't you? Or have you forgotten what you owe me?'

'No.' I sighed. 'I haven't forgotten.'

What I owed this crippled old man was nothing less than my life. When I had come into our master's household – after the Chief Minister had snapped me up as a bargain in the marketplace – I had been helplessly in the grip of the

Four Hundred Rabbits, the gods of the sacred wine. The twenty cloaks my master had paid me for my liberty had gone, every last stitch, on the roughest, sourest and cheapest drink I could get. When the money had run out and I had given myself up to servitude, in accordance with the bargain my master and I had struck, I still had no thought beyond the next gourd. It was Costly who had seen me through it, whose wasted, bony arms had held me as I had shivered and struggled and cried out for just a drop, just a taste of fermented maguey sap on my tongue.

I could never forget what he had done for me. He would never let me.

I told him of everything I had seen and heard that evening. It took a long time, but the old man was still awake at the end.

'So old Black Feathers was banging on about his father again? You amaze me. I've known our beloved Chief Minister a lot longer than you have, young man, and if I had a bag of cocoa beans for every time I've heard one of those jealous tirades about his father, I could have bought my freedom years ago.'

'But Lord Tlacaelel's been dead nearly forty years.'

'Yes, and his son's never moved out of his shadow. Not surprising, is it? Four emperors deferred to Tlacaelel. He was their equal. Montezuma treats his son like a servant – even though one of his wives is old Black Feathers' daughter! How often do you suppose our master has to listen to tales of his father's exploits in war – or even worse, gets asked to tell them himself? Now what's his own most famous military achievement – can you tell me?'

I could, because we had had this conversation before, but in order to humour my companion I had to pretend to think about it before answering: 'Well, there was that time he and Montezuma went off to war, but Montezuma decided he wanted the servants of his own household killed, and sent old Black Feathers home to see to it. Not exactly glorious.'

'No, not the sort of thing you want to tell your grand-children about – especially since the Emperor didn't trust him not to balls it up and sent spies after him to check. And every time he visits that great big palace next to the Heart of the World he must tell himself: "If only my father hadn't turned down the throne, all this would be mine!"'

'Our master's jealousy isn't really my problem,' I reminded Costly as I squirmed into a less uncomfortable position under my cloak. 'It's the sorcerers I have to worry about.'

'Don't you think there's a connection? What was it he told you – he wanted something that wasn't his father's?'

'True, but he also said the Emperor was afraid of him.'

'Why? He's too old to be any threat. If Montezuma died tomorrow the throne would go to his brother, Cuitlahuac. Our Chief Minister and our Emperor both know that.' The old slave sucked noisily on his bare gums. 'I'd lay odds old Black Feathers was lying to you.'

'He would,' I said drily. 'I'm meant to be spying on him, remember?'

The old slave persisted as I rolled over on my mat. 'Whatever's happened to these sorcerers, it's not just because of some feud between old Black Feathers and Montezuma. It's got to do with something our master wants – something his father never had. Now what might that be, I wonder?'

ONE REED

1

I did not want to go to the Cuauhcalco Prison, but since I seemed to have no choice, I steeled myself to visit it.

If I could have remembered the time I had spent there clearly, I might never have been able to face going back at all. I had been so far out of my head with drink – and then with the anguish of not being able to get a drink – that it now seemed mercifully remote. The jumble of memories that assailed me as I approached the blank stone wall of this deliberately neglected corner of Montezuma's palace was bad enough. Once again I felt the rough hands of the parish police dragging me to my feet, simultaneously knocking the gourd I had been guzzling from out of my hands. I heard my own voice protesting hoarsely, not at their manhandling as they carried me to the prison but at the waste of good drink pouring away into the dust. I tasted the sourness of my own vomit again, just as I had the morning I had woken up in my cage, dimly aware, even while I shook the wooden bars and howled for some sacred wine, that the stuff had finally done for me.

I smelled the place again, before I even set foot in it: hot, still air reeking with puke, piss and dung, and a vile septic stench from the cell next to mine, whose occupant had been slowly starved until he was too weak even to twist his emaciated frame to reach the small puddle of urine he had been drinking from.

I saw the daylight as it had been the day they brought me out, unbearably bright, so that I had to squint to see the Emperor on his dais and the crowd gathered before him at the Heart of the World, all waiting to find out who, among that year's crop of drunks, had been chosen to have their skulls smashed in by the Constables.

Remembering all that, and knowing it had probably been even worse than I remembered, it was as much as I could do to enter the prison's narrow, barely lit hall and look along its lines of wooden cages.

Rainwater had pooled on the flat roof and dripped into the cages. The rushes strewn on the floor had absorbed all the moisture they could and now floated uselessly in shallow puddles. The floor was criss-crossed by thin streams of liquid stained with filth from the overflowing pots the prisoners were given to relieve themselves in. The only light came through tiny apertures set high in the walls: not enough to show you where you were putting your feet, but enough to reveal the misery on the faces of the prison's handful of desperate inmates.

Each prisoner huddled naked on the floor of his cage. There was a sameness about them, each one alone, unable or unwilling to speak to his neighbours, surrounded by the smell of his own and others' ordure – reduced to everything an Aztec was not.

'They're drunks, mostly.' The Emperor's major-domo, the *Petlacalcatl*, dismissed most of the wretches in his care with a single word. 'Don't feel too sorry for them, they've only themselves to blame. And these are the worst offenders – the ones their own parishes couldn't handle. Still, you'd know all this, wouldn't you?'

'What do you mean?'

My tone must have been too sharp, as he gave me a curious

look. 'I thought you were Lord Feathered in Black's man. He is the Chief Justice, isn't he, after all?'

'Oh . . . yes, yes, of course . . .'

'Anyway, it's up to him and the other judges what happens to this lot. They'll let most of them off with a good talking-to in front of Montezuma's palace and having their heads shaved in public. The others . . .'

The others would be beaten to death, but for any of them the public humiliation, the casting-out from society of a man brought up to value reputation more than life, might be the worse punishment. I looked at the nearest prisoner, hoping his face would tell me which of his possible fates he dreaded more, but he had his eyes fixed on the ground.

'We had some more interesting characters,' the major-domo went on. 'But you know all about the sorcerers, of course.'

'The men who escaped? They really were sorcerers, then?' I asked innocently.

'They must have been, to get out of this place. Turned themselves into birds and flew out through the windows.'

Having seen the windows, I thought nothing much bigger than a hummingbird could have got through any of them, but I kept this to myself.

'That's what I came to talk to you about,' I said. 'Lord Montezuma wanted me to see where the sorcerers had got away from, so that I could see what manner of men we are dealing with. He would want me to eliminate all the mundane explanations first, though.'

'Lord Montezuma?' He sounded surprised, and when he stared at me his eyes were pale discs in the prison's gloom. 'The Emperor sent you? But I thought you said you were the Chief Minister's man?'

'The Emperor asked the Chief Minister to find out what happened,' I explained, 'and then he asked me.'

'He asked you himself?'

'Yes.'

The man looked at his feet. His toes turned over some rushes. I wondered why he seemed to be prevaricating; after all, I could hardly be the first person to ask him these questions. What difference did it make who had sent me? To encourage him, I added: 'And so when I ask you a question, it's as if Lord Montezuma were asking it, except I personally don't have the power to have you dismembered if you don't tell me what I want to know. Now, are you going to answer me, or do I have to suggest to the Emperor that he interrogate you in person?'

The major–domo let out a theatrical sigh. 'All right. I suppose it can't hurt if I run through the whole story from the beginning. These men – they'd been rounded up from all over the place, fingered by the headmen of their villages, I think, and brought in by order of the Emperor. He interrogated them personally.'

'What about?'

'What do you think?' The man lowered his voice to an awed whisper. 'The omens!'

The cages on either side of me seemed to be getting closer together and the ceiling seemed to be descending towards my head, but it was something more than the prison's suffocating heat which started the sweat running down my cheeks.

Montezuma had spoken of omens, of portents, but everyone in the city knew we had been beset by these things for years. We had all seen strange lights in the sky and thousands had fled their homes when the lake mysteriously boiled over. We had heard rumours as well, too many to dismiss. It was said that a man with two heads had appeared in the city and vanished when he was brought before the Emperor. A woman had been heard crying in the street, calling out, 'O my sons, we are lost! My children, where shall I take you . . .?' The Emperor himself, it was claimed, had seen a strange bird with a scrying-glass in its head, and had been terrified by what he saw when he looked into it: men riding on the backs of deer – armed men, with beards and pale faces.

You did not have to believe all of these stories to be convinced that something strange and terrible was happening, or about to happen.

'It sounded to me,' the major-domo said, 'as if the Emperor was afraid of some huge disaster, and just wanted some sorcerers to look into the future and give him a straight answer about it. That's why he had them rounded up, I think, so that he could consult them without the whole city knowing what they were talking about. He was asking them whether they'd had any visions.'

'And had they?'

'Of course not! If they had been able to predict the sort of catastrophe the Emperor had in mind they would have been fools to own up to it. How do you tell an emperor his realm is about to perish? They just kept saying they'd seen nothing. In the end Montezuma ran out of patience, had them thrown in here and sent me along the next day to question them.'

'What did you find out?'

'Nothing! All they'd tell me was that whatever was going to happen would happen and that a great mystery would come to pass – not exactly helpful. Montezuma was so angry that he kept them in here on starvation rations and then sent me back to interrogate them again. But that was when . . .'

The major-domo licked his lips. His voice seemed to have dried up and he had to clear his throat before continuing.

'We had a double guard on the place, because the Emperor was so troubled about these men. The guards were all men I'd known for years, men I'd trust with my children's lives, and none of them saw a thing. They'd all gone – flown away like . . . well, like bloody birds!'

'How did you explain that to the Emperor?'

'How do you think? I had to go and tell him his most important prisoners, the ones he'd taken a particular interest in, had vanished into thin air. What would you have done?'

'I suppose I would have either run very far away or grovelled a lot.'

'Yes, well, I just told him he might as well have me cut to pieces there and then, because there was no sign of his prisoners and none of my guards had seen or heard a thing. I thought I was a dead man. He's had people disembowelled and their wives and children strangled for less, but I got away with it somehow.' He paused thoughtfully. 'It's not as if he wasn't angry, mind you. If he ever catches those men, he's going to make them suffer – and anyone else who gets the blame for their disappearance. But I was lucky. It never seemed to occur to him that it might be my fault – not that it was, of course!'

I eyed him sceptically. 'So what did the Emperor think had happened?'

'That they'd used magic to escape, of course.'

So the Emperor had done as any Aztec would in his position. If you needed the favour of the gods, you might go to a priest, but sometimes that was not enough. Perhaps the war-god and the rain-god at the summits of their pyramids seemed too remote from the affairs of men. Perhaps what troubled you was the work of some malignant spirit whose name you did not even know. Then, if you had a dream that needed interpreting, or were about to set off on a long journey or try planting your beans too late in the season, you would go to a sorcerer.

Sorcery came at a price, however. It meant dealing with strange, unnerving creatures who could easily do you more harm than good. If the sorcerers Montezuma had questioned were genuine then they may have been able to tell him what the future held. Obviously he believed they had not dared to, and had used their powers to escape him.

And the more convinced he was that they had seen his future, the more desperate he would be to get them back.

I examined the nearest empty cage. 'Let's leave magic aside, for the moment. If I were shut up in here, how would I get out?'

'You wouldn't!'

'No, but just suppose I were to try it.'

He sighed. 'Oh, all right. To begin with, there's no door. You'd have been dropped in through the trapdoor on the roof – see it? Once you were inside we'd have weighed it down with a stone slab and no way would you get it open. Don't even think about pushing it out of the way – we won't stop you, but trust me, it won't budge.' He gave me a nasty grin. 'Shall I shut you in and let you try it for yourself?'

'No!' I stepped hastily away from the cage. I could still remember the wood creaking under the weight of that stone slab. 'I'll take your word for it. So I'd have to have someone open the trapdoor from outside.'

The major-domo looked suspiciously at his inmates, a couple of whom had lifted their heads and seemed to be taking an unwelcome interest in our conversation. He raised

his voice deliberately. 'Forget it! To begin with your accomplice would have to get in past my guards – and I've told
you, they were doubled up that night. He'd have to find the
right cage, open it and let you out, and do all this without
being spotted. What's more, he'd need help shifting that
stone. Then he and his mate would have to sneak you out,
again past my guards, who wouldn't have missed them going
in in the first place! There's only one way in or out of here,
you know, and you've seen how small the windows are. Oh,
and on this occasion, he'd have had to do the same trick five
times.' He looked about him smugly, as though he had forgotten that in spite of everything a number of his prisoners
had managed to slip away. 'I tell you, it couldn't be done!'

'Who's allowed in here, besides your guards?'

'Nobody! Apart from the judges, of course, if they want
to question the prisoners – and the work details who come
in to clean up when it's their parish's turn at the job.'

I could not help grimacing. Forced labour was a part of
the common man's lot and most would cheerfully tackle
dredging a canal or hauling stone to the site of a new public
building, but for a people who liked to keep themselves
clean, mucking out the prison would be a different matter.
'I suppose you're going to tell me they're always escorted?'

'All the time! We count them in, we watch them and we
count them out again. Face it, there are only three ways out
of here. The rats eat you, the judges let you out, or . . .' He
lowered his voice again. 'Or you use sorcery! That's what we
told the Emperor, and he believes us!'

I asked the major-domo whether I could question his
guards.

'Go ahead,' he said indifferently. 'It's the same shift we had
on duty when the prisoners went missing, but they won't be
able to tell you anything I haven't.'

Each of the guards had been hand picked for two qualities: being able to wield a huge cudgel and being able to tolerate enough boredom to crush the mind of anybody that had one to crush. I could not credit any of them with great powers of observation, but I could not imagine any of them falling asleep on the job either. Each of our conversations was a repeat of the last, with me staring up into a slack-jowled, thick-jawed, heavy-lidded face that bore all the expression of one of those masks of human skin the priests wore to impersonate the god Xipe Totec at the Festival of the Flaying of Men. It would go something like this:

'What did you see the day the prisoners went missing?'

'What prisoners?'

'The sorcerers.'

'The sorcerers?'

'Yes, the sorcerers – the ones the major-domo says turned themselves into birds.'

'Oh, the sorcerers!'

There would be a pause.

'Well, what did you see?'

The guard I was questioning would turn to one of his colleagues – preferably the one I had last spoken to.

'Did you see anything, mate?'

'When?'

'When those sorcerers went missing.'

'Sorcerers?'

'Yes – you know.'

'No.'

'No what?'

'No, I don't know.'

'The sorcerers – the men who got out. When that happened, what did you see?'

There would be another pause.

'I didn't see anything.'

The guard I was questioning would turn to me in triumph.

'See? He didn't see anything either. I reckon they must have flown away, like bloody birds!'

After three attempts at this I gave up. I had found out as much as I was going to here.

2

I stood outside the Cuauhcalco Prison, savouring the midday sunshine, which had dried up the last of the rain, the clean air and the newly swept earth under my feet.

I watched the Aztecs around me, the men and women strolling or hurrying through the street or paddling along the canal beside it. I sought out things that distinguished the passers-by from the wretches in the prison. I looked at the men's cloaks with their bright colours and bold patterns, each announcing its wearer's rank and achievements, and at the earrings and lip-plugs sported by those entitled to them. I looked at the skirts and blouses of the women, no two alike in their rich embroidery, at the yellow ochre on their faces and at the ways they wore their hair – loose or cut short or braided, or done in the formal style that was the emblem of respectable Aztec womanhood: divided and bound at the nape of the neck to leave two ends projecting over the crown like a pair of horns. Here and there a distinctive figure would appear – a master from a House of Youth with his temples shaved, a tangle-haired priest with his soot-stained face and arms and his ocelot-skin tobacco pouch, a noblewoman with a cotton scarf. When I looked down at my own apparel – a plain, functional cloak and breechcloth, with none of the cheap brash jewellery or feather-work that slaves sometimes had to put on to suit their owners' tastes – I felt comforted. I was among my people, and I was as good as they were, or at least I would be as soon as I could have a bath.

Something stirred the crowd: a subtle movement, like the ripples on still water a fish swimming just below the surface makes. Peering between the jostling bodies, I followed the disturbance to its source near the walls of Montezuma's palace, and caught sight of the heads of a little group of men moving purposefully towards the steps my brother and I had gone up the evening before.

There was something familiar about the movement, and the bodyguards' casual way of parting the crowd to let their master through. Then I saw a flash of yellow as the hem of his cloak brushed the lowest of the steps leading to the Palace's interior.

I glanced irresolutely in the direction of my master's house before I made up my mind what to do. He had released me so that I could obey the Emperor's command and visit the prison. I had a little time in hand, and there were things I had to say to my brother.

Lion shared his section of Montezuma's palace – the Constables' Chamber, something between an apartment and an armoury – with his fellow executioners. They were all commoners whose deeds had earned them their rank, and their quarters reflected their origins. They had all been brought up in little adobe houses with no furniture except a few sleeping mats and a wicker chest. The walls of their quarters now groaned under the weight of feather-work wall hangings and animal skins that half hid their vivid murals, while it was hard to find a place to squat for the low tables and high-backed leather-covered chairs cluttering the floor. The honours heaped on my brother and his colleagues for their prowess in war had given them expensive tastes.

It took me a long time to persuade the sentries to let me in, and by the time I found him, he had settled his powerful frame comfortably into a chair and was drinking chocolate. I could see from the fine froth in his bowl how much trouble had been taken in its preparation. It would have been beaten for a very long time, carefully seasoned and served at just the right temperature.

He glared at me over the rim of his bowl. 'You'll pardon me for not offering you any. I wasn't expecting you.'

'It's all right,' I said lightly. 'I bet you had them put pimentos in it. I hate pimentos in my chocolate. How's the hand?'

'Fine.' Under its heavy bandages his left hand looked gratifyingly stiff and swollen. 'Nothing hot piss and honey couldn't cure. What do you want? Have you been to the prison?'

'I have.'

'What did you find out?'

'The sorcerers aren't there any more.'

He slapped his bowl angrily on the floor, sending a tiny dribble of expensive chocolate over the edge. 'You think this is funny, don't you?'

'No, as it happens, I don't. I don't find being put up as the stake in some game between the Emperor and the Chief Minister very funny at all.'

'So get Montezuma his sorcerers,' he replied unsympathetically, picking his drink up once more. 'The game'll be over then.'

'It's not that simple. My master says he hasn't got them. The Emperor seems to have got the right idea about that Bathed Slave who killed himself yesterday – he was one of

the sorcerers, but my master says it's the merchant, his
owner, who's holding them.'

'And you believe him?'

'Not necessarily. But I'll talk to the merchant and find
out.' I watched him drinking luxuriously. If he had come
across me dying of thirst I would not have put it past him to
drain a gourd full of water in front of me just to add to my
suffering, but then I might have done the same to him.
'There's something I want to know first, though. Whose
idea was it to give the Emperor my name?'

The cup hid my brother's face. He said nothing.

You are spoken of most highly, the Emperor had said.

'It was you, wasn't it?' The suspicion had planted itself in
my mind while we were at Axayacatl's palace. In the hours
since then it had sprouted and put down roots. 'You bastard!
This is all your doing, isn't it? You got me involved in this.
Why?'

'Why did I bring you to the Emperor's notice?' My
brother drained his bowl and laid it carefully on the ground
between us. 'Why do you think? So that you might have a
chance to make something of yourself! I told you yesterday –
you can repair some of the damage, give your family something to be proud of.'

'For sure, they'll be proud to see me flayed alive for going
against my master,' I retorted bitterly, 'and that's only if the
Emperor's right and old Black Feathers really does have the
sorcerers. What if he doesn't? What's the Emperor likely to
do then?'

My brother frowned. 'But your master does have them!
The Emperor as good as said so.'

'Only because someone put the idea in his head. Now I
wonder who that was?'

'What are you saying?' My brother gripped the sides of

his chair so tightly that I heard the woven canes crack under their hide covering. Something had dislodged his mask: suddenly he was not the renowned warrior taking his ease but the boy I had known as a child, our father's favourite son, who became the man he was because he grew up more scared of failure than death.

'I don't understand why you're so convinced that my master is hiding the sorcerers, and so determined that I should be the one to find them. I don't believe this has anything to do with our family. They gave up on me years ago, Lion, and nothing I do now is going to make any difference to them. You had some other reason for wanting me brought into this. Some reason of your own.'

He picked up his chocolate bowl then, looked at it absently, saw it held only a shallow puddle of froth at the bottom, and put it down again.

'All right,' he said at last. 'I'll tell you what I know. I think – I mean, I heard – well, you know what the army's like for rumours.' He was not looking at me. He seemed unsure of himself: not like my brother at all, more like a gauche lad recklessly embarking on a funny story he had picked up in a House of Youth without really knowing how to begin or end it or whether he should be telling it in the first place. 'Montezuma told you he asked the Chief Minister to find these men when they escaped. I'm not sure exactly what your master did about it. It was all a big secret, but there were warriors involved – I heard there were warriors involved. I heard someone say he'd talked to someone who'd been hand-picked for a special mission by the Chief Minister. Apparently he had to go to a village near Coyoacan.' He paused. 'Coyoacan,' he repeated, as if wanting to make sure I had caught the name of the place.

'And what happened there?' I remembered another

expression our emperor had used: *Extreme measures*. What had that meant?

'He . . . he didn't want to say.' He looked up then, and there was something in the way he stared at me, through eyes that seemed obscured, as though they had somehow withdrawn into his face, which made me think twice about asking any more questions.

Eventually he added, in what for him was a quiet voice: 'All I can tell you is this. I think the Emperor's decided the reason your master came back from that village empty-handed is that he wanted to.'

I looked into my brother's eyes again, but could make nothing out in their darkness. He was concealing something, and if I knew him at all, you could roast him over a slow fire before he would say what it was. One thing was obvious enough, though. Whatever he had seen or heard that was haunting him so, he believed I could do something about it – even though he could not bring himself to tell me what it was.

'You think I should go to Coyoacan,' I said at last. 'You want me to see for myself what old Black Feathers did, don't you?'

3

It was no great distance from Montezuma's palace to the Chief Minister's house, through streets that now, in the early afternoon, were largely empty. After parting company with my brother I walked home slowly, giving myself just enough time to work out how many kinds of trouble I was in.

Thoughts were still chasing each other around my head when I reached my master's house. I was so caught up with them that I did not see the big man until I almost walked into him.

'Yaotl!'

The voice was familiar: it belonged to Handy, my comrade in our encounter with the priests.

I greeted him like an old friend. Anyone who was neither old Black Feathers nor his steward was a welcome sight. We sat in a quiet corner of my master's patio and drew our cloaks over our knees while we exchanged pleasantries. He asked me where I had been. I replied by asking him what he was doing here.

'Carrying a message. Come to think of it, you might like to hear about it.'

I wondered what sort of message he could have to deliver here.

'The same young lad who put me on to that last job

sought me out in the marketplace. They must have been impressed, in spite of what happened, hey? It turned out they wanted me to go all the way to Pochtlan to pick up this letter . . .'

'Pochtlan?'

'Yes, odd, isn't it? You'd think they'd have found someone in Tlatelolco market, where they'd have had more choice, but anyway . . . Guess who it was from?'

'No idea.'

'Shining Light.'

'Really?' Considering what I had been through on the young merchant's account the day before and what I had heard about him from my master since, any news of him was bound to get my attention. 'What did it say?'

'How would I know? I'm just a commoner, I got my schooling at the House of Youth, and you know they don't teach reading there. I was just told the message was an urgent one for the Chief Minister. I'd sort of hoped to see him – never met a great lord before.' He suddenly had the half-hopeful, half-anxious manner commoners often adopted at the prospect of meeting their rulers. 'As he was out when I got here, I had to give it to the steward, though . . . was that right?'

'Oh, yes.' The steward could be relied upon to pass a letter straight to my master – and to hang around afterwards in the hope of overhearing its contents. 'It'll get to his Lordship, don't worry.'

'Good. Shining Light seemed very anxious about it.'

'You saw him, then? I thought he'd vanished off the face of the Earth, yesterday. What else did he have to say for himself?'

'We didn't have time to talk. He was in a rush. He was just setting off in his canoe. He was actually sitting in it when he gave me the letter. It looked as if he had a long way to go, judging by what he had with him – bags of provisions, toasted maize, stuff like that – the sort of stuff you'd take on a long journey.'

'Hang on!' That could not be right, I thought. I glanced quickly up at the clouds chasing each other briskly across the sky and noted the promise of fresh wind and rain in the evening. 'You're telling me you saw Shining Light setting off on a long journey today – on One Reed?'

'That's what it looked like. I know what you're going to say – it's not the most auspicious day he could have chosen. I thought it was strange too, especially for a merchant. This sorcerer I go to every time the gods lumber us with another child, he tells me merchants are some of his best clients. They're so superstitious they never go anywhere without consulting the Book of Days.'

One Reed was a day influenced by Tezcatlipoca: the Mocker, the Enemy on Both Hands, the most unruly and capricious of our gods. There could hardly be a worse day for setting out on a long journey. 'I wonder where he's going?'

We sat silently for a moment, each wrapped up in his own thoughts. Shining Light had left in a hurry, it seemed, but he had still had something to tell my master so urgent that Handy had to trot halfway across the city for the sake of it.

'Yaotl?'

'Sorry.' I looked up. 'I was thinking.'

'I was just asking if you knew of any work going around here? I thought I was on to a good thing with Shining Light, you see, but if he's gone away, then I'm short of an employer . . .'

I looked at his muscular arms and recalled his efforts of

the day before. What had happened had not been his fault, I thought generously, any more than it had been mine. 'I'll suggest my master bears you in mind,' I promised.

I went to see the Chief Minister the moment I finished speaking to Handy, to tell him about my visit to the prison.

In the event my master paid scant attention to my conversations with the major-domo and his guards. I put his distracted air down to the fact that he was in a hurry. He had just come from Quetzalcoatl's round temple in the Heart of the World and was due back there, to carry on the ceremonies and sacrifices that attended One Reed; for One Reed, besides being presided over by Tezcatlipoca, was also the Feathered Serpent's name day. The old man still wore his regalia, the white robe edged with black feathers that he had taken his name from, and he fiddled impatiently with a piece of paper on his lap. He did not show me the paper but I assumed it was the letter from Shining Light that Handy had delivered. He kept looking down at it and then at me in a speculative way that I did not like. It was almost as if its contents concerned me, and as if my worth were somehow being weighed against them.

When I had finished speaking he tapped the paper on his knee nervously and asked: 'What am I going to do about Shining Light?'

'My Lord, I was going to see him today, but Handy says he's gone away.'

'Gone away – a merchant, going on a journey on an unlucky day like One Reed? Rubbish! He'll be hiding somewhere – and no wonder! He must have a pretty good idea what I'm going to do to him – that's if the other merchants don't get their hands on him first!'

'Then you want me to go to his house today, after all?'

'Yes. No,' he corrected himself hastily. He looked at his letter again, and a curious half-smile appeared on his face, as if a pleasing thought had just struck him.

'I think it's too late to go today. Go, by all means, but leave it till tomorrow.'

'As you wish, my Lord.' I had no urgent wish to go all the way to Pochtlan that afternoon.

'Is that man Handy still around?'

'Yes – I believe he's looking for work.'

'Good! Tell him not to go anywhere. I will have a letter for him to carry and we'll make it worth his while if he delivers it tonight.'

TWO JAGUAR

1

The next day found me in Pochtlan, the parish in Mexico's northern district of Tlatelolco so famous for its merchants that it had given its name to their whole class — the Pochteca.

Most of the Pochteca's houses were neither palaces nor hovels. Their plain walls had been crafted to return a stranger's gaze impassively, saying nothing about the people who lived behind them. I knew each would be much the same inside. There would be a square courtyard, lined with rooms on two sides, with the remaining open space filled with flowering plants, kept for their beauty and scent, and turkeys and small dogs, kept mostly for food. The family rooms would be home to three or four generations, from little children playing in the courtyard to their grandparents and great-grandparents, who would be kneeling on their sleeping mats, telling stories and looking forward to their next drink of the sacred wine they were allowed to indulge in freely.

I had been born in a house that looked like these; much smaller admittedly, but laid out in the same way. However, the resemblance between the houses here and the one I had grown up in ran no deeper than the coat of whitewash on the walls.

The dwellings here might look ordinary, and their inhabitants might go about in short, rough, undyed cloaks with their hair loose, but you would find no more wealth and power in any house in Mexico except a great lord's palace. The Pochteca were long-distance traders whose caravans of sweating bearers brought us long green quetzal plumes, bales of cotton, cocoa beans, chillies, rubber, gold, silver and jade and countless other luxury goods.

In the process the merchants naturally made themselves and the Emperor rich. They also served the Emperor as spies, emissaries and *agents provocateurs* in the endless campaigns to keep his subject peoples in line and the tribute houses stocked. For the services they had rendered him, Montezuma's ferocious predecessor, Emperor Ahuitzotl, had granted the merchants special privileges and had called them his 'uncles'. Most Aztecs, envious and suspicious of their wealth, had less affectionate names for them, which explains why the merchants' characteristic demeanour was so humble.

The slave who greeted me at Shining Light's house was barely polite. After staring at me for so long that I began to wonder whether there was something wrong with his eyes, he showed me into the courtyard and told me to rest there, among the foliage plants and empty flower pots of a winter garden. He offered me something to eat, although when I turned to him to accept he had vanished, leaving me to the courtyard's only other occupant.

An old man sat with his back to an immaculately whitewashed wall, against which the dull mottled brown of his ragged cloak stood out like a stain. His head was bowed, and he seemed to be asleep. A thin trail of saliva ran from a corner of his mouth across his chin.

I shifted my weight indecisively from one foot to the other while I wondered how to get into the house without causing offence. The slave seemed prepared to leave me where I was, alone save for the unconscious old man, for the rest of the day.

Apart from being a lot quieter, the courtyard was much as I had imagined it. Its freshly swept stuccoed floor was already warm beneath my bare soles and its walls gleamed in the morning sunshine, making the doorways into the interior of the house resemble dark cavities. Wicker screens covered some of the doorways, and if anyone apart from the old man was at home, I thought they must be behind one of those.

I started towards the nearest of the screens.

The voice cut me off before I had gone two steps.

'If it's money you're after, don't bother. We don't keep any here.'

The other man in the courtyard had raised his head and was watching me. His stare had a vague quality that made me think he was looking past me, until I noticed that his eyes were filmed over with age. There had been nothing vague in his voice.

'I want to speak to Shining Light,' I informed him brusquely. 'Do you know where he is?'

'You want my grandson? Oh, I was right, then. It is money you're after! You're still wasting your time, though. You're welcome to look, but you won't find so much as a bag of cocoa beans.'

I reappraised him hastily. I had assumed this piece of human litter was some broken-down old slave that the merchant's family tolerated out of sentiment and because they expected death to relieve them of him shortly. A second glance did little to change my impression of him, but if he was Shining Light's grandfather then he might well be head of the household and so entitled to some respect.

I believed what he said. Merchants hid their wealth. They kept it in secret warehouses, often using each other's, so that no one else could ever be quite sure who owned their contents. Anything they kept in their own houses would be carefully concealed behind false walls. If I had been interested in the merchant's money – whether he kept it in the form of cotton cloaks, bags of cocoa beans, little copper axes or goose quills filled with gold dust – I would have known better than to look for it here.

'I'm not after money,' I assured him. 'I just want to speak to Shining Light.'

'Aren't you that man he does business with down at the ball court – what's his name, Misty?' He meant Ayauhcocolli, whose name meant a Curling Mist. 'I assumed you were him, come to collect.'

'I was sent here by the Chief Minister, Lord Feathered in Black', I declared importantly. 'He's the one who has business with your grandson – not some petty criminal.'

The old man laughed, sending a shower of spittle across the courtyard. 'The Chief Minister! Young Shining Light's surpassed himself this time, then, if he's managed to get into trouble with him! I wish I could help,' he added, wheezing while he got his breath back, 'but my grandson isn't here.'

'Then I'll wait here until he returns.'

'We don't know when he'll be back.' This was the voice of the slave, who had come back bearing a plate of the stuffed maize cakes known as tamales. He stood in front of me, offering them as politeness dictated, although his surly expression made it clear that this was as far as his courtesy extended. 'You might as well go home.'

I looked from the slave to the old man. 'No one said he was in trouble. I was just told to speak to him about the Bathed Slave he presented at the festival, that's all.'

'Oh, that,' the old man mumbled. 'I might have known. Nochehuatl here's right, though: Shining Light, my grandson, he's gone away and we don't know where he's gone or when he'll be back.'

'Well, do you know anything about his offering?' I demanded. 'Where did he get him from?'

'I don't know anything about it,' he said firmly. 'It was nothing to do with me. Look,' he added with a touch of impatience, 'you're talking to the wrong person. My daughter handles our business now. It's her you need to speak to.'

'Then may I see her?'

'Sure. You'll have to wait, though. She's got the chiefs of the merchants' parishes with her at the moment.'

He gestured to Nochehuatl, miming the action of upending and draining a gourd full of liquid. As the scowling slave, whose name meant 'Constant', went to fetch his drink, the old man said: 'You can keep me company, in the meantime.'

The old man's name was Icnoyo, which meant 'Kindly'. He told me this as he pulled the maize cob out of the neck of the gourd to let the contents splash freely into his mouth. As an afterthought he offered it to me. He seemed surprised, although not offended, when I waved it away.

'It's against the law,' I pointed out primly.

He laughed. 'Not for me, son. I won't see seventy again and I'm a grandfather, I'm allowed as much as I can hold!'

As he tipped the gourd up again I decided I had better ask him something before he fell into a stupor. 'You think your grandson owes this man Misty money? Is that why he went away?'

'Could be. I've heard him mention the name – and Shining Light spends a lot of time hanging around the ball courts.'

'So he's a gambler?'

'You could say that. Aren't we all?' There was a trace of bitterness in the old man's voice. 'You know the mistake my daughter made with that boy? He was born on Two Rabbit, and you understand what that means.'

'Prone to drunkenness,' I responded automatically, like a student answering an examination question on the Book of Days. I had spent much of my youth in the Priest House poring over screenfold texts, committing to memory the fate of every man and woman ever born, on pain of a beating if I later got any of them wrong. I could still recall the stiffness of the bark paper under my fingers and the crackling sound the pages made when I turned them over. I had no trouble recognizing the destiny prescribed for a man born on Two Rabbit: to be ruined by sacred wine. I wondered how his parents had chosen his name. An exemplary life: I knew only too well how hard that would be to live up to.

'That's right. But believe it or not, our Shining Light never touched a drop, except when he had to as part of a festival. He was never let near it, because his mother was so terrified he would fall victim to his fate. But she didn't realize there are other vices that can seduce a man.' He sighed and upended the gourd, draining it once and for all. 'You can't blame her, poor girl. He was the only one she had, and with his father gone . . .'

'His father? What happened to him?'

The old man closed his eyes. He sat like that, neither looking at me nor speaking, for so long that I wondered if he had been taken ill. I was on the point of doing something – shaking his arm to rouse him or calling for a slave – when abruptly he opened them again and said one word.

'Quauhtenanco.'

I had been a very young man when the inhabitants of the province of Xoconochco in the far South-west had risen against the Aztecs, killing some merchants and besieging the survivors in a town called Quauhtenanco. The merchants had held out for four years, beating off their attackers and making captives of many of them, and when a young general named Montezuma had come to their rescue at the head of the Aztec army, the merchants could only apologize to him for his wasted journey.

Quauhtenanco was no mere symbolic victory and the merchants secured more than just their own lives. The province of Xoconochco was the key to the hot lands in the South, whose wealth included rubber, cocoa, emeralds and above all feathers — the long, soft, shining green quetzal feathers that Aztecs coveted more than anything and could get nowhere else. It was chiefly for this that Emperor Ahuitzotl had granted the Pochteca their privileges, including the right to dress as warriors and offer slaves to the war-god at the festival of the Raising of Banners. If Shining Light's father had helped win them their status, especially if he had died in the process, then I could see why Shining Light had been allowed to sacrifice a Bathed Slave at the festival.

'We were there together, Xippopoca, Shining Light's father — my son-in-law — and I,' the merchant's grandfather explained. 'Shining Light was only a baby when we set out, so he never knew his father, and his mother . . . well, she had no word of us for four years, and then I came home, laden down with the spoils of war and gifts from the Emperor's hand, and her husband didn't. I'm not sure she ever got over it.'

'What do you mean?' I asked. 'Quauhtenanco was twenty years ago. She can't still be in mourning, surely?'

'I don't mean she breaks out weeping every day,' the old man said impatiently, 'but maybe having only the boy left made her a little over-protective. I've sometimes wondered if, well . . .' He tapped the gourd absently with his fingers, making a hollow drumming sound, and frowned as he searched for the right words. 'I sometimes think she's trying to smother the lad, and it hasn't always been for the best. How she'll cope now Shining Light's gone, I don't know — but look, you might be able to judge for yourself.'

Out of the corner of my eye I saw something move, and I heard the sound of a wicker screen being drawn aside from a doorway.

'I think she can see you now.'

A little group emerged, blinking, into daylight. Their faces had all been tanned like old leather by years of exposure to sun and wind, and they all had plain cloaks, lank hair and a proud, stiff bearing. As the seven of them walked silently past us towards the courtyard's street entrance I realized they must be the leaders of Tlatelolco's merchant parishes. Despite their lack of cotton cloaks, lip-plugs, feathers or sandals, these were among the richest men in Mexico.

Just as the last of them was about to leave, he paused and looked back at my companion.

'Kindly,' he said curtly, 'your grandson has gone too far this time.'

'Tell it to Oceloxochitl.' The old man suddenly sounded weary. 'I don't care any more.'

'We've told her,' the other man assured him. 'She knows we've only been as patient as we have because of the way his father died. When Shining Light comes home,' he added ominously, 'his account will be settled.'

2

The servant showed me into a small room that I guessed was an antechamber, used for receiving formally those guests the household chose not to be intimate with. Conventionally pious images of the gods decorated the walls: I recognized Ohmetecuhtli and Ohmecihuatl, Two Lord and Two Lady, who allotted our birth-dates and, along with those, our destinies. A low table, spread with delicacies — savoury tamales, stuffed tortillas, fruit and assorted sweetmeats — stood in the middle of the room.

The only other furniture was a large reed box. It lay open, displaying its contents. They looked like an elaborate suit of clothes: I recognized a colourful, feather-bordered jacket, obsidian sandals and wooden earplugs. They puzzled me at first, until I saw the lock of hair lying in the middle of the heap, and then I understood: these were the clothes the Bathed Slave had danced in during his last days and nights. Afterwards they would have become his owner's most treasured possessions, to be kept as long as he lived and burned and buried with him when he died.

Shining Light's mother knelt on a mat beside the box. She greeted me with conventional courtesy.

'You are out of breath, you are hungry. Rest. Eat.'

I sat opposite her, mumbling something polite as I gathered

my cloak around me. I accepted a honeyed maize cake and munched on it to give myself time to think.

Kneeling, with her head inclined, lit only by whatever sunlight managed to slip past the screen at the doorway, she gave little away. By what I could see – the silver strands in her dark hair, which lay loose upon her shoulders, the lines etched in shadow about her eyes and mouth, her dark, unpainted skin and bright, unstained teeth, the sombre, formal patterns of her skirt and blouse – I judged that she was a respectable woman in her early middle years and that she was in mourning. I presumed this was for her son, since I knew the merchants' womenfolk went into mourning whenever their men set out on a long journey.

'I am Oceloxochitl. You are Lord Feathered in Black's man? You are welcome here.' She spoke in a deep, clear voice, and deliberately, like someone used to choosing her words carefully.

'Thank you, madam. I am his Lordship's slave, yes.'

'What does the Chief Minister require of my poor household?'

'I wanted to speak to Shining Light.'

'Then, sir, you have come too late, and I am sorry your journey has been wasted. My son left on a trading venture yesterday.'

When she looked up her gaze was steady and unblinking. There was no catch in her voice and no tears had left tracks on her cheeks. Only a hand, trembling slightly as it strayed towards the reed box beside her, might have betrayed grief or a need for reassurance.

'Why yesterday?' Disbelief made my voice sharper than I had intended. 'Why on a day like One Reed?'

'Why do you think?' Her voice cracked like a dry branch collapsing on a fire. 'He had to go away, don't you understand? They'd have killed him if he'd stayed.'

'Who'd have killed him – his creditors?' I remembered what the merchant's grandfather had said about Misty. Perhaps he was not the only one Shining Light owed money to.

'I'm talking about the merchants! You were at the festival, weren't you? You were there when that slave ran away and killed himself. It was the disgrace of it. My son knew he could never show his face among his own people again. He left the city the next day. He knew it was a bad day, at a bad time of year, and he had neither proper provisions nor his elders' blessing. He knew he could drown in the lake, be killed by robbers or eaten by bears or pumas, die of cold in the mountains or heat in the desert. We merchants have lived with this knowledge for generations. Shining Light's own father was killed by barbarians.'

She would not let herself cry or raise her voice, but I could not miss the way her fingers caught and twisted the fabric of her skirt.

'You don't know where he went?'

'He didn't say, but it may have been in the East – somewhere like Xicallanco. He talked about Xicallanco before he went.'

Xicallanco! 'A long way away,' I said, while I tried to remember where I had heard of the place recently.

'Oh, yes. The farther the better!'

'I suppose,' I reflected, 'by the time he gets back from a place like that, there's a chance it will have been forgotten – the Bathed Slave and everything.'

'He won't come back.'

'You think he's gone into exile?'

'I think he'll die.' She whispered the words, hissing at me in a voice that sounded like air escaping between hot coals on a brazier. 'The same as his father. He died when our son was a baby.'

'I know. Your father told me. Your husband must have been a very brave man. I'm sorry you lost him.'

'It was a long time ago,' she said matter-of-factly. 'But yes, he was. He was worth ten of those so-called warriors.' A brief smile surprised me. 'Thank you for saying so.'

I remembered what her father had told me about her and Shining Light. I wondered whether I could get her to confirm it, or explain what he had meant about things not always having been for the best.

'It can't have been easy for you all these years – on your own, with your son growing up.'

The woman gave me a curious glance. 'It hasn't,' she conceded, 'but merchants' wives are used to coping. We have the family business to run, while the men are away for months or years at a time. We're brought up to it. And we weren't poor. The Emperor was very generous, you know. After the merchants got back from Quauhtenanco he sent round boat-loads of maize and beans, and cloaks of cotton and rabbit's fur. We were never going to go hungry, even when my father got too old to go abroad himself. And now Shining Light is ready to start trading on his own account.' She turned her head away sharply and added in a voice suddenly thick with tears: 'Or he would be, if this wretched thing hadn't happened!'

'You mean the sacrifice.'

She bit her lip but said nothing.

'That's what the parish chiefs were here about, wasn't it?' I probed gently. 'They were angry about what happened. What did they have to say?'

The woman struck the floor next to her with her open right hand, making a ringing slap. 'What do you expect they said? Do you know what an honour it is to be selected to offer a Bathed Slave at the festival? A merchant spends his

whole life cringing before the warriors, going about barefoot and wearing a rough old cloak instead of nice cotton
and ducking out of the way of some oaf he could buy ten
times over, and then for one day a year there is this chance
to show we are as good as they are. For someone as young as
Shining Light to be chosen, and then to show us all up the
way he did – is it any wonder they were angry?' Agitation
made her teeth grind together. 'You know what I had to do
just now? I had to listen to seven old men lecturing me on
the disgrace we've brought on our people, and demanding
to know where Shining Light is now and where he got that
slave from in the first place. And I've had to take all that and
try and defend my son and pretend I knew what he was up
to, when I never did, and do it all by myself because my
father's drunk himself into a stupor again and the ungrateful
little sod's run away and left me!' She ended with a deep
shuddering breath and something like a sob.

'You don't know where Shining Light got his Bathed
Slave from, then?'

She gave a loud sniff before replying: 'He told me he got
him at the big slave market in Azcapotzalco.'

'You didn't believe him.'

Oceloxochitl looked down at where her hands lay
clasped on her knees, between the folds of her skirt. 'He left
off buying him until very late – too late to train him properly. And when the parish chiefs wanted to inspect him, and
advise Shining Light on how to present him, he kept fob-
bing them off. The truth is, I don't know where that slave
came from.' She tilted her chin up until her eyes glinted in
the sunlight. A faint huskiness, a hint of pride, came into
her voice. 'But I will tell you this. I was with my father
when he presented a Bathed Slave at the Festival of the
Raising of Banners, in the first year the Emperor allowed

the merchants to make an offering, and he was nothing like Shining Light's creature. He danced up the steps ahead of us, the way the poets say they should, and he died like a warrior. I know how these things should be done!'

Her fingers unlaced and laced themselves in her lap. I watched her thigh lift and settle again under the thin material of her skirt, betraying a sudden restlessness, and wondered what feelings came with the thought of that sacrifice, so many years before. Perhaps she pictured herself as a young woman, ascending the Great Pyramid, with the sounds and smells and thrill of death around her, and ahead of her the man her father was sending to die, mounting the last few steps with a triumphant cry on his lips, shedding chalk-dust from his heels as he climbed.

I had an unsettling vision of her as she must have been in the moment when her father's slave gave up his life, her lips parted, her cheeks flushed, her eyes shining, the breath caught in her throat. I had seen enough sacrifices to know how it had been, the animal joy that no man or woman with blood in their veins could help being caught up in. It was not bloodlust but a more basic thing: the presence of death and the affirmation of life, two things that our traditions taught us could never be separated.

'I know too. I used to be a priest.'

She looked at me with renewed interest and I saw the dark colour that had spread over her face and the quick pulse in her throat. I wondered whether she in turn saw me as a young man, when I had been one of the temple's mysterious, glamorous servants, with my crown of feathers and my cheeks daubed with blood and ochre. She frowned. 'But now you're a slave – how did that happen?'

The question shocked me back to the present. I did not want to talk about this.

'My master needs to know where your son's offering came from,' I said clumsily. 'He needs to talk to Shining Light . . .'

'Why?'

I opened my mouth to reply and then shut it again. What could I say, when for all I knew old Black Feathers might just then be amusing himself deciding what parts of her son's body he would like to have severed with a dull knife? I heard myself mumbling: 'He's concerned that it went wrong. After all, he sent me to help.'

'And a lot of help you were too!' she said bitterly. 'If you hadn't let that slave get away when he did, it might have been all right . . .'

'There was nothing I could have done!'

'My son would have been better off hiring another escort, like that big commoner Handy,' she went on, ignoring me. 'Two men like him might have been able to hold the slave.'

'I didn't ask to be there!' I protested. 'I don't even know why I was there in the first place! Whose idea was it to send me, anyway? Did your son ask for me?'

'How should I know? I've told you, I had no idea what he was doing.'

'So you don't know what dealings he had with my master?'

'Until yesterday, I wasn't aware that he'd ever had any!'

'What about the man he placed his bets with – Misty?'

My last question seemed to strike her like a blow. She leaned forward sharply as if someone had stabbed her in the stomach. She sat up again just as abruptly, but kept her eyes on her knees as she answered me in a voice that was suddenly very small: 'My son doesn't share all his . . . business affairs with me. Why should he?'

'But he did use him? He did put money on the ball game through him?'

I watched her shoulders shudder momentarily beneath the thin fabric of her blouse. 'I don't know. Yes – he probably did. Look, I'm tired. I had the parish chiefs here all morning, and now you come asking questions that I can't answer.' Her eyes were no longer glistening, merely hard and defiant. 'If the Chief Minister wants to talk to my son, then he had better go and look for him. But you can tell him Shining Light isn't here. He's gone away to die. See what your master makes of that, slave!'

3

A small canal ran alongside the merchant's house. I lingered by it for a while, toying with the idea of hailing
a canoe and so saving myself a long walk back to my master's
house in the centre of Tenochtitlan. I felt tired and dispir-
ited: I could not claim to have achieved very much here,
beyond establishing that Shining Light was not at home and
that his mother appeared to have less idea of where his sacrificial victim had come from than I had. I did not even
know whether to believe her when she claimed her son had
gone into exile.

It was quiet here. The walls around me were the colour
of sun-bleached bones, and for all I could tell held as much
life within them. The water at my feet sparkled in the late
morning sunshine. I gazed at my reflection, wondering what
Oceloxochitl had really seen when she had looked at me.

Had I imagined the way she had looked at me while we
were talking about the death of Bathed Slaves? Many
women found priests alluring. They found us intriguing and
sinister, for our ancient hymns and bloodstained knives, our
black robes and long, tangled hair. They thought us brave,
because we fasted and bled ourselves and confronted the
gods every day and the creatures that frequented the darkness
every night. And they could not have us, for we were celibate, and that only made us more fascinating.

Oceloxochitl was a handsome woman, much the same age as myself, and something about her had snagged in my heart and was refusing to be dislodged. Perhaps it had been her fierce pride in what her late husband had done, or her refusal to surrender to grief or rage, or her defiance towards the Chief Minister's messenger. Perhaps it had been something in that moment we had shared, dwelling on the long-ago death of her father's slave. She was named for that boldest of flowers, the tiger Lily, and for a moment I thought that if I had just seen its deep red and brilliant yellow petals for the first time, I should not have been so struck by them. I turned the name over on my tongue: 'Lily . . .'

Then I allowed the face in the water an indulgent smile. A man who had sold himself into slavery had no ambition, no desire, no will of his own. He had given all that up, and now just had fantasies, and they were safe enough.

Two faces smiled back at me.

I nearly fell in the canal. Recovering hastily from the fright, I stepped back and looked at the new arrival in the flesh.

He was dressed as a priest. Skulls and stars adorned his long black mantle. An ocelot-skin tobacco pouch dangled on his chest. His hair was as long as mine, although not as dirty as a priest's hair would often be: matted and filthy with moss growing in it. Fresh blood, drawn from his earlobes, lay congealing on either side of his neck.

For a moment I had the unsettling feeling that I was seeing myself, a dozen years younger, until the surprise wore off and I began to see the differences.

To begin with the stranger was taller than I was, although he was stooping to bring his face on a level with mine. More interesting than that was the sooty paste covering his face and body. All priests wore this to stain themselves as

black as the night that was their habitat, but this man had
gone further than anyone else I had seen. He was caked in
the stuff. It had rubbed off on the hem of his mantle and
collected as a smattering of black dust at his feet. It had
cracked around his eyes and mouth, showing slivers of
brown skin underneath, but elsewhere it had been applied so
thickly it obscured the features underneath like a mask. I
could not even tell the man's age, because he had laid the
soot on so heavily that it would have hidden any lines on his
face.

Still smiling, he said: 'Looking for a boat?'

He was mumbling. Priests often did, owing to their practice of sacrificing their own blood by sticking cactus spines
through their tongues.

I looked around quickly. There was no one else beside
the canal, although a canoe floated on the water a few paces
away. A boatman stood in it, leaning on his pole with his
back to me. He was young, an unblooded youth's lock of
hair still falling down the nape of his neck.

'You can share mine,' the man beside me added.

I found the sudden appearance of man and canoe disturbing.

'Thanks.' I tried not to sound ungracious. 'I might walk
back to Tenochtitlan, though.'

The smile vanished, splitting off a few flakes of soot as it
did so. 'You might not.'

Something jabbed me below my ribcage. I tried to back
away, only to find one of my arms seized in a grip like an
alligator's bite. I felt a sharp pricking against my stomach and
looked down at the knife. It was made of brown metal, like
copper, but darker. I had never seen anything like it.

'What's this about? Let me go!'

The grip on my arm tightened.

'The boat.' The man with the knife jerked my arm, twisting me around to face the canoe. Struggling to keep my balance, I could do nothing about trying to escape before I felt the knife again, now prodding me in the small of my back.

As we moved towards the boat, its occupant turned around.

He was Nimble, Misty's son – the boy I had last seen and heard taking bets on a ball game from my master.

I thought it was a robbery at first. Perhaps Kindly had not been altogether wrong after all, I thought, assuming that the black-faced man with the knife was Nimble's father, Misty. Perhaps it was true that the merchant owed him money. If he had heard about the young man's departure he might have been in a hurry to collect it before it was too late, and perhaps he thought I had beaten him to it.

'Look, you've got this all wrong. I haven't got anything.'

'Shut up and get in the boat. Call out to anyone and you're dead.'

I was made to clamber into the centre of the canoe under the youth's watchful eye. The black-faced man got in behind me. As soon as he had settled himself, with the blade of his knife resting against the side of my neck, the youth pushed off from the side of the canal.

'What's this about?' I demanded. 'Where are you taking me?'

My assailant's breath stirred the hair on the back of my head but he said nothing, so I tried the boy instead.

'He doesn't say much, your father, does he?'

The youth had nothing to say either. He was concentrating on the canal's banks and the pole in his hands. He handled the canoe skilfully, avoiding the occasional oncoming craft with nothing more than a slight curl of his lip and an almost imperceptible twist of the pole.

'We're heading out of the city,' I observed. I might as well have been talking to myself. I lapsed into silence, trying to decide what to do while I watched the scenery changing slowly around me.

The canal merged into the broad waterway that spilled into the lake at Copolco on the eastern edge of Mexico's island. Soon the houses gliding by on either side of us would be replaced by fields: chinampas, the artificial islands that our farmers had taken to cultivating when they had run out of dry land, and which now surrounded the city.

I watched the houses and fields slipping past me with an odd feeling of detachment. The knife was still scraping the skin at the back of my neck but I was not afraid. What was happening to me was not real. It was too bizarre: to have been sent to Shining Light's house by my master and then kidnapped by the man with whom my master bet on the ball game and his boy. It was obviously not a robbery, since they had made no effort to search me for valuables. What were they planning to do, then – hold me against my master's gambling debts?

I considered raising the alarm despite the threatened consequences, but there was no one to call to. The houses were silent: most people must either be at home, out of sight and earshot behind the faceless walls of their courtyards, or have gone to the market. The fields looked no more promising. I knew there would be little work being done in these man-made wetlands now, with the earth too hard to dig when it was frosty and too soft when it was mild, and if there was anyone about I would be lucky to see them through the thickly planted willows bordering each plot.

My only chance, unless I steeled myself to take on the

youth, the man and the knife alone, was the open lake, where there were always plenty of boats and a shout carried a long way – provided I ever got there. All I could do in the meantime was to try to get them talking. I thought it might distract them at least.

'Do I have to guess what all this is about?'

That drew as much of a response as I expected it to.

'All right, then.' I tried to keep my tone bland and conversational, while my eyes darted about, searching the fields on either side for an opportunity to get away. 'You aren't thieves, I know that. So it's me you're after, isn't it? But why?' I paused. The boy went on plying his pole impassively and the knife stayed at my neck. 'No, you won't tell me that. All right, then, how did you know where to find me? Was it the woman who told you where to look, or the old man? But they'd never have got a message to you in time, not unless you were right by their house already. What about the Chief Minister?'

The knife twitched.

'Isn't old Black Feathers one of your best customers? What's he going to say when he learns you've made off with his slave?'

From behind me a thick voice said: 'I told you, this is too dangerous. We should do him here.' I thought it sounded more distinct than before, as if the effort of talking like a priest was becoming hard to maintain.

I tried to shift my weight forward a little so that I could throw myself at the boy if either he or his father made a move, even though I knew the knife would be deep in my flesh before I could stir a muscle.

The youth turned to look at me and let his eyes linger on my face, as if he were looking for something there.

'No,' he said. His voice sounded too old for his years. 'We mustn't.'

I felt the other man's tension through the metal pressed to my skin. I recognized fear or suppressed anger or a mixture of both and wondered how long I had before he got desperate enough to use the knife. 'We're taking enough chances with him as it is. The longer we let him live the riskier it gets. I should have killed him beside the canal!'

'But . . .'

'But nothing!' The strain had come out into his voice now, which was suddenly high pitched, almost strangled. 'Who do you think I'm doing all this for, anyway? If it wasn't for you, I wouldn't be on this boat at all!' The cold pricking at my neck vanished and the knife blade appeared at the corner of my eye as he waved it in the youth's direction. I started to turn my head, to flex the muscles in my arms and legs ready to spring. 'Don't argue with me! We kill him when I say so!'

The glittering metal swung fully into my sight. I saw shock and alarm in the boy's eyes, and realized too late that the knife was arcing towards my throat.

A strong hand seized my hair and yanked my head backwards, stretching my neck like a sacrificial quail's.

'No!' The young man almost screamed, dropping his pole as he threw himself towards me. 'Please! You mustn't! Not until we've asked him – we've got to know!'

He was too slow. His fingers barely brushed Misty's arm before the blade struck my taut skin.

It stayed there, quite still, for a moment that seemed to stretch into days. I was distantly aware of a stinging sensation and the warm, wet feeling of blood running from a shallow cut down the front of my neck. Much closer to me seemed the youth's wide-open, imploring eyes, just a hand's breadth from my face.

'Please,' he begged in a whisper.

The knife wavered a little as the hand holding it relaxed.

'You really want me to spare him?'

'Yes . . . at least for now.'

'At least for now.' The man behind me slipped once more into his slurring parody of a priest's voice. 'All right. You win. He can live until he's told us what you want to know. Then we'll kill him.'

4

At Copolco we turned south to pass along the western edge of the island towards Tenochtitlan. The boy swapped his pole for a paddle and put a little distance between us and the shore. Whether this was to make it easier for him to avoid running aground or harder for me to escape I did not know, but both he and his companion seemed to relax a little. The knife returned to the side of my neck.

I had not tried to start another conversation. Nearly having my throat cut had made the danger I was in all too real, and I held my tongue for fear of provoking Misty again. I suspected that if he and his son renewed their argument over me, the boy might not win it so easily the second time. Still, as the land receded, I felt I could risk a glance over my shoulder.

The Sun lay low over the mountains, throwing the far shore of the lake into shadow. The water's surface was calm, the bulk of the island of Mexico and the dyke beyond it sheltering it from the winds that sometimes stirred up the great salt lake to the east. Canoes dotted it, although none was close enough to be worth calling out to.

Ahead of us, like a long low wall barring our way, was the causeway connecting Mexico with the small city of Tlacopan on the western shore of the lake. By the time we got there it would be thronging with traders, day-labourers and artisans heading home for the night to their towns and villages on the mainland. Every so often they would stop the traffic to open the wooden bridges that pierced the causeway at intervals, in order to let boats pass from one part of the lake to another. While the bridges were closed a mass of canoes would build up around them, drifting aimlessly about like reeds scattered over the water while they waited for them to open again. If we found ourselves in the middle of such a crowd, I thought hopefully, then anything might happen.

The nearer shore was all willows, sedges and rushes, with here and there a wooden landing stage or a little adobe house whose whitewashed walls glowed pink in the light of the setting Sun. Once or twice the flat summit of a pyramid appeared above the tops of the willows, with smoke drifting lazily from the temple that crowned it. The greatest city in the World lay just behind this quiet green verge, but here there was no one to be seen.

I heard a faint splash as the paddle was dipped into the water, and my view of the shoreline shifted abruptly as we turned towards it. With a sudden feeling of dread I realized we would not, after all, be crossing the causeway.

In an effort to see where we were going I twisted my head around too quickly and was rewarded with a sharp stinging at the side of my neck as the man behind me reminded me of the knife. He uttered a low, wordless growl as I turned hastily to face the youth again. The boy's face had suddenly turned a little paler than before, and I saw strain in his narrow eyes and tightly compressed lips.

We were entering a little sheltered cove – probably nothing more than a gap between plots of reclaimed land. There was no one else about – nor would there be by now, I thought, with dusk falling – but we did not quite have the cove to ourselves. There was another boat here, tucked away among the sedges, although I caught only the briefest glimpse of it.

We must be close to our destination, I realized, and if I was going to get away now was the time to do something about it.

'Is this it? Have we arrived yet?' I must have sounded like a small child being taken on a long boat trip, whining from boredom and hunger after the honeyed maize cakes had run out, but I was only hoping to distract them both for long enough to try for the knife.

The only answer I got was a tense silence, broken only by the sound of water lapping against the side of the boat.

The boy stood up in the stern, with his paddle poised a hand or two above the water, but he did not dip it in. He was staring at something behind my head.

His lips moved but for a moment no sound came out.

From somewhere behind me, I heard a voice. It was strangely muffled and I could not make out the words, but it was surely a voice.

The man behind me turned towards it, unthinking. I felt the knife leave the side of my neck and I moved. I threw myself forward, launching myself at the boy: in the narrow space of the canoe it was the only way to go.

'Look out!' he shrieked, raising his paddle.

His father went for my hair again, but this time he was too late, because I was already moving. He seized a lock, bunching it in his fist, but my own weight tore it out by the roots. I heard it rip horribly over my own scream of pain but I was still moving. I hit the youth with my shoulder. He fell over backwards and I landed on my knees on top of him, my arms flailing wildly at his face.

I must have hit the boy three or four times before his father dragged me off him. Yet again he had my hair, using it now to haul me backwards onto my haunches as he bared my throat once more for the knife.

'No! No! No!' I heard Nimble's urgent cries over my own howl of pain and the sounds from behind me, the loud splashing as of something heavy moving about in the water and that voice, clearer now but still unintelligible.

'I've got to kill him!' The voice behind was almost shrill. 'Can't you see what's happening? We can't deal with him as well! Get rid of him now! What else can we do?'

The youth was on his feet again. His face was bloody from my attack and his eyes were wide and wild and he had the paddle in his hand, raised much too high above the water.

'We can do this!' he shouted.

With my hair gripped in Misty's fist I had no chance of dodging the blow. I could only watch as the flat of the paddle's blade swung in towards me, to smash into the side of my head.

I have seen flying men among the barbarians in the East — among the Huaxtecs and the Totonacs. Of course, the flying man does not truly fly like a bird: he is really an acrobat, whose act consists of jumping off the top of a tall pole, many times his own height, on the end of a long twisted rope. As he falls and the rope unwinds he seems to swoop through the air in ever-widening, giddying circles, until he hits the ground at a staggering run.

After the boy hit me with the paddle I felt like one of those acrobats, with the world spinning crazily about me, around and around and up and down, and the roaring in my head was like wind rushing over my ears as I soared skywards with stomach-wrenching speed before plunging back to Earth to drop, sprawling, into the bottom of the boat.

For a moment I had no idea where I was or how I had got there. I could not hear anything over the roaring noise and I could not open my eyes. I tasted blood: it filled my nose and mouth and stopped my breathing. My scalp seemed to be on fire and someone was battering the side of my head with a flint axe and my bowels were churning.

I panicked. My arms and legs hit out and thrashed madly. One of my knuckles struck the wooden side of the canoe, yielding a jolt of acute agony that I noticed even over the pain in my head and my guts. The flat of my hand found the same surface again and felt its way to the top and clutched it spasmodically.

Clinging to the canoe's side and hauling one-handed got me, somehow, onto my knees. My other hand batted at my face and came away wet. It rubbed some of the blood away from my eyes and out of my eyelashes where it was fast congealing. I coughed and choked. I opened an eye, too briefly to see anything. I thought I heard someone shouting.

I tried to stand then, too quickly, because the world was still rocking from side to side, and when I put an arm out to grab something to steady myself there was nothing there. Without uttering a sound, I toppled out of the violently pitching canoe into the freezing waters of the lake.

It was like falling through a sheet of ice, so cold I could not feel how cold it was, and as dark as a cave. I could not think. I could not move. My body was trying to swim, seemingly without any impulse from me, but all I could do was twist about, as helpless as a sick fish. For a horrible moment I thought some water monster had got me; then I found my cloak had wrapped itself around me and pinned my arms to my side.

I had another moment of unthinking panic while my arms strained against the heavy, wet cloth and my legs kicked uselessly. I wanted to scream but there was no air in my lungs and my mouth and nose were full of blood and water.

Into my mind flashed a vision of the fate of those who drowned, who were destined to spend the afterlife in the rain-god's paradise, a place of ease and abundance where the rain was warm and the harvest never failed.

Perhaps that vision calmed me. I stopped struggling, just at the moment when the sodden fibres of my cheap cloak finally gave way and I was able to free my arms.

With the last of my strength, I struck upwards. The tattered remains of my cloak caught around my ankles and I kicked them angrily away. I looked up, opening my eyes for the first time in the cold fresh water.

I could not see the surface. A large dark shape loomed above me. Just as I realized what it was my head hit something hard.

I had come up under a boat.

I pushed against the rough, pitted wood with both hands, desperate to be free of it before the dizziness that was starting to come over me became too much and I forgot which way was up. I felt movement through my palms: the whole great mass stirring sluggishly and little tremors shooting through it, as if the vessel above me were full of people running from side to side. I was half drowned, I thought, and must be hallucinating: the canoe had not seemed so large.

Then the shadow over my head was gone, and I was on the surface, gulping air in great anguished whooping gasps.

At first I could hear nothing except my own breathing. I trod water, while I looked around me for the shore. I had to make for it as fast as I could, but my strength was almost gone and the cold was creeping deep into my bones, bringing with it a strange lethargy.

I became dimly aware that there was some sort of commotion going on. I heard shouts of anger or alarm. With my ears still full of water I could not make out any words and I was not listening anyway, but then, for all my growing indifference, came something that made me look up.

'Yaotl!' The voice was still indistinct but I could not mistake my own name. 'Nimble! Where's Yaotl?'

I peered up the boat's side, listening to the shouting and the sounds of running feet.

A face appeared above me.

The youth and I stared at each other, both too astounded to speak or move. I saw streaks of blood on his cheeks and neck. It had not had time to dry since I had hit him.

'Yaotl!' the voice cried again.

The face vanished without a sound.

I swam for my life.

5

The shore here was man made, the edge of a chinampa plot held together with stakes and willows. There was no easy, shallow beach for me to flop onto like a stranded fish and crawl up. On the other hand there were plenty of tangled willow roots for my numb, slippery fingers to cling to as I hauled my protesting body onto relatively dry land.

I had no idea whether anyone had followed me from the boat. I had not heard anyone, but I did not care. I was too exhausted to do anything except collapse, face upwards, in the middle of a muddy field.

The Sun had set. The sky was darkening, turning a deep blue, and the willow branches overhead were dark jagged shadows, shot through with stars that were steady bright points in the thin, clear winter air.

If I stayed here I might freeze to death, I thought dreamily, but I could just lie still for a moment, listening to the faint rustling of the bare branches as they swayed gently above me.

I closed my eyes.

They snapped open again.

Something was moving through the branches.

I peered straight up, looking for the movement again, wondering whether I had fancied it. Then I both saw and heard it: a large bird, its wings beating madly as it took off from a bough just above me, seemed to dither in midair and dropped heavily onto a lower limb. A little shower of broken twigs fell around me, followed by a couple of large feathers drifting downward.

The bird perched, swaying uncertainly back and forth. Something about its brief, awkward flight made me think it was unused to being airborne.

I tried to get up for a closer look. I slipped in the mud under me, landing hard on my backside, and swore.

The bird took fright. It exploded into the air, showering me again with debris from the trees as it crashed through the branches around it, and streaked off into the night, cawing loudly, and then there was nothing left but a few scattered feathers and the sound of its raucous voice over the water.

I do not know how long I stood there, staring after it. It was long enough for the Moon to come up because, when I picked up one of the long, stiff feathers and examined it, I noted how it glistened in the silver light, and how deep was its red colour.

I was trembling by then, but not from the cold. It was a natural reaction, I told myself, even for one who had been a priest, when confronted with a message from the gods: for the bird had to have been an omen.

I had not mistaken its cries as it had flown away. I had heard them before, in the moments before the boy had hit me with the paddle. Now I knew them for words. But what kind of bird could utter human speech?

'Save us!' it had cawed, over and over again. 'Save us! Save us! Save us!'

I had a long walk home from the chinampa plot. I staggered and sloshed my way across one waterlogged field after another, scrambling in and out of the icy ditches between them where they were too wide to jump, unsure whether I was heading the right way or just going around in circles.

When I reached my master's house I was exhausted, cold, wet, hungry, filthy, in pain and furious. I had had long enough to think about what had happened to me to ask myself what it meant, and to come up with the only possible answer. I stamped up the steps towards my master's private apartments, intending, if I had to, to burst in on him there, because by now I was too enraged to care what he might say or do to me.

I found old Black Feathers at the top of the stairway, sitting under his magnolia tree, enjoying a quiet smoke under the stars before turning in for the night. He had his eyes closed, but opened them at the sound of my footsteps.

He sat bolt upright. His eyes started from their sockets, his hands flew out in front of him as if to ward off an attack, and the pipe fell from his mouth and struck the floor with a clatter. He made a faint noise far down in the back of his throat.

'You seem surprised to see me,' I said, pausing significantly before adding, 'my Lord.'

A thin streak of smoke rose from the dropped pipe into the air between us. Neither of us made any move to pick it up. I would normally have retrieved it as a matter of course, but I was in no mood to tonight. My master seemed to have forgotten about it.

'You didn't think I'd be back today, did you? Were you expecting to see me again, ever? What did Misty want with me, anyway?'

His hands dropped onto his knees. He relaxed a little against the back of his chair. A puzzled frown took the place of his stupefied stare, deepening the lines permanently etched in his forehead.

'Misty?' he echoed.

'Yes, my Lord. We both know what sort of dealings you have with him, and why his son comes here. You sent me to Pochtlan and they knew exactly where to find me. That's what you wanted Handy for yesterday, isn't it – to deliver the message? What happened – did the team from Huexotla let you down? Was he collecting his winnings? And why me?' I added, my voice rising with bitterness. 'It's not as if you couldn't spare the money. Am I that useless?'

Ordinarily I would never have got away with such insolence, and if repeated it would have given my master a lawful reason to put a wooden collar round my neck and send me to the market, where the only likely buyers would be priests looking for sacrificial victims. This time, however, all he could find to say, over and over again, was: 'Misty?'

'You can't pretend you didn't know he'd be there.' As I told him what had happened to me I watched his frown deepen. When I finished there was a long, thoughtful silence.

'Misty,' my master murmured to himself, for the last time. 'But that doesn't make sense . . .'

Then he seemed to pull himself together. The frown lifted and he coughed once to clear his throat.

'I don't understand your story, Yaotl, and frankly I don't believe it.'

'But you know it's the truth!'

'Silence!' he roared, his hands gripping his knees and his knuckles suddenly turning white with fury. 'Who do you think you're talking to? Have you forgotten who I am, slave?' He was trembling with rage, and in spite of myself I took a step away from him. 'I tell you to go and find the merchant and what happens? Not only do you fail to do what I told you, but you come barging into my presence, unbidden, looking and smelling as if you've been sleeping in a ditch, and have the temerity to tell me what I know or don't know! I could set you to work in the quarries for this – that would teach you some manners!'

'But my Lord, I . . .' I spluttered, but then fell silent, my indignation failing in the face of his anger. In a few words old Black Feathers had re-established our relationship of master and slave, reminding me that I was his man and not my own.

'I'm sorry, my Lord,' I mumbled.

He took a deep breath and let it out slowly. The trembling subsided.

'I don't pretend to know what you've been up to,' he said at last, 'but from the look of you, you've obviously been through a lot.' I had lost my cloak, my breechcloth was torn and sodden, dried blood caked my face and neck, my legs and feet were black with mud, and a small puddle had formed on the stuccoed floor around me. 'In fact,' he went on, 'I wonder if you haven't been overexerting yourself. Perhaps you ought to rest. After all, it's not as if you've got anywhere nearer to finding Shining Light, or the sorcerers, for that matter. Yes, that's it. You can spend tomorrow resting, and see if you get any fresh ideas.'

It was my turn to stare as I realized that I was being dismissed from his sight, and that as far as my master was concerned our discussion was over.

I crept away down the steps. It was hopeless to argue. If my master knew I was telling the truth but was denying it for some reason then nothing I could say would make him change his mind. In any event, what was I going to suggest – that he take my kidnapping up with Misty, when I was convinced the two of them had connived to bring it about in the first place?

As I headed back to my room, however, I was left with the uneasy impression that he had ordered me to rest because he wanted to keep me in his house, within easy reach, while he made up his mind what to do with me.

6

I crawled onto my sleeping mat, grabbing a rough old blanket with numb fingers and pulling it over my painfully cold limbs, and lay down, too exhausted to care that I was still caked in mud and blood.

'Where have you been all day?'

I groaned. 'Don't you ever sleep?'

'How can I?' Costly grumbled. 'I threw my blanket off during the day, when it was too hot, and now I can't reach it. I'm freezing! Also, no one's been around to give me my medicine, and I haven't been able to go all day.'

Swearing under my breath, I got up and found the old slave's blanket for him. It was too late for him to have the revolting infusion he took to open his bowels, but I found the gourd anyway so that I could give it to him first thing in the morning. I swirled the liquid inside it around and judged that he had enough to last him a couple of days.

'That's better. Now you can lull me to sleep, telling me what you've been up to.'

I told him. I wanted nothing better than to slip into unconsciousness myself, but I was too uncomfortable. A violent shivering had come over me and my head was throbbing. At the same time the numbness that had come over my toes and fingers from being immersed in icy water and

exposed to the evening's chill was wearing off and they felt
as if they were on fire.

My companion's only response was: 'So you fancy your
chances with the widow, then?'

'Don't be ridiculous,' I growled between teeth clamped
together to stop them chattering. 'Apart from the fact that
she's from a Pochteca family and I'm a commoner and a
slave, she's got no reason to like me. She thinks I'm part of
the reason her son ran away.'

'And she's not your type anyway,' he added mockingly.
When I ignored him he went on: 'Still, I'd be more worried
about this man Misty. You really think our master gave you
to him to settle a bet? It seems a roundabout way to go
about it, though.'

'That was my first thought. Even he might not get away
with handing me over openly. I thought staging a kidnapping might be the easiest way of doing it without risking
exposing himself.' The explanation sounded plausible, but I
had already worked out that it was nonsense. It was simply
too much trouble to go to for the sake of a trifling debt.
'Besides, he seemed remarkably eager to kill me. I'd not
have been worth much to him if he had!'

'But his boy wanted to spare your life,' the old slave
reminded me.

'He let me go,' I replied wonderingly, remembering that
blood-streaked face peering at me over the side of the boat.
I could not make sense of any of it. The boy had played his
part in my abduction, and he had hit me with the paddle,
although he had plainly done that so that his father would
refrain from taking the knife to me. But why had he not
called out when he was watching me treading water and his
father was shouting for me?

'What about this bird, then?' Costly interrupted my

thoughts. 'You say it talked – that could be an omen, could-
n't it? Either that or it was a sorcerer who'd turned himself
into a bird. Say, you don't suppose . . .?'

'It wasn't one of the men I'm looking for. I'm sure they're
just charlatans. I don't think real sorcerers would have let
themselves get shut in the prison in the first place, and
anyway the bird I saw looked too big to get between the bars
of one of those cages. A sorcerer would have turned himself
into something tiny, like a hummingbird or a swift. An
omen, though . . .'

I hugged my blanket uneasily. There had been many
omens seen in Mexico of late. The Emperor had described
some of them to me but there had been others: two-headed
men, a disembodied female voice crying out in the streets at
night, lightning striking the war-god's temple. 'It could be.
An omen of what, though?'

He let out a breathless, croaking laugh. 'That's an easy
one to answer! Take a leaf out of the Emperor's book – get
a sorcerer to tell you!'

'Very funny.' At last the shivering was beginning to subside. I rolled over, intending to sleep, but the old man was
not finished.

'No, I mean it,' he persisted. 'Why not hire a sorcerer to
interpret the bird? It might be the answer to all your questions.'

'I don't know any sorcerers – not real ones, anyway.'

'No problem. There's a man I used to go to, name's
Cipactli, he lives in a village down near Coyoacan. Just mention my name and he'll . . .'

I sat upright once more. 'Did you say Coyoacan?'

'I know it's a long way, but if you start early enough . . .'

'Coyoacan.' The name recalled my brother's face, and the
thing hidden in its shadows when he had mentioned it. I
shivered, although I had forgotten the cold.

'Of course,' Costly went on, 'he doesn't come cheap. The genuine article never does.'

'I haven't any money, you know that.'

'Then use some of mine. There's some good cotton in that chest over there, easily enough to pay for a consultation.'

The chest he meant was the small reed box that contained our possessions. In my case they were pathetically few – a single worthless souvenir from my days as a priest, a couple of badly worn maguey fibre capes and breechcloths and little else. Costly had a little more: some money in the form of cloth and cocoa beans and a couple of bone nose-plugs, as I recalled. The money was what he had saved, as most slaves did if they could, against the day when he might be able to buy his freedom.

'I can't take that,' I said.

He sighed. 'Yaotl, what do you think I'm going to do with it? Buy myself back from old Black Feathers? What good would that do me? I can't walk and there's no one out there to look after me. I'd starve – I might as well be a slave and eat. I was . . .' I heard him swallow, as if trying to get rid of an obstruction in his throat. 'I was going to leave it all to you anyway, so you might as well take some now. Consider it an advance on your inheritance!'

I could not think of anything to say.

I had spent years fetching and carrying for the old slave, putting food in his toothless mouth, giving him his medicine and cleaning up the results, turning him over in his bed when he was too weak and stiff to move himself and above all listening to his incessant complaints, and in all that time it had never occurred to me to expect anything more from him than what he had already done. Yet what made my eyes sting now was not his generosity in leaving me all he possessed. It was the thought that if I ever came into his money, it would be because I was never going to hear the old man's whining voice again.

'Thank you,' I managed eventually.

The only answer was a loud snore.

THREE EAGLE

1

I left my master's house before dawn, without speaking to anyone. The Chief Minister had not got up and I wanted to be gone before he learned I had defied his order to rest. I took some of Costly's money with me, although I had no intention of paying any of it to a sorcerer.

Handy, the commoner, lived in Atlixco, a parish in the east of the city. It was right on the edge of the lake and, but for the dyke that shielded the city from storms on the great salt lake beyond it, would probably have been awash in brackish water three or four times a year.

I arrived at the house early in the morning, to find the place already in uproar.

There appeared to be children everywhere. The youngest, yelling and whooping, chased turkeys and little dogs around the courtyard, in an elaborate game whose object seemed to be to herd the creatures between two human thigh bones, stuck upright into the ground, and into the bath house. Two older lads stood near by, trying to look grave and grown up, even though they were transparently yearning either to join in the game or to break it up by seizing the bones – the proudly displayed remains of the two enemy warriors Handy had captured with his own hands – and using them to beat their siblings unconscious.

The youngsters looked at me just long enough to register

my existence and then ignored me altogether. Their older brothers tracked me curiously as I crossed the courtyard and made for the family's private rooms.

The big commoner stood in his doorway, wearing an even older cloak than the one I had first seen him in and a harassed look.

'Lively lot!' I congratulated him. 'Are they all yours?'

He glanced over my shoulder. 'I don't know. How many did you see?'

'I think seven.'

'In that case no – a couple of the youngest are my brother's. We've got nine,' he went on apologetically, 'but the oldest girl's married and her sister and two of her brothers are at the House of Youth. Itzcoatl and Mazatl won't be far behind them – that's if I haven't suffocated the whole brood by holding them all head down over burning chillies first, of course! Excuse me.'

He was back a moment later, having righted one of the thigh bones, pulled a couple of small children off an even smaller one, dragged a fourth child out of the bath house and roundly scolded the two eldest, although whether this was for inattention or just for the sake of it, I could not tell.

'You won't believe it, but we're expecting another one!'

'You must like children.'

'I can't help my fate.'

'Nonsense! He adores them!' The speaker was a young woman who had just bustled out of the house with her arms full of cloth, the coarse stuff we sometimes used for blankets. She looked from me to Handy. 'Are you going to introduce your visitor?'

'My name's Yaotl.'

'Yaotl? Oh, I know! I heard all about the business on the

Pyramid. How awful for you! And for the poor man who owned the slave!'

'Most of the city heard about it, Atototl,' Handy said drily, 'many of them from you! This is my brother's wife,' he explained. 'They've got a room across the courtyard, although Atototl spends most of her days in ours, gossiping with Citlalli.'

'Your wife needs someone to help her prepare for her lying-in.' She grinned at me. 'We have to be patient with him, poor man. He is feeling the strain at the moment!'

A pained expression crossed Handy's face. 'If you're looking for your two, you'll probably find them in the bath house, and if there's a dog with them, I'd like it back!' To me he added: 'You can see why I have to spend so much time and money on sorcerers, with all these birthdays to interpret.'

'Ah, that's what I came about.'

'Birthdays?'

'No, sorcerers. I've got to go and see one.'

'What, you want me to recommend . . .'

'No, I know who I want to see: a man from Coyoacan. But I've got a lot of money with me for his fee, you see, so I was wondering if you could come with me – just in case I run into trouble on the way. I'll pay you, naturally.'

The big man looked dubiously at me. 'Trouble? What kind of trouble?'

'You know – thieves.'

I had spent much of the night mulling over the answer to this question, and in the end had decided to lie. It would be too difficult to explain what I expected to find at Coyoacan when I did not know myself, and I did not want my brother's dark hints to put Handy off. Besides, I thought, if I started mentioning warriors and the Chief Minister he would only ask for more money.

He pursed his lips thoughtfully. 'Coyoacan's a long way. It'd take the best part of a day to get there and back. I mean, I expect I could do it, but . . .'

I sighed. 'All right. How much do you want?'

However much it was, it was going to be worth it. If Lion had been telling the truth about Coyoacan, then there was no knowing what might happen, and I might need a strong right arm.

Coyoacan lay on the mainland at the south-western corner of the lake, just at the end of a causeway.

We took Handy's sons, Itzcoatl and Mazatl – Obsidian Snake, or just Snake, and Buck – with us. 'No scholars, either of them,' confided their father, 'but then neither am I, and they'd cause more trouble if I left them at home.'

I was aghast at the thought of taking the boys, but their protests against being left behind effectively drowned out my own. 'They'll be all right,' Handy said when I remonstrated with him. 'It's not as if anything's likely to happen to us. I feel quite bad about taking your money for this, really.' He was in a good mood, apparently looking forward to his day out. I felt an urge to tell him the real purpose of the trip but I suppressed it. After all, I told myself, he was probably right, and nothing was likely to happen. I did not want him turning back and leaving me to go to Coyoacan on my own.

To change the subject, I asked him about the letter he had delivered for my master.

'No idea what it said. I told you, I can't read.'

'Where did you take it?'

'Back to Pochtlan – the house of that merchant, Shining Light.' He hesitated at my sharply indrawn breath. 'I suppose it was a reply to the letter I brought him.'

'Who did you give it to?'

'A household slave – miserable old sod. I asked him what the letter was about, just out of curiosity, but he said his eyes were too far gone to read anything.'

The boys had not made a promising start, slouching sulkily behind their father and quarrelling over whose turn it was to carry the bag with our lunch in it. They were just too young for the House of Youth, and no doubt that is where they would rather have been, hero-worshipping their older brothers, learning how to handle a spear or a sword and hanging on every exaggerated word of some scarred veteran's exploits. They plainly did not think taking a long walk with their father and an unkempt slave was a good use of their time.

They cheered up when we put the city behind us and headed south, because we let them know who we were hoping to see.

'A sorcerer! Will he use a dead woman's forearm to put us all into a trance?' asked Snake keenly.

'No, he won't,' I said firmly. 'Only the wicked kind of sorcerer does that. This one's just going to interpret a dream for me, that's all.'

We carried on in silence after that. We wanted to save our breath for walking, and once we were out on the causeway there was so much to see that even the boys found little to say.

It was a fine winter's day. A light breeze had blown the morning mist away and now stirred the water around us, breaking up the sunlight on its surface and the shapes and shadows of the life underneath. It was easy to imagine terrible things lurking down there – huge fish with jaws full of glistening teeth, the creature we called the Ahuitzotl that outraged the bodies of the drowned – but then you could look up and see the boats and feel reassured. There were more boats than you could count, of every size from one-man canoes to big transports and houseboats whose crews lived all year round in rough, cramped shelters on their decks. Many sat low in the water, weighed down by the people and goods they carried between the island of Mexico and the little whitewashed towns and villages dotting the shore around it.

And you could look over your shoulder at the city. On a clear morning, when the Sun picked out the brilliant colours of its temples and made the white walls of its houses and the snowy caps of the mountains beyond them gleam, no Aztec could look at it from a distance and not be moved. You could forget about the people who lived there; I could forget capricious masters such as the Chief Minister, bullies such as his steward, the Emperor, my father and my brothers and everyone else who had blighted my life over the years, even Misty and his son. From here I could see only the place, and it was the most beautiful thing on Earth: the city my people had built from nothing in just a few bundles of years.

Almost regretfully, I turned back to the road. There was not much traffic. A few individuals sauntered or ran, according to their business. We passed a caravan on the last stage of its long journey from the South, weighed down with exotic goods, the bearers sweating under tump-lines that chafed their shoulders and bit into their foreheads. Trotting briskly in the other direction, so that we had to move smartly out of their way when they caught us up, was a squadron of warriors. They were mostly unblooded youths, judging by their plain cloaks and the loose locks of hair at the backs of their heads, although their captain was a veteran, a Shorn One. They were off to war, or to threaten war: they had heavy packs slung over their backs on top of which their gaudy feathered shields and wooden swords bounced awkwardly. The obsidian blades set into the swords' shafts glinted in the sunlight. The big floppy straps on the Shorn One's sandals clapped noisily on the road.

'Grand sight, eh?' Handy broke our silence as he and his sons stood gazing after the warriors. The boys' mouths were agape. 'They'll keep the tribute houses filled up. Wish I was young enough to go with them. Handy with a spear, I was. Still am. You should have seen . . .'

'I know,' I interrupted him too sharply. 'I've seen enough warriors' handiwork, believe me.' I watched the little cloud of dust the squadron had kicked up spreading and settling back on the road. I had been like them once, dreaming of a Flowery Death in battle or on the sacrificial stone. Then, like all young priests, I had gone to war and seen what it was really like: the trussed captive wriggling helplessly at my feet, the wounded man holding his severed arm and grinning at it in disbelief, the eagle warrior lying dead in the mud, his gorgeous plumage blackened and matted with blood. Above all I remembered the confusion, the captains shouting themselves hoarse and nobody listening, the bewildering sense that life's rhythm had been suspended and Tezcatlipoca alone knew who had won and whether it mattered.

War, I thought, was for young men who had no time for the future and old men who had forgotten the past. The rest of us just had to grow up.

2

According to the old slave, Costly, Cipactli's village lay just outside Coyoacan. Skirting the town itself, we found ourselves walking up a gentle slope, between narrow fields edged with tough, fleshy, broad-leaved maguey plants. The maguey had been planted in rows running across the hillside and their robust leaves and strong roots shored up the earth above them to form shallow terraces. Scattered among the fields were thatched huts made of mud bricks.

'People live in them,' said Buck knowingly.

'No they don't!' his brother cried indignantly. 'They're too small. I bet the men from the town just put them up to shelter from the Sun in, when they're working in the fields.'

'You two,' growled their father, 'don't know you're born! And keep your voices down. People do live here, so be polite about them. Not much happening,' he said to me.

I glanced warily up towards the crest of the slope and down towards the town and the lake. 'I can't see anyone at all,' I said. 'Should it be busy at this time of year?'

'It's always busy,' the big commoner assured me. 'You should try some honest toil in the fields! Look over there – there are some winter squashes they haven't got in yet. They'll lose them if they don't get a move on.'

The fat vegetables lay, apparently neglected, among their tangled foliage. Just beyond them was a low, dark mound that I took to be earth until I saw a dark plume lifting from its surface in the breeze, and recognized the blackened and pulverized remains of mud bricks embedded in its surface.

Despite the Sun's warmth on my back I felt a sudden chill.

'What happened here?' I asked slowly.

The big commoner's brow creased in an expression of concern as he looked at the heap of ash. 'It probably belonged to whoever was growing those squashes. I expect someone kicked over a hearthstone and the Old, Old God took offence and burned the place down.'

I laughed nervously. 'I hope it wasn't Cipactli's.'

'Me too, after coming all this way. We'd better have a look around. Maybe we can find someone to tell us where this sorcerer lives.' He raised his voice to call his sons to order, but they took no notice. They were busy bickering and pushing each other about.

'Told you they were houses,' Buck taunted his brother. 'You're so stupid you wouldn't know a house from raccoon shit.'

Snake replied by aiming a sly kick at his brother's leg and then, very prudently, running away. I could not help smiling as I watched him go. He was the younger and, I suspected, the smarter of the pair, and he had my sympathy for that. I had been a little bit like him once.

'I don't know what I'm going to do with those boys,' Handy grumbled. 'The sooner at least one of them gets some manners beaten into him by a Master of Youths, the better.'

'Leave them to it,' I said. 'Let's find our man and get it over with.'

'All right. You two!' he called. 'We're going up the hill. Mind you look after that bag or we'll all go hungry!'

I kept looking over my shoulder as we climbed the slope towards the nearest house, as if I expected to see someone following us, but apart from the two boys chasing each other between the rows of maguey plants there was nobody in sight.

The house was a shabby affair of crumbling mud bricks and mouldy thatch, with a soiled cloth screen in the doorway that flapped listlessly in the breeze because no one had bothered to secure it at the bottom. The back and sides were surrounded by trash: shattered plates, maize husks, chipped obsidian knife blades, gnawed bones, a broken turkey pen. At the front squatted an old woman, her face tanned by a lifetime in the fields to a leather mask that gave nothing away as she watched us walking up the hill.

'Cipactli? Never heard of him.'

Handy looked at me. I looked away, in case the sense of foreboding I felt showed on my face.

'You must have done,' the commoner said. 'He's a sorcerer. He lives here.'

'There are no sorcerers here,' the old woman snapped. 'Never have been. You got the wrong village. Go away.'

Handy took a step backward, repelled by her sheer hostility. 'What's going on here, Yaotl?'

I shot a nervous glance at the heap of ash down the hill behind us. Was it my imagination, or had something disturbed it? The plume I had seen earlier had become a large black cloud that hid the ruin itself. My stomach lurched as I realized there was no sign of either of the boys.

I turned back to the old woman. 'Who lived in that house?'

The leather mask stayed fixed in place. Only her eyes responded to my question. They blinked once.

She hesitated for what seemed like ages before saying, slowly and quietly but distinctly: 'I can't remember.'

Handy and I stared at each other. We both opened our mouths to speak at the same time, but shut them again when we heard a sharp, shrill cry from the hillside below us.

'Father!'

3

Handy got there first, as might have been expected, racing across the fields while I was still trying to work out where Snake's cry had come from.

By the time I caught him up the three of them were standing in the middle of the burned-out house. The two boys looked safe and healthy, apart from being coated from head to foot in dark grey ash. Snake was grinning and his older brother was scowling. Their father stood between them. His face had changed from an anxious parent's to that of a judge trying to arbitrate a particularly intractable dispute.

'I found it!' Snake was saying.

'But you wouldn't have if I hadn't pushed you into that heap of ash!' his brother retorted indignantly. They reminded me of novice warriors standing over their first captive and squabbling over which of them deserved the first prize, the torso and right thigh.

'What have they found?' I asked.

Handy handed it over without speaking. I hefted it in my palm. It was surprisingly light and burned almost black but there was no mistaking it.

It was the lower jaw of a human.

'No wonder they never got those squashes in,' I remarked.

'Should we look for the rest?' Snake asked.

His father looked dubious, but his brother was already rooting around in the ash and rubble after a souvenir of his own. Before either of us could restrain him he had let out a triumphant whoop and was tugging enthusiastically at another blackened fragment. This one was a collarbone.

'Handy . . .'

'I know,' he said. 'I don't like this either, but there's no stopping them now!'

'Why hasn't someone picked up the bones?' I asked. I would have expected the dead man or woman's family to have had the remains cremated or at least put in a jar and buried near by. To see them casually tossed about disturbed me. A warrior killed or taken in battle could expect his grinning, fleshless skull to moulder on a skull-rack and his thigh bones to end up on show in his captor's house, swelling his glory, but someone who had died in a stupid accident such as a house fire deserved gentler treatment.

Assuming it had been an accident.

'This happened a while ago,' I added. 'Hasn't anyone been here since?'

'Perhaps there isn't anybody – maybe the dead man had no family.'

'Or maybe his family didn't dare come looking for his remains.'

The other man was not paying me much attention, however. He was watching with a mixture of pride and exasperation as his boys turned their quarrel into a race to see who could gather up the most human fragments in the shortest time. 'Look at those two! If I could get them to work that hard in the fields we'd never be hungry again!'

Flakes of ash and clouds of soot billowed around us as Buck and Snake worked. By some unspoken agreement, whenever either of them found a bit he dropped it on his own heap beside the ruins of the house. I wondered how they were planning to judge the winner: were they going to count the bones or weigh them?

I stepped across to Snake's heap and decorously placed the jawbone on it. I gave the heap a second glance as I straightened up. Something did not look right. I bent down again and extracted a bone.

'Snake.'

He came over, his intelligent face turned up towards mine.

'Do you know what this is?'

'It looks like a thigh,' he said accurately.

'Where did you find it?'

He considered the question as gravely as an old gardener being asked to pick out the best spot to plant dahlias in. 'Over there,' he said eventually.

The outline of the house could just be made out beneath the ashes. The place he indicated was just outside it. Judging by the fragments of pottery and other detritus that could still be seen there, it must have been the household's rubbish heap.

As I went to examine it his father joined me. 'What's the matter?'

'Take a look at this.' Handing him the thigh bone Snake had found, I knelt down and began raking through the ashes.

'It doesn't look as badly burned as the others.'

'No,' I agreed. My fingers closed around something hard and jagged. 'Nor does this,' I added as I pulled it free and stood up.

'Hey,' Buck protested, 'that's not fair! I might have found that!'

'Shut up,' his father snapped.

'That's another jawbone, isn't it?' observed Snake. 'How come it's so much smaller than the first one I found?'

'Because it's a child's,' I told him, 'and so is that thigh bone your father's holding. I think it might be a good idea if we all had another look at the little collections you two have made, don't you? Let's see exactly what you've got.'

We sorted the bones out. The process of turning their heaps into skeletons enthralled the boys far more than their contest had, and in no time we had assembled three incomplete specimens.

'This must be a tibia, so it goes here . . .' Snake was saying, placing the bone as precisely as a feather-worker gluing a plume onto a ceremonial shield. 'Father, have you noticed both the small skulls are broken?'

His father stood next to me. 'What do you make of all this?'

I looked at the bones. Two of the reconstructed skeletons were noticeably smaller than the third. 'A man or woman and two children. What's odd is that the adult's bones look more badly burned than the children's. And your son's right – his skull, her skull's in one piece and theirs aren't. Why do you suppose that is?'

'I don't know. I wonder how the place got set on fire. It must have been pretty quick, to get all three of them. A spark from the hearth catching the thatch, maybe?'

'Maybe.' I began pacing around the perimeter of the demolished house. What had been the interior had been churned and trampled by boys looking for bones, but some of the soil and ash outside was relatively untouched, except at the back around the rubbish heap. I scanned the ground around my feet, hoping it still held some clue to what had happened, although I had no idea what I was looking for until I found it.

'I suppose the roof would have caved in,' Handy was saying, 'and maybe it caught them all unawares, but that still doesn't explain why the children's bones are almost white.'

There was something half buried in the earth, near where the doorway would have been: a flash of bright colour among the greys, blacks and browns around me. I dropped on one knee to get a closer look.

'And then again, where . . . Yaotl? What have you found?'

I scraped the ash off the thing and lifted it carefully, holding it between finger and thumb as if it were a venomous insect. It was made of leather, dyed yellow, slightly charred at one end and badly frayed at the other, and large; oversized, in fact.

I showed it to Handy. 'A sandal strap.'

'That's funny,' he said. 'I doubt if many people from around here own a pair of sandals. It doesn't tell us what happened, though.'

I had already worked out who the sandal must belong to, and it was as much as I could do not to turn and run down to the lake and all the way along the causeway back to Tenochtitlan.

'It gives us a pretty good idea.' I looked nervously up and down the hillside once more. 'This fire wasn't an accident. And whoever left this strap wasn't making a social call. We'd better think about getting out of here – the sooner the better.'

'I don't understand.'

'Then look at this strap again.' I waved it in front of him, scattering flakes of soot. 'It's too big for any sandal you or I are ever likely to wear. Ask yourself who wears sandals with big, floppy straps. Remember the Shorn One we saw on the causeway this morning?'

'The Shorn One,' Handy said dreamily. 'They're the greatest warriors in the army, you know, along with the Otomies.' Abruptly he seemed to wake up. He stared at me with his mouth hanging open in astonishment. 'No, wait, you can't mean . . .'

His expression hardened as he added, in a dangerous voice: 'Yaotl, just what were you expecting to find here?'

I had been dreading this moment. As quickly as I could, and keeping my voice low so that the boys could not hear me, I told him what my brother had told me, adding the story of my abduction and the bird and Costly's suggestion for good measure. 'So you see,' I concluded lamely, 'I was hoping to see a sorcerer, really I was, it's just that I thought something might have happened to him.'

'And now you've got us involved with the army! You idiot!'

'Keep your voice down – do you want the boys to hear?'

'Why do you think I'm so angry? What am I going to say to their mother, have you thought of that?'

'I did tell you not to bring them.'

Handy's answer to that was a furious growl and a stamp of his foot which showered ash over us both. 'I knew you were bloody trouble as soon as I set eyes on you,' he muttered. 'So what happens now? You reckon they'll be back?'

'How do I know?' I could almost see the column pounding up the hill after us, the wind ruffling their feathered shields and tunics as they ran, their swords' obsidian blades glittering in the sunlight, their teeth bared like a hunting animal's. 'I think we should get out of here as soon as we can.'

'Oh, don't worry about that, we're off as soon as I've found our lunch bag. You needn't think we're sharing it with you! Buck! Snake! Which of you had the food?'

'He did,' said Buck without looking up from his work.

'Snake?'

'I left it over there,' the younger boy said casually, 'under one of those maguey plants, near where Yaotl's standing now.'

Automatically I peered into the shadow cast by the nearest plant and those on either side of it. 'Are you sure? I can't see it here.'

Handy swore. 'I don't believe this! I tell you boys to do a simple thing . . .'

'But it was there!' Snake's voice was an outraged squeal. 'I put it there when you went up the hill!'

I stepped over to the row of plants and stood on the edge of the little bank of earth above them. 'It's probably just fallen over into the field below us,' I said, pulling two broad glistening leaves apart and peering into the space between them.

Two round pale eyes stared back at me.

Startled, I stepped back, letting the leaves flop back into place to cover the eyes again. Then I recovered myself, plunging into the foliage once more just as the owner of the eyes began to move. Dropping Handy's bag, he scuttled along the edge of the field, keeping his head down level with the top of the bank.

'Thief!' I yelled. 'There he goes! Catch him!'

The boys liked a live quarry even better than old bones. They exploded out of the wrecked house in a shower of dust and ash and hurled themselves straight at the bank, diving over it to emerge just in front of their prey.

Confused by their joyful cries, he stumbled to a halt. He might have got away if he had turned and fled straight down the hill immediately, since for a moment Buck and Snake were as surprised and disoriented as he was. He left it just too late, though, and even as he was turning to run Handy appeared at the top of the bank, roaring like a bear, and threw himself on him.

'Got you! And if you've eaten all our tortillas . . .'

His captive said nothing, although since the big man was lying across his chest this was not surprising.

I let myself gingerly down the slope and picked up the bag. 'I think it's all here,' I said. 'Let's go!'

Handy began to get up, although he kept one knee on the would-be thief to pin him down. 'I want a quick look at this one first.'

Then a strange expression came over the big man's face. As he looked down at the child he had caught – and he was just that, I realized, no more than nine or ten years old – Handy's eyes and mouth opened wide, while at his sides his fists clenched and unclenched in a gesture of indecision. He did not seem to know whether to fight or run.

'Handy?'

'Father?' Snake's voice sounded small. 'What is it?'

Abruptly his father seemed to make up his mind about something. Bending down, he scooped the captive boy off the ground and shoved him under one arm like a freshly killed turkey. Before any of us could react, he was off down the hill at a brisk trot, with the child's head dangling upside down at his side, bouncing so low it almost scraped on the ground.

'Come on, then!' he called out over his shoulder. 'Let's get out of here!'

His sons and I could only stumble after him.

'What's happening?' I called out. 'I know we're in a hurry, but . . . Wait for us!'

As I caught him up he turned to me and said, without breaking his stride: 'Can't you see the family resemblance,

Yaotl? Look at the ears, man! You and I – we killed this boy's father!'

I saw the family resemblance. Even upside down, flapping up and down as his head dangled from the crook of the commoner's arm, the boy's ears were unmistakable. When I had last seen them I had been climbing the steps on the Great Pyramid, and they had protruded from the head of the man in front of me: Shining Light's Bathed Slave. It was not just the ears. The child had the slave's scrawny physique and the same air of resignation.

'You're telling me this boy's father was Shining Light's sacrifice? Slow down! What was he doing filching your lunch?' I gasped.

Handy stumbled and ran towards the causeway, leaving us to keep up as best we could. He ran with the child jammed uncomfortably under one arm. The child's eyes were open but he made no sound. Either there was something wrong with him, I thought, or he must be very brave. In his place, I would have been howling.

'How should I know? All I know is we've found him. We've got to get him home. Don't you see, Yaotl? He can tell us who his father was and where he came from. The merchants will want to know that. They'll want to know where Shining Light got the Bathed Slave who let them down so badly. There'll be a reward!'

There might be more than that, I thought, as we raced past the low stone walls marking the outskirts of Coyoacan and onto the broad, flat, hard earth roadway that led out across the lake to Mexico. What would happen, I wondered, if anyone – some passing merchant, perhaps, or a member of my master's entourage – happened to recognize the son of Shining Light's offering wedged under Handy's arm?

Halfway along the causeway I stumbled to a halt and tried to call out to the others, to urge them to throw the boy in the water and forget they had ever seen him.

They ignored me. Either I was too out of breath to make myself heard or they were just not listening.

4

'Citlalli,' Handy said confidently. 'She'll know what to do.'

His wife gazed at him in astonishment as he dragged the child into the house.

'I thought you went out to have an omen interpreted. Who's this? And how did you manage to get yourselves into such a state?'

At daybreak, the women of Handy's household made tortillas, swept the courtyard and washed the faces of the idols. The rest of the day, they wove. Citlalli was too big to use a backstrap loom by now, however, and so she divided her time between turning maguey fibres on her spindle and supervising her elder daughters and nieces. This still left her free to take a keen interest in what we were doing.

Her husband looked at his own legs as if he had not noticed they were coated in muck from the knees down. 'We found this urchin skulking around the village. He tried to steal our lunch!' He gave her a severely edited account of the day's activities, which she listened to with mounting incredulity.

'So you failed to find the sorcerer and you let those boys get themselves covered in grime and soot playing with bones?' she said mildly, when he had finished. From the way her gaze passed over us all I felt I was comprehended in 'those boys'.

'Yes,' Handy admitted.

'Well, you know where the brushes are. If you think I'm cleaning up after you in the morning, you're mistaken. Now, this child . . .' Citlalli's speech sounded brisk but the skin around her eyes was creased with laughter. I decided I liked this woman: bringing nine children into the world had not eroded her sense of humour. Star, her name meant, and she had the bright cheerful manner to go with it, although she was not laughing when she examined the child.

Handy was eagerly explaining his idea to her. 'You remember the Bathed Slave who ran away and then jumped off the edge of the Great Pyramid? This is his son – I'm sure it is. What do you think the merchants would give to find out where he really came from?'

The subject of this discussion squatted in the middle of the room where Handy had put him, with his thumb in his mouth, listening wordlessly while we reminded each other how his father had died. He shivered slightly, although it was not a cold day.

'The merchants aren't going to find out anything from this child if he starves to death,' Star said crisply. 'I don't suppose any of you has any idea when he last ate?'

Her husband and I looked at each other self-consciously. 'He didn't tell us he was hungry,' I protested.

She gave me a look that would have wilted a cactus. 'Why do think he was after your lunch, then? And it's hardly surprising if he hasn't told you anything – he's obviously scared out of his wits.' She pulled herself to her feet, ignoring her husband's belated offer to help her up, and extended a hand to the child. 'Come along. There are fresh tortillas and honeyed tamales – do you like tamales? Of course you do, everyone does. Now, that's better . . .'

Casting a reproachful glance at us over her shoulder, she

led the child out of the room, holding him by the hand that she had somehow coaxed out of his mouth. She took the still unopened lunch bag with her.

Buck and Snake were not the sort of lads to squat at their father's feet when the food had just been taken out of the room. They scampered hastily after their mother and the boy. A moment later we heard her scolding them for leaving muddy footprints in the courtyard.

'Handy,' I began.

'Well, the food's gone,' he said mournfully, 'but I think I can find us something to drink. Wait here.'

'We need to talk,' I told his departing back.

He returned a moment later with two bowls made of the cheap orange-and-black ware you could find in almost every house in Tenochtitlan. They had water in them, although I caught myself wishing it was something else.

The commoner drained his bowl at once, smacking his lips appreciatively. 'I needed that! Now, you were saying we needed to talk?'

'About that child. I don't think you should be so eager to go running to the merchants as soon as you've heard his life story. And I certainly wouldn't tell anyone where you found him.'

He rocked back on his heels, frowning. 'I just thought the chief merchants, or maybe your master, since he had something to do with Shining Light . . .'

I put my bowl down deliberately so as not to smash it on the floor in frustration. 'Don't you realize what happened in that village?'

'Why don't you tell me?' he replied coolly. 'All I know is three people got killed in a fire, and if we'd been there at the wrong time it might have been seven!'

'They weren't killed in the fire — at least, not all of them. Look: the grown-up's bones were burned worse than the children's, and we found the children outside the house. So she died indoors, with the place blazing all around her. Her children were in the rubbish heap with their heads broken. They must have been killed first and left outside when the house was burned.'

'"She"? How do you know it was a woman?'

'I'm guessing, but we know what became of Cipactli, and he wasn't there. So I suppose the three we found today were his wife and children. That's what the Chief Minister did — when the sorcerers got out of the prison he had the army go after their families. And judging by that sandal strap I found he wanted a thorough job done, because he hand-picked the very best. Now, do you really want to go proclaiming this in the streets?'

'No, I don't!' Handy said in a hurt voice. 'I just thought the boy . . .'

'The boy whose father just happens to have been Shining Light's Bathed Slave. Isn't that a bit of a coincidence — having him turn up while we're picking over the remains of a massacre? Why do you suppose that happened?'

Handy stared sulkily into the bottom of his bowl and waited for me to answer my own question.

'We found the boy there because it was his own house we were turning over. He was hanging around the ruins because he had nowhere else to go. If you're right about Shining Light's Bathed Slave, and he was the boy's father, then that would mean . . .'

I stopped as I pondered exactly what it would mean.

If Handy was right, then it was indeed the Bathed Slave the warriors had been after. If my brother was right then that put my master's role in all this beyond question. The house had been visited by the men he had sent to find the Bathed Slave. Obviously they had not found him, but they had not been content to go away empty-handed. They had killed three members of his family and burned his house to the ground, and they had done it all on my master's orders.

No grown-up Aztec male was a stranger to killing. We killed enemy warriors, or better still dragged them to the tops of our pyramids and offered them to the gods, knowing that they would do the same to us if they could, and believing in the reward the gods had in store for them: to escort the Sun on his journey through the morning sky and after four years to be reborn as hummingbirds or butterflies. When the gods demanded it we even killed women and children, but what we rarely did was to kill wantonly. Human lives were too precious for that; or else why would the gods have valued them so?

The slaughter of ordinary peasants, the subjects of a town so close to Mexico itself, seemed to me an act so audacious, so desperate, so utterly lawless that the man who could order it must be capable of anything. At that moment I did not much care why he had done it. All I could think about was what it meant for me – for his slave, the man most at his mercy.

Who, I asked myself, could protect me from a man like that, once he decided I had let him down once too often, and the trouble he would put himself to by explaining my death away was less than the trouble of keeping me alive?

Only the Emperor himself, I knew, and I also knew that Montezuma would not trouble himself for a moment about the life of a slave unless I gave him what he wanted: the sorcerers. But all I could offer him now was a tongue-tied boy who, from what I had seen and heard, could not even tell us his own name.

★

Night had fallen by the time I left. The boy was still with Star. He had eaten something but for all our coaxing had still not said a word. Handy urged me to stay, but I knew I had to get back to my master's house. I was going to have a difficult enough time as it was, explaining where I had been.

I was going to have to explain it to Lion, too. My brother had sent me to Coyoacan, and as I walked slowly home, treading carefully to avoid straying into the dark waters of the canal beside me, I rehearsed how I was going to tell him what we had found.

But what had we found?

The warrior who had left his sandal strap at the house had been one of the army's elite, perhaps either a Shorn One or an Otomi, the kind who would kill to order and never ask why. Who else would the Chief Minister trust to wipe out a whole family quickly, efficiently and without making a fuss?

As soon as that question occurred to me I saw a possible answer, and it was so abhorrent that I had to stop walking for a moment to fight the wave of nausea that threatened to engulf me.

My brother was one of the army's elite. The strap could easily have been his.

It was my brother who had told me about the warriors going to Coyoacan. I had thought at the time that he knew much more than he was letting on, and that he seemed strangely unsure of himself, as if afraid of saying too much. He would always obey orders and he would carry them out with ruthless dispatch. Yet he was one of the most pious, upright, unbending men I had ever known. What had been done in that village was something he would surely never have stooped to, no matter who ordered it.

'No.' I swallowed a couple of times. 'He couldn't . . .'

I walked on slowly, unable to dismiss the appalling thought until I rounded the last corner before my master's house and had it driven from my mind by the sight of yet another death.

5

A broad canal ran past the front of the Chief Minister's house. His Lordship could alight from his canoe and climb straight up the steps to his private apartments if he chose to. It was here that I had been hailed by the steward three days earlier, before that tense interview with my master at the top of the steps. Tonight my intention was just what it had been then: to find my sleeping mat and curl up on it under my cloak.

As soon as I saw the steps I knew this was not going to happen. They were covered in people standing or sitting on them, making them look like the tiers of stone seats surrounding a ball court.

Several pairs of eyes turned on me for a moment, before swivelling back silently towards the canal. As soon as I had climbed a little way up the steps and turned around to get a good look at the water, I saw why.

From behind me, someone said: 'His Lordship should be back soon.' There was a general murmur of assent, as if our master's arrival would help.

Without taking my eyes off the thing floating in the water, I said: 'Has anyone sent for a priest?'

With neither my master nor his steward to be found, and the rest of the household seemingly paralysed by fear, I found myself taking charge.

I had them moor boats across the canal in two places, so as to keep the stretch opposite my master's house clear of traffic. Then the two priests who had been sent for went out into the middle of the waterway in a canoe with a long pole to fish the dead man out.

'If it's a drowning, it's our job,' one of them reminded me. The bodies of the drowned, like their souls, belonged to the rain-god and no one except a priest could handle one.

'Just get the body back here,' I said wearily. 'His Lordship will want to know who he is and what happened to him on Earth, not where his soul is going.'

The priests had no trouble finding the body. It was floating in plain sight. It must have been dumped in the water earlier that evening, perhaps as soon as it had got dark, since otherwise someone would surely have seen it being left. Getting it out proved unexpectedly hard, however. The priests kept catching it with their pole only to find that it would not move. It was only after nearly capsizing their canoe twice that they stripped off their cloaks and started delving into the water to find out why.

Seen from the shore in starlight, the priests' sooty bodies, long black hair and stick-like limbs made them look like cranes hunting fish on the lake.

Once they had located the rope, it took only a few moments to haul the stone up. It had been tied to the body's ankle and used as an anchor.

They heaved the body over the side and into the bottom of their boat. They gave it the briefest of examinations before heading back towards the bank. As they scrambled onto dry land their relief was visible in their faces.

'You were right to call us, but it's not a matter for us, after all,' the younger of the two told me. 'He didn't drown. His throat was cut.'

That explained why he and his colleague were relieved, for it meant they would not have to bury the body. Those who died by water were not cremated but interred, normally in their own courtyards, in a sitting position. Getting them that way, when they were as often as not slimy, bloated, stinking and half eaten by fish, was not a pleasant task.

'Someone fetch a torch,' I commanded, peering over the side of the boat.

The dead man was naked. It was easy to see that he had been thin, almost emaciated. The hair plastered to the side of his head was long. His eyes and mouth were wide open, as if in terror.

The throat had been slashed cleanly across. That may have been the fatal wound, but it was by no means the only one. The body was covered with strange marks, like scars of varying sizes, from tiny punctures to tracts of ugly puckered flesh.

'Not been in the water very long, if you ask me,' the young priest said conversationally, peering over my shoulder. 'He's not swollen up, and the skin's barely discoloured. Doesn't smell too bad, either.'

I stretched a hand out behind me, without a word, and someone put a pine torch in it. I clambered into the boat. The priests had got the head and torso aboard but left the feet dangling in the water. I pulled them over the side one at a time, looking closely at the rope tied around one of the ankles as I did so.

'Whoever decided to leave a corpse floating opposite my master's house meant us to find it in the morning,' I observed.

'You think it was some sort of message?' It was the young priest again. He was no fool, I thought, as I considered the idea.

'Part of a message, at most,' I replied. 'A corpse by itself doesn't amount to much of a message, does it?'

I looked at the naked body, frowning. After what I had seen that day it was hard to feel anything for this unknown victim except bewilderment. Had he really been killed just to convey a message? And if so, where was the rest of it – the key to whatever threat or warning he represented? I thought of a letter, but there was no obvious place where one could be hidden. My eyes roamed over the torso and limbs, searching for some pattern in the wounds covering them, but there was nothing there. Then I looked at the head again and saw the answer.

'I wonder . . .' I reached down and parted the dead man's long, lank hair. It was wet and sticky and clung to my fingers like cobwebs as they delved into it. They brushed against an ear, and the slick skin behind it, and something else – a coarser, less pliant surface than the skin. Of course, I thought, as I drew the little cloth square out and unfolded it, it would not be paper. Paper would have disintegrated in the water.

Sure enough, someone had drawn on the cloth. It had been hastily done and the ink had got a little smudged but the message was clear enough for me to read. It was simple enough: just a name-glyph.

'At least we know his name, now.'

Then I looked at the drawings again. A single spot, a skull, a crude little stick figure wielding a sword and standing on a path decorated with chevrons.

'Cemiquiztli Yaotl.' I mouthed the words over and over again like an idiot, while the cloth shook in my hands.

'Cemiquiztli' meant 'One Death' and 'Yaotl' meant 'Enemy', but taken together they spelled out my own name.

'Is this someone's idea of a joke?' I demanded. I began

climbing out of the canoe, too shocked to look where I was going. 'Did someone tell you to put this with the body?' I waved the piece of cloth in the priest's face.

The priest was not there any more. The face opposite mine as I stepped onto the edge of the canal was my master's. Next to him was his steward. They were both staring at me, their expressions comically alike, with their eyes starting from their heads and their lower jaws slack with amazement.

The steward recovered first. Stepping delicately around our master, he reached for the cloth square, plucking it from my hand.

'I think we'd better have this, Yaotl.'

The Chief Minister seemed to have lost the power of speech. He kept staring at the body in the bottom of the boat with his mouth hanging open like an imbecile's. His steward silently pressed the note from the body into his nerveless fingers. Someone else took the torch from me and held it over my master's head so that he could read it.

He ignored the note as if unaware that he had it. He seemed oblivious to everything around him except the corpse. Nobody else dared to speak, even in a whisper, and so the only sound was his own breathing. It did not sound healthy – quick and shallow and with an ugly rattle in it.

Finally he broke the silence himself. 'Who did this?' he gasped.

'My Lord,' the steward responded in his most simpering tone, 'perhaps the note I gave you . . .'

My master glanced down at the piece of cloth he was holding as if noticing it for the first time. He looked at the body again, and then turned his sharp, glittering eyes on me. It struck me then that they never seemed to age: however lined his face and frail his body got, they were always the same, as though made out of some hard, bright, imperishable stuff like jade or polished marble. Now their gaze was hooded, malevolent and calculating, and made me feel as cold as if I, and not the corpse, had spent the evening floating in the canal. The fear that had assailed me at Handy's house came back redoubled.

'Cemiquiztli Yaotl.' My master's lips moved soundlessly over the name.

'M-my Lord,' I stammered. 'We found that note on the body – the body was in the canal. I had priests sent for . . .'

'Yes, yes, I know all that.' My master looked at the note again. 'Why has it got your name on it?'

'I don't know,' I replied in a wretched whisper.

'I do.' The grim certainty in his words matched his expression. When he looked at me again his lips were pressed together in a thin line. 'Huitztic!'

'My Lord?' the steward responded eagerly.

'Escort Yaotl to his room – and make sure he stays there until I send for him!'

'But . . .' I began, but the Chief Minister did not want to hear me. The old man who had had a whole family done to death in Coyoacan quelled my protest with a glare, while his sneering steward propelled me out of his sight, a calloused hand clamped firmly on my arm.

My master's last words seemed to hang in the air behind us.

'Cemiquiztli Yaotl! I will deal with you in the morning!'

6

'You get in there and stay put,' the steward snarled as he shoved me through the doorway. 'I've got to talk to Tochtli.'

Tochtli, whose name meant 'Rabbit', was one of my master's litter-bearers, a large, dim man who had been in my master's household since boyhood and had risen eventually to a mindless, menial job that suited him perfectly. He had had the misfortune to cross our path as the steward was dragging me back to my room, and had been ordered to come with us. The Prick had no intention of spending the rest of a winter's night huddled in the open courtyard watching my doorway, and thought poor old Rabbit would be the ideal deputy.

I slumped against the wall in a corner of my room, with all thought of sleep gone. I had come home that evening with my mind in turmoil.

Why had a message bearing my name been left on the body? Did it have something to do with the sorcerers? I felt that it must, but could not see what.

There had been something about the dead man himself – but I would have to see his body again to be certain, and I could hardly do that, I told myself gloomily, while I was confined to my room.

And I suspected that by the time they came to let me out of here it would be too late.

'So what have you done this time? And what's Rabbit doing out there?'

On any other night I would have dreaded the sound of Costly's voice, but tonight it was a relief to hear he was awake. It gave me a chance to share my troubles instead of brooding on them. The old slave lived for gossip and devoured every word eagerly.

As soon as I had finished he said astutely: 'So let me guess. You think the body in the canal might be one of those sorcerers the old man's so anxious to get his hands on, is that right?'

'It could be,' I said. 'I'd need to look at it again – and that still wouldn't tell me why it had my name on it.'

'How many people know your full name?'

I stopped to think. It was a good question. My name included the date of my birth. That was information no Aztec would give away freely, in case a sorcerer got hold of it and used it to bewitch you. 'Not many. My family, of course, our master, a few of the people I was at the Priest House with . . .' I pounded my knee in frustration. 'That's it, isn't it? That's all the suspects! The person who killed the man in the canal – he can only have been someone who knows my name! And if there is some connection with the sorcerers he might lead me straight to them. All I have to do . . .'

'Is get out of this room,' he capped my sentence drily. 'You won't find out a lot from in here.'

'I know,' I said mournfully. 'How do I get past Rabbit?' I could picture the litter-bearer on guard opposite our door-way, no doubt wishing he was curled up on his own sleeping mat rather than squatting in this chilly courtyard, but wide awake nonetheless and not about to let his master down.

'Rabbit?' the old man scoffed. 'I've known him since he was a boy. You leave him to me. Let's just get him in here, shall we?' Before I could react he had raised his voice to a loud croak and was calling the litter-bearer's name.

A suspicious-looking face appeared in the doorway. 'What do you want?'

'I don't want anything,' responded Costly cheerfully. 'We just thought you might be more comfortable in here with us than freezing your balls off out there in the courtyard!'

Rabbit scowled. 'What's it to you if I would?'

'Oh, come on.' Costly put on an air of hurt innocence. 'We all know it's nothing personal between you and Yaotl.' That was true enough: I had never thought of the litter-bearer as anything other than an amiable buffoon. 'You just had the bad luck to get picked on by that arsehole of a steward. But if you're going to keep an eye on Yaotl, you might as well do it in comfort from where you can see him, don't you think?'

The face in the doorway took on a puzzled frown as Rabbit tried to work out what Costly was after. 'I'm not sure . . .' he began.

'So where's the harm? Besides,' the old slave added, lowering his voice mischievously, 'I'm fed up with hearing Yaotl's problems. You could tell me yours, for a change. Say, how are things between you and the wife now?'

This appeared to have a disastrous effect. It was followed by the briefest of pauses and then the single word 'Fine', and Rabbit's head vanished.

'You idiot!' I hissed, but Costly seemed unperturbed. 'So the old trouble hasn't come back, then?' he called out after the other man.

A moment later Rabbit was back. He took two steps into the room and growled at Costly: 'No, it hasn't! And I'll thank you not to mention it in front of him!'

The old slave cackled lewdly. 'Oh, don't worry about Yaotl. He used to be a priest, and you know they never do it at all – he hasn't the faintest idea what we're talking about!'

I kept silent. 'Still, I'm glad to hear everything's working properly now. It's funny, though: I was thinking about you just the other day, and remembering when I had the same trouble myself. I had to go to a curer for some medicine . . .'

'Did it work?' The eagerness in the litter-bearer's voice told its own story.

'Work? It was like walking around with a lump of hardwood between my legs! I never even had to use it all. Probably still got some, somewhere.'

I could not believe even Rabbit was stupid enough to fall for a simple ruse like this, but he was obviously desperate. 'I don't suppose it still works, though,' he said nonchalantly.

'Oh, I should think it's gone off by now,' the old slave agreed. 'And it probably never would have worked in the first place unless you invoked the right gods when you took it. It wouldn't be much use to me now, anyway! But if you had still been having problems – well, I'm just glad to hear you aren't.'

There was a long, awkward silence. Then Rabbit said nervously: 'Look . . . I mean . . . I'm fine now, no problem at all, but if it ever came back, well . . .'

'Actually, come to think of it, the stuff might even be poisonous by now. No, forget I mentioned it . . .'

'How much do you want for it?'

'I wouldn't dream of selling it to you.'

'How much?' Rabbit demanded again, this time with an edge to his voice.

Costly sighed. 'I told you, I can't sell it to you. But look, at your own risk . . .' I could not see what he was doing in the darkness of his corner of the room but I could hear him rummaging for something beside his sleeping mat, followed by the faint sloshing of liquid in a gourd. 'I'll give it to you. But I really think . . .'

'Thanks!' Rabbit almost snatched the gourd from him. 'If this works, I owe you one!'

A moment later he was gone and the old slave's body was heaving up and down on his mat in time to his convulsive wheezing laughter.

'Was that what I thought it was?' I said.

His mirth brought on a fit of coughing. 'That moron!' he spluttered when he could draw breath. 'He'll drain it to the dregs! By midnight his bowels will be flowing like the aqueduct! You've got all the time you need, now.' The laughter overcame him again. 'Oh dear!'

I like to remember Costly that way – laughing so much he could hardly breathe.

It helps me to forget what happened afterwards.

It was easy to work out where they had taken the corpse from the canoe. My master would not want to be concerned with it, and the steward had neither the brains nor the imagination to do anything other than the obvious.

I could assume it would not be left where it was. The obvious thing to do with the body was to move it before it stiffened, but it could not be taken far in the middle of the night. In any case, I thought, my master and his steward could have no idea where to take it, unless they knew where the dead man's family was or who his friends had been. They would have had it carried as short a distance as possible and left somewhere convenient, from where it could be got away from the house as soon as the Sun came up.

Few households were ostentatious enough to have torches burning through the night, but my master's was one of them. I took one and hurried to the front of the house, to the room where the litters were kept, near the foot of the broad steps up to the patio.

As I ducked through the entrance, I realized that the steward had not let me down. The body was there. In fact, as I straightened up, I saw that it was altogether too much there. Lifting the torch, I saw the dead man's shadow projected, much larger than life, against the far wall, hunched over the angular shape of a litter. Not even the torch's flickering, however, could account for the way the shadow flowed and changed shape as the corpse got to its feet.

I dropped the torch, which fell at my feet, turning the dead man's shadow into a dark streak that shot up the far wall until it loomed over me. The torch went out. It did not matter: there was already one burning in the wall above my head. I stepped back, my hands groping behind me, looking for the doorway. The moment I found it, I intended to run.

Then the dead man spoke.

'S-sorry. I shouldn't be here. I'll go now.'

It was the voice of the young priest, one of the pair that had brought the body out of the water. As soon as I heard him I made my eyes take a fresh look at the scene in front of them.

The dead man cast no shadow to speak of. It was the priest who had frightened me, suddenly getting up from where he had been squatting by the litter because he was as startled as I was. The corpse sat in the litter itself, propped against the tall wicker back of its chair with his eyes closed, looking quite peaceful apart from the hideous gash at his throat and the way his jaw hung slack and open. He was still naked. Surrounded by the heron feathers and paper streamers that decked my master's plainest litter, and swaddled in the rabbit's fur covering its chair, he looked more pathetic than when he had just been pulled out of the canal.

I bent down to retrieve my torch. It was just as well it had gone out. Otherwise it might have set fire to something. Any of the embroidered cotton canopies resting against the walls, or the shining blue and green feathers that bordered them, some as long as my arm, could have caught in an instant.

I studied the priest. As light and shadow danced around and behind him his soot-stained face remained uniformly dark. Watching his eyes shift from side to side as he sought a way around me to the door, I had the unsettling feeling that I might have met him before that night.

'Who are you?' I asked.

'Yolteotl,' he replied. 'I'm a priest of Huitzilopochtli.' There was no tremor in his voice. Instead there was an unnatural stillness, a conscious control that betrayed his fear as eloquently as if he had been begging for mercy. He seemed even younger than when we had spoken by the side of the canal. He had been right: he should not be here. He should be in the Priest House or watching over a temple fire and offering his blood to the gods.

I asked the obvious question.

Realizing he was not going to get past me, he seemed to relax a little. 'I was curious.' He indicated the body. 'About him.'

I took a step towards him and grinned. 'That makes two of us!'

The priest moved aside to give me a closer look at the corpse, and hovered over my shoulder as I examined it. It occurred to me afterwards that he could easily have got to the door then, had he chosen to.

After a few moments he said: 'It's the wounds, isn't it?'

I grunted assent. I was looking at the neck, probing the edges of the gash with my finger. The skin around it was cold and unyielding and dry, as if there was no blood left in the body.

'This would have killed him, no doubt about that. I wonder what it was?'

'A sword?' he hazarded.

'Maybe. It's a very clean cut – too clean for a flint knife. It must be obsidian.' That would argue for its having been a sword, I knew, a flat shaft of fire-hardened oak with rows of obsidian blades set into its edges. 'It's quite shallow, though, isn't it?' I imagined a sword swishing through the air and slicing through a neck or a limb at the bottom of its arc. 'I think it was a knife or a razor. A sword-blow would have taken his head off.'

'Not if whoever was using it didn't have much space to swing it in.'

I glanced back at the young priest peering eagerly over my shoulder. I had been right to think he was no fool, I thought, but his brains were going to get him into trouble one day.

'You're right,' I said. 'So either it was a knife — made of something sharper than flint — or he was killed in a cramped space. Or both. No reason why it can't have been both. The less space you have to work in, the more likely you are to prefer a knife.' I tried to imagine the cramped spaces I knew: small rooms, steam baths, the niches at the backs of temples. If you were going to murder somebody it made sense to do it somewhere enclosed and private.

I took a step away from the body to survey the rest of the wounds.

'What do you make of these marks?' I asked.

The skin seemed to have shrunk and turned grey, bringing the punctures, slits and blisters into a gruesome kind of relief.

'I don't know,' he said. 'But it was done on purpose, wasn't it? Just before you came in I was thinking it looked like he'd been pricked with maguey cactus spines and beaten with burning sticks, the way they do in the Priest Houses.'

'Why would anyone have done that?'

'To punish him?'

'Maybe.' I knew that was why the priests did it. The memory could still make me squirm. 'Maybe it was to get him to talk.' I looked from the dead man's ravaged skin to his face. His eyes were still open and clear and glittering in the torchlight. Their irises had not begun to blur as they do after death. What might they have seen that someone would use torture to learn?

I looked curiously at the priest.

'Why did you want to see the body again?'

'I kept thinking about those marks. I thought I'd seen something like them before.'

I had thought the same. It was what had brought me here.

'I have the honour to serve the god at the great temple in the Heart of the World,' the young man explained. 'I was there at the Festival of the Raising of Banners, when the merchants were presenting their slaves to be sacrificed to the god. One of them had scars like this – pricks, scratches, burns. I noticed them when we stretched him over the stone. I remember . . .'

'So do I,' I said. 'He was dead before he got to you, wasn't he?'

When the priest gaped at me he looked a little like the corpse. 'How did you know?'

'I was there. He jumped off the temple steps halfway up. We had to haul him all the way back to the top, and then we had a job persuading Peynal and the Fire Priest to accept him.' I remembered Yolteotl now as the young acolyte who had greeted us at the top of the steps. 'I saw the scars too, when the body was being butchered.'

'It was you, then! I remember, now. The one with the mouth! It's strange, isn't it? You bring us an offering with these scars on it, and a body turns up here in the same state, right in front of your master's house. What's going on?' His eyes narrowed as he looked at me. I kept mine fixed on the body in the chair.

'I don't know,' I said slowly. 'I'll have to think about it.'

I was still thinking about it when the young priest remembered where he was supposed to be and left. I was still thinking about it when the torch sputtered and went out.

I went on thinking about it in darkness.

I could not simply return to my room and wait to be sent for. I had to get out of the Chief Minister's clutches, but that would not be enough. I had to find the sorcerers quickly and deliver them to Montezuma before my master caught up with me. Then I could throw myself on the Emperor's mercy, and if he inclined his heart towards me, I might survive.

So all I had to do was track down the sorcerers! I might have wept from sheer desperation, but I suddenly saw how I was going to do it – and at the same time, catch the killer of the man we had found in the canal, and find out why my name had been left on him.

The dead man had been half a message, but my name had been the other half. Either the message was for me – although if it was, I did not understand it – or it was about me. Either way, I reasoned, I would have to answer it. All I had to do was reply, and the killer would come for me.

And the killer would lead me to the sorcerers. Shining Light's Bathed Slave had been treated in the same barbarous way as the dead man beside me, which meant the same person had had them both at his – or her – mercy. The Bathed Slave had been one of the men my master and the Emperor were seeking, and I felt sure the man in the canal had been another. If he had been kept in the prison on starvation rations it was no wonder he was thin.

Now Shining Light, even if he was the killer, had probably not sent that gruesome message, because he was not one of the few people who knew my full name; but he must know the person who had, and they must be working together. I remembered what my master had said to Misty's boy: '*Do I just have to watch those men being killed, one by one, until he chooses to tell me what he wants?*' The Bathed Slave had been a message too, of a sort, and the body in the canal a reminder.

Whatever lingering faith I might have had in the story of Shining Light's exile died then. Whether his mother had genuinely believed what she had told me I did not know, but in any case I decided I would have to confront her with the truth.

I did not have time to go calling on every person who knew the date of my birth, few though they were. In any case, what was I going to ask them – a few old priests and my own relatives? Were they likely to confess all to me, the man who had been slung out of the House of Tears and brought disgrace on his family?

Far better, I thought, to find the merchant, and get to the killer through him.

I looked down at the corpse in the litter, now faintly visible in a thin stream of twilight through the doorway. Seeing his wounds again, I shivered as I contemplated the danger I was inviting, trying to set a trap for whoever had done this to him.

'I don't know who you are,' I heard myself saying, 'but we have something in common. I promise you, I'll catch our enemy.'

The sound of brooms sweeping the road outside and a faint burning smell that might be cooking fires told me the Sun was about to rise.

FOUR VULTURE

....

1

When I slipped out of the room with the litters the sky was still a deep blue. Somewhere within the house tortillas would be cooking. I felt a pang of hunger at the thought and found myself sniffing the air. Sure enough, I caught the expected hint of smoke, although it did not smell altogether right. Instead of the wholesome odour of maize dough on a griddle, the air bore an acrid tang that I could not quite identify.

I reminded myself that I had to get out of here and off to the merchant's house as quickly as I could. I wanted to look in on Costly, however, and I thought that if Rabbit was still incapacitated then I should be able to sneak across the court-yard our room opened onto, ignoring the women sweeping up imaginary dust with their brooms, and vanish indoors undisturbed for a few moments.

As I peeped cautiously into the courtyard I realized it was not to be that simple.

Nobody was sweeping the earth floor, although this was a duty owed to the gods and always done before dawn. I looked quickly up at the sky to see whether it was earlier than I had thought, but it was not. It was as if the women had been told to stay away this morning.

The burning smell was stronger here. A whiff of it stung the back of my nose, forcing me to suppress a sneeze.

Rabbit was there, squatting in the middle of the court-yard. He had his back to me, and so I could not tell what state he was in. He was not alone: a second man stood beside him, with his feet braced slightly apart, and, like Rabbit, gazing at the doorway into my room. In the slowly gather-ing daylight, I noticed a wooden pole slung over his shoulders.

There was no way I could get past them. Nonetheless I hesitated, looking at the two men while I convinced myself that it was best just to leave quietly. I wondered what they were doing here, and I was curious about that wooden pole.

I was just about to turn away when I realized what it was they were both watching so avidly.

Through the doorway into my and Costly's room, ten-drils and then clouds of smoke were coming.

Without thinking I dashed into the courtyard as the clouds became a billowing grey wall that threatened to hide the doorway altogether. 'Hey!' I called out. 'There's some-one in there! We've got to get him out!'

The old slave could not walk. Without help he was going to be burned alive, unless he choked to death first. I broke into a run, calling again to the men in front of me: 'Come on! Move yourselves! What's wrong with you?'

Neither Rabbit nor his neighbour seemed to hear me at first. They seemed intent on the smoke, which had started issuing from the room next door to mine as well. I was almost on top of them before either of them reacted to me. Rabbit tried painfully to get to his feet; the other man whirled.

'You!' he cried.

At that moment the smoke caught them both. Costly's medicine must have weakened Rabbit badly because he sud-denly bent double around a fit of agonized retching that left him on his knees. His companion fared a little better, keeping his feet despite the dry cough that suddenly racked him and made him stagger. Then the smoke reached me too, stinging my eyes like a blow and stopping the breath in my throat, before I could gulp any of it into my lungs.

I staggered blindly to a halt, gasping: 'Burning chillies! You bastards!'

Through the tears I watched the man stumble towards me. He could see less than I could, but he knew my voice. 'What are you doing there?' he gasped.

It was my master's steward, and the pole he was carrying was a wooden collar, the kind used to stop cheap and unreliable slaves running away from the marketplace.

Holding onto the slave collar with one hand, he fumbled towards me with the other. I kicked him. He dropped the collar to free his other hand and blundered, still blind, towards me, but I had dodged out of his way. I kicked him again, harder, on the side of the knee as I passed him. He fell over.

I went for the collar. It was awkward and heavy and not designed as a weapon but it was all either of us had. As the steward tried to get back to his feet, I swung it as hard as I could against the back of his head. He tipped silently over onto his face.

A noise beside me reminded me of Rabbit. He was trying to rise, supporting himself with one hand while the other batted ineffectually at the curtain of smoke enveloping him. He stared blindly in my direction with eyes that were raw and streaming. When I hit him with the collar, he collapsed next to the steward and lay still.

The whole fight had been silent. It had not attracted any attention: I glanced swiftly around the courtyard but there was still nobody around.

I badly needed to breathe. I ducked, trying to get under the waves of smoke, and ran parallel to the wall, away from the direction the fumes were drifting in, until I could stand and fill my lungs without burning them. I took great, whooping breaths, blinking rapidly at the same time to clear my eyes.

Looking back, I saw that the dense clouds pouring from the two doorways had thinned to a fine haze, with puffs and twisting strands of smoke drifting lazily through it. I hoped the fire was burning itself out, but it made no difference to what I had to do.

Taking a deep breath and wrapping my cloak around my face, I ran back to my room and plunged into the acrid, searing darkness.

Involuntarily, I dropped the cloak covering my nose and mouth to rub my streaming eyes. It made them worse. I could not breathe, with or without the cloak. I could not see. I staggered around and tripped over something soft, crashing to the floor and jarring my knee so hard I had to bite my tongue to stop myself from screaming and letting the fumes into my lungs.

On my hands and knees, I turned around to find out what I had fallen over. It was a body. I hit it roughly, twice. I shook it. I found a fold of skin and pinched it cruelly. There was no sign of life.

Disoriented, I could only blunder about before the air in my lungs ran out and I either escaped, passed out or started to choke. I rammed the wall with my head. Exploring it with my hands, I found something unexpected: a hole, just over a hand's width across, at floor level. I thrust my fingers through it incautiously, snatching them back as soon as they met the fierce heat of the fire.

The steward had set it in the next room, after poking a

hole in the plaster separating it from Costly's and mine. I could imagine him working quickly and quietly so as not to disturb either of us before he had time to get back outside. Rabbit, anxious to keep his dereliction of duty to himself, would have assured the steward that I was still in the room, and the Prick, having decided to take no chances, had tried to smoke me out rather than risk going in after me. I was meant to be driven into the courtyard, coughing and weeping, and yoked securely before I came to my senses.

I wondered whether either the steward or our master had spared Costly a thought.

As I backed away, my heels fetched up against the wicker chest.

I spent the last of my air in a gasp of relief. Knowing where the chest was positioned meant I could find my way out. I got up, grabbed the chest in both hands and stumbled from the room, barely noticing when my shoulder smashed into the edge of the doorway on the way out.

Outside I dropped the chest on the ground and collapsed, panting, on top of it. I could not stay here, I knew, but the need to rest, to gulp down clean, fresh air, was too strong. I lay there, slumped over the chest, until I heard the women's voices.

'What's up with these three?'

'Isn't that Huitztic?'

'What's that funny smell?'

I raised my head reluctantly. There were two of them, girls I knew vaguely as members of the household, concubines of my master or one of his relatives. I had the feeling their fathers were minor provincial kings who had parted with them under the terms of some treaty or other. Now they both carried brooms, and were eyeing the steward and me as critically as our fathers might have done if they had found us asleep after daybreak.

'It's Yaotl!' one of them cried. 'What happened? Why are Rabbit and the steward lying here?'

A quick look at the sky, which was lightening steadily, reminded me I did not have much time. Soon the Sun would be up and the courtyard would be full of people, including my master. At some point, too, the steward and Rabbit would wake up, since I was sure I had not hit either of them as hard as I should have done.

'Aren't you two late?' I mumbled, as I pulled the lid of the chest open and began rummaging inside it. From the top of the Great Pyramid, the bellowing of a conch-shell trumpet warned us that the Sun was up.

'We were here ages ago,' one of the girls protested, 'but the steward sent us away. Very rude about it, too, he was.'

'And now here he is, lying in the middle of the courtyard. He'll have to move, I want to sweep that bit.'

'Can't you go around him?' I suggested wearily. 'Surely the gods won't mind just this once.'

I looked at the contents of the box with a feeling of despair. The few items of value were smoke-damaged beyond hope of repair, but I was past caring about that. They had been Costly's, and he was dead, and I could not even weep for him because I had no tears left and no time now in which to shed them.

There was only one thing in the box that I wanted, but I could not see it. A cold band tightened around my chest as I thought that maybe the steward had been there before me and plundered the chest before setting the fire in the next room. Even as I was telling myself that what I was looking for was too small to see and must be buried under all the things stowed on top of it over the years, I was clawing frantically at the chest's contents with both hands, tossing cheap jewels and faded feather-work fans carelessly aside in my haste.

'Hey! What are you doing? We're not picking all that rubbish up as well!'

When I found the thing, at the very bottom of the box where I had left it years before, my eyes closed with relief. It was too small for me ever to wear again, of course — so small that I could hide it in my fist when I brought it out of the box, with the old coarse cotton reassuringly rough against my palm.

The stinging smoke had all cleared by now. Still a single tear forced its way past my eyelids as I sat by the almost empty box, remembering.

There was nothing more I could do for Costly now, but I knew what he would have wanted me to do. He would have wanted me to use the chance he had given me by getting clean away as fast as I could, and then following my plan to catch the killer of the man in the canal, find the sorcerers and get them to the Emperor.

For I could see the purpose of the message now — the message that had had a dead man as one part and my own name as the other.

It had been me that Shining Light or his ally or both had wanted all along. Between them, they must have the sorcerers in their power. They must have organized the attempt to kidnap me, using Misty and his son to do the deed, and then when I escaped they must have killed one of the sorcerers and sent his body to my master as a reminder. My master had already tried to deliver me into their hands once; this time he must have ordered his steward to make absolutely sure I was handed over in such a state that I could not run away again.

But who was Shining Light's confederate, and how had they got Misty and his son involved in their schemes? For a moment I thought Misty might have been the man who wrote my name on a cloth square, but then how, I asked myself, would he have known my name, any more than Shining Light himself did?

There was another question whose answer I could not begin to guess at, although I knew that as long as it remained open I would never be able to sleep easily in Mexico again: why me? What had I done that so many people – the merchant, his mysterious ally, Misty, my master and his steward – were prepared to kill, suffer disgrace and exile and incur the Emperor's wrath for the sake of it?

I got up slowly.

'You may as well pick it all up,' I said to the girls, gesturing towards the stuff scattered around me. 'Some of it might be salvageable. Anything you can use is yours. We won't be needing it any more.'

2

Noon found me in Pochtlan, contemplating a stone wall at the rear of the merchant's property.

I was not about to announce myself at the gateway. I had a simple message to deliver, but I wanted to make sure it got to the right person: to Shining Light's mother, Lily. The only way to be sure she received it, before either my master sent men to fetch me home or the merchant himself or his allies tried to kidnap me again, was to speak to her face to face. I wanted to come upon her without warning, surprise her with what I had to say and get away in time to plan my next move. That meant sneaking up on the household, and the obvious way to do that was to climb over the courtyard wall.

I knew I ought to wait until nightfall before attempting it. On the other hand, while I might just survive getting caught doing this during the day, to do it at night would be a sure way of being taken for a sneak thief. Besides, there was an ash tree growing next door, one of whose stout limbs dipped temptingly within my grasp before reaching across to shade the courtyard of Shining Light's house, and there was no one about.

Seizing my opportunity, I scrambled up onto the limb. Further good luck greeted me on the far side of the wall, much of which was covered with a mature passionflower whose woody stems gave me a soft and silent landing in the courtyard.

It was as I had seen it before, except that there was no old man slumped against the wall. There was no one about. Not even a dog stirred.

I breathed a sigh of relief and stepped across to the nearest doorway. The screen had been pulled away from this one and lay propped against the wall beside it, so that I could walk straight in.

The room was empty.

I cursed myself for an idiot. Of course it was empty: why else had the doorway been left uncovered? I turned to go, but something made me turn back.

There was something odd about this room.

It was hard to see what it had been used for, since it had no more furniture than most Aztec interiors. There were a couple of badly frayed mats and a broken wicker box. Daubed on the walls were a few stylized figures, noticeably cruder than the ones decorating the room I had been received in. The odd thing was that the walls were only half painted. The back of the room, the half farther from the door, was bare, and the division between the two halves was a straight line. Either it had been left that way on purpose or there had been some physical boundary that had been painted up to and that was no longer there.

When I inspected the line closely I could see what had happened. The false wall had been knocked away cleanly and the remains of the plaster swept away, but the traces of it were clear enough.

'So you did hide your wealth here, after all,' I muttered. 'I wonder where you put it all?'

'I wish I knew, too,' said a voice from behind me. 'But

like I told you before, if you want to talk business, you'll have to ask my daughter.'

Fright made me yelp like a dog. I jumped and tottered forward a couple of steps into what had been the hidden part of the room, before regaining my balance and turning to face the old man.

Shining Light's grandfather stood in the doorway. His face was hidden in shadow but his bent frame and the sour smell of sacred wine that clung to the air around him were instantly recognizable.

'What are you doing here?' I asked, absurdly reproachful. 'I thought you were all asleep!'

'Had to get up for a piss. Saw you skulking about, thought I'd come and see what you were up to. Besides,' he added, as though the thought had just occurred to him, 'shouldn't I be asking you that question, Yaotl? How did you get in?'

Drink and age had not dulled his mind too much, I noted, as he seemed to have no trouble remembering who I was.

'The servant let me in.'

'No he didn't. You climbed that ash tree over the back, didn't you? I ought to have made them cut it down years ago. In summer the kids use it to steal passion fruit off that wall.'

I was still standing in the bare half of the room. 'You told me there was no money here,' I said, adopting the reproachful tone again as I looked at the space around me.

'There isn't. There used to be.' Disconcertingly, the old man seemed not to mind being questioned by someone who was on the face of it a burglar. 'My grandson took it all away. I gather a friend of his found a better hiding place for it. But as I keep saying, you'll have to ask . . .'

Another voice interrupted his. It was a man's but sounded as querulous as an old woman's. 'What's going on? Who're you talking to?'

Kindly glanced sideways at the newcomer and then stepped back to let him see through the doorway. As he did so the sunlight fell on his gnarled face, revealing a lopsided grin.

'It's an old friend of yours, Constant,' he said, as the servant who had let me into the house on my previous visit peered myopically into the room. 'Yaotl, the Chief Minister's slave.'

'Yaotl!' The servant jumped back as if I had just stung him. 'Him! All right, I'll go and tell the Parish Chief. We'll have him taken away!'

'There's no need.' The old man laid a restraining hand on the servant's arm. 'I'm sure Yaotl was just going – weren't you? I dare say he only wanted a word with Lily.'

'Yes, I do!' I said eagerly.

'Well, you can't have one,' the servant informed me curtly. 'She's not here.'

'Where is she, then?' Somehow it had not occurred to me that Shining Light's mother would not be at home, patiently waiting for me to slip over the back wall so that I could deliver my message to her.

'Mind your own business,' rejoined the servant instantly.

'Why do you want to know?' the old man asked mildly.

I hesitated, fearful of saying too much, although it occurred to me afterwards that my presence was revealing enough by itself. 'I want to tell her something that will interest her.'

'He's lying,' growled Constant.

'Only a bit,' said the old man. 'He came here for a reason, and I don't suppose it was to steal our wealth from us. If your master was after money,' he added, looking shrewdly at me, 'I imagine he'd just have demanded it.'

'I'm not working for the Chief Minister now,' I said hastily.

'Really?' The old man looked thoughtful. 'Well, in the end it's up to my daughter whether she wants to listen to what you have to say or not. She makes up her own mind about everything else. Oh, shut up!' Kindly directed his last words at the servant before turning back to me. 'Try the ball court in Tlatelolco.'

What would a respectable merchant's widow be doing at a ball court? 'You mean Lily has gone to pay off her son's gambling debts?'

Or was her motive more sinister than that? I had to face up to the possibility that, whatever Shining Light was up to with Misty and Nimble, his mother was in on it too. If you wanted to arrange a discreet meeting then the ball court, thronging with gamblers, was the obvious place.

The idea of her conspiring with my kidnappers was enough to make me shiver.

'You said your daughter didn't know there were other vices that could seduce a man,' I said bitterly. 'I take it she knows all about them now!'

Shadows fell across the old man's face as he looked away. 'Some of them, anyway,' he muttered.

3

I raced to the ball court, anxious to outpace the news of my coming. If Lily really was talking to Misty then I wanted to surprise them.

By the time I got there, sweating and breathless, a game was already in progress. It was a fine day for it, sunny and warm, but not excessively hot, and a recent light drizzle had been enough to dampen the dust in the ball court without softening the mud floor. As I approached I could hear the thump of the solid rubber ball as it bounced off the court's brick walls and the players' bodies.

It was hard to get near the stone seats overlooking the court for the mass of people surrounding it. They were as quiet and well behaved as any gathering of Aztecs, but the business being carried on in whispers among them was being conducted with such intensity that I feared to interrupt it. I found myself edging between little knots of people talking earnestly of odds and prices and swapping gambling tokens.

Eventually I managed to climb up onto a stone seat and join the crowd looking down into the ball court itself.

The court was a long, narrow strip of hard earth at the bottom of a deep pit between high brick walls, with shorter strips at right angles to it at either end. Back and forth within the court ran two teams of tough-looking young men, whose hairstyles and scars showed that their bodies had been hardened by war as well as exercise. They wore abbreviated breechcloths and leather pads on their knees and elbows, and they hurled themselves at the ball as if their lives depended upon keeping it in the air – as well they might, for this game could be played to the death, and if the players ever forgot that, they only had to look at the lurid and bloody friezes on the walls above them.

The ball itself was a dark blur among the jostling bodies, taking a solid shape only in the instant when it was stopped by a hip, a thigh or a buttock. The players were not allowed to use their hands or feet, except to spring off the ground when they fell. Splashes and streaks of blood on the earth showed where players had fallen and got up again. The air above the court was full of the smells of blood and sweat, mixed with an elusive animal scent of high excitement.

You could not help getting caught up in the game. We spectators leaned forward, craning our necks to follow the ball's flight and the hurtling, crashing bodies of the players. Nobody cheered, called out or even spoke above a whisper, even when a player did a full somersault to catch the ball at an improbable angle and drive it off the wall and into his opponents' half of the court. We could never lose sight of the fact that this was more than a game: it was a sacred ritual, one of the ways through which the gods revealed their will, and the dark-robed priests stationed on either side of the court were not just there to award points and punish fouls.

Some of those watching the game would be hoping it would tell them their fortunes. Others hazarded more than their fate, or less, depending on your point of view. Spread out before us, between us and the court, were money and goods of every kind: bags of cocoa beans, loads of cloth, copper axes and quills full of gold, jewelled lip-plugs and other adornments, fresh squashes, turkeys and quails, folds and sheets of the best paper from Amatlan or Amacoztitlan, and the most precious and delicate thing of all: feathers. Right in front of me was a bundle of the most beautiful scarlet feathers, the kind the merchants and tribute-collectors got from distant provinces far to the south, but as stiff and full of colour as if they had just been plucked.

The only rule about betting was that the stakes must be displayed in full view of the players. This was the law my master had broken with his secret wagers with Misty. The reason for it was connected with two small stone rings, not much more than a hand's breadth across, set into the walls of the court at twice a man's height. A team that managed to get the ball through one of them would win everything that had been staked on the game. I had never seen this happen, and I knew no one who had.

The man who had performed the somersault picked himself up, hobbled about for a moment and then hopped to the back of the court while a team-mate rushed forward to intercept the ball. One leg was already swelling up: after the game they would have to let the pooled blood out with obsidian razors.

I reminded myself that I was here to look for someone, not watch the game, but when I glanced at the tiers of seats opposite and around me I saw only the sort of crowd these events usually drew. Most had the short, coarse cloaks and tonsured hairstyles of commoners who had never taken a captive and never would. A few, occupying seats reserved for them at the front, were more gaudily dressed, their lips and ears punctured by jewels that glittered as they chatted to one another. The ball game attracted the very poor, pinning all their hopes on one big win, and the very rich, who could afford to lose. None of the spectators obviously had anything to do with the merchant class and its discreet wealth. And none of them was female.

Perhaps she had been here and left, I thought. I tried asking my neighbours.

I could not see the face of the person on my right, as he was leaning forward in his seat with his eyes fixed on the game being played out below us, but I could tell that he had not yet had his head shaved to mark his first capture of an enemy warrior. He wore no cloak, and from the sleek muscle coating his shoulders and back, I thought he might be a ball-player himself. I had more luck catching the eye of the commoner on my left.

'Come to a lot of these games?' I asked conversationally.

He grinned. 'Whenever I can. Whenever the Governor's team from Tlatelolco are playing, anyway, but I try to catch all the games – even crappy practice sessions like this one. You?'

'Oh, you can't keep me away.' The players were taking up their positions, ready to contest the next point. Sweat made their bruised bodies glisten, where they were not caked with dust, and the earth under their feet was mottled with their drying blood. It would not have occurred to me that this was anything other than a competitive match.

'There's a good crowd here,' I said casually, keeping up the pretence of having a conversation until my neighbour's attention strayed back to the game.

'Not bad,' he said noncommittally.

'I was wondering . . .'

He turned to me in exasperation. 'Are you watching this or not?'

I edged away from his glare. 'Sorry,' I said. 'It's just that I was looking for someone.'

He gave the ball court a longing glance before deciding that the quickest way of getting rid of me was to answer my questions as concisely as possible. 'Well, who is he, then?'

'She, actually. Her name's Lily.'

He fell into a furious fit of coughing. As soon as he recovered he said: 'Oh, so it's like that, is it? You picked an odd place to meet her, then. Wouldn't a garden have been better?'

'Better for what?' I stared at him, suddenly confused. I wondered whether he thought I had been planning an assignation, and then realized that that was exactly what he had thought because it was what I would have thought as well, had I been in his place.

'Well, you know . . .'

'No, I don't,' I snapped. 'Look, I'm not talking about a pleasure girl – she's a merchant's widow and the mother of another.' I felt a sudden urge to pitch him over the backs of the seats in front of us and all the way down into the bottom of the court, just to wipe the knowing, lascivious smirk off his face. 'Now have you seen her or not?'

Indifferent to my anger, my neighbour turned back to the game. 'Sorry, friend, but I can't help you . . .'

I did not hear whatever else he might have had to say.

It had been just a blur of movement out of the corner of my eye, but the play had sent a ripple of appreciative murmuring through the crowd and one or two of the spectators were standing. The ball had come to rest on the short strip running across one end of the court and the team whose half it was in were standing around it. Judging by their gestures and the fragments of agitated speech that drifted up to where I sat, they were exchanging views among themselves about how it had got there and whose fault it was.

'Oh yes!' The burly youth on my right was one of those

on their feet. He turned to me. 'You saw, didn't you? That was a classic! The ball can't have been more than a hand's breadth off the ground when he returned it! That . . .'

His voice tailed off as he saw me staring at him. Then the shock of recognition widened his eyes until they were as round as the ball.

It was Nimble, Misty's son and messenger.

He made an inarticulate noise and turned, trying to scramble out of his seat and clamber up over the tiers above us.

'Hey!' cried someone in the row behind me. 'Sit down! We can't see!'

'You can't get out this way. What do you think you're doing?'

I reached up, grabbed the lock of hair hanging from the back of the youth's head and yanked it firmly. He howled in pain and staggered backwards.

'You heard them,' I growled. 'Sit down!'

He slumped back in the seat next to me and glowered at me.

I said nothing. I was so astonished to see him there that for a moment I could think of nothing to say. I could only stare and marvel at the god Tezcatlipoca's sense of humour. It was hard to believe that even the capricious Lord of the Here and Now would be so perverse as to put this youth, of all people, in the seat next to mine.

'Are you going to let go of my hair?' he asked, his accented voice suddenly sounding as young as his years. 'It hurts.'

I gave it a malicious tug, watched him wince, and let go. 'Don't get any ideas,' I warned him. 'You and I are going to talk.'

'Yes.' His tone was almost eager. 'Did I hear you say you were looking for Lily?'

If he had been sullen or truculent I might have listened to him, but his treating this as a conversation annoyed me. 'I'm going to ask the questions!' I snapped. 'You can start by telling me what you meant by kidnapping me the other day!'

'We didn't mean you any harm! We just wanted to talk to you!'

'What do you mean, you didn't mean any harm? What was the knife for, then? What about the body in the canal? You didn't mean him any harm, either?'

'Body?' Frowning, he managed to look puzzled. 'What body?'

'The one we found last night, floating outside the Chief Minister's house – with a little message asking for me to be delivered to the sender. Which I nearly was, yoked like a slave at the market. And I was lucky – there's an old man lying dead, back at my master's house, because of your little gesture!'

'I don't know what you're talking about!'

'I bet you don't! Like you don't know why the man in the water was covered in burns and cuts and bruises, the same as the poor wretch Shining Light forced to imperson-ate a Bathed Slave – or are you going to tell me you didn't know about that either?'

To my surprise he made no effort to bluster. He looked at a place between his feet and mumbled: 'Look, that wasn't my idea. I'd no idea he'd go so far. I thought we could get them to talk if we just showed them the cactus spines, waved the fire under their noses . . .'

'Them?' I echoed. 'You mean the sorcerers?' Then, remembering that, although the men around us were engrossed in the game, this was a public place, I lowered my voice. Whispering my questions made me feel uncomfortably like a conspirator. 'The men who got out of the Cuauhcalco Prison? Where are they?'

He raised his head again, before turning it quickly as if he were looking over his shoulder. 'I don't think I can tell you.'

'Well, if you don't tell me, you can tell the Emperor! Have you ever been inside the prison? Do you want me to describe it to you?'

'I can't tell you!'

'Where's your father?'

The boy stared at me. 'My father?'

'Yes, your father. Misty!'

'My father?' he said again, his whisper now barely audible. Then, for no obvious reason, he started giggling.

He carried on giggling while I sat and gaped at him. He covered his mouth with his hand and giggled into it. I might have struck or shaken him but I was too shocked by his reaction to do either. He was still giggling when a sudden commotion broke out in the ball court, followed by a roar from the spectators around us.

Distracted, I jumped up to find that everyone else had done the same.

It took a few moments to find a position from where I could see past the people in the row in front, but then I saw that the players and the officiating priests were all standing about, their faces upturned and all looking equally bewildered. The ball lay in the dust in the middle of the court, inert and seemingly forgotten, as if it had served its purpose. It had gone through one of the stone rings set at the top of the wall.

A strange silence descended over the crowd. It was as if their voices had drained away as fast as the blood from their faces.

But when I turned towards him, the boy had gone. He

had slithered away between the legs of the standing spectators like a water snake among rushes.

Many years ago, the defeated side would have lost much
more than the game. Their captain, at least, would have
been bundled up the steps of the nearest pyramid, where the
last thing he saw on Earth would have been the black face of
the priest who took his heart out.

I lived in more civilized times, when the losing team
merely had to be hustled out of the ball court and got away
as fast as possible to avoid being torn apart by a furious
crowd of disappointed gamblers. Theoretically the winners
had the right to pillage the losers' clothing and possessions
and the onlookers' as well, but in practice that was the least
of anybody's worries.

There was no point running after the boy. If I was lucky,
I would find him later, trampled to death by the stampeding
crowd, who otherwise would sweep him along with them.
At moments like this the restraint we Aztecs habitually
imposed on ourselves was abandoned, replaced by the ugly
ferocity that so terrified our enemies. As the only spectator
with no stake in the game, I kept my place until the last of
the crowd had gone and the dust they had stirred up had
begun to settle, only cringing slightly when two sandalled
warriors trod on my legs in their haste to get after the losing
team.

I stood up and looked into the court. The winners were
still there, looking, if anything, even more bemused than
their opponents had.

'Congratulations,' I called out.

One of the players – the captain, I supposed – looked up
at me imploringly.

'Look, we're really sorry. We didn't mean it to happen.'

I had gathered up my cloak and was about to leave, but now I paused. 'What are you talking about?'

'You must have lost a fortune. But it wasn't us, not really. It was the gods – it was Tezcatlipoca.'

The dust made me sneeze. 'Don't worry about it. I didn't . . .'

'And that other lot,' one of the other players added, ignoring me. 'They shouldn't have put so much topspin on the ball, in that last rally. How were we to know where it was going to end up?'

'And the ball was harder than usual.'

There was a note of genuine fear in their voices. Perhaps they were afraid of what would happen when the crowd gave up its pursuit of their opponents and came back for the men who had actually knocked the ball through the ring, but I guessed it was more than that. A god – almost certainly Tezcatlipoca, the perverse and capricious Lord of the Here and Now – had touched their lives and probably changed them for ever. I knew how they felt. He had intervened in mine enough times, seldom to the good, but I doubted that I had felt more desperate and afraid than they did.

'It was a fluke. We're professionals, you know. We were going for a points win.'

'Come on, let's get out of here.' The captain looked up at me again. 'You can keep your clothes. You can even have your stake back, if you want.'

'I didn't have a bet,' I replied.

'You didn't?' He looked relieved. 'Well, that's all right, then.'

The players began climbing the steps leading out of the court, talking quietly among themselves, perhaps about how they were going to get their newly won wealth home before any of its former owners tried to steal it back from them.

I decided to ask them about Lily, on the off chance that one of them had seen her.

The captain laughed. 'Are you joking? We have enough to do keeping our eyes on the ball, never mind looking at girls!'

A couple of his team-mates laughed with him, but one of them – the youngest looking, a lad barely out of the House of Youth – paused on the steps and touched his lips thoughtfully with his fingers.

'There was one, though.' He glanced nervously at his captain, who was glaring at him, and added hastily: 'I only noticed her because she was the only woman – she stood out in the crowd. And not one of your pleasure girls, either. Middle aged, I thought, and really plainly dressed, like a commoner's wife or a merchant's.'

The breath caught in my throat. 'Where is she? Which way did she go?'

The youth lowered his head unhappily before his captain's silent reproach. 'I don't know. Last time I looked, she'd gone.'

I made myself breathe again. 'Never mind,' I said. 'At least I know she was here.'

I turned to go.

'You only just missed her, though,' the young man called after me. 'She was sitting in the same place you were.'

4

So now I knew for sure that the woman had gone to the ball court in order to speak to Nimble. For some reason she had then left straight away, vacating the seat next to his, which was how we had found ourselves sitting next to each other. The gods had had no hand in it after all.

It was easy to work out where the boy had gone: assuming he had been swept along with the crowd running away from the ball court, I merely had to follow a broad trail of footprints, broken feathers, tortilla crumbs and pipe ash. And he knew what I wanted to know: where the sorcerers were.

The trail ended a little way away, at the entrance to Tlatelolco market. A surprisingly small group of ball game spectators was milling around there, in front of one of the gateways in the long, low wall that stretched away on either side, surrounding the marketplace. A few were already on their way home, creeping away self-consciously, while some of the more patient formed an orderly queue and shuffled in under the watchful eyes of the market policemen guarding the entrance. A vague air of collective foolishness hung over the rapidly dwindling crowd and made itself heard in the subdued voices muttering around me. It felt as if, having seen the ball game end so unexpectedly and run from the scene in such a panic, nobody was quite sure where to go next.

As there was no sign outside the market of Misty's boy, I joined the queue at the gateway. If he was trying to hide from me, I thought, there was no better place to do it than the vast, overcrowded sprawl that was Tlatelolco market.

The market was in its way as much the heart of our world as the sacred plaza in Tenochtitlan to the South. Between forty and sixty thousand people were drawn to this place every day. They came to buy or sell, or just to stare; to walk quietly up and down the seemingly endless lines of pitches and admire the goods on display and watch and listen to their fellow Aztecs. Much of our subject peoples' produce ended up here, either through extortion or by trade with towns many days' march away. Here, laid out on mats, guarded for the most part by middle-aged women, merchants' wives, mothers and daughters, was everything you could ever want to buy.

Each type of merchandise had its own place. Some nestled in the shelter of the colonnades lining the marketplace. Most faced the narrow lanes that threaded their way through the market's vast space – lanes lined with pitches that might be generations old. Here were animal skins – jaguar, otter, jackal, deer and badger – hides, both tanned and untanned, maguey fibre cloth and cotton. There were cheap sandals made of sisal and expensive ones of jewel-encrusted leather. Here were tobacco and chocolate and every sort of mushroom. There were cooked food and raw ingredients: kidney beans, vanilla, sage, chillies and squashes, maize flour and amaranth, turkeys, live dogs and mounds of tripe, frogs and water-fly eggs. Here were gourds, plates and wooden and clay pots and jugs. There was everything you would need to build a palace: ropes, timber, mortar and stone, tools of flint, bone and obsidian, labourers for hire to do the work. Here was paper for writing and for offering to the gods. There were boat-loads of shit from the roadside privies, lining the canal that skirted one side of the marketplace, on sale for manuring the city's fields and gardens.

I wormed my way through the jostling crowd that filled the spaces between pitches, mumbling apologies when I ducked between a customer and the trader he was haggling with. I poked my head among the colonnades, peered rudely into the faces of passers-by and craned my neck to stare over their heads, but there was no sign of Nimble.

'Are you buying, or what?' The stallholder had to shout to be heard over his merchandise, wooden cages full of live ducks quacking and squabbling.

'I'm looking for a boy.'

He glanced over his shoulder at the noisy, shuddering crates behind him. 'You're obviously in the wrong place, then, aren't you? Try the slave dealers!'

I stared at him. 'No, you don't understand . . .'

'But if that's your taste,' he added nastily, 'I'd be very careful who you ask. They burn people alive for that sort of thing, didn't you know?'

'But I don't want . . .'

'You don't want to buy a duck, that's all I care about. Now fuck off before I call the police!'

I soon gave up asking for the boy. His name meant nothing to any of the busy, impatient people I mentioned it to, and his description yielded nothing but strange looks and the sort of abuse I had got from the seller of waterfowl. But I searched the slave dealers' section of the market anyway: it was close to one of the gateways and I thought I might as well look there on my way out, although I was half-hearted about it by now, tired and footsore and resigned to walking back to the merchant's house in Pochtlan.

The moment I entered this grimmest part of the market, I felt I had made a mistake.

I had been more fortunate than many. No slave merchant had lashed me to a wooden collar to stop me running away or dressed me up in a fine cloak and breech-cloth that would be stripped away the moment I was sold. I had not come to the market as part of a subject city's tribute payment or as punishment for some petty crime of my own or to release a debt. Because I had offered up my freedom voluntarily, I had been spared some of the worst indignities of slavery, and I had had four witnesses on hand, as the law required, to ensure that, when I was sold, a fair bargain would be struck. There had been a few that insisted on looking in my mouth and feeling my limbs to ensure they were sound, but most had been able to tell at a glance that I was no labourer, and treated me accordingly. The servant who had bought me for the Chief Minister had been looking for someone who could act as a secretary, and if it worried him that my stare was a little vague and my complexion a little ruddy and my breath tainted with sacred wine, no doubt he had put it all down to nerves.

My experience of being sold as a slave had not been pleasant, then, but it might have been worse. For all that it was hard to watch them being put through their paces: the men made to prance mechanically through their dance steps to a rhythm beaten out by a hired drummer, the women spinning listlessly. It made me wonder what was going on behind those dull eyes, and whether it was what I had known all those years ago: a bitter mixture of self-reproach, self-pity, fear of the future and anger about the past and whatever sequence of poverty, misery and bad luck had reached its end in this awful place.

'Can I help you?' The traders here were more polite, since their merchandise was more expensive than most.

'I'm looking for . . .' I stopped myself in time, remembering the response I had got enquiring about the boy elsewhere. I tried a different approach. 'I was looking for a merchant's widow named Lily,' I explained. 'She may have had a young lad with her.'

The slave dealer frowned. 'Lily? Oh, excuse me.' His drummer had his rubber hammers poised over a two-toned drum. 'We won't need that, he's not buying. And you lot,' he growled at the slaves whose feet had already started shuffling automatically through the dirt, 'get your slack arses back in line, if you don't want the skin beaten off them!'

He turned back to me. 'I know Lily – Kindly's daughter, isn't she? Xippopoca's widow? Isn't she the one whose son caused all that fuss at the festival, just the other day, when his Bathed Slave went mad and jumped off the Great Pyramid?'

'That's right,' I said ruefully, wondering whether there was anyone in Mexico who had not heard of the incident by now.

'You aren't likely to find her here,' he said, not unkindly, 'unless she's buying. Her family don't deal in slaves. They sell mostly luxury goods from the South: quetzal feathers and so forth. Have you tried the jewellers?' He looked along the aisle I was standing in, towards the next section of the market, where sellers of pretty things held them up to be admired, making them flash and glitter cheerfully in the afternoon sun. My eyes followed his hungrily, desperate now to be away from the sight and smell of his human merchandise. 'Try over there. If she's been in today, they'll know about it.'

I almost ran towards the jewellers' quarter of the market.

I soon found myself walking between rows of reed mats spread with gold, silver, amber, jade, turquoises, emeralds and feathers. Some jewels were loose, others set into bracelets, others carved into ornamental lip-plugs and earplugs. Some of the gold had been made into pendants or arm bands, some into plates, some packed into goose quills in the form of gold dust, as a handy form of currency. Some of the feathers were sold loose, some made up into shimmering mosaics and some fashioned into headdresses, whose blue cotinga and roseate spoonbill plumes would float above the wearer's crown while iridescent green quetzal feathers trailed gracefully behind him.

I paused by the feathers. This was the place to ask about Lily. I did not just have to take the slave dealer's word for that. Exotic feathers were imported from the South, from places such as Xoconochco, where I knew the woman's family had interests.

In any case the feathers themselves were worth admiring. The centrepiece of the display in front of me was a ceremonial shield, a leather disc pasted with blue and red feathers depicting the water monster we called Ahuitzotl, with its teeth, claws and scales picked out in gold. On the mat next to this was a great mass of scarlet feathers, sold in bunches, and they caught my attention because they reminded me of the bunch I had seen displayed in front of me at the ball game. These were fresher, however. They were among the best I had seen. Their colour was as vivid as the Sun and the air stirred them as if they were still attached to a bird in flight.

'Do you like them?' the stallholder asked. 'My cousin supplies them. They're our speciality.'

No Aztec could resist such beauty – as glorious and fragile as life itself. 'They're lovely. What are they, red spoonbill?'

'Scarlet macaw. These are the tail feathers.'

'Where does your cousin get them from?'

The stallholder was a young man, perhaps an apprentice merchant impatient to be allowed to accompany his elders on his first foreign venture. As he grinned ingenuously up at me he reminded me of Shining Light. 'Family secret,' he said.

'Oh, really? What family would that be, then?' I asked, a little too eagerly.

The stallholder's grin faded. 'These belong to Kindly and his grandson – why do you want to know that?' His tone was suddenly suspicious.

'I might have something for them,' I replied cryptically, 'or for Lily. Have you seen her? She manages the business, I gather.'

'Up to a point,' mumbled a new voice behind me.

I spun around but I knew who I would see before I had moved a muscle. I had heard that voice only briefly but I was never likely to forget it.

Misty was standing a few hands away, leering at me from beneath the layers of soot that caked his face more thickly than ever. One hand was concealed under his cloak. I could guess what it held. I could feel the skin on the back of my neck shrinking at the memory of that strange metal knife.

'What would you have that Lily might be interested in, then?' His voice was as indistinct as ever but there was no mistaking its edge of threat.

I looked quickly around for Nimble and found him. He was walking towards us, a tuna cactus fruit in his hands, and gaping at me in frank astonishment. An instant later he broke into a run. 'Stop!' he cried.

Misty turned sharply to face him. The knife slipped into view, its keen blade a streak of light as it caught the sun. To my amazement he waved it at the youth. 'Stay out of this!' he shouted. 'If you don't want . . .'

I threw myself at him.

I went for the knife arm but he was sideways on to me and it was on the far side of his body. As I reached across him to seize the weapon the elbow of his other arm shot upwards and jabbed me under the chin. The blow was not hard – he was off balance, staggering backwards under the force of my attack – but it put me off my stride and gave Nimble time to reach me before I could try again. Howling, the youth seized me by the shoulders and dragged me backwards. I tried to tear myself free but he snagged my legs with his own and brought me crashing painfully to the earth.

I was on my knees then, with my enemies standing over me. In the moments I was waiting for the knife I was only dimly aware of what they were doing. I had a vague impression of jostling bodies and raised voices.

'I'm going to kill him now!' The pretence of mumbling like a priest had vanished, as it had once before, on the boat. Now I thought his speech was familiar, but I could not place it. There was too much happening.

'No! You mustn't!' the boy protested. 'We've got to know!'

There was the sound of a blow, a sharp, youthful cry, and one of the shadows over me had gone.

It sounded as if Nimble had lost the argument.

Something massive and blunt bore down on the small of my back, pressing me into the dusty floor: Misty's knee, pinning me down.

'Now,' he hissed, 'I've been waiting for this!'

Suddenly I heard Nimble's voice again. It was choked and tearful and shrill but quite clear: 'Look out! Here she comes – Lily!'

'What? Where?'

The weight vanished from my back as my assailant leapt

to his feet. I got up and ran blindly, before he had time to turn on me again with the knife.

'I can't see her — you're lying! You stupid little sod, he's getting away!'

I heard Misty's sandalled feet slap the earth as he gave chase, but I had too long a start on him.

So he gave up the pursuit and thought of something else.

'Stop!' he cried. 'Stop, thief!'

I looked up just in time to see two tall, muscle-bound figures emerging into the aisle in front of me. They both halted at once, staring at the scene in front of them while they made up their minds what to do. Then they too started running.

I skidded to a halt so fast I scraped skin off my bare heel. I had a knife-wielding madman at my back, crying 'Thief'. Bearing down on me were two of the market police, whose work included arresting thieves. I had no time to think about what I was doing: if I had, I would not have been so stupid.

I tried to leap across a mat full of jewels and feathers into the next aisle. I thought I could run, then, get clear of the marketplace and keep running until I found a place to hide. All I did was land on my face and scatter precious stones around me like spilled corn.

I scrabbled desperately there while an old woman's voice screamed into my ears and blows rained down on my back and head. The blows were still falling as I was hauled to my feet, some of them now catching me in the side, under my ribs, and driving the wind out of me as my arms were wrenched out of the way. The old woman screamed some more obscenities and then something as heavy as a wall hit the side of my head, and I passed out.

SIX KNIFE

1

A woman's voice said: 'Don't move.'

I was not about to try. It seemed to me that I had made the effort once, a long time ago, but pain and nausea and a sinister scraping sound from somewhere inside my body had made me stop.

Besides, I knew I was going to die soon. Why bother moving, when it could not help? I considered giving up breathing, because it hurt my ribs and achieved nothing except to prolong the pain, but I kept forgetting. I would be about to pass out when a bright shaft of pain like an obsidian knife stung me awake.

'Take it easy!' It was the woman's voice again. A weight was laid on my shoulder, pressing it gently but firmly to the ground.

'Can you open your mouth?'

'Mmmph?'

I could not speak because my lips were numb and the tongue behind them was swollen through having had my teeth driven through it.

'Try to drink this.'

I could not see what she was offering me because my eyelids were bruised, pulpy masses that had gummed themselves shut.

'It will help your ribs.'

Liquid trickled onto my mouth. Some ran over my cheeks and down my chin. It was as sour as vomit and burned my throat.

I coughed. The pain of coughing made me gasp.

'Have a little more,' said the deep, seductive voice.

I was too feeble to fend her off or stop her pouring more of her fetid brew into me. I was too feeble even to retch.

'Sleep, now,' she said.

I slept.

I woke up.

I could open my eyes a little. All I could see were vague shapes, shadows and pools of light blurring into one another, and everything tinged with red. It was hard to make any sense of what I was looking at until I thought of closing one eye. Then the world stopped spinning long enough for me to work out that I was indoors somewhere and that from the way the shadows fell it must be either late afternoon or early morning.

Pain sliced through my skull, forcing me to shut both eyes again. I moaned.

Someone moved near by: my ears, although they were singing, picked up the slightest noise, such as a maize ear being dropped in the street outside, or somebody's joints creaking as he stood up. A hand at the back of my neck lifted my head, while another laid something warm over my brow, a thick paste that stung when it was pressed into place. I moaned again. As the stinging subsided I felt brisk, efficient fingers tying on a bandage.

'Can you speak?' It was the woman's voice again.

'Mmmph?'

'It's all right. Rest. You're safe here.'

★

When I woke up again I was alone in a small room with only an evil smell for company.

I lay on my back in the middle of the floor, staring at the ceiling. I could just about unglue my eyes now, although there was little to see but grey plaster. When I turned my head to look at a wall I saw more of the same, apart from a couple of large irregular smudges. I remembered the light drizzle there had been recently and thought of damp. They were going to have to renew the thatch on the roof before the real rains began in the summer, I told myself, while I turned my head the other way.

Opposite the smudged wall was an odd pattern of little lights, like stars but more regularly spaced and less distinct. I frowned as I tried to make them out. I blinked and stared at them, and gradually they became two identical sets of lights placed side by side, and in the space between them was a pain like a wooden peg being driven into my skull. My stomach lurched.

My head rolled back of its own accord, leaving me staring at the ceiling again. I shut my eyes and swallowed convulsively, to stop the gorge rising in my throat, and I lay still, in darkness, until the agony and nausea subsided.

I waited until all I was left with were a dull throbbing in my head – a familiar pain that I seemed to have had always, its regular beat almost reassuring, as though I needed it to remind me I was still alive – and aching ribs that protested every time I drew breath.

The smell worried me. Even the poorest houses in Mexico, one-roomed hovels perched on stilts over the marshes on the fringes of the city, were cleaned every day, but this room stank like a dog left for dead in a badly kept latrine.

I decided not to move my head again, but to try looking at my surroundings out of the corners of my eyes, the way a

rich man looks at a beggar. That seemed to help. I could see
no furniture of any kind, but I now knew what the little
lights were. When I was not seeing double, there was just
one set of them. They were daylight showing through the
gaps in a wicker screen. They were the room's only illumi-
nation, just enough to paint everything around me a
washed-out grey colour.

The lights were all equally bright. That meant the Sun
was not shining straight on the doorway. I wondered how far
it had moved round and then realized I did not even know
what day it was.

I let out a soft moan as a fresh wave of sickness rolled
sluggishly over my stomach.

Where was I and how long had I been here?

The appalling truth began to take shape in my befuddled
mind even before I glanced at the wall opposite the doorway
and realized that what I had taken for dark smudges were
really paintings, their colours turned to shades of grey in the
gloom, but still recognizable if you knew them. They were
Two Lord and Two Lady. I had last seen them in this room,
the day I had come looking for news of Shining Light, when
the young merchant's mother had received me as graciously
as she could and told me her son had gone into exile.

Then I realized that a voice I vaguely remembered hearing, crooning softly at me while my wounds were dressed
and vile medicine was poured into me, had been Lily's.

I tried to sit up then. What stopped me was not the
sudden, crippling pain or the sensation of broken bones
grinding against each other, but the fact that I had been
strapped to a board, so tightly that I could scarcely inflate my
lungs.

I flopped back on the board with a gasp. I was trapped
and at the mercy of my enemies.

I had set out wanting a killer to come for me, and meaning to use the merchant's mother to bring it about, but not like this – when I was wounded and as helpless as a newborn.

And the bad smell, I realized with a shudder, was my own.

Pain and despair made me groan aloud.

In answer came footsteps in the courtyard outside, the scraping sound of the screen being pulled aside and a tide of light that flooded the room, washing their grey pallor from the faces of the gods.

'What's going on?' I tried to say. What came out was: 'Mmmph?'

The only response was a grunt of effort as I was picked up, sleeping mat and all, and carried through the doorway. My bearers took me through the afternoon sunshine into a shady place, where they propped my board against a wall.

When the feeling that the blood inside my head was sloshing violently back and forth had begun to ease off, I looked around cautiously.

Lily's father was sitting in the middle of the courtyard with his back to the trunk of an old fig tree, watching me balefully.

'I hope you appreciate that you're in my place.'

'Mmmph?'

'I'm sorry, you'll have to speak up. My hearing isn't what it was.'

I tried again, eventually managing something that sounded more like 'What – am – I – doing – here?'

'Well, they had to move you out of the room, so they could clean it. It looks as if my daughter's looked after you all right, but I'm told you've left dried blood and piss and the gods know what else all over the place. And I suppose they had to get you upright as well, or else you'd have got pneumonia.'

A man and a woman crossed the courtyard, he carrying a bowl of water and she a broom. The man was Constant, the servant I had met before. Judging by his expression, he was no better disposed towards me now than he had been then.

I made a noise that must have sounded like a question.

'I don't know,' the old man said, 'but they seem to have given you a good working over. Lucky for you Lily went to the market instead of coming straight back here.'

'Lily?' I gurgled. 'The market?'

'Why, yes – don't you remember?' He looked me up and down. 'Maybe you don't. Well, what she told me was, after she'd finished her business at the ball court – where you went looking for her, remember? – she had someone to see at the market. Then she saw a fight going on near one of our pitches: you and a priest. You were on the ground and the priest had a knife, but then something distracted him and you managed to run away. You didn't get very far.'

His casual words brought the whole thing back – the black-faced man chasing me with his cries of 'Thief', the police heading me off, the blows driven into me from all sides as I was hauled to my feet. I felt as if the ground were sinking under me and my eyes began to roll.

A look of alarm crossed the old man's face. He snatched up the gourd beside him. 'Constant! Quick, the man needs a drink!'

'What happened to the priest?' I gasped weakly.

The male servant who had been cleaning my room emerged, saw the gourd Lily's father was proffering, and slouched sullenly towards him.

'Give him a mouthful of this, it'll pick him up,' the old man ordered. 'The priest? He ran off, apparently. My daughter said she ran up to the stall he'd been standing by, to ask him what he was shouting about, but he vanished into the crowd before she got there. By then everybody was too busy watching you being beaten up to be able to tell her where he'd gone.' He grinned pitilessly. 'You don't know how lucky you were. The police were all for hauling what was left of you straight off to the courthouse, where they'd probably have had you beaten to death on the spot. Fortunately my daughter managed to convince them that you hadn't actually stolen anything, so they let you off with a good hiding.'

Without a word the servant snatched the gourd from the old man, walked over to me and pressed its opening against my battered lips.

It was sacred wine.

I had once sworn never to touch the stuff again. On the other hand, at that time I had not been beaten unconscious, unaccountably rescued and cared for by a woman I thought of as my enemy, and then strapped to a board and stood up in the corner of someone's courtyard like a trophy.

I shut my eyes and swallowed the drink as gratefully as a baby devouring his mother's milk.

'Are you awake?'

The room was dark. I shared it with shadows that moved around me like coyotes prowling around a wounded deer.

'Yaotl?'

I rolled my eyes towards the voice.

The shadows were moving because someone was carrying a torch around the room. As the dark figure lifted it into a bracket in the wall, they stopped, settling down in the corners, suddenly as tame as little pot-bellied dogs.

'You must be hungry: you haven't eaten for days. You must try some of this.'

It was only as she knelt beside me, tipping a tortoiseshell bowl towards my lips, that I recognized the void in my belly and realized how long it had been empty of anything except the old man's sacred wine. The thought made my stomach heave.

Lily was feeding me maize gruel, insubstantial stuff, unseasoned except for a little salt, but as it oozed down my throat my head jerked forward out of her hand and I spewed gruel and sacred wine and thin sour juices down my chin and onto my chest.

She snatched the bowl away but kept her hand behind my head, supporting me until the retching stopped.

'It's all right,' she cooed. 'It's all right. Relax. We'll try some more later.'

Putting the bowl down, she gently let my head fall back, and stroked my forehead while my breathing gradually slowed.

I closed my eyes. I did not want to sleep. I wanted to get up and get out, away from the ministrations of this disquietingly kind woman, whose son and his friends were killers who wanted to mingle my blood with their other victims', but I was too tired. If I could just rest for a moment, I thought, I could gather my strength until the woman left me alone, and then think of a way out of here.

I must have slept a little.

Perhaps I merely dozed, but it must have looked like sleep to her.

With her hand still resting on my forehead, she was whispering: 'My boy. Oh, my poor boy,' in a voice now choked with tears.

SEVEN RAIN

1

I woke up after sunrise, alone, to the sound of rain.

Lily's house was as plain as befitted a merchant, but it was well made and the roof did not leak. I could lie, dry, warm and snug on my mat, and enjoy listening to the rain rattling on the wicker door-screen and dripping steadily from its frame.

My head felt better, although my ribs still yelped with every deep breath. I felt a curious sense of calm, as though the stout walls of this strange house could protect me from the dangers circling me. It was as if the city, with its constant rush and bustle, had somehow left me behind in this quiet, still place, and taken with it the Emperor, my master, Misty and his son and their anonymous ally, the one who knew my full name. Even Shining Light seemed safely far away, although this was his own home. It had begun to occur to me that if his mother had really meant to kill me or hurt me she had had ample opportunity. I let myself think that I might have been wrong about her. Perhaps her interest in me had not been so sinister, after all.

My peace was shattered when the screen was pulled aside and two figures hurried into the room.

The man said: 'I'm wet through, Lily. I hope you're going to make this worth my while.'

'You know you will enjoy our hospitality,' she reassured

him smoothly. 'We have venison as well as turkey. And I'll see to it that you have a change of clothes.'

That seemed to mollify him. 'All right. I'd better have a look, then. We'll see how these ribs have set. I don't suppose there's any chance of keeping a torch alight long enough to bring it in here, is there?'

The torch was brought and held aloft as he advanced on me.

If I had not been tied up I might have squirmed out of the way. Obviously the stranger was one of the many varieties of curer. Even good curers were frightening, and good or bad, this man was no exception. Although he was short and stocky and kept making nervous, fussy movements with his head and hands, still his face, featureless against the torchlight except for the whites of his eyes and his glittering nose- and lip-plugs, loomed over me like a thundercloud. When he took a knife out, a thin sliver of obsidian, I felt my mouth go dry.

'Now then . . .'

I winced even before he began slicing at the bandages around my chest.

'Still tender, eh?'

'Yes,' I croaked.

'Thought so. These things are always worse on the third day. And we couldn't get you to swallow your ground lizards in hot urine, when it would have helped.'

'The third . . .' I gasped, incredulous.

'Why, yes. You were brought here on Four Vulture – that's right, isn't it, Lily? And it's now Seven Rain.'

He stood up for a moment, fingering the cloth pouch that hung from his neck before leaning over me again and blowing into his cupped hands.

A cloud of fine powder flew into my eyes, nose and throat. My eyes stung and watered and I sneezed.

'What are you doing?' I gasped. 'What was that?'

'Yauhtli.'

'Yauhtli? But that's what they give to . . .'

'. . . Sacrificial victims at the festivals of the Fall of the Fruit and the Arrival of the Gods, just before they throw them in the fire. Of course it is. You need something to dull the pain. Now be quiet: I need to call upon a god.'

His powder did not dull the pain by very much. He worked to the sound of his own voice, chanting a hymn to Quetzalcoatl, the patron god of healers. I gritted my teeth, noticing at the same time that I had lost a few, and writhed on the mat. My hands found and grasped the edge of it, crushing and splitting the reeds between my fingers.

Lily came and took one of my hands, squeezing it gently. I was too surprised to return the pressure or pull my hand away, so I just let it lie limply in hers until the curer was done.

'He's mending well,' he announced. 'I've drained some more blood off him. He can try a steam bath in a day or so, and I'll give you some herbs to give him when he does, to help the swelling in his face. Don't let him go out of the house or the courtyard. I'll make up some snake's tongue in case he starts coughing and you must keep putting the poultices on his chest. Oh, and give him an enema if his stomach swells up.' He looked down at me. 'You're lucky to be alive, let alone mostly in one piece.'

He looked at the doorway. 'Has it stopped raining? Good. I'm hungry!'

'I don't understand what you're complaining about,' she snapped. 'At least I found you a real doctor. Or would you have preferred some quack of a sorcerer throwing maize kernels up in the air and lying about your fortune?'

'It wouldn't have hurt,' I mumbled.

'It wouldn't have worked!'

I was no longer strapped to a board. The courtyard had dried out enough for a mat to be taken outside and placed by a wall for me. I had been helped out of the room and eased painfully onto the mat, and now watched Lily pacing back and forth in front of me, the hem of her skirt flaring about her ankles as she turned.

'He's the best doctor I know of, as well. He learned his craft with the army . . .'

'Doing what? Finishing off the wounded?'

She threw her arms up in frustration. 'Why didn't I leave you where I found you? He attended you when I brought you here, you know. You ungrateful, ignorant little man, you owe him your life!'

'I understood I owed you that much,' I said, 'but I don't know why.'

The woman looked as if she was trying to make up her mind about something. She had her eyes fixed on a point somewhere above my head and her toes kept twitching as if she were about to take to her heels. One hand plucked absently at a loose thread on her blouse.

'What were you doing at the market, Lily? You were sitting next to Misty's boy, Nimble, at the ball court, but you left early. I followed him into the marketplace but lost him, so I thought I would look for you, or news of you, instead. I got as far as your family's pitch and was attacked by Misty himself. Now it turns out that you were there too. Why? What are Misty and Nimble to you?' It was a longer speech than I had set out to make and the last two words came out in a painful croak.

There was a long silence, and at the end of it a barely audible snap as the thread the woman had been tugging at gave way.

'Misty?' She whispered the name to herself. 'I don't understand. The man you were fighting with was a priest.'

'It's a disguise. He and the boy were there together. So were you, but why?'

I looked directly into Lily's face. Her eyes were narrowed, although whether in anger or disquiet or puzzlement I could not tell.

'Is that all you want to know?' she asked quietly.

'Well, no,' I replied. 'What I really want to know is . . .'

What was I doing here? That was what I wanted to ask, but I was not given the chance.

Lily flared. 'How dare you question me in my own house! Do you know what I've done for you? I had to talk the police out of throwing you in the canal, among the manure boats. I had to pay off the owner of the pitch you demolished. I had to send a runner to tell Constant and a couple of bearers to come and get you. I've sat over you for three days and cleaned you up and endured your stench and paid for the best doctor, and what thanks do I get? Who are you, to pry into my business? What were you doing following me around anyway?' She had begun pacing again; now, as though the question had only just occurred to her, she broke her stride, pausing thoughtfully for a moment before rounding on me again.

She bent towards the mat I lay on, put her face close to mine and hissed dangerously: 'Tell me why you were looking for me. Tell me now, or I'll have you thrown out of my house!'

I tried to scuttle away from her like a scorpion retreating into a crack in a wall, but it still hurt too much to move. If I needed a reminder that I was still helpless, that was it.

'I wanted to give you a message,' I said weakly.

'What message?'

'It's for your son – or for Misty, or his boy. But . . .'

'You know my son's not here,' she said coldly, straightening up and moving away. 'I told you the first time we met, he's gone away.'

'I didn't think he had, though. I thought he and Misty and Nimble were still in touch. I thought you were taking messages between them. Wasn't that what you and the boy were doing at the ball court?'

'No!' she cried vehemently. 'It was not! I mean, who said we were doing anything . . .' She stumbled to a confused halt.

I waited, listening in silence to her quick, agitated breathing. I was not about to ask any more questions and risk being thrown out into the street.

Eventually she said, in a low, guttural voice: 'My son gambles. It isn't a secret. He has given more of his family's wealth away to Misty than I care to remember, and there are still debts. They have to be paid, do you understand? Merchants trade on their reputation: we would be ruined if they were not honoured. So, yes,' she went on, forcing each word out between clenched teeth, 'I did go to see the boy, to pay some of what my son owed his father, but I have never met the father and what I told you about my son is true – I will eat earth!'

Then, keeping her eyes on me the whole time, she slowly knelt down, touched the ground beside her with a fingertip, and solemnly brought the fingertip to her lips.

I tried not to react. I tried not to show my shock at the woman's impiety, or surprise at the extent of her desperation, because I was convinced she was lying.

'What was the message?'

'Message?' I repeated absently.

'The message you wanted conveyed to my son.'

I hesitated. I was in no fit state to confront a ruthless killer now. On the other hand, I realized that what I had intended to say really did not matter. It was my name that had been found on the body in the canal. It would be enough for Lily just to tell her son or his allies where I was.

Perhaps she would not betray me to them, though. I clung once more to the thought that she had saved me in the marketplace and brought me here and nursed me and done nothing to hurt me when she had ample opportunity. Perhaps the best way to dissuade her from going to my enemies was to tell her what she had demanded to know.

I described all that I had seen and done since the day I had met her son, at the Festival of the Raising of Banners. By the time I had finished my throat was dry and my head was throbbing with the effort of remembering it all, but I got a strange sense of relief at having had someone to tell the story to, even someone I did not trust.

'So my son's Bathed Slave was a sorcerer,' Lily said wonderingly. 'But I don't understand how Shining Light got hold of him.'

'Neither do I. I wondered if he had got him from Misty, but it could just as well have been the other way round, and either way I can't see how he fell into their hands.' I studied her for a moment until the pain between my eyes forced them shut. 'What was going on between your son and Misty? Was it just gambling, or was there something more?'

She looked at me sharply. 'What do you mean by that?'

'Nothing,' I replied hastily, alarmed by her tone. 'But I know Shining Light had one of the prisoners, and Misty and Nimble had another, and they were both treated the same way before they died, and I can't see why. And my name comes into it somewhere, and I can't see why that is,

either . . .' I ended on a groan as the pain in my head was
starting to make me dizzy.

The woman stood up abruptly. 'You need to rest.'

'But . . .'

'And I have work to do,' she added in a voice that did not
invite argument.

As she walked away I remembered something.

'Lily.'

I heard her footsteps falter. 'What?'

I looked at her as levelly as I could, through eyes squinting with pain under droopy, puffy lids. She stood with her
weight on her left foot and the right slightly raised, a muscle
in the ankle twitching as it made up its mind whether to
take the next step or not, and looked at me over her shoulder with her eyebrows drawn together and her lips pursed
thoughtfully, as if she was trying to anticipate my next
words.

'Thank you for saving my life,' I said.

Lily's work included rousing her aged father, who found it
difficult to get up in the morning. Soon after she left me the
old man appeared, stumbling into view on the arm of a servant, bearing a sour look and a gourd full of liquid.

'Not against the tree. There's a knot in the wood, it's like
an arrowhead between my shoulder-blades. Put me against
the wall, next to the slave, there.'

As soon as the servant was out of sight he pulled the
maize cob out of the neck of his gourd and upended it into
his mouth, smacking his lips when he was done. When he
turned to me the smell of his breath matched his expression.

'You're still here, then? Well, as my daughter seems to
have taken a fancy to you, I'd better make you welcome.
Have a drink!'

I felt myself recoil as he thrust the gourd towards me, even though part of me wanted to seize it from him and drain it in several gulps.

'Come on,' he snapped impatiently. 'It's all right. You're ill and I'm old. We might as well both make the most of it!'

Eyeing the gourd suspiciously, I licked my lips because they suddenly felt dry. 'Why do you drink so much?'

He took a thoughtful nip at the gourd.

'Put it this way,' he said. 'Do you keep dogs?'

'I expect my master does. My father used to, although my eldest brother sends him so much turkey and venison these days that he probably doesn't have to. Why?'

'Ever wonder why they lick their balls?'

The question was so unexpected that it made me roar with laughter, and then, of course, cough, gasp and groan with pain. When the tears had cleared from my eyes the old man was looking at me steadily through his filmy eyes.

'It's because they can,' he explained, matter-of-factly. 'Now do you want a drink or don't you?'

My chest hurt. I told myself it was for medicinal purposes, and that made it all right.

My memory of the rest of that morning is obscured by pain and sacred wine.

When I had drunk, it had been to make the days pass more quickly. Kindly clearly felt that, having reached the age when drunkenness was allowed, he had a sacred duty to make up for a lifetime's restraint. He drank with the kind of determined concentration that I had seen on the faces of novice priests learning to recite old hymns from memory.

While I still could, I tried to remember why I had come to the house and gone looking for his daughter in the first place, and before the drink had completely paralysed my already swollen tongue, I tried to tease some information out of him.

'Tell me about your grandson.'

'What about him?'

'Has he always been a gambler?'

Kindly frowned at me over the curved surface of his gourd. 'I suppose so. You know how it is: they start off as kids playing Patolli for beans, on a board scratched in the dirt, and it goes on from there. But I think it's only in the last couple of years that it's got really serious.'

'Since he met Misty?' I was guessing.

He appraised the gourd for a moment before reluctantly handing it to me. 'Could be.'

'You see, what I think,' I said as I took a swig, 'is maybe there's more between them than just gambling.'

The lined and leathery face grew dark.

'What makes you say that?' he asked slowly.

'I just mean that sacrifice of his,' I said carefully, wishing neither of us had drunk so much. 'I saw what state the man was in. He'd been tortured – beaten with burning torches and pricked with cactus spines. He wasn't in any condition to be a Bathed Slave. In fact I don't think anyone would have given a bag of cocoa beans for him, let alone presented him to a god. But he's not the only man I've seen in that sort of state.' I found myself explaining again about my kidnapping, the body we had found floating in the canal outside my master's house and the message that had accompanied it. While I spoke I put the drink down between us and I noticed that the old man made no move to pick it up until I had finished. His head was nodding on his chest, but it was nodding in time with my words, and he spoke up promptly when I had finished.

'So Shining Light's sacrifice and the body you think Misty

had something to do with were both treated the same way?' he mused. 'Why would that be, though? Do you think my grandson gave his . . . associate a slave as a way of settling a gaming debt?'

'That wouldn't explain why he was tortured,' I pointed out, 'nor where either the man in the canal or your grandson's offering came from to begin with.'

'Nor what they want from you,' the old man added. 'It's interesting that whoever left that message used your full name, isn't it? I can't see how my grandson would have known it. Misty I wouldn't know about.' He stroked the neck of the drinking gourd thoughtfully. 'Did you ask Lily about any of this?'

'She didn't seem to want to discuss it. Got quite angry, in fact.'

'I'm not surprised.' He gave the gourd a thirsty glance and then pressed it to his lips in a sudden, almost convulsive movement.

'You have to understand, I don't know this Misty,' he gasped, in mid-gulp. 'Never met him. But anyone Shining Light takes up with would have to be a nasty piece of work. Torture, you say? Well, that sounds about right. He and my grandson should make a fine couple, in that case.'

I stared at him as he took another long drink. 'I don't understand.'

'That's why my daughter was upset,' the old man said bitterly, when he had finally pulled the gourd away from his face. 'Bad enough losing her husband to a bunch of savages, but to have her son burned to death for sodomy as well, that would be too much!'

'Shining Light and Misty?' I said incredulously.

'Why not? Misty has some hold on my grandson, and it's not just money. He's the one I was telling you about, who persuaded Shining Light to move all our property. It all ended up in Misty's own warehouse. As I said, I've never met the man, but he sounds like my grandson's type: vicious. I told you once there were other vices that could seduce a man besides drinking, didn't I?' He waved the gourd at me theatrically. 'It's not just the gambling, you see. I think Shining Light's tried everything once. And he always had a cruel streak – I caught him once, he had one of Lily's dogs in a sack with a turkey, I think he wanted to see which one would come out alive. Maybe they dreamed up this business with the sacrifice together as a kind of sick joke.'

'And Lily knows about this?'

'She knows what her son's like, yes. But you can't blame her for not wanting it talked about, can you?' He took up the gourd one last time, tipping it to let the last drops of liquid run into his mouth. 'If it got out that her son liked boys instead of girls, he'd be killed and we'd be ruined.

'In fact,' he added, turning a grin on me that had no humour in it whatsoever, 'I wouldn't let my daughter know I've even told you. She might kill you herself, just to keep your mouth shut!'

2

'**A**s if having one drunkard in this house wasn't enough! Do you think I saved your miserable life just to provide that disgusting old sot with company?'

The sound of Lily's voice was like a hard rubber ball bouncing off the inside of my skull, although the words themselves seemed to come from far away and to be in a foreign language that I could just about understand with a lot of effort.

'He is your father.'

'He could be the Sun, the Turquoise Prince himself, with a crowd of warriors dancing around him, and he'd still be a disgusting old sot! At least he has an excuse!'

'So do I,' I ventured.

'Oh no you don't. The doctor prescribed snake's tongue for you, not sacred wine, and that's what you're getting. Here!'

I sniffed at the proffered bowl, which contained a brownish liquid. I knew it was not literally made of snakes' tongues but of a herb called *coanenepilli*, which was used to treat chest pain. I had learned that much at school. They had not taught me how vile its smell was, but I assumed its taste could not be worse. I was wrong.

'You might have mixed it with atolli, or honey, or something,' I spluttered.

'I might,' she conceded, taking the bowl back. 'Maybe I will, next time, if you learn to grow up!'

It was getting towards evening, and a chilly breeze had got up and driven us indoors – Kindly to collapse, unconscious, on his mat, and I to endure Lily's pet curer's revolting medicine and a lecture on the perils of drink.

The stuff cleared my head, at least. I looked at Lily, who had knelt opposite me, by the open doorway, so that the sunlight that came into the room fell on her. She looked different, somehow, although I could not at first see why.

'Tell me something, Lily. If I'm not your father's drinking companion, what am I doing here?'

'Getting better, of course. You were in such a bad way when the police had finished with you that I couldn't see what else to do with you, except bring you back here.'

'So you felt sorry for me? Look, I don't want you to think I'm ungrateful, but if some beggar comes to your door offering withered chillies or stale maize cakes for sale, do you buy them? I doubt it.'

She surprised me by looking hurt: she gave an audible sniff and turned her head away sharply. As she did so the sun caught her cheek and I realized what was different. Although her hair was still streaked with grey, her skin looked clearer and paler than before.

On her the effect was so surprising that I could not help remarking: 'Ochre?'

She looked at me again. 'I beg your pardon?'

'You've painted your face.'

'What do you mean? Oh, I see! No I haven't,' she corrected me primly, although she could not quite suppress the smile that wanted to form on her lips. 'Even if I had any reason to put on make-up, I couldn't, not while my son's . . . away. It's like being in mourning, for us,' she added in a low voice. 'This is only axin ointment, for the cold. It stops my skin drying out at night.'

Her half-smile did not chase the lines around her mouth and eyes away. If anything they deepened, but they looked now as if they might have been etched there by laughter as well as pain. They made me wonder how she could be in happier, more relaxed times.

Since we seemed, just for a moment, to be able to speak to each other, I tried putting my question again.

'Why am I really here?'

She sighed. 'Why do you think? I wanted to ask you about Shining Light's sacrifice. Then when I saw you in the marketplace, I thought it was a gift from the gods.'

'We were both lucky, then,' I said sceptically.

'I had to speak to you, because I thought you could tell me about the offering – tell me something that would help me work out where he came from and why he did what he did. I know why my son would have had you with him, you see. He never told me, but it's obvious enough. He knew he had not prepared the sacrifice properly, and he thought it would help if he had someone who knew all the rituals.'

'I assumed that was what I was there for,' I conceded, 'but I don't understand how he fixed on me. He might have got a real priest to advise him, and there must have been enough of his own people, merchants, that he could have turned to. Did your son ask my master for me in particular, or did my master volunteer my services?'

'I've no idea.'

I followed my own train of thought. 'Shining Light got my name from somewhere. What would have made him go to the Chief Minister? A mutual acquaintance? They both had dealings with Misty.' I noticed Lily's sharp intake of

breath at my mention of the name, but I carried on thinking aloud. 'So Misty, or that boy of his, Nimble, could have
suggested my name – but what for?' I groaned aloud, not
from the pain of my wounds but from a much older, more
enduring anguish. 'It's not even as if I'm a priest! I'm a
scribe, a secretary, a messenger, a dogsbody, a whipping boy
for my master's vicious dog of a steward. I haven't set foot in
a Priest House in a dozen or more years – what use could I
have been anyway?'

Lily said nothing. She was staring at me.

Then I realized that I had been almost shouting, with my
fists clenched like a baby's and the muscles of my face
clenched in an angry mask. With an effort and some pain I
made them relax.

'Sorry,' I muttered. 'Sometimes it's not so easy, remembering.'

She leaned forward into the room and laid her hands on
her knees.

'What happened to you, Yaotl?' she asked earnestly. 'You
were a priest. You belonged to the gods. You belonged near
the sky, in the mountains, on the summits of the pyramids.
What made you give all that up to become another man's
possession?'

'Perhaps the gods gave up on me,' I said lightly. It hurt,
merely thinking about this subject. 'They do that, you know.
They're easily bored. They will raise a man up as high as
Popocatepetl only to hurl him down again, and if it's going
to happen to you then it's no use trying to prepare for it, or
complaining. And I was dedicated to the most fickle of them
all, Tezcatlipoca. Why do you think we call him 'the Enemy
on Both Hands'?'

'Something drove you out of the temple,' she insisted.
'What was it – a woman? An argument with another priest?'

'It was a long time ago.' Being asked these things now was like being pricked with maguey spines. 'It doesn't matter any more. Please, let's just forget it.'

'You don't want to tell me.' The woman sat back again, withdrawing from me a little, apparently feeling that my reserve was a poor return for her hospitality. 'Well, it's up to you.' She looked towards the doorway, as if making up her mind to leave. 'But I don't know that I believe you when you say it doesn't matter.'

She stood up and stepped quickly out of the room, to return a moment later clasping something small.

Before she came over to me, taking my hand and extending it, palm upwards, to drop the object into it, I realized what it must be, and from different directions joy and fear tugged at my heart.

For a long moment I just stared at the thing in my hand, unable to speak. Only when I could no longer see it for the tears in my eyes did I manage to croak: 'This was mine – I thought I'd lost it.'

'When I got to you in the marketplace, you had your fist clenched around it. The doctor said we'd have to cut your fingers off to get it away from you, but you let it go eventually, once we'd got you to sleep.'

It was a child's necklace: an infant's, so small that it would barely have gone around my wrist.

'You know what this is,' I said hopelessly.

'Of course I do. We send our children to school at the Priest House as well, you know. A merchant travelling abroad has to learn how to be his own priest, his own healer, his own scribe, an ambassador for his own city.' She took the little cotton loop from me delicately and examined it, threading it between her fingers. 'It's so small, isn't it? You were given this when you were just days old, and the priests took it and hung it up in the temple as a sign of your dedication to the gods.'

It was still hard to speak. 'It was all they left me with,' I mumbled.

Memories, suddenly released, tumbled over each other in my head: the calculated cruelty of the priests, the temples with their reek of incense and slaughter, the hymns and prayers I still knew by heart, and the confusion, anger and despair that had ended it all. I could live without such memories, cheerfully abandoned years before, with the traces washed away by a cleansing tide of sacred wine. I had been happy to leave them bound up in a tiny necklace at the bottom of a trunk.

But now I had the necklace in my hands, and the woman who had returned it to me wanted me to share my memories, and in some way I felt she had a claim on them.

Besides, I realized, surprising myself, I did not want her to go.

'Do you know . . .' My voice faltered.

She turned her head. 'Yes?'

'Do you know what happens during the month of Eating Maize and Beans, before the festival?'

3

'The month of Eating Maize and Beans: it's a time of testing. Summer is coming and if the rains fail, the city will starve, the way it did sixty years ago, when even the nobles had to sell their children for want of food. If a priest falters in a song or a sacrifice, Tlaloc may just go away from us – empty his rain-clouds on the far side of the mountains, perhaps, and water our enemies' fields instead of ours. The priests have to be prepared for the festival. They have to be culled. Any who aren't up to it have to be weeded out.'

'You failed the test?' she enquired gently.

'I passed the test! I passed it every year from when I was seven years old!

'Let me tell you what happens. You have to remember that this is all done during a fast, when there is nothing to eat but a few maize cakes at noon. Now, at twilight we make an offering before the hearth in the Priest House. It's nothing much – dough balls, tomatoes, peppers, something like that. The important thing is that whatever we offer has to be round. It has to be something that will roll about the moment you so much as look at it, because that's part of the test. You have to pile the offerings up in front of the fire and if they don't stay just where you put them – if they roll over, or worse if the pile collapses – then you're in trouble.'

'What sort of trouble?'

'I'll come to that – there's a lot more to it. When that part's all over, you strip and make a blood offering.'

I remembered drawing the thorns through my earlobes, feeling the old, numb scar tissue reopening and watching the blood, the water of life so precious to the gods, as it ran over my shoulders and arms.

'Then you run to the lake. It's the middle of the night and the water's as cold as the Land of the Dead, but you all have to jump in, from the youngest to the eldest. There was always a lot of shouting and splashing about, and some people tried to tell me it was to attract the gods' attention or frighten away the lake monster, but I think we were really just trying to stop ourselves freezing to death.

'Then it's back to the Priest House, to sit and shiver until noon. You're allowed to sleep, but in the night it's too cold for sleep, and in the morning the prospect of food keeps your eyes open.

'They feed you at midday – nothing but a few maize cakes, as I said, with some tomato sauce, and that's part of the test too. You've failed the moment you spill or splatter a drop. You try it, when your fingers are numb with cold and your hands are trembling, and all you want is to shovel those maize cakes down your throat and then go to sleep.'

'We owe so much to our priests,' said Lily. I gave her a sharp look, but from her dreamy expression I could tell she meant it.

'You haven't heard the half of it! You don't go to sleep in the afternoon, you go to work. You get sent out to Citlaltepec to gather reeds.'

'I think I've heard about this. Isn't that when the priests attack passers-by?'

'On the way back, yes, if they're stupid enough to be

out on the road. Hardly surprising, is it? You have a gang
of priests, half starved, exhausted, and facing five days and
nights of this misery, all in the name of keeping the crops
watered, and they come across some ungrateful bastard
with a full belly and a warm cloak who thinks his maize
and beans just spring out of the ground by themselves – of
course they're going to beat the crap out of him!'

I paused, surprised by my own excitement, the quickness
and shallowness of my own breathing and the look on Lily's
face. Her skin had coloured a little under the ointment and
she was watching me steadily with her lips slightly parted.
She was imagining herself as one of us, I thought, feeling
our hunger and fatigue and nervous exhaustion, and the
release we had got from those few joyous moments of
licensed violence.

'Was that part of the test, as well?'

'I suppose it must have been. If you could vent all that
anger on some stranger and come back to the temple in
good order, ready to start again in the evening, then you
might stand a chance . . . Oh, and one final thing. Whoever
is last back to the Priest House . . .'

'Fails the test?'

'That's right.'

'So what happens if you fail?'

'Someone will denounce you. They'll point to the chilli
that rolled into the fire, the tomato stain on your breechcloth, your head nodding on your chest when you should be
attending to your duties. You'll be hauled up before a senior
priest and made to pay a fine – to your accuser.'

'To your accuser?' She stared. 'But that's mad! You'd all be
accusing each other all the time!'

'Why, yes, of course we were. How else do you think we
passed the time? It was a game; it was the only thing that

made the whole thing bearable.' I could not help smiling at the memory: how we would run back from the lake, too cold, wet, tired and absorbed in our own wretchedness to notice what was going on around us, and yet how soon the squabbling would start the moment we were settled on our mats in the Priest House. Pale eyes would probe the gloom, ready to pick up the slightest lapse, and soon harsh, triumphant cries, spirited denials and bitter recriminations would shatter the strained silence. I remembered how especially sweet it had felt to secure a fine from the man who had denounced you the day before. 'The amount you paid depended on how wealthy you were, so it was the great lords' sons who were denounced most often. Since my father was a commoner and we had no money anyway, I used to do rather well.' By the time the festival began I would have a bundle of cotton capes and fine jewels wrapped up in my cloak, all things of no real use to me except as tokens of my triumph over my fellow priests.

I had known and savoured that triumph every year I was a priest, except the last.

'Of course, the fifth day was different.'

I closed my eyes, as if that would keep out the sights of the last day before the festival in my final year at the Priest House. I had to stop myself clapping my hands over my ears in an effort to shut out the sounds as well.

From a long way off, I heard Lily asking me a question.

When I opened my eyes again, they would not meet hers, but were fixed on her hands, which were kept still by gripping her knees through her skirt.

'It had stopped being a game by the fifth day. It was serious. There were no fines and the rich fared the same as the poor. Make a mistake during the first four days and it would cost you nothing more than a couple of cloaks and a bit of ridicule, and you knew you'd get the sods back in the morning. On the last day it would cost you everything.

'They'd drum you out of the priesthood. They'd drag you by the hair and the ends of your breechcloth to the edge of the lake, throw you in and push you under till you were half drowned, you couldn't see, you were puking salt water. Men who'd been your friends since childhood would be the first to kick you in the head, and the last as well. Then they'd leave you, and if you were lucky, sooner or later someone would go and tell your family where you were.'

And sooner or later, I reminded myself, your family would come and take you home, and that had been the worst humiliation and the harshest punishment of all.

4

Nothing stirred in the house, but I knew that the city beyond the walls – that vast, outrageous lumping together of houses, hovels, temples, priests, warriors, traders, men and women, dogs and turkeys – never truly slept. Even now priests would be tending the temple fires, warriors examining the feathers on their costumes, merchants reckoning their wealth, men and women fighting, making babies, sleeping, stirring and dying. The gods would watch every movement, like players intent on a game of Patolli – and Tezcatlipoca, the Mocker, the god who held us in the palm of his hand, would be musing on where the counters should fall next.

At that moment, the room I was in felt like the only still place in the universe.

'What was your mistake?' the woman asked.

It was years since I had dared ask myself that question, but now the words slipped out painlessly, like a splinter that has worked its way to the surface of your skin.

'I didn't think I'd made a mistake. I'd been tested over so many years by then that the fifth day didn't frighten me. There would always be one or two who failed – novices, children whose fathers should never have pledged them to the Priest House in the first place, or old ones who were simply past it – and I remember feeling a bit sorry for some of them, after it was all over for them. But I felt confident enough. Maybe too confident.

'And it was such a small thing! Just one of those tiny green tomatoes, and all I had to do was add it to the pile in front of the fire. I did it, too, without disturbing any of the others, but just as I was about to let go, something stung the back of my neck.

'I don't know what it was, but it felt like touching the edge of an obsidian razor, or being scratched by the sharpened end of a reed or a cactus spine. It didn't really hurt, but it made me snatch my fingers back, and, well . . .'

My fists clenched involuntarily at the memory.

'I didn't see that tomato roll. I turned round to face the others, to ask what was going on – who had scratched me, or thrown or blown something at me – and then I saw it in their faces. They were all looking past me at the offerings in front of the fire, and I don't think anyone in that room was breathing.'

I had not turned back to look at the offerings again. There had been no need. The shock and then the certainty I had seen in the faces around me had told me enough.

I had not thought to argue, fight or flee when they came for me. I had just waited, like the most compliant of victims, sitting passively before the fire that it had been my life's work to tend.

'You never knew who distracted you?'

I lifted my eyes to Lily's face to find that it was blurred by tears. When I had blinked them away I saw, to my surprise, that her eyes too were glistening.

'No, and I don't know how – a clay ball blown through a reed, the sharp end of a goose quill, a small stone – Lily, I don't even know for sure that it was a human act. Suppose it was a god? I think that was what I believed at the time, and that's why I didn't protest.'

And it would be just like Tezcatlipoca, who was said to look with particular favour on slaves, to choose such a perverse way of setting the course that would make me, eventually, one of his creatures. But men and women were a tool the gods used, and in my heart I knew that whatever had touched me that evening, all those years ago, had been propelled by a human hand.

I could not sleep. I tossed and turned on my mat, kept awake by the pain of my wounds and questions that had lodged in my head and were refusing to leave.

What had really happened the day I had been expelled from the Priest House? I had always accepted it. It had been my fate, ordained by the highest gods, Ohmetecuhtli and Ohmecihuatl, as they had presided over my naming-day; if not that, then I had just been another victim of Tezcatlipoca's caprice. Talking about it now had shaken me, stirring up long-buried memories that would not be put down again until I had looked at them afresh.

Had there been a man with a reason to hate me?

I pictured a face, stained all over with soot, with long, matted hair and temples streaked with fresh sacrificial blood: a priest's face, unrecognizable as an individual's. Only the eyes, white against the black-painted skin, might have enabled me to put a name to it, but another vision distracted me from them: another face, seemingly hovering behind the first, less distinct, pale, or perhaps tinted with yellow ochre.

I sat up, as if that would bring the faces into clearer focus.

'I know you,' I muttered.

A noise from outside the room dispelled the vision and sent me, in spite of my pain and the stiffness in my limbs, scrambling towards the doorway.

The moon and the stars shone through the fine haze made by hearths and temple fires, and my breath was a glowing cloud in front of me as I peered outside. I drew my blanket around me and shivered. There would be a hard frost in the morning.

I heard the noise again: a faint rustling, the sound a skirt might make as its wearer gathered it up to walk quietly across the courtyard.

A slight figure slipped from the shadows, crossed a pool of light and vanished into the darkness again.

Few Aztecs would go out in the dark alone. To come across almost any creature of the night – an owl, a weasel, a coyote, a skunk – was to stare your own death in the face; and worst of all were the monsters we conjured out of our own heads. Not many would willingly venture into streets haunted by a headless torso whose chest opened and shut with a sound like splitting wood, by men without heads or feet who rolled, moaning, along the ground, and by fleshless skulls with legs.

I, however, had been a priest. At night I had patrolled the hills around the lake, with my torch, my censer, my conch-shell trumpet and my bundles of fir branches to burn as offerings. It had been my task to face and drive away these monsters, so that my people could sleep soundly on their reed mats. The night no longer held any terrors for me.

Hoping I was still hardened enough against the cold to stop my teeth chattering, I discarded my blanket and followed the woman across the courtyard.

Hiding in the shadows, as she had, I saw a pale, unsteady light in the room nearest to where I had seen her vanish. She had gone to the most important room in the house – the kitchen, where the hearth was.

I stepped up to the door.

The hearth was much more than a cooking fire: the three hearthstones were sacred, a shrine both to Huehueteotl, the old, old god of the fire, and to Yacatecuhtli, the Lord of the Vanguard, the merchants' own god. A merchant's travelling staff, wrapped in stiff, heavily stained paper, was propped against the wall behind the hearth. The woman knelt in front of it, with her head bowed so that her face was hidden and the flames cast a huge hunchbacked shadow on the wall behind her.

She had something in her right hand. It glittered in the firelight as she lifted it to her right ear. It was a sliver of obsidian, the sharpest kind of blade we knew.

Its polished surface flashed once as she cut into the ear-lobe.

The woman's blood ran over the obsidian, quenching its sparkle like water tipped on glowing embers.

With her left hand, Lily held a little clay bowl up to the side of her head. She held it there for a moment, before stretching her hand out over the fire and tipping the pooled blood into the flames. She shook the bowl once to get the last drops out, and put it aside.

Then she took a strip of plain white paper and laid it against her wounded ear. She pressed on it to squeeze out more of her blood, so that when she took it away again it showed black in the poor light of the hearth. She looked at the sodden, limp scrap for a long moment, and then stood up.

I knew what she was going to do. She had sacrificed her

blood to the Fire God; now it was the turn of her own personal god, the patron and protector of the merchants.

Yacatecuhtli's offerings were not burned. The merchant's mother was not about to throw his gift of her blood into the fire. Instead, she went to the travelling staff propped against the wall and solemnly wound the paper around its middle, adding one more bloodied layer to its binding.

She spoke to her god.

Yacatecuhtli was always there for a merchant, embodied in the travelling staff he took with him everywhere. The traveller would stick his staff in the ground by the fire when he made camp, so that he would see it when he woke and remember his god and be comforted. He would lean on it as he walked from one end of the World to the other, drawing strength from his god as he crossed deserts, forests and swamps and lands filled with hostile savages. If he died on his travels, they would be burned together at the top of a tall hill.

Lily's voice was too low for me to distinguish more than a few words, but I heard enough before I came away, treading as softly as when I had approached.

It was not the words themselves which had impressed me. 'Only a boy,' she had said, and 'Keep him safe': not much of a prayer, addressed to the god all merchants entrusted their safety to.

If anything was going to move the Lord of the Vanguard, I thought, it was not the words of Lily's prayer, but the desolate, dry sobs that had forced themselves out between them.

'Are you awake?'

Moonlight fell through the doorway across the floor. The woman's elongated shadow lay in the midst of it, the head just touching the edge of my mat.

'Yes.' I had jumped so visibly on hearing her speak that there was no point in pretending otherwise.

Her skirt was like a dark cloud against the light on the floor, and when she turned towards me her toenails glinted like faint stars.

'Why did you follow me across the courtyard?'

'I didn't know it was you.'

She came up to the head of the mat, so that I was looking up at her face, hooded by shadows. I hauled myself up on my haunches.

'You might have been anybody,' I added. 'You might have been my master's steward or Misty, come back to finish what they started. Why were you so furtive, anyway?'

She knelt beside me, bowing her head as she had before the fire.

'I didn't want my father or the servants or . . . or you to see me. I didn't want you to hear me praying.'

I recognized the woman I had first met, the day my master had sent me to enquire about Shining Light. Her voice was low and guttural, as if there were some obstruction in her throat, and the strands of her hair caught by the moonlight shook a little, but there was the same composure, the same reluctance to show or share a sorrow that she could never quite successfully conceal.

I should have challenged her then. I should have confronted her with the truth: that her son had not left the city, that he and Misty and Nimble, his boy, and some nameless other had conspired against my life, and that I was sure she was a part of it all, because I did not believe her story about meeting the youth at the ball court to pay off Shining Light's debts. That is what I should have said.

I did not, because all of a sudden I had forgotten my terrors and suspicions, and remembered only what I had heard and seen that evening: the woman's bleak little prayer, her trembling hands wrapping the travelling staff in paper soaked in her own blood, the grief and fear that seemed real even if she had been lying to me.

'You really don't think he's coming back, do you?'

'No . . . yes . . . I don't think so.' I barely heard the words, but then she gave a loud sniff.

The sound was so childish that I could not help myself: I reached out for her, extending my arms to her at the same time as she turned towards me to hide her face in my bony shoulder.

Even racked by tears, she was discreet, muffling her sobs against my chest until at last they subsided and she lay quietly across me. I murmured what I thought were soothing words and stroked her hair awkwardly.

'He had to go away, do you understand? They'd have killed him if he'd stayed – after what happened.'

'I know.' She was still talking about the merchants. In spite of everything I wondered whether she really did believe her son had fled their wrath after what had happened to his offering at the festival.

'I know what people think of him. But he's not a monster. He can be so kind. He has so much love, if only people would try to understand him. He's just a boy, a bit wild, with no father to guide him. His father would have taken him in hand. They'd have gone on trading expeditions together, to the Mayans or the Zapotecs or the Yopi. I think that's what Shining Light always wanted, you know, to be like his father, a hero for his people . . .' She broke off with a sob.

In the moonlight she was a vague shape in my arms. I could smell her faint, clean woman's scent better than I could see her.

I touched her hair. 'Lily . . .'

My touch broke the spell. All of a sudden she collected herself. 'It's getting late. It's going to be a cold night. I'm sorry – I did not mean to burden you with my family's troubles.'

She got up stiffly. I reached for her again, catching the hem of her skirt with my fingers. She hesitated a moment too long.

She knelt beside me for a long time, saying little, absorbed in her own thoughts.

At last she said: 'Do you remember Quauhtenanco?'

'I remember the Pochteca coming home.' The whole of Mexico, or so it had seemed at the time, had gone out to greet the victorious merchants, lining the causeway between the southern shore of the lake and the city to cheer the little group on for the last stretch of their journey.

'I couldn't believe he was lost.' There was no need to ask who she meant. 'They sent runners ahead, of course, so we knew who had come back alive and who hadn't, but I kept telling myself there must have been a mistake. So I stood there at the side of the causeway, staring at their faces as they came past, while everybody was shouting and cheering and telling me how proud I must be.'

'I was there too.' At the head of the crowd, by Emperor Ahuitzotl's orders, had been the Fire Priests, the great lords and the Constables. I had been there too, among the priests, my formal cape billowing around me as I blew lustily into my shell trumpet to add to the din.

'They'd almost all gone by before I saw him.'

'"Saw him"?' I repeated, confused. 'You mean Xippopoca? But I thought . . .'

'He looked so old,' she went on, as if I had not interrupted her. 'He was carrying this trophy – only a feather banner, but from the way he stooped under it, it might have been a block of granite. I couldn't see his face. It was his cloak I recognized – it was torn and dirty, but I'd have known it anywhere, because I'd embroidered it myself.'

I knew what she was going to say after that. I had seen him too, shuffling along at the end of that line of gaunt, grimy, exhausted men until he heard a voice he knew, somehow making itself heard over the crowd's roar, and he had paused, raised his head and smiled.

'I had little Shining Light in my arms, and I held him up and shouted myself hoarse before I realized – but when I saw it was my father, wearing my husband's cloak . . .'

'You wished he'd died instead.'

'I wished I'd died, so I would never have known what it was to feel like that! I waited four years for Xippopoca to come back to me, and for just a moment I let myself believe he had – can you imagine what that was like?'

'Your father just walked on, didn't he? He had to follow the procession. I saw. He couldn't meet your eyes.'

'Four years,' she said again. 'And so many years since then.'

'There's been nobody else?'

'No. There might have been – I've had offers.' She uttered what might have passed for a laugh. 'I'm a wealthy widow, what do you expect? One of the old men you saw the other day, even he's . . .' She ended the sentence with a shudder. 'But it never seemed to matter, being alone. I had the family business to look after, you see, I had Shining Light – but now there's nothing.'

Clear, unblinking eyes searched my face.

'Do you understand me?' she whispered.

I wanted to answer her but my mouth was suddenly dry. I felt desire and a kind of fear, both at once.

Then we held each other again, but this time it was different.

It was not like being with a pleasure girl. To feel my own heat returned was like watching a flame reflected in an obsidian mirror: a thing known but strange, unpredictable, elusive, uncontainable.

Afterwards she giggled like a young girl.

'You didn't learn how to do that in the House of Tears!'

'It was a skill they didn't teach.'

Our priests were celibate, pledged to the gods, but they sometimes strayed. The Emperor, Montezuma, had been a priest, and it was hard to imagine that a man like him, with all his wives and concubines, had never had a girl in all the time he had been at the Priest House.

I had strayed myself, letting my feet wander towards the market when the madness overcame me. It did not matter, so long as you were discreet, and if you came back laden with shame and sure that your betrayal showed as plainly as blood smeared on the face of a statue, then that was between you and the gods. It was different if you were caught, naturally.

'So, are you going to tell me about her, then?' the woman wheedled in my ear.

'Not much to tell.'

I thought of my visits to the market, of hastily arranged, fleeting encounters that I would promptly try to forget. It was always the market – it was too dangerous to visit the beautiful, lithe creatures from the official pleasure houses, who danced with the warriors and were reserved for them. I knew solid peasant girls, slaves too clumsy to dance and die at the festivals and foreign women stranded, lost and hungry in the midst of a strange, vast city.

'There was one girl in particular,' I recalled dreamily. 'She was a foreigner. She called herself Miahuaxihuitl.' It was an unlikely name, meaning 'Turquoise Maize Flower' in Nahuatl. 'She said she was a Huaxtec, and she dressed as one – you know, the brightly embroidered blouse and skirt and her hair braided in coloured cloths wound with feathers. I don't know whether she really was one, though.' The Huaxtecs were a famously hot-blooded race, and I had always suspected Maize Flower had merely been playing on their reputation for inventiveness on the sleeping mat. 'I was calling on her regularly at one time. It all ended in tears, of course.'

I spoke casually, but what I felt in that moment was horror.

Remembering the last time I had seen the girl and what she had told me then was like being accused of a crime I had committed years ago, and thought I had got away with. It was like looking down and noticing for the first time that the road I had been carelessly ambling along was bordered on both sides by deep chasms that would swallow me as soon as I put a foot wrong.

'Yaotl? What's the matter?'

My muscles had stiffened, involuntarily pushing her away. She must have felt the cold sweat that suddenly came over me.

'It's nothing,' I said hoarsely. 'Just something I remembered. I'm sorry. I can't talk now – my ribs hurt.'

I saw again the faces I had pictured earlier that evening, before I had followed Lily across the courtyard. I knew whose they were now, and wished I did not.

I lay still in her arms and tried to stop myself from shivering. Neither of us spoke for a long time.

Eventually I slept.

EIGHT FLOWER

1

I sat up with a start.

It was morning. The screen had been drawn back and sunlight streamed through the open doorway, around a dark figure whose shadow fell across my sleeping mat.

I stared stupidly at the shape for what seemed like hours, lying with my head on one side, waiting for sleep to wear off, before realizing there was someone else in my room.

'Who . . .?'

Lily did not move. 'I think you should tell me what really happened.'

'What?'

'When you were thrown out of the Priest House, Yaotl.' She spoke in a bleak monotone, like somebody reciting a passage learned by rote. 'Tell me who hated you enough to want you expelled, and why.'

Carefully, mindful of my sore ribs, I levered myself up on one elbow.

'I don't understand. Why do you want to know?'

'Just tell me! I brought you into my house. I've fed you and treated your wounds and . . . and . . .' She seemed unable to bring herself to mention the rest. 'It's just one thing I want to know – don't you think you owe me that much?'

This was bewildering. 'I really don't know. I'd tell you if I could, honestly.'

'Was it over a woman?'

'You're never jealous?'

'Don't flatter yourself.' She stamped her foot. 'Just answer me! Was it that woman you were telling me about – Maize Flower?'

'Lily – what's all this about?' As sleep receded, along came the memory of how the woman had treated my wounds, and how she had been, lying in my arms in the night. Something had happened since then: she had left me to wake up alone, and come back with a purpose that I did not understand.

In the way she leaned towards me, with her hands at her sides bunched tightly into fists, there was an almost childish air of desperate determination, as if there was something she absolutely must have that was just beyond her reach.

All of a sudden I thought I knew what that something was.

'This is about your son, isn't it?' I said slowly. 'They've got him, haven't they – Misty and his boy? They've kidnapped him – the way they tried to kidnap me! And now they're threatening you. They made you tell everyone he'd gone away, so the chiefs of the merchants wouldn't come looking for him. They wanted me – they wanted to know something about me – and now they've told you to find it out for them! That's what this is all for!'

Then the woman's face, which had been set as firmly as a statue's, seemed to crumple, and she hid it in her hands and burst into tears.

'My son had no money, do you see? And he owed that wretched man Misty so much. It ended up that he would do anything he asked him to. Misty made him take that Bathed Slave. I don't know where he got him from, or why Shining

Light had to sacrifice him to the war-god, but he did it, and afterwards he had to go and see Misty, to tell him what had happened. I think my son thought he had done all he had to. But he never came home. Before he went, he told me to give out that he'd gone away, because after the sacrifice he wouldn't be able to show his face in Tlatelolco for a long time. A couple of days later I got the first message.' She looked into my eyes, blinking rapidly. 'I had to keep up the pretence that my son had gone away. And I had to report to the boy — I had to tell him if I saw you.'

'Why, though? What do they want from me?'

'I don't know.'

'And now you want me to tell you about . . . about the girl in the market.' A chill came over me, as it had the night before when I remembered how Maize Flower and I had parted.

She looked down so that her hair fell limply over her face. 'I had to see the boy this morning. I told him what you told me last night. He told me to find out more.' With a despairing sob, she added: 'Yaotl, please! They'll kill him if I don't tell them what they want to know! It's such a little thing to ask, but it could be worth my son's life!'

I did not want to. I did not want to drag this one event out of the tangle of petty and not so petty rivalries, squabbles and feuds that had been life at the Priest House. I did not want to examine it in all its painful detail and endure all that guilt and loss again.

I listened to the woman's sobs and watched her shoulders heaving and realized that I had no choice.

Two boys had been born on the same day — One Death, in the year Nine Reed. One Death was the day-sign of Tezcatlipoca, and each of the boys bore one of the god's many names.

One was called Telpochtli, which means the Young Man. The other was called Yaotl, the Enemy. Both their fathers had promised them to the priests a few days afterwards, and that was as much as they had in common.

'Telpochtli was from a noble family,' I explained. 'He could have been born on one of the Useless Days at the end of the year and he'd still have ended up a priest. My father's just a commoner, and if I'd been born on any other day I'd have gone to the House of Youth like my brothers.'

'And you were friends?' Lily's tone had softened a little, now that I seemed to be telling her what she had to know.

'Friends? I don't know. No, how could we be? He was a rich kid, surrounded by other rich kids. They'd accept him without question. They'd never accept me: I only survived by being smarter than they were, which didn't make them like me any better. All the same, Telpochtli was taken into the Priest House the same day I was. He was always there. And we both knew, as soon as we knew each other's birthdays, that our fates couldn't be separated.'

We had practised telling fortunes together, testing each other on the Book of Days. We had raced each other home with our bundles of sticks during the festival of Eating Maize and Beans, and joyously denounced each other in the evenings – although only during the first four days when it was a harmless game. We had gone into battle as novice warriors together, and on our first time out – when it was permissible to cooperate to bring down a captive – we had been in the same team.

It turned out we had even shared the same woman.

'That was Maize Flower?' Lily asked.

'Yes, although I didn't know it at the time. To tell you the truth it was a surprise to find out that he'd been to see a girl at all, because I didn't think he was the type – a bit too serious, more wrapped up in his service to the gods than me, I thought. But I found he was visiting the marketplace regularly too. He couldn't keep it from me for long. I never told anyone, naturally. Sometimes we made excuses for each other when the other couldn't be found. I didn't know who his girl was, though.'

'But you found out.'

I did not want to go on with the story. I lifted my eyes from Lily to the edge of the doorway behind her and kept them there, trying to pretend I was alone, until the effort became too much and I became aware of her gaze fixed expectantly on me as if she were willing me to tell her something she already knew.

'I found out,' I whispered, 'when she told me about the child.'

She gasped. 'You had . . .?'

'No,' I replied, a little testily. 'At least . . . Lily, I'd been seeing her for months, but I thought we'd been too careful. I suppose it could have been mine, but why should it? Why not Telpochtli's or anybody else's? Why did she have to pick on me?'

I had long ago decided not to dwell upon the possibility that I might have fathered a child. I had suppressed all thought of him or her, banishing the notion from my mind as I had once effectively banished the unhappy pleasure girl from my life. Only at unguarded moments, or in my dreams, did the thought of my son or daughter sometimes come back to haunt me: a charge that was never proved, never dropped, and to which I had no answer.

'I laughed at her when she told me, but she just said it had been put in her womb by Tezcatlipoca, and so it didn't matter who the father was. If she went to the Head Priest and said it was me, he'd believe her.'

I remembered how my jaw had dropped when Maize
Flower had made her announcement, and how quickly I had
turned over possibilities, calculations and plans in my mind,
grasping the danger I was in long before she threatened me
with it.

'I didn't think she'd go to the priests. After all, she'd be in
almost as much trouble as I would. But I didn't know! I was
trying to reason with her, and then I tried to buy her off. I
offered her ten cloaks, which was more than I had and twice
what a husband would've given her on her wedding day.
Then she started getting hysterical. I couldn't really make
out what she was saying through the tears, but there was a
lot of nonsense about trust and love and men and women
being stronger than the gods. Stronger than the gods! That's
a good one to remember next time you hear that the lake's
flooded and swept a score of houses away.'

Maize Flower had kept lunging towards me, trying to
grasp the hem of my cloak, and I had kept backing away,
turning my face away from hers as if afraid she was going to
bite me. Then, suddenly, she had seemed to give up, and had
slumped, sobbing, in a corner.

'Why don't you just go?' she had cried.

'Maize Flower . . .' I had begun, awkwardly stretching a
hand towards her, only to have it knocked blindly away.

'Save your breath! What do I need you for anyway? It's
not even as if it's your child, you pathetic little fart! Do you
think I'd risk the real father's life by going to the priests? Just
get out! I don't want to see you again!'

Lily said: 'That must have been hard to take.'

'Do you think so? Just then I think I felt more relieved
than anything else. It did hurt,' I conceded, 'but that came
much later. At the time I just got out as fast as I could, with
the insults ringing in my ears.

'I couldn't understand most of what she was saying – I think by then a lot of it was in her native language – but there was one phrase I do remember, because it was so odd. It was something like "Just as good as you!" Not "better". This other man, whoever he was, was definitely "just as good".'

'And you never saw her again?'

'No. But I didn't see much of Telpochtli either. He vanished soon afterwards.

'Before he did, though, he came to see me. He didn't say much. He just came up to me – I remember this clearly, it was in the middle of a fast, and I was sitting over my one bowl of maize porridge for that day – looked me in the eye and said: "You know, don't you?"

'I had a mouthful of porridge and couldn't speak.

'"Don't think you've seen the last of me, you peasant. It may take a while, but we'll pay you back!" he said, and then he kicked my bowl of porridge clean across the room, spilling the lot, and walked off.'

'You think he knew about you and Maize Flower?'

'More to the point, he knew I knew about him. It must have been him, mustn't it? Who else was just as good as I was – no better, no worse? Who else but the man who shared my birthday?

'He must have run away soon afterwards. And I never found out what happened to Maize Flower, but she was gone next time I went to the market. Perhaps they went off together. At the time, I hoped they had – I thought it must mean the child was Telpochtli's and not mine, after all.

'It wasn't long after that when I left the House of Tears myself – but you know about that. It never occurred to me at the time, but it must have been one of Telpochtli's noble friends that got me slung out!'

★

'What will you do now?' Lily asked.

By the time I got to the end of my tale she had relaxed. She fetched food and water for me and knelt in the corner of the room, with her skirt folded under her knees, watching me through red puffy eyes while I nibbled at the edges of a tortilla.

'I don't know. Obviously I can't go back to my master, and I can't very well stay here, can I?'

She lowered her eyes but said nothing.

I sighed. 'I wasn't talking about what happened between us last night. I just meant that Misty and Nimble obviously know where I am now. They've attacked me twice. It's only a matter of time before they come after me again.'

'The boy knows, yes,' she conceded. 'I'm not sure about his father.'

I frowned. 'I don't understand how that can be. Anything you told Nimble would get straight back to Misty, surely?'

'I'm not sure,' she said thoughtfully. 'Look, this is what happened. After I saw Nimble at the ball court, on Four Vulture, the day you were attacked and brought here, I went to the marketplace. I'd left a young cousin of ours in charge of one of our pitches and I wanted to make sure everything was all right. You spoke to him, I think.'

'The lad selling feathers? Yes, I did.'

'Nimble caught up with me there after the game ended. He was quite flustered. He said he'd seen you at the ball court, and that you were looking for me. He wanted me to be sure to inform him if I saw you. As if I needed telling!'

I smiled grimly. 'And you've been faithfully reporting on me ever since.' Bitterness welled up in me then, forcing me to add: 'I suppose you went to him this morning, didn't you, and told him all about last night? Was that what you had in mind – getting me to whisper my secrets in your ear on the sleeping mat so you could run straight to that boy with them?'

'No!' She recoiled as if I had just struck her. 'No, it wasn't like that! It was . . .' She lowered her voice. 'You know what it was.'

'I know what it sounded like! I should have known better, shouldn't I?'

'How dare you!' She was so angry she was spitting. 'What do you think I am? Do you think I'd give myself to any serf or slave just to hear the filthy details of some squalid fling with a pleasure girl in the marketplace?'

I said nothing for a moment. I did not know whether I dared believe her, but then I thought that it hardly mattered anyway, since there was no question of my staying here. My own anger failed in the face of hers. After everything that had happened to me I had little enough left of pride, and what there was was hardly worth fighting over.

'I'm sorry,' I mumbled. 'I just thought . . . it's been so long, you see . . .' I sighed wearily. 'You were telling me about the boy and his father.'

She frowned and bit her lower lip. 'There's something going on between them. I don't know what it is, but it was the last thing Nimble said to me. He told me to watch out. He said he never meant for anyone to get hurt, but he didn't think he knew how to stop it any more.'

And just a little while before, in the ball court, the youth had said much the same thing to me: how he had not thought his father would go so far as to have Shining Light's Bathed Slave killed on the Pyramid, and how he had not known of the body in the canal. At the time I had dismissed his words out of hand; but he had quarrelled with his father over me in the marketplace, and there had been that strange incident on the lake as well, when he had seen me in the water and said nothing.

'I had the feeling,' Lily went on, 'that the boy was afraid of something, because he kept looking over his shoulder all the time. I wondered if it was his father.'

'Misty was close enough,' I said, 'along with that knife of his. He's crazy, isn't he? The boy would be right to be afraid. It doesn't explain why he tried to save me, though, or why his father wants me dead.'

The explanation struck me before the words were out of my mouth. When I saw it, all the muscles in my face went loose, my eyes widened and my mouth fell open, and it was only afterwards that I noticed I was staring past the woman at nothing like a slack-jawed imbecile.

'Yaotl?' she asked, alarmed. 'What is it?'

'Oh, Quetzalcoatl,' I said softly, vainly invoking the god of wisdom, 'I've been such an idiot!'

'What's the matter? What are you talking about?'

'Telpochtli!'

'What about him?'

'That's who he is! Of course!' I groaned. 'My enemy — who else would hate me enough to want me dead?' I put my hand to my forehead and drew it down over my eyes as though clearing them of something that had obscured my vision, like cobwebs. 'Do you see? After I saw the message that had been left on that body in the canal, I thought Misty and Nimble must have an ally who knew my full name, but they didn't need one. Misty knew it all the time — because Telpochtli was born on the same day I was, and he and Misty are the same man!'

It was Lily's turn to stare. 'I don't understand — I thought you said Telpochtli had left years ago — before you were thrown out of the Priest House.'

'He did. He must have come back. But it makes such perfect sense – he disguises himself as a priest because that's what he used to be; and because under all that soot he could be anybody, so there's no chance of me or any of his other contemporaries recognizing him. It explains why he wanted to know how I left the Priest House, and about Maize Flower. He's obsessed – and he really hates me, enough to want to kill me with his own hands.'

'So why doesn't his son want you dead as well?'

'I don't know. Perhaps he just doesn't hate me as his father does. Perhaps he thinks it's all getting out of control.' There was another possibility, I knew, but the moment it occurred to me I felt the horror again, the chasms opening up around me, the accusing voice calling my name.

I could not bring myself to name that possibility out loud, but Lily did.

'Or perhaps he thinks he's your own.'

'No,' I said instantly, and as firmly as I could for the trembling that had come over me. 'No, I don't believe it. Maize Flower told me the child wasn't mine – she said that, remember? And Telpochtli took her with him. He'd never have done that if she was carrying another man's child.

'He's not mine. He can't be. He's not!'

Lily stared at her hands resting in her lap and I munched my tortilla absently.

The woman broke the silence by reminding me that I had not told her what I intended to do now.

'Go away, I suppose,' I said dully. 'When I came looking for you it was to give you a message for your son, but that was when I thought I was fit enough to take my enemies on. Now I need somewhere to hide from them, at least until my ribs have healed up. It's too dangerous to stay here.'

'I know.' Lily had the good grace to sound regretful.

'What about you? What are you going to do?'

'I have to see the young man again,' she said, avoiding my eyes. 'I'll have to tell him what you've told me – about the pleasure girl and leaving the Priest House, I mean, not the rest. I hope . . .' She faltered, took a deep breath and carried on: 'I hope it's enough to get Shining Light back. They can't keep him for ever, surely?'

I took a sip of water and watched her over the rim of my bowl. She looked tired, and as long as her son was away she was not allowed to disguise the deep shadows under her eyes with make-up. I wondered how much sleep she had had since he had been gone. I had seen her in so many moods in such a short time, I thought: proud, kindly, passionate, angry, distraught.

I remembered her father's warning not to mention her son's tastes. I sighed, realizing that if what I suspected was true then I was going to have to make her angry again. I had no choice, however: I had to know.

'What exactly is your son's relationship with Misty?'

Her expression froze.

'What do you mean?'

'I know your merchandise was taken to his warehouse. Your father told me.'

Lily let out a long shuddering breath. 'Misty convinced Shining Light it would be the ideal place to hide our stock. No one would ever know where it was, he said. I told the boy he was a fool, but he's a man: it was his decision. He wouldn't listen to me, and my father wouldn't intervene. And he owed the man so much money. Now – it's like living on sufferance. I don't know where this warehouse is. Shining Light couldn't tell me – he doesn't know where it is himself! I just used to hope my son and Misty didn't fall out

and Misty would let us have enough of our own property to
live on. Now, though . . .'

'Are Shining Light and Misty lovers?'

I was not prepared for what she did next. Suddenly she
was across the room with her hand in my hair and wringing
it so savagely that I spat a mouthful of bread on the floor.

'Don't you dare ask me that! Never, ever! Do you understand?'

'Yes!' Pain and surprise forced tears from my eyes.

She twisted the hand in my hair still further. 'Do you
understand?'

'Yes, I told you, yes!'

She let go. 'Just remember what's at stake for us. Shining
Light and I were honoured for his father's sake, but that's all
over now, since . . . well, you know what's happened. And
now that parasite, Misty, has got his hands on my son and
our wealth, all we have left is trade, and until Shining Light's
back and can go abroad there's precious little of that. If
anyone outside my family ever hears that my son is . . . my
son is a . . .' She swallowed, unable to say the word. 'You
know what would happen. If he showed his face in the city
he would be burned alive and I would never be allowed to
trade again.' Lily put her face very close to my face then,
close enough that her breath on my cheek felt like a kiss, and
hissed: 'I will kill to prevent that, do you hear me?'

She resumed her place in the corner. I took one last ten-
tative bite at the tortilla she had given me, but although I
chewed and swallowed it dutifully I found I had lost my
appetite.

NINE ALLIGATOR

1

'**Y**ou're restless today.'
     I had come out to sit against the fig tree but could not relax. Instead I tried to loosen up my limbs by walking around the edge of the courtyard.

Kindly felt no need of exercise.

'I wish you'd go and do that somewhere else,' he complained, 'or at least walk round the other way. You're making me dizzy!'

I turned around to limp in the opposite direction. Out of the corner of my eye I saw Constant hurrying towards the street entrance.

'Why don't you have a drink?'

I surprised myself by refusing. 'I need to think.'

'Suit yourself.'

What was I going to do? I had told Lily I would have to go away, but where could I go? I fantasized about trying my luck abroad. It would have to be somewhere remote. I thought about the far East and toyed for a moment with the idea of living among the Mayans. I could learn their barbaric tongue, cut a farm out of their impenetrable forest, catch fish on the Divine Sea and comb the beaches for some of the strange things that had been washed up there in recent years, such as that box full of clothes my brother had shown me.

Forget it, Yaotl, I told myself. You're too old!

Constant reappeared, with another man scurrying behind him. He disappeared indoors before I got a proper look at him.

My mind kept returning to the things Lily and I had talked of the day before. I tried to remember Telpochtli, but after a dozen years or so all that came to mind was a priest, emaciated as we all were from the fasts, his face obscured by soot and dried blood. The pleasure girl I could recall a little more clearly: her braided hair swinging provocatively around her shoulders, the red flash of her cochineal-stained teeth when she smiled . . .

There had been a thousand girls in the market just like Maize Flower: why had I kept going back to her?

'Anybody would think you had woman trouble,' muttered Kindly sardonically.

'Maybe I have.'

He laughed: a short, harsh, barking sound. 'Never my daughter? Well, good luck to you. You'll need it. I was wondering why she'd taken to wandering around the courtyard at night.'

'It's not like that at all,' I said impatiently. 'She thinks I'm a nuisance – no, more than that. A threat.' My scalp itched where she had twisted my hair.

Kindly groaned. 'You never repeated what I told you about Shining Light?'

'I had to,' I said helplessly. 'I have to find out what Misty is up to. He's tried to kidnap me twice, remember?'

The old man mumbled something into his drink. It sounded like 'Idiot'.

Constant's harsh voice cut across my thoughts. 'Yaotl! Come here!'

The servant was standing in the entrance to my room. Behind him, half hidden, lurked the shadowy figure of the stranger who had come in with him.

'What do you want?' I felt a twinge of foreboding. Who was the stranger?

'Time for your medicine!'

'What medicine?'

Constant stepped outside, giving me room to pass indoors and leaving the stranger behind him. 'How should I know what medicine?' he answered testily. 'Am I a physician? This man says the mistress sent for him, so get on with it!'

There was a snort of laughter from Kindly. 'Better go, then, son. Once my daughter's taken it into her head that something needs doing, you don't want to start asking questions!'

'But I don't need any medicine,' I protested, although I limped towards the door anyway. 'Lily didn't tell me anything about this.' And I could not ask her, as she had left the house before I had woken up.

She had gone to talk to Nimble. She had made no secret of it.

Now here was this stranger, claiming she had sent him to give me medicine I had not asked for.

Dreadful, cold certainty gripped my bowels as I realized this could hardly be a coincidence.

I had left it too late to run away. The confrontation I had sought when I first went to look for Lily was about to happen, and whether I felt strong enough or not, I had to face my enemy now.

Constant muttered: 'Just get in there, you ungrateful little sod. The gods know what this is costing. She must have spent three times your worth keeping your miserable body and soul together already!'

Kindly laughed again.

Ignoring them both, I stepped through the doorway.

★

'Yaotl.'

The voice was like claws scrambling up my backbone. He was still talking like a priest, sounding as though there was something wrong with his mouth. I supposed it must have become a habit.

He squatted in the shadows, in the corner of the room. I sidled away from the doorway, keeping as much distance between us as I could and wishing the room were larger. I wondered whether he still had his knife. Fresh from the whitewashed brightness of the courtyard, my eyes told me nothing about him.

'What do you want?'

I heard a brief, unpleasant, throaty laugh. 'To offer you some medicine!'

'No you don't,' I said tautly, fighting to suppress the panic that was threatening to render me speechless. 'I know who you are. I know what you've come for.' At my sides, my fingernails dug into my palms. I forced my clenched fists to relax slightly. I had no idea what was going to happen, or when, or how to prepare for it.

'Oh, but I think you'll like this medicine, Yaotl – it's mostly sacred wine!'

A hand snaked towards me out of the gloom, bearing a small gourd whose contents sloshed faintly.

I looked at it the way you might look at a live scorpion. Then I glanced through the doorway, as if reassuring myself that I had an escape route – a mistake, as the glare of the courtyard at midday blinded me again to whatever was to be seen in the room.

'Come on, Yaotl,' said the voice coaxingly. 'I'm offering you a drink!'

The gourd was unstoppered. I could smell the contents, heady and sour. It smelled like good sacred wine, although there was a hint of something else, a slightly bitter under-tone.

'I don't want it!' I cried. 'Just tell me what you want from me!'

Misty erupted out of the darkness. He slammed into me, hurling me backwards onto the floor, and the gourd was jammed against my lips, its contents running down my throat so that I must either swallow them or drown.

'Come on, drink it, you bastard!' he hissed.

Punching and kicking did no good. My hands and feet flailed uselessly in the darkness above me. The man holding me down was far too strong for my wasted, injured muscles. With a gourd jammed against my lips I could not even call for help. He held it there until it had emptied itself into me and then wrenched it away and tossed it aside.

'*Teonanacatl!*' I spluttered. There was no mistaking the taste of the little mushrooms we called the Food of the Gods. 'This is obsidian wine!' I tried getting up again but there was a hand weighing me down like a rock on my chest. 'Why?' I gasped.

'I think you know. You said it yourself: you've drunk the obsidian wine, the stuff they give captives before they die!'

I could feel the stuff reaching my belly, hot and indigestible, like a tortilla snatched straight from the griddle. I had to get rid of it before it started to spread through my veins, and the mixture of sacred wine and sacred mushrooms loosened my soul and deprived me of my will. I struggled furiously, contracting my stomach muscles and gulping air in the hope of making myself sick and expelling the poison.

'Not that I made you drink it because I'm going to kill you, Yaotl.' Misty spoke in a throaty whisper. 'I'd rather have you fully conscious. I want you to know exactly what's happening to you, I don't want you to miss a thing . . .'

I could feel myself weakening, the weight on my chest turning from a rock to a boulder, my head spinning, the tips of my fingers starting to tingle. Was it the drug or lack of breath which was doing this? Saliva filled my mouth and I swallowed it, bolting it down with more air as I fought to clear my stomach.

'But I made a promise, see? I told Nimble I wouldn't kill you until you'd told us what he wanted to know. So I've given you something to get your tongue working. In a moment you won't be able to help yourself.'

I bit my tongue to add blood to the fluid and air I was forcing into my stomach. The voice came to me over the roaring in my ears like the voice of a god speaking from the back of a cave.

'Do you remember the Priest House, Yaotl? Do you remember Telpochtli, and the girl in the market? You're going to tell me all about her – what you did with her, everything!'

The mushrooms were beginning to work. I thought I heard footsteps and voices, a long way away, and someone calling my name: 'Yaotl! What is it? What's happening?'

I opened my mouth.

The twisting in my belly caught me by surprise, doubling me up with such force that the hand was thrown from my chest, and out of my mouth the poison, the sacred wine and the mushrooms and everything else poured in a jet that caught the other man just as he was struggling to keep his own balance.

As he cursed me I used the last of my strength to roll over and cry out, in a strangled voice, 'Help! Help! Murder!'

Constant must have been waiting outside. I wanted to call out a warning but had no breath left to do it. My enemy hurled himself at the slave, barged him out of the way and raced into the courtyard, but I knew from Constant's cry that he had hit him with something more than his fists.

I staggered outside, my feet catching on Constant's prone body and splashing through his blood.

'Help! Murder!' I croaked again. 'Stop that man!'

The floor of the courtyard rose and fell beneath me as I blundered drunkenly across it, until finally I lost my footing and the ground came up and hit me in the face.

I lay there, with the sun-heated ground hard against my cheek and my voice still bleating vaguely about murder, until it occurred to me that no one was responding.

I got to my knees and looked around.

Kindly had left his seat by the wall and was bending over Constant. Without looking round he said: 'Forget it. You were much too slow. He's long gone.'

I stood up. My stomach heaved. The walls seemed to rush in towards me and then recede equally fast. I took a couple of steps towards the fig tree and leaned on it gratefully.

'Didn't you try to stop him?'

'You must be joking!' He straightened up, putting a gnarled hand to the small of his back. 'I'd be as dead as he is.' He prodded Constant with his toe. 'That's if I could have got near the man in the first place, and there was no chance of that.'

I stepped cautiously over to the body.

'Did you get a good look at him, at least?'

'With eyes like mine? I haven't had a good look at anything in years. Besides, I was listening to you howling and watching Constant's blood running away. I can't be everywhere.'

'You didn't see him at all?'

He sighed impatiently. 'Tall man, long untidy hair, face blacked up, puke all over his cloak. Is that enough?'

I looked at the body curled up at our feet. 'I'm sorry,' I added belatedly.

'So am I,' said Kindly. 'He may have been a bit of an old woman but he had his uses. You knew where you were with him.' He tried bending down towards the body again, groaned, thought better of it and stood up. 'My daughter will miss him. Look, make yourself useful and turn him over for me, will you?'

I obliged, although my head was still swimming. It took a little effort as the dead man was stuck to the floor with congealing blood. As he flopped over on to his back I heard Kindly give a triumphant growl.

'Thought so! What do you think of that?'

He did not have to show me what he meant. A knife jutted from under Constant's second rib. To pull it free I had to jerk it up and down, feeling it scrape against bone as I did so. When it finally sprang out, like a decayed tooth from its socket, I saw that its blade was like nothing else in Mexico: a long glittering sliver of brown metal.

I held it up, grasping it gingerly between thumb and forefinger, and shivered. I knew this blade well: it had been held against my neck all through the long canoe journey from this house to the cove where I had seen the bird. It had come out at the marketplace, too, and on both occasions it had only been Nimble's defiance of Misty which had stopped it from being used. This time, I reflected sadly, the boy had not been around to prevent it.

'It's bronze,' said Kindly. 'It's like copper, only much harder. The only people who know how to make it are the Tarascans — it's a secret they don't share with anyone. They won't even trade the stuff, it's so precious.'

'So it's come a long way.' I put the knife down next to the body. 'That man was no Tarascan, though.'

Constant's eyes were wide open. As I looked at him I thought that even by Aztec standards I had seen a lot of dead people lately.

'That should have been me, shouldn't it?' I said.

'It should,' said Kindly regretfully. 'He was coming to help you, you know. He heard something amiss, so he went to investigate. He'd just got to the doorway when that madman came out, stabbed him and ran off. Constant was just in his way.'

I could hardly see the wound, despite all the blood. 'He knew what he was about, didn't he? Straight for the heart.'

'I need a drink.' The old man began walking slowly back to his place by the wall. A gourd lay there where he had dropped it.

I limped after him, to stand over him while he threw the liquid into the back of his throat and gasped with relief. He did not offer me any. I did not mind that in the least: after what had just happened, the thought of sacred wine made my stomach turn over.

At last, pulling the gourd from his lips with a sucking noise, he turned to look at me again, through eyes narrowed with disgust.

'So who was that man? I take it he wasn't a doctor.'

'He was your grandson's associate, Misty.'

'Misty?' He looked speculatively at his gourd, no doubt realizing for the first time that there was nobody to replenish it for him now. 'Misty? Here? Why?'

'Your daughter sent him,' I told him grimly. 'So what he told Constant was half true. She told him where he could find me – and I don't suppose for a moment she thought he was coming here to cure me of anything!'

I looked around me at the immaculately swept court-yard, all silence, cleanliness and order apart from a body lying in a pool of blackening blood in one corner. I did not know what to do. My bones still ached from the beating I had had, my head still swam from the sacred wine I had drunk, and I had nowhere to go. I knew only that if I stayed here I would be killed.

'I'm going,' I informed Kindly curtly.

'Wait!'

The urgency in his voice brought me up short. 'What is it?' I asked suspiciously.

He waved his empty gourd towards Constant's body. 'Aren't you going to clean up the mess? Someone will have to explain this!'

I started walking again. 'You merchants police your own affairs, don't you? Sort it out among yourselves. Only don't involve me!'

I left, almost believing that could be the end of the matter.

2

With nothing to give to a boatman I made my way through the city on foot, keeping well away from anywhere where I might be recognized. Fortunately I left Pochtlan at the hottest part of the day, when there were few people about. At last I stood beside the canal that trickled past one wall of the yard, staring at the little house I had grown up in and wondering whether it had been worth the journey.

With the Chief Minister presumably looking for his errant slave, it would not be safe to stay at my old home, and I had certainly not come for sentimental reasons. I was not here for a rest either, although my bones and muscles throbbed, my stomach still felt as if it had been kicked and my head did not belong on my shoulders.

It was not as if I expected to be made welcome anyway.

I had no choice, however. I had tried seeking out Shining Light and the men I had thought were his allies and the attempt had nearly cost me my life and left me feeling betrayed and humiliated. Now I had another confrontation in mind, one which might prove as dangerous as the one I had just survived. I was going to look for my elder brother, to challenge him with his complicity in the killings in Coyoacan, and demand to know just what it was about the Chief Minister and the sorcerers that he knew but had held back from me.

I dared not go near my brother's quarters at the Palace, for fear of being seen by my master or his servants. The only other option was to come home.

I watched an old woman emerge from the yard to empty a clay pot briskly into the canal. She had hair the colour of ash, skin like old paper and arms and legs so thin they looked as if a child could snap them. Clad in an old blue skirt and blouse and limping on swollen joints, she looked frail and pitiable, although in reality she was neither.

She shot a curious glance at me before turning back into the house but showed no sign of knowing who I was.

'Mother?'

She was almost inside the yard before she stopped to glance over her shoulder.

'What do you want?' She might have been talking to a stranger, and an unwelcome one at that.

'You know who I am.' I started towards her. She half turned in my direction but took another step into the yard.

'Do I?' she replied coldly. 'I don't know. You look a bit like my youngest son, Yaotl the drunkard, but you can't be him. He's a slave in the Chief Minister's household.' She spat the word 'slave' at me as though a fly had landed on her tongue, but made no move to stop me as I walked towards the entrance to the house.

Halting nervously on the threshold, I asked her where my father was.

'Chapultepec,' she informed me grudgingly, 'along with your brothers – except Lion, of course. They were called up to work on the aqueduct – good, honest toil!' This was her way of reminding me that I was exempt from being conscripted into a work gang, as any commoner might be, only because I was a slave and my labour belonged to my master.

'I don't expect them back tonight – now, isn't that lucky for you?' she added with a sneer.

So I would not have to see my father, after all. What I had to do here was going to be fraught enough as it was, without the furious recriminations that would have been bound to accompany such a meeting. I felt a surge of relief, barely tempered by my mother's adding: 'They took the last of today's tortillas with them in their lunch bags when they left this morning, so you needn't think you're going to be fed!'

'Yaotl!' My sister Quetzalchalcihuitl – 'Precious Jade' – was making paper in the yard, using a wooden beater on strips of fig-tree bark stretched over a stone. 'What are you doing here?'

'Thanks for the welcome,' I replied sullenly. 'I've walked a long way, you know. I need a rest.'

'You smell revolting and you look as if you've been in a fight.' She sniffed elaborately.

I sat down facing her. 'It's a long story, Jade,' I said wearily. 'I'm too tired to tell it now, though.'

My mother emerged from the house carrying a copper mirror that had hung on one of the walls since I was a baby and a bowl of the rich maize porridge that we called atolli. The smell reminded me how thoroughly I had emptied my stomach a few hours before. 'I was going to give it to the dogs,' she said, 'but since you're here you might as well eat it. I don't suppose slaves eat very well.'

As I gobbled the porridge my sister said: 'I hope that doesn't go the same way as your last meal. Or had you given up solid food?'

'Give it a rest, Jade,' I mumbled between gulps. 'I haven't had a drink in years.' I told myself that Kindly's gourds had not counted, because I had been sick, and of course the drink Misty had forced on me had not counted either.

All the same, there was no denying that it had been real sacred wine that had passed my lips and warmed my belly. I seized on the memory of that last mouthful, the gourd jammed against my lips, the bitterness of the mushrooms underlying the sacred wine's sour taste, and told myself that was what it was really like, and I never wanted to touch the stuff again.

I felt my stomach contract and hurriedly pushed the bowl of atolli away.

'What's the matter?' asked my mother. 'Don't you like it?'

'Not used to home cooking,' my sister suggested. 'He's been living on delicacies from the Chief Minister's table. Good, wholesome food makes him throw up . . . Why don't you give him the mirror, Mother? Show him what he's become!'

'Look, I'm just full, that's all . . .' I heard my own voice tail off as the mirror was dangled in front of me.

The eyes, with their deep brown irises shifting from side to side, I could accept as my own, even if their lids were heavier than I remembered. It was the blue-black marks around them, the swollen and bent nose, the shapeless ears and the thought of whatever lay under my cloak that I had not dared look at which scared me.

'All right,' I breathed, 'so I'm no beauty. So there was a fight. It wasn't my fault!'

'I'm surprised you can remember anything about it,' snapped my sister.

'So how did you look, the last time Amaxtli hit you?' I retorted viciously. My brother-in-law could be as free with his fists as my sister was with her tongue.

'That's enough!' My mother had had years of practice at

putting down our arguments. 'Yaotl, I hope you didn't come here just to start a row. What do you want?'

'I need to speak to Lion.'

My mother and my sister looked at each other. My mother said, in what for her was a subdued voice: 'You're in trouble again, aren't you? Is it that serious?'

'My life is in danger.'

'It would have to be more serious than that!' said Jade.

'Look, will you help me, or what?'

'We will send a message to him,' said my mother stiffly. 'Whether he'll come is another matter. He doesn't love you, Yaotl.'

'I know that.'

My sister said: 'In the meantime, you can clean yourself up. Have a bath. Yes, actually that's a good idea – have a bath. It will get you out of our sight for a while!'

I looked at the dome-shaped bath house, at the soot stain against one wall and the hearthstones that showed where the fire was built up to heat the interior. I thought about shedding my filthy clothes, the dust of the city and the strange face I had taken on – the face of a fugitive – and exchanging them for the dark, private, steamy world of a sweat bath.

'Who's going to make the fire up?' I asked, dubiously.

'I will,' said Jade firmly. 'Don't worry – it will be nice and hot. Trust me!'

Jade was as good as her word, banking up the fire against the outside of the bath house expertly until the stone set into the wall to conduct the heat inside glowed a furious red.

'Do you want me to come in and switch you?' she asked, grinning mischievously, as I took off my clothes.

'No thanks.' The thought of what my sister might do with a handful of long stalks made me uneasy, and besides, I just needed to think. There is nothing like a sweat bath for making you take a fresh look at your life. You cannot run, fight or talk in a sweat bath. You can only think.

I thought about the people I had met since the Festival of the Raising of Banners, and saw their name-glyphs and faces floating in the darkness around me.

First was Shining Light: an affable young man who, according to his grandfather, practised every vice there was except one. Kindly had thought Shining Light was Misty's lover, but was Misty's hold on Shining Light really so strong that he could induce him to part with his fortune? How had he persuaded the young merchant to offer the war-god, at the cost of his family's good name, a bewildered, emaciated, mutilated prisoner?

That led me to Misty. His name-glyph had no face to go with it, for I had only seen it so caked in soot that his features were indistinguishable, but replace the Serpent in the Mist that represented his assumed name with the glyph meaning the Young Man and it all seemed clearer. Was he really my old rival, Telpochtli? If so, then Telpochtli had taken both my master's and Shining Light's money, had been Shining Light's lover and was now the merchant's captor. If the hand that had marked the body of Shining Light's offering had done the same to the corpse in the canal, then Telpochtli had the sorcerers too. Had everything he had done really been to avenge an incident a dozen years ago? A childish sense of unfairness pricked me: it had not even been my fault!

Now I was caught between this madman and my master, who was so desperate to get the sorcerers back that he would willingly trade me for them. The thought of old Black Feathers' face, scored by decades of bitterness with lines like cracks in a dry stream bed, reminded me that I still did not know why the Chief Minister wanted the sorcerers back so badly that he was prepared to defy the Emperor to get them.

There were two people whose names and faces I tried hard not to see.

One was Lily. I had wanted her, but in getting what I wanted had plunged myself into a nightmare of betrayal and loss, as my enemies had used her to leach my secrets from me and then try to kill me. It meant nothing to me that she had done what she had to protect her son's life. She had lain in my arms in the night and waited until the next day to let me know it had been for a price. I could not think of her without feeling my teeth grind furiously together.

The other I found it hard to think of at all: Nimble. If his father was really Telpochtli, then his mother was surely Maize Flower. The youth was the right age for that; however, I knew, despite all the care I told myself we had taken, that Maize Flower's child was as likely to be mine as anybody else's. If he thought so too, was that why he had saved me from Telpochtli and why he had seemed to Lily to be afraid of him? But if that was so, then why was he with him at all?

I had never wanted to acknowledge that Maize Flower's child might be mine, but now I had seen him and spoken to him and I owed him my life twice over. A boy who might be my son had grown up almost to manhood. I had not seen it; I knew neither where he had had his upbringing nor who had had charge of it. I felt like a man suddenly elevated to the status of a great warrior who had been caught running away from a battle, and just as suddenly had his precious cloaks and quetzal feathers and gold and amber lip-plugs and his place in the Eagle House taken away again, and the knowledge of my loss made me weep until I had cried myself to sleep.

And once asleep, I dreamed. I dreamed of the dead: of

Costly, choking his life away on the fumes from the steward's fire, of Shining Light's Bathed Slave and the boy Handy and I had found skulking around the ruins of his burned-out house, of the children and their mother who had died there and of the man the priests had fished out of the canal, his body still bearing the marks of his torture.

They seemed to crowd around me, all talking at once. 'What about us?' they said. 'We didn't ask to be involved in this. Does anyone care about us?'

It is always a mistake to fall asleep in a sweat bath.

I awoke from one nightmare into another: a hot, dark, airless, cramped space with something yanking my ankle as ferociously as a dog tugging at a bone or the water monster dragging a doomed sailor down to his death. I howled. I called on the gods, the Emperor and my mother to save me. I kicked out, my hands reached vainly for the smooth wall enclosing me, and I hit my head on the entrance to the bath house.

The afternoon sky drenched my eyes with daylight, but when I squeezed them shut I saw little sparks twinkling like stars.

'What's up with him?' demanded the voice I had come to hear and had been dreading.

'You probably woke him up,' Jade replied.

'Maybe he was having a nightmare,' my mother suggested.

'I hope not,' said Lion sourly. 'I'd have hated to interrupt . . . Are you with us yet, you lazy toad?'

I sat up. The yard spun around me. I shook my head to clear it and wished I had not as my ears started to ring.

'I was having a bath,' I said unnecessarily. I stared at my brother. There was something wrong with his appearance. I closed my eyes, thinking in my befuddled state that I might be imagining things, but when I opened them again he was still there and still looked the same.

'Why are you dressed like that?' I asked.

He had shed the long yellow cotton mantle of the Guardian of the Waterfront for a cloak of maguey cloth that barely covered his knees. His hair fell down his back, loosely tied with a piece of cord instead of his customary white ribbons. Plain bone keepers had replaced his ornate lip and earplugs, and his face was unpainted. His feet were bare. It was my brother, but not as I had known him for years, and the moment I registered this I realized that scarcely anyone else in the city would recognize him now. I knew he must feel this keenly. Unless he was calling on the Emperor, when dressing down was obligatory, it was unthinkable for a man of my brother's rank to shed his hard-won regalia – all the more so when he had been born a commoner.

His fingers plucked distastefully at the ragged hem of his cloak.

'I think you might tell me why, Yaotl. It seems I have to put on a disguise just to visit my fool of a younger brother, in case half the army follows me with a mind to butcher my entire family. What did you want to run away for? You realize the Chief Minister's got men out looking for you, don't you? They've even questioned me! Of course, I told them there was no point looking for you here. Yaotl hasn't been home in years, I said. There's no way he'd be stupid enough to go back there now, when he knows he's a wanted man. Obviously I overestimated you!'

'Why do you think I ran away?' I replied defensively. 'People kept trying to kill me!'

He cast an expert eye over my naked body. I squirmed self-consciously until my sister passed me a clean breechcloth.

'So I see,' he commented, as I tied the breechcloth with as much dignity as I could manage. 'They haven't made a very good job of it. What do you expect me to do about it?'

'You can tell me what happened at Coyoacan.'

My brother suddenly managed to look both shocked and uncomfortable, like a man who has found a hornet buzzing around under his cloak.

'What do you mean?'

'You remember what the Emperor told us, Lion. My master took extreme measures to find the sorcerers. I remember what you said as well, about the warriors he sent to Coyoacan. I thought at the time you knew more than you were telling me. But you told me to go there, so I did. I saw the house that got burned down. I saw the bodies – the children, and the woman. I found everything you wanted me find.'

'What are you talking about?'

'I wondered why you took such care to make sure I knew where to look, but didn't want to tell me what had happened there. You wanted me to see for myself what the Chief Minister had done, but you didn't want to tell me about it in case I started asking how you knew so much. Only I found more than you bargained for at that house: I found traces of the warriors who'd called there. I found a strap off one of their sandals – one of those big floppy things, like what you normally wear. It was badly frayed. I suppose it was worn out and came off when someone trod on it, but then you wouldn't bother dressing up for an outing like that, would you?

'Were you one of them? Did you kill those people?'

'Yaotl!' my mother cried, appalled.

My brother said nothing. His jaw began working dangerously. His face had gone dark red with anger.

I had done it now: I had accused him and gone too far to withdraw. 'Lion, since we last met, I've been threatened with a knife, abducted, nearly asphyxiated, beaten up and poisoned. I've found one body floating in a canal – all right, I know you had nothing to do with that one, but I've raked over the burned remains of three others, and I know it was the army that killed them. You didn't tell me very much, but I've seen enough to work some of it out for myself. You are one of the Emperor's executioners. Was it your handiwork I saw? Why, Lion? At least tell me that. I know one of the sorcerers was taken from that house. Why did his family have to die?'

My brother's pent-up fury exploded then. He was a skilled warrior and fast, in spite of his years. He leapt towards me in a blur of speed and I felt the blow, a stinging open-handed slap to the side of my head, before I saw it coming. As I cowered under him he bellowed: 'Who do you think you are, to talk to me like that? Am I going to be questioned by a slave, a drunk, a loser like you?' Then he rounded on my mother and sister. 'As for you – you brought me here just to listen to this? I had to traipse halfway across the city dressed like a tramp in case the Chief Minister had me followed and all for what? So this idiot could accuse me of murder to my face?'

'Sit down!'

My brother had been trained to issue commands and had spent years in the army honing the skill, but there was something much older and deeper in the way my mother spoke. It stirred something planted in him when we had both been little boys, and he had always been the first to come meekly to order, even though he was the eldest and the biggest. He subsided now as quickly as he had flared up.

'I'll tell you who he is,' our mother reminded him. 'He's

your brother and my son. Now get away from him, and then,' she went on in a dangerous voice, 'I want to hear you answer his questions.'

'Mother,' I began, but she turned on me too.

'And you, Yaotl, try and keep a civil tongue in your head!'

Lion sat, glaring at me from under heavy, sulky eyelids.

I took a deep breath and tried again.

My mother was right: I ought to choose my words carefully. Lion was one of the most respected and feared men in the city. The gaudy finery in which he and others of his rank vaunted themselves could be got only from the Emperor's hand, for valour on the battlefield. This was why clothes and jewels were so important to us: if you saw a man like my brother in the street you would not need to ask how he came by his wealth, and you would know either to be polite to him or keep out of his way. Yet Lion had abandoned his public face to come and see me. He had done that for a reason, but I knew better than to forget what it was costing him.

'I'm sorry, Lion.' The unexpected apology lightened his expression a little. Even my mother sighed happily. 'But I have to know what my master did and why. You remember what the Emperor told me to do. I've got to find the sorcerers now and get them to him and tell him what his Chief Minister has been up to at the same time. If I can't do that then I'm likely to suffer a worse fate than the people in that village.'

My brother shot a brief glance at my mother, who was watching him impassively, like a judge waiting to hear a witness's evidence.

The most extraordinary change came over his face. It went from the deep red of overripe tomatoes to the colour of an uncooked sweet potato. It seemed to sag, as though all the strength had drained out of it and left the skin hanging unsupported on the bones beneath. Suddenly it felt as though we were looking, not at a famous warrior, but at a common man old before his time.

He turned his face towards the sky and shut his eyes. When he opened them to look at us again, there was something I had never expected to see: a tear running down his cheek.

'I don't know why.' He was barely whispering. 'I was never told. But until we talked to the Emperor that day, Yaotl, I thought the orders had come from him. I will eat earth for that!' He touched the ground with a fingertip automatically.

'So it's true, then,' my mother stated grimly.

'I tried not to let them suffer! I made the men take the children outside – they never knew what happened to their mother, or she what we did to them. I didn't have a choice, do you understand?'

For a long time none of us answered him. My sister stared resolutely at the strip of bark in front of her, although she had not touched her bark-beater since I had emerged from the bath house. My mother's face might have been carved out of granite.

At last I made myself say: 'I think you'd better tell it from the beginning, Lion.'

'I didn't want to be there,' my brother mumbled. 'It's not exactly soldiering, is it? Stringing up women and bashing their children's brains out, like you'd swing a fish you'd caught against a rock to stop it flopping about.' Out of the corner of my eye I saw my sister wince.

'Why'd you do it?' I asked.

'Don't be stupid! We were under orders. Anyway, the

Constables – we're the Emperor's hard men, aren't we? What was it to us, any more than cracking the heads of drunks in front of the Palace?'

I chose to ignore that. 'You thought the orders came from the Emperor?'

'Who else? I didn't hear him issue them, but . . .' My brother sighed heavily. 'Look, I'll tell you how it was. We weren't told anything about these men. We weren't even told their names. We just had to find the village headman and bring in the man he took us to.

'We went into Coyoacan mob handed – a full squad of twenty men, a lot just to make an arrest. We met up with the headman and his party outside the village well before daybreak.'

'What did they tell you?' I asked.

'They didn't tell us anything at all! But you pick up things. I heard the word "sorcerer" whispered a couple of times, when they thought we weren't listening. When I heard that, I thought we were wasting our time. I assumed any sorcerer worth his salt would have known we were coming for him and would have vanished like the mist before we got there. He wouldn't need to be a sorcerer, for that matter – you try moving a squad of fully armed warriors through a village in complete darkness without making a noise. They must have heard us on the other side of the lake.

'In the event, though, we picked him up without any trouble at all. We even had men stationed at the back of the house, in case he broke the wall down and got out that way. It was only one of those little crude one-room mud huts, I could have knocked the wall through with my elbows. We needn't have bothered. The headman just stood at the door and called him, and out he came, as meek as you like.'

'What did he look like?'

'Little scrawny specimen. Not what you'd call impressive, except for his ears. I think I'd know him again, just from the ears.'

'What happened to the man then?' I asked.

'We marched him off to the Cuauhcalco Prison. We didn't think about him any more once we'd brought him in. Why should we? I was just relieved we hadn't had to break any heads. Like I said, this sort of thing isn't exactly soldiering – not what they hand out cotton capes, tobacco and turquoise lip-plugs for, anyway.

'So when they told us to go back . . .'

'When was that?' I asked eagerly.

'Not long after the arrests. I wasn't happy, nor were my men, but orders are orders, and he made it very clear what we had to do. Whatever the man we had taken had done, it meant his family had to die and his house had to be razed. It had to seem as if he had never existed.'

'He made it very clear? Who?' I asked, although I thought I knew the answer.

Lion looked appealingly at my mother. She told him to go on in a voice I could barely hear.

'He spoke to us in person. He didn't take long – I had the feeling he was in a hurry because he had the same orders to issue to all the other squads who'd been involved in the round-up, and all in person, as if he couldn't entrust the task to anyone else. It was your esteemed master, Yaotl: the Chief Minister himself, Lord Feathered in Black!'

He glanced at each of us in turn, as if to gauge the impact his revelation made on us. If he had expected shock he was disappointed. My mother and sister seemed not to have moved a muscle since he had begun speaking, while I had known what he was going to say before he said it. The three of us looked back at him in grim silence.

Lion drew a hand across his face, and then stared at it, as if surprised to see it had come away wet.

'We hanged the woman in her own doorway. That's what he told us to do. I hit her over the head first, when she wasn't looking, so she wouldn't know and the children wouldn't hear her struggling. I told my men it would make them easier to deal with.' Suddenly he snarled like a trapped beast trying to ward off its tormentors. 'Do you think we wanted to do this? The Chief Minister told us to swing the children's heads against the outside wall. I had no choice: my men had all been there when the Chief Minister gave us our orders. He meant it that way, didn't he? If my men hadn't heard him, it might have been different, but what else could I do?'

'What else did you do?' I asked.

'We searched the house for other occupants. Then we torched it. Even the house had to go, don't you see? To give the villagers the idea the people who lived there never existed and weren't to be spoken of.'

I leaned forward, unable to keep the urgency out of my voice. 'You got all the occupants? You're sure of that?'

My brother gave me a strange look: the sort of look a drowning man might give to someone he has just seen on shore carrying a rope. 'All the occupants . . . why do you ask?'

I hesitated, unsure how far I could trust him with news of the boy Handy and I had found. 'I just wondered if anyone might have escaped.'

'I accounted for the whole family.'

'You're sure?'

'Oh yes,' my brother assured me in a voice brittle with self-reproach, 'every last one.' He took a deep breath before going on: 'Except the one I rescued.'

'Rescued?' my mother, my sister and I cried in unison.

'Maybe we didn't search the place as well as we should have done. I think that's what made me turn back, just the feeling that we'd missed something. I pretended I had a stone in my sandal, sent the rest of the lads on ahead and doubled back into the village.

'Everyone had run away, of course, and so there was nobody in the place except me and whoever was screaming inside the burning house. I know, I should have left him – but I was sick of the whole business by now. So I got him out, just before the roof fell in. It wasn't easy, either – he kept kicking and screaming, right up until I dragged him past his mother's body. I had to push her legs out of the way.' He looked thoughtful. 'Funny, he stopped screaming then.'

'You disobeyed orders?' I was struggling to reconcile the image of a man dragging a terrified child from the burning, collapsing shell of his home with everything else my brother had told us. 'What if you'd got caught?'

'Then your master would have had me cut to pieces, wouldn't he?' he snapped.

'Where's the boy now?' my sister asked anxiously.

'No idea,' Lion told her. 'The moment I put him down he ran for it.' He sighed. 'I don't blame him. The poor kid was probably as frightened of me as he was of the fire.'

I remembered the boy's silence and how not even Star's coaxing had persuaded him to talk. Now it seemed more important than ever to get some words out of him.

While I was thinking about this, a row was developing between my brother and Jade.

'I don't care whose orders you thought you were following!' my sister shrieked. 'Don't you have a mind of your own? Couldn't you see what you were doing was wrong?'

'You don't understand,' Lion replied feebly. He looked to

my mother to intervene but she just looked away. 'You haven't been in the army. You don't know what it's like.'

'Not even Yaotl would have been that stupid!' Jade was brandishing her bark-beater like a warrior waving his sword as he taunts the enemy. 'At least he'd have thought of a way out of it!'

'I got the boy out,' Lion protested. 'I risked my life to save him – doesn't that mean anything? What else could I do?' Then he rounded on me, snarling: 'This is all your master's fault!'

'Don't try to blame Yaotl for this, Lion,' my mother warned. 'It sounds as if you should have told him all this days ago.'

'He couldn't,' I said, surprising myself with my own mildness. 'It was the shame of it, wasn't it, brother? Especially when you realized old Black Feathers had duped you into thinking you were doing the Emperor's bidding.'

'At least you might have looked after the boy!' my sister said. 'What do you suppose happened to him?'

'I don't know,' my brother muttered wretchedly.

'I do,' I told him. 'And I've just thought of something you could do to make amends and maybe get back at my master too.'

I told them what I had seen and done since the Festival of the Raising of Banners.

I told them as much as I thought fitting. I saw no need to mention the night I had spent with Lily, but, to make sense of the rest, I was forced to stumble through an account of my visits to Maize Flower, the girl in the marketplace.

My sister silently rolled her eyes skywards at that point in the tale. My mother's expression remained unmoved, as if nothing she heard now could affect her any more. Lion listened to everything I said with his eyes half closed. Perhaps he thought following my story would help him make sense of his own.

My mother's voice was the first to break the silence after I had finished.

'So it comes to this. All the while you were supposed to be devoted to the gods, you were running around with some cheap whore from the marketplace.'

'Not all the time,' I said defensively, 'and she wasn't especially cheap.'

'And you didn't even have the sense to make sure you didn't get her pregnant!'

'Now wait a moment!' I cried. 'I didn't get her pregnant! That was Telpochtli – you heard me tell you what she said!'

'And you believed her?' It was my sister's turn. 'I take back what I said, Lion – Yaotl's even more stupid than you are, after all!'

My brother stiffened but did not answer her. Instead he looked thoughtfully at me.

'Let me see if I've got this right. You're saying Telpochtli – that friend of yours at the Priest House, the one who vanished before they could stone him to death for fornication – really ran off with the girl you'd both been seeing, and they had the child she told you about, and now he's going around pretending to be a priest and taking bets on the ball game, with the boy in tow?'

'They must have come back to the city years after they left,' I confirmed. 'Nimble was brought up abroad, in exile. The lad still has an accent.' I wondered where he had acquired it – among the Tarascans, perhaps? That would explain the bronze knife. 'Telpochtli can't use his own name, of course, and he goes about in disguise. Whenever I've seen him, he's been so heavily blacked up he might be anyone.'

'But Telpochtli was a priest! What's he doing, taking illegal bets for a living?'

'I was a priest — what am I doing as a slave?' I responded crisply. 'Telpochtli's been living outside the law ever since he left the Priest House. You said it yourself: he could be stoned to death. What has he got to lose?'

'So what do you want to do now, go and denounce them all to the Emperor — your master, Telpochtli and his lad?'

'The young man might be your nephew,' my mother warned him.

'No he isn't!' I insisted. My mother's and my sister's willingness to believe the child had been mine made me uneasy. 'All the same, I don't think it would be a good idea. The Emperor wants the sorcerers, not a tall story about his Chief Minister. Telling Montezuma that old Black Feathers doesn't know where those men are because he lost them, when we have no more idea of their whereabouts than he does, won't help us at all.'

'So what can we do, then?' I noticed that all of a sudden Lion and I appeared to have become allies. I had mixed feelings about that: the renowned and mighty warrior was not going to be content to take directions from his disgraced younger brother for long. 'Go looking for Misty, Telpochtli, whatever his name is?'

I grimaced. 'That hasn't done me a lot of good so far! Besides, I don't even know what he looks like under all that soot — not after all these years, anyway. I'd rather concentrate on the sorcerers. I think we ought to find out what my master's interest in those men was in the first place — what any of them might have done that would have made him go after his whole family. The boy you saved from the burning house is the only person I know of who might be able to tell us that. As far as I know, he's still at Handy's place. He wasn't talking when I left. He may have said something since, of course, but if he hasn't, it will be because Star's too gentle. I have a feeling what he needs is a fright, to shock it out of him.' I looked steadily at my brother. 'Seeing you again ought to do it.'

'That sounds brutal,' my sister objected.

'He could be right, though,' Lion replied. 'Might even help the lad, in the long run. Boys from the House of Youth get like that sometimes, the first time they follow the army to war and see the darts flying and real wounds. They come back and won't talk about it, and that's not good. You want to go and see your friend Handy tomorrow, then?' The prospect of doing something, however small, to repair the damage he had done had given him back something of his old briskness of manner.

His pride had taken a beating, however, and was obviously still suffering under his mother's and his sister's reproachful looks. He soon announced that he was tired and wanted to go in and rest. I imagined him sitting awake all night, with his face to the wall, now scowling, now twisted with grief and regret, now frowning in bewilderment at the position he found himself in.

'You, in the meantime, can make yourself useful,' my mother said, handing me a bark-beater.

'What?' I cried feebly. 'You let my brother go in and rest and expect me to do women's work?'

'You're eating our food, you can share our work,' said my sister. 'And leave Lion alone – can't you see he's suffering?'

'So am I! I've still got the bruises – and I haven't killed anyone!'

I wondered how it was that my brother's offence seemed to have been so quickly forgiven, but then I decided to forget it. I was never going to be the favourite son.

TEN WIND

1

My friend Handy, my brother had called him, but judging by the way the big commoner greeted us at dawn the next day he clearly saw our relationship differently.

'You're the last person I need to see,' he said before I had opened my mouth. 'Sod off, and take your grubby mate with you.'

I took a step back from his threshold and stared at him in astonishment. I resisted the temptation to turn and look at my brother to see what he made of Handy's appraisal. I was dressed in my usual short maguey fibre cape and breechcloth. Lion had let his appearance deteriorate still further since the previous day: now he wore only an old breechcloth that looked as if a pair of dogs had been fighting over it.

'Listen,' I protested, 'you haven't given me a chance to explain.'

'Explain what?' He turned back into his house. A mass of human hair, dangling from the ceiling, brushed the top of his head and he swiped at it angrily. It was an old war trophy, taken no doubt from the owner of one of the thigh bones decorating his courtyard. 'What's there to explain? Exactly how I'm going to be put to death, just for being seen talking to you? I'd rather not know!'

'But we just wanted to talk to the boy!' I called from the doorway.

That brought Star waddling into the room from the courtyard with urgent shushing noises. 'Be quiet, you fools! Do you want the whole city to know?'

Handy turned back to me with a helpless gesture. 'You see, now? I wouldn't have to put up with this if I hadn't listened to you. Now I have this extra mouth to feed and the moment anyone so much as comes round the corner at the end of the street, we have to stuff the lad in a maize bin in case it's that steward of your master's.' He sighed in exasperation. 'Look, you might as well come in. Snake! Where are you? Run on ahead and tell them I'll be late.'

'Thanks. My master's steward? What would he be doing here?'

'Giving me orders. I work for Lord Feathered in Black now.'

'What?' Lion and I cried simultaneously. I looked quickly at my brother and then even more quickly away again. 'As what?' I added weakly.

'As a handyman, a messenger, a general dogsbody. Lord Feathered in Black needed someone he could rely on, especially after his most valuable slave had gone missing. I'd been carrying messages to him for that merchant, Shining Light, and I suppose he thought I was reliable.' Handy caught me glancing nervously at the doorway. 'Oh, don't worry. I'm not about to turn you in. But you see how awkward this is for me. How would I explain it, if I was found talking to some runaway?'

I could see how awkward it might be for him. More to the point, I could see how fatal it might be for me. 'Of course,' I said as smoothly as I could. 'I quite understand. Lion, we'd better forget the boy.'

'Lion?'

Snake had been on his way out but mention of my brother's name stopped him in his tracks.

There was a long silence while Handy and his son stared at my brother, my brother glared at me and I tried to avoid looking at anyone.

I might have guessed that one of Handy's sons, a boy just too young to have started his training at the House of Youth, would know every famous warrior in Mexico by name and many of them by sight. I would have bet he knew the name and rank of each of my brother's captives as well.

Snake went on: 'But you're . . .'

So much for my brother's disguise. 'Yes, he's the Guardian of the Waterfront.'

'That's fantastic! Incredible! Father . . .'

To my amazement, Handy immediately prostrated himself before my brother and nudged his son into doing the same. Only Star stayed upright, looking at her menfolk as if she thought they had gone mad. In a slightly muffled voice Handy said: 'My Lord, my house is at your disposal. It is a wretched place, and I would not insult you by offering it to you, but I know you have had a long journey, you are tired . . .'

My brother was clearly used to this sort of attention. 'Sir, you are too kind,' he began, in his most self-deprecating tone. 'Indeed, I am sure such generous hospitality is more than I deserve, a mere humble servant of the Emperor, and I could never presume . . .'

'Now wait a moment!' I broke in. 'Lion, we're here for a reason, remember? Have you forgotten what we came here to ask?'

'Yes,' said Star drily, 'what are you here for, exactly?'

At that moment the boy from Coyoacan appeared,

attracted by all the fuss. Ignoring the rest of us, he went straight up to Star.

'What's happening?' he asked.

'Nothing, Ehecatl,' she said soothingly. 'These men were just . . .'

Then he noticed my brother. He screamed.

Star wanted to get the boy out of our sight, but my brother would not have it, and Handy, forced to choose between them, sided reluctantly with the Constable. The woman submitted less than graciously to her husband's will, planting herself by the door with a fierce scowl on her face and an arm draped protectively around the child's shoulders. The moment we left the house, I suspected, Handy was going to wish he had never been born.

'Of course he talks,' she informed me coldly. 'All it needed was a little kindness.'

'Have you asked him about his father yet?' I enquired, with a nervous glance at my brother.

'No, and I'm not going to. He'll tell us about that in his own time, or not at all. What do you want to do – beat it out of him?'

I had been contemplating doing just that, but it was my brother who answered.

'We didn't come here to hurt anybody.' He spoke to her more gently than I would have thought possible for him; but then I often forgot that he had children and grandchildren of his own. 'But we have to know what this boy may have seen or heard. It's for his own sake as much as ours.'

'And if he won't answer your questions?'

'Then we'll have to go away again.' My brother quelled my objection with a look. 'He's suffered enough already. Believe me, I know.'

Star looked as if she was about to say something, but to everyone's surprise it was the boy who answered. He looked straight at Lion and said: 'You came to our village with the soldiers.'

My brother hesitated for a long time before replying: 'Yes, I did.'

Star looked at the boy in alarm. 'Are you sure you want to talk about this now?'

The lad ignored her. 'It was the old man, wasn't it?'

'What old man?' my brother asked.

'The old man,' the boy repeated doggedly. He seemed to take little notice of anything any of us said. 'He made you do it, didn't he?'

My brother had more discretion than I would have given him credit for. Another man might have ended the discussion there, by seizing on the child's words as proof that what had happened was not his fault, because he was merely acting under orders. All Lion did was to ask once more, very cautiously, who the old man was.

'He came to the village on foot,' Ehecatl explained, 'but I know he was important because the headman had to stand outside the house while they talked. But I knew you could hear things through the wall at the back, if you stood in the right place.'

'Old Black Feathers,' I breathed. 'It all makes perfect sense.'

'What were they talking about?' Star asked gently. For all her concern for the child, she was as intrigued as I was.

'I didn't understand it all. The old man kept asking questions. He wanted to know about something. Men with pale skins and beards had arrived somewhere in the East. He said something about a place called Xicallanco. He wanted to know . . .' The boy's voice faltered.

'Yes?' I leaned forward eagerly.

'The old man wanted to know if the pale men ... if they really were men, or if they were gods, and if they were men, whether anyone who traded with them would earn fame and riches.'

'And what was the answer?'

'I don't know. I didn't catch it, but I heard the old man say: "You don't have very long." And he said something else: he said other people might come and ask the same questions, and not to tell them anything.'

Handy, Lion and I exchanged glances, but before either of us could say a word the child's composure suddenly cracked, and he burst into tears and hid his face in the folds of Star's skirt. As she held him, speaking soothing words and rocking him like an infant, we heard his muffled voice crying: 'And they did, didn't they? They came back to kill us all! They took my father and then they came for us – my mother. Why? Why?'

The last words, bawled into Star's lap, were barely intelligible. She held the boy, cooing and smoothing his hair with her fingers.

After a glance at me, my brother spoke softly to the boy. 'Your father kept his word to the old man, lad, that's why. He didn't tell the other people what they wanted to hear.'

'All right, Yaotl,' my brother challenged me, after Star had led the sobbing child across the courtyard to the women's room, 'you said it all made perfect sense. It makes no sense to me at all, so you'd better explain.'

Lion, Handy and I squatted together in the courtyard, keeping the morning air's lingering chill away with tortillas still warm from the griddle. These were a treat, and I was sure Star only let us have them in deference to my brother's rank. Handy had lent him his best cloak too, although on Lion the old patched two-captive warrior's mantle that I had first seen the commoner in somehow looked still more incongruous than a bare loincloth.

While we ate, I repeated for Handy's benefit the story I had told my mother, sister and brother the day before.

'The old man the boy saw was my master,' I said. 'It has to have been him.'

'But why?' Handy asked. 'Why would the Chief Minister be skulking around sorcerers like some lovelorn girl wanting her fortune told?'

'It sounds as if he wanted to know how a trading venture would fare,' added my brother, 'but he's not a merchant. Why should he care about a trading venture? It's not as if he needs the money!'

'True,' I said. 'I don't think it's about money.' As I considered my brother's words it came to me that the Chief Minister had given me the answer himself, in the evening of the day Ehecatl's father had died. 'It's about renown. He wants to be as famous as his father, and he wants to put one over on the Emperor at the same time. Lion, you remember what Montezuma told us about the East? Pale men with beards, pyramids on the sea. And you showed me that box yourself, the one full of cloth finer than cotton. The Emperor wanted the sorcerers to tell him whether the strangers he'd heard about were men or gods. His Chief Minister obviously thought he'd find out before the Emperor did. The Emperor mentioned Xicallanco. So did old Black Feathers, when he went to see the sorcerer. So, for that matter, did Lily. She told me her son used to talk about the place, and I don't see why she should have been lying about that.'

'But what's some trading post in the East to your master?' my brother asked.

'It's not the place that interests him,' I replied, 'but the reports that have come from there: these pale men from the East. My master thought the way to lasting fame was through these strangers, whoever or whatever they might be; and he wanted it for himself, and the Emperor was to know nothing about it. He obviously couldn't go to see them in person. He needed an agent, someone he could rely on to keep his mouth shut – and someone who wouldn't cause a stir if he turned up in a place like Xicallanco. Who else but a merchant, a Pochteca? Famously secretive, and as for going abroad to deal with exotic foreigners – well, that's what they do, isn't it? And it turned out that the man he dealt with at the ball court, Misty, knew just the man – another of his clients. He's the link, you see, between old Black Feathers and Shining Light.'

'So the Chief Minister and the young merchant made a deal?' Handy suggested.

'That's what I think. I suppose the Chief Minister paid off Shining Light's debts and Shining Light agreed to go to Xicallanco for him. Probably old Black Feathers put up some capital for the venture too – goods to exchange for this wonderful cloth, whatever. And he consulted sorcerers – the way you would before any venture like this, only he did it very, very quietly.

'But then two things went wrong.'

'Montezuma had the sorcerers arrested,' my brother pointed out.

'That was the first, yes. The Emperor decided he wanted to talk to the sorcerers himself! My master must have been terrified when they were rounded up. He'd have had to get them out of the prison, just to make sure they didn't compromise him. I suppose he just ordered the major-domo to release them into his custody. He's the Chief Justice, he could do that. That explains why the major-domo was surprised when I came along afterwards, as the Chief Minister's slave, asking how they'd managed to escape. Then when the major-domo found he'd been ordered to act against the Emperor's wishes he panicked, and said it must be magic. The Emperor more or less believed him, but in any case by then his Chief Minister had got the sorcerers out of his reach. What could he do with them then, though? He wasn't going to kill them, not if he still wanted his questions answered, and he couldn't just let them go. He needed somewhere to keep them, in case they talked. It was too dangerous to use his own house. I suppose he asked his partner in crime, Shining Light, who said put them in his warehouse. The only thing is, everything Shining Light owns . . .'

'Telpochtli!' breathed Lion. 'So that's how he got hold of the sorcerers! And their families – no witnesses, right?'

'Of course. The Chief Minister had to make sure no one could describe him coming to see the sorcerers, especially once they were out of the prison and beyond his control. So he got the Emperor to give him the job of finding them and used it as an excuse to have their families killed.'

Handy bit his lip. 'But why the sacrifice?'

'Yes,' added my brother, 'and why the body in the canal outside your master's house? You thought that was a message from Telpochtli. What's that got to do with these strangers in the East?'

'That's the other thing that went wrong,' I said. 'Whatever was going on between Shining Light and Telpochtli, it all changed, around the time of the Festival of the Raising of Banners. Then Shining Light became Telpochtli's prisoner. Telpochtli had already got his hands on the sorcerers, along with the rest of the merchant's property, and he'd started torturing them. I suppose he wanted the answers to old Black Feathers' questions himself. Then he used them to blackmail my master. Old Black Feathers wanted them alive, so he started delivering them to him dead. As for the sacrifice . . .' I remembered what the merchant's grandfather had told me, how Telpochtli – or, as far as he was concerned, Misty – and Shining Light might have dreamed the whole business up together as a kind of sick joke. 'It was the audacity of it, that was the whole point. They were telling my master they could do anything they wanted.' To have the peasant die at the summit of the Great Pyramid, and so publicly, and be powerless to intervene – unless he wanted to risk exposing his own dealings with the sorcerers – must have provoked my master beyond enduring. 'They even sent Nimble to him as a messenger, to make sure he knew what had happened!'

'Ehecatl's father played his part well,' observed Handy, 'considering he wasn't supposed to be there. How'd they persuade him to be so cooperative?'

'There are ways. I've seen it done often enough: sacred wine, bathing, exhaustion, hunger, more sacred wine . . . after enough of the sort of treatment they give the Bathed Slaves, I doubt if he'd have known his own name, and he'd have done anything you asked him to. And before that, remember, he'd been hauled off to the prison, sprung and then tortured. He wasn't cooperative right at the end, though, was he? He had enough of his own will left to run away. And he did have a prophecy for old Black Feathers, after all. He wanted me to tell the old man about the big boat.'

'I still don't see why Telpochtli was prepared to kill the sorcerers and threaten your master to get you,' Lion said. 'Was it really all over something that happened at the Priest House all those years ago?'

'What else can it be? For some reason he seems to blame me for what happened to him and the girl from the market.'

'Doesn't make sense to me,' said Handy. 'It wasn't your fault they had to run away, was it?'

'No, and I can't pretend to understand it either. I suppose Telpochtli started out being jealous, and over the years it must have become an obsession.'

'Besides,' the commoner added, as though the thought had just occurred to him, 'I thought you priests were all supposed to be impotent – aren't you supposed to stick so many cactus spines and obsidian razors into your parts that you can't get it up anyway?'

This drew a short, harsh laugh from Lion. 'No,' I said coldly. 'We used to draw blood from our penises, but only the real fanatics went further than that. I certainly didn't. I always thought Telpochtli might be the type to do it, but I guess he wasn't.'

'Does it really matter what started all this?' my brother asked impatiently. 'We have to decide what we're going to do now. Which of them do we go after – Telpochtli or the Chief Minister?'

My brother could be alarmingly direct, especially when he had an end in sight or, as now when his pride had been wounded, a score to settle.

'Both of them,' I said. 'We still need to get the sorcerers to the Emperor before we can denounce my master, and we need Telpochtli to lead us to the sorcerers.' I considered for a moment before going on. 'I think we go back to Lily's house now – you and me, Lion. It's just possible she was able to tell Nimble enough to get her son released, but if she wasn't, Telpochtli won't be able to resist having another crack at me. That's where you come in, brother. You can protect me if he tries another trick like yesterday's . . . What's the joke?'

A wintry smile had appeared on Lion's face. 'I was just remembering,' he said drily, 'how I told you not to expect me to save your worthless hide this time!'

I looked at him seriously. 'You will, though, if you have to. You owe me. I went to Coyoacan for you. I found the boy.'

My brother's face darkened, but whatever he was about to say was interrupted by a sudden noise. An argument seemed to be going on outside the courtyard.

Handy cocked his head to one side for a moment, listening.

'It's Snake,' he announced. 'Why's he making such a row?' He stood up and took a step towards the doorway. 'Who's he arguing with . . . Oh, shit!'

My brother was on his feet too, running for the women's room. 'Star! Quick, the maize bin!'

I was left alone with my head darting about like a turkey's, looking for somewhere to run or hide. I thought briefly about the bath house, but I was too late to reach it in time and it would have been too obvious a hiding place anyway.

'Handy!' called a voice I knew only too well. 'Congratulations! You've caught our runaway!'

I let my arms go limp at my sides as I watched an old adversary striding through the entrance to the courtyard towards me, with Snake plodding disconsolately at his heels.

It was my master's steward.

2

I let the steward drive me out of the courtyard like a stray dog, submitting meekly to the blows falling on my shoulders and back. He was so pleased with himself for having caught me that he did not stop for whatever business had brought him to the house.

'That canoe there. Go on, move!' He propelled me towards the canal beside the house with a vicious shove. Floating there was the canoe he had obviously come in, a little two-man craft with a boatman in the stern. He looked up in alarm when he realized that he had a second passenger. Then he recognized me and his expression changed, first to wide-eyed amazement and then to a broad grin of pure joy.

My heart sank. The boatman was none other than Rabbit, my master's litter-bearer, the man Costly had fooled into taking his medicine while he was supposed to be watching me and whom I had last seen sprawled on the ground after I had hit him with a slave collar.

'In!' the steward roared from a hand's breadth behind me.

He kicked me as I was stepping into the boat. I had one foot on the bank and one in the bottom of the canoe and his foot swung up between my legs. Pain exploded in my groin and shot up into my guts, driving the breath out of me in a high-pitched whistle. I crashed into the bottom of the boat, rocking it violently and sending spouts of water over the sides.

'You've got worse than that to come,' the Prick assured me.

Rabbit gripped the boat's sides to steady himself. 'I haven't got room for both of you!'

'Oh yes you have,' the steward growled as he stepped over me into the canoe's bows. 'Yaotl won't take up much room lying there like that. If he's any trouble, we can always chuck him overboard!'

'Where are you taking me?' I gasped as soon as I could speak.

'Why, home, of course. Lord Feathered in Black will be so glad to have you back. He's missed you!'

'Pleased to hear it,' I croaked, for the sake of having something to say. There was one thing I urgently had to tell the steward, and then I did not care if I never spoke to him again. 'Listen . . .'

'In fact, we've got a surprise prepared for you.'

I put my hands on the bottom of the boat to try to lever myself into a more comfortable position. Maybe, I thought, I could throw myself overboard and swim to freedom, as I had when Telpochtli had kidnapped me. 'A surprise?'

'Oh yes. It's good that we found you when we did, though, because it wouldn't have kept – would it, Rabbit?'

The litter-bearer said nothing, probably because he was concentrating on keeping the overloaded canoe afloat.

'Huitztic, listen,' I said. 'Don't you want to know what I was doing at Handy's house?'

'Oh, all in good time. Don't spoil things by telling me everything at once, Yaotl – I'm looking forward to beating it out of you!'

'I'm still looking for the prisoners – the ones the Emperor and our master told me to find,' I said carefully. 'The man

Shining Light offered to the war-god at the Festival of the Raising of Banners, he was one of them. His Lordship knows this. I wanted to find out if Handy remembered anything about him.' At all costs I must not give the steward or my master any reason to go back to the commoner's house, at least until Lion and Ehecatl were safely out of the way.

'That's very interesting,' the steward said insincerely.

'He didn't know anything. In fact he didn't want to speak to me at all.'

'Well, you can tell it all to Lord Feathered in Black. I'll be sure not to cut your tongue out until afterwards!'

My weight was on my hands now. I noticed the canoe was still swaying, and Rabbit was muttering under his breath as he strove to control it. It occurred to me that with a little effort I could tip it over, spilling all of us into the canal.

A sandalled foot stamped on my right hand, sending me sprawling once more into the bottom of the boat with a cry of pain.

The steward bent over me. 'Not thinking of leaving us, were you?'

They dragged me to the rear of the Chief Minister's house, depositing me in a heap in the middle of the courtyard outside my own room.

The Prick prodded me with his foot. 'Up you get.'

Cautiously I hauled myself upright. The steward was behind me and Rabbit facing me, and behind Rabbit was the doorway into my room. The big litter-bearer looked surprisingly unsure of himself, continually glancing over my shoulder as if looking for cues from the steward. Neither man said anything.

I licked my lips, which had gone dry. I could think of nothing I could say or do that would not make matters worse.

Eventually the steward's patience ran out.

'Nothing to say, Yaotl? You were really talkative in the canoe. I thought we weren't going to have any fun with you for a moment there.'

'What do you want to know?' I was looking at the man in front of me, who did not look as if he was having fun at all.

'Know? I don't want to know anything! I want you to hold out on us for as long as you can. I'm looking forward to hurting you, Yaotl. So's Rabbit here – even more than me. He hasn't forgotten who earned him the beating he got after you escaped!'

He pushed me then, not very hard, but hard enough to send me staggering towards Rabbit.

I knew this game. It was like the ball game, with me as the ball, being bounced from one to the other a little harder each time until I ended up rolling around on the floor, a helpless pulpy mass of flesh and broken bones, with hands and feet slamming relentlessly into me. Rabbit got off to a poor start, though, reacting too late to push me back to the steward, so that the big man and I ended up standing face to face, staring into each other's eyes.

I managed a feeble grin. 'You haven't done this sort of thing before, have you?'

I heard the Prick's brisk step behind me an instant before he hit me in the kidneys.

I went down in front of Rabbit with a scream of agony. I lay there, writhing helplessly as the pain spread through me like fire from the small of my back.

'I enjoyed that. Go on, Rabbit, your turn.'

Still dazed with pain, I barely felt the foot thump into my side.

'Go on, you can do better than that! Remember what the shit this bastard and his mate gave you did to your guts!'

Rabbit kicked me again, harder, making me grunt. I rolled over towards the steward, who jabbed his foot into the place where he had hit me a moment before. I squealed. I arched my back, exposing my still-tender ribs to Rabbit's foot. He was getting into his stride now, and his next kick set me coughing and choking and spitting blood.

'Careful! Not too hard – we want him to be able to enjoy his surprise!'

'What do you want to know?' I gasped. 'You might at least tell me that!'

'Oh, we're not ready for that yet. This is just a taster!'

Priests became inured to pain. As a boy in the Priest House I had had cactus spines driven into me and been beaten with burning torches for the slightest offence. I had drawn my own blood from my tongue, ears, arms, legs and penis every day, reopening the same unhealed wounds time after time. I had endured extremes of cold, throwing myself into the lake at midnight and sitting, still wet, naked and shivering, until daybreak.

At some point while the kicks and punches were raining down on me, some instinct from those days, long buried through lack of use, came back to life, and I stopped hurting. I could still feel the blows but it was as if they were being driven into someone else, someone I could watch indifferently as he lay twitching and groaning on the ground in front of me.

Eventually it occurred to me that they were not trying very hard. The steward and Rabbit could easily have killed me if they had had a mind to, but for all the obvious relish with which they pounded the body lying between them, they were restraining themselves. The steward kept warning the other man not to go too far, before carefully delivering a kick that drove a gasp of pain from his victim but broke no bones.

Eventually the man on the ground stopped struggling. There seemed no point in staying awake after that, so I fell asleep.

I became aware of a curious rattling noise. I could not work out when it had begun, but it seemed to go on and on and to come from everywhere, or from nowhere in particular. I drifted in and out of sleep, but it was still there whenever I woke up, its rhythm scarcely seeming to vary.

The noise began to irritate me vaguely. I rolled over to get away from it, thinking to escape back into a silent, dreamless sleep.

That was when the agony started again.

It was not much at first, just a sharp stinging when my bruised hip touched the ground, but it was like what happens when a stone dropped into a pool breaks the surface and the leaves and twigs around it vanish as well. That one careless movement pulled down whatever fragile wall my mind had built around my body's pain, and in a moment I was writhing in anguish, each spasm sending a fresh, excruciating jolt through me until I wanted to scream.

A horrible gurgling sound forced its way through the fluid that clogged my throat.

I forced myself to stop struggling, to lie still and try to keep the pain away, as I had when I was being beaten.

I was bitterly cold and shivering uncontrollably, and suddenly I recognized the rattling noise that had first woken me: it had been my own teeth chattering.

I forced them to stop so that I could listen.

I could hear footsteps and familiar voices. One said, 'I think he's awake now.'

Another replied: 'Throw another pot over him, to make sure.'

I tried raising myself on one arm. It was hard because something was holding me down and it took all the strength I could muster to tear myself free of it. Only when I felt and heard the stuff peeling off my bare skin did I recognize it as my own dried blood.

I tried opening my eyes. The effort yielded only more pain and an unbearable swirling brightness. I sank back to the floor and moaned softly, and then tried again, this time squinting and blinking at the tall, dark shape that appeared in front of me.

Eventually it resolved itself into a man carrying something bulky in both hands. It took a moment of befuddled thought to recognize Rabbit holding a heavy clay pot.

I understood then why I was so cold. He had been tipping water over me to wake me up, and he was just about to do it again.

I opened my mouth to speak, to beg him to stop.

The contents of the pot hit me in the face as I drew breath, sending nasty, brackish water streaming into my nose and mouth. I collapsed again, spluttering and retching.

'So good to have you back with us,' said the steward, from somewhere behind me. 'Are you ready for your surprise now?'

Between them they got me up and, picking their way through the pools of blood and other things that marked the spot in the courtyard where I had lain, they dragged me to the entrance to my own room.

'Here you are, Yaotl,' the steward growled as he shoved me into the room. 'Do give your friend our love, won't you?'

My legs would not hold me, and so I fell on my knees, biting my tongue to hide yet another sudden jolt of pain.

'My friend?'

I peered into the relative gloom of the room, wondering what he had meant. Then, suddenly, I saw it, and for a moment I was speechless, lost in the sheer joy of learning that someone you had given up for dead is still alive.

'Costly!' I croaked as cheerfully as I could. 'You old rogue, you'd live through anything!'

The old slave was on the far side of the room. He looked better than I had seen him in years. He was sitting up with his mouth wide open – how like him, I thought, yawning nonchalantly while I was being beaten half to death.

'Am I happy to see you!' Tears pricked my swollen eyelids as I forced myself to stand, to get across the room to embrace him. 'Old friend, I thought they'd done for you . . .'

The truth hit me just a moment before the steward did.

It was not a hard blow, only enough to send me staggering forward a couple of steps until my balance went and I pitched forward on top of the old slave's body. Vainly I threw my arms out to save myself, but too late, and the dead man and I collapsed in a heap, my arms around him like a lover's, his cold skin against mine, his loose jaw snapping at my ear as it swung shut.

They left me alone after that, squatting and shivering in the room that had been mine, in surroundings that might have been comfortingly familiar but for the soot stains on the walls, the lingering smell of roasted chillies and the body slumped beside me.

I did not try to pick Costly's body up. There was nothing I could do for him. I could not even weep, and if my eyes stung it was from the beating I had had, not grief. I felt numb and passive, listening idly to the sweepers complaining while they cleared up the mess I had made in the courtyard outside while I waited for someone to come and get me.

How long it was before the familiar, hated figure appeared in the doorway I have no idea. It may have been a few heartbeats, or the best part of a day.

I barely looked up at the steward, not caring enough to return his gaze or look defiant.

'What did you think of your surprise, then? Told you it wouldn't keep. It's a good job we found you when we did, though, it would have started to smell soon!'

I said nothing.

He let out an exaggerated sigh. 'Lost your sense of humour, have you? Well, I hope you haven't lost your tongue too. I think his Lordship is ready to hear what you have to say now!'

The steward and Rabbit hauled me to the foot of the stairway leading to my master's apartments. They dragged me into the interior of the house and dumped me unceremoniously at my master's feet.

He said nothing to me. He sat in his high-backed reed chair, looking at me the way a man might look at a bowl of stew if he suspected the meat was rotten. I said nothing to him. What would have been the point?

A girl appeared at the edge of my vision, carefully stepped around the quivering mess on the floor and passed my master a clay smoking-tube. Its end was already lit, and as he drew deeply on it the room filled with the complex aromas of a rich man's tobacco – the leaf itself, the resinous scent of liquid amber, bitumen and a hint of vanilla.

'My Lord . . .' It was the steward's voice.

'You may go, Huitztic. You too, Rabbit. I will send for you if I need you.'

Then the Chief Minister and I were alone: a frail old man and his runaway slave who he must know had every reason to wish him harm. Considering the state his servants had left me in, however, my master had little to worry about. It took an effort just to raise my head far enough to look into his eyes, to find them veiled by the thin cloud of pipe smoke that hung in the air between us.

It was hard to know what I felt. There was grief for Costly, suddenly made sharp and fresh again by the steward's cruel trick, anger at what had been done to both of us and, naturally, fear. Yet none of these was overwhelming, none of them strong enough to make me want to do anything. I was still numb. Contemplating the dangerous, hateful old man in front of me, I felt nothing so strongly as a kind of helpless bafflement, and it came out in a single word.

He took the pipe from his mouth and frowned, looking surprised by my question.

'"Why", Yaotl? You ask me "Why"? Why do you think? You ran away, after poisoning my litter-bearer and assaulting him and my steward . . .'

'They tried to kill me!'

'Nonsense. They merely wanted you to go with them, that's all.'

'And what they did today, and that sick joke with Costly?'

'Huitztic can be a little heavy-handed sometimes.' My master chewed his pipe thoughtfully before blowing a thin jet of smoke decorously out of the corner of his mouth. 'This really didn't have to happen.'

So that was how it was going to be, I thought. I might have known that the Chief Minister of the Aztecs would not demean himself by threatening and bullying a slave. He could leave that to his henchmen, and himself show me every kindness, hoping that I would open up to him as I never would to his steward, no matter how hard he hit me. I half expected him to share his pipe with me. Then he did.

'Why don't you have a smoke – you'll feel better. If my steward had really been trying to kill you, would we be talking now?'

My fingers accepted the smoking-tube almost of their own accord. I took an uncertain puff. As a priest I had used rough, heady tobacco that seared my lungs and made my head spin and got me into the ideal state of mind for some of our ceremonies. This was different, the stuff young lords had packed into their pipes when they paraded themselves in public. I breathed in the smoke, losing myself momentarily in the scent and taste of it until I remembered who and where I was and gave the pipe back.

'You must understand that a man in my position simply cannot afford to have his most valuable slave disappear the way you did. I would be a laughing stock. At the very least I am going to have to have you formally admonished, and you know what that means.'

'Oh yes, my Lord.' It meant that I would be subjected to a ritual harangue about my shortcomings as a slave before at least two witnesses. This was not a fearsome punishment in itself, except that the third time it happened I could be sold, and as a slave known to be habitually recalcitrant I would be bought for only one purpose: as a very cheap gift for the gods.

'Good. Well, now we've got that distasteful subject out of the way, I want you to tell me what you've been doing since you ran away.'

I told him what I dared. I had been to the ball court in Tlatelolco, seen the boy there and been attacked by Misty. I had been taken to the merchant's house in Pochtlan, and there Misty had attacked me again. I had not gone home to Toltenco. I could not deny having been to Handy's house, of course, since the steward had found me there, but I explained that to my master the same way I had to his steward, by claiming I had wanted to talk to Handy about Shining Light's Bathed Slave.

I realized that he probably did not believe I was telling him the whole truth, and that it did not really matter. Each of us was playing a part. He was pretending to be my genial, indulgent master and I was pretending to be his loyal slave. That would last while I kept up the act on my side and he still had a use for me.

He did not interrupt my story. At the end of it he sat in thoughtful silence, watching a perfect smoke ring curling and flattening out as it rose towards the ceiling before slipping like a ghost through a small opening high in the wall.

'Misty,' he murmured at last. 'You think he is really an old enemy of yours from your days in the Priest House – what did you say his name was, Telpochtli? And he's the one who's trying to use the sorcerers to blackmail me into giving you up to him?'

'My Lord, yes. Hasn't he been sending you messages, demanding that you hand me over? There was one on the body we found floating in the canal.'

A puzzled frown creased my master's forehead. 'Misty, sending me messages? I don't think so.' He put the smoking-tube down beside him delicately. 'Let me show you something.'

The Chief Minister of the Aztecs got slowly to his feet and made his way over to a small reed chest under the little window. As he bent towards it a shaft of sunlight caught his face, picking out in shadow every line that nearly forty years in office had etched into it.

'Ah! Here it is. I want you to look at this.'

As he lowered himself back onto his seat he held out a single sheet of paper.

'It's a letter. Why, it's from Shining Light!'

'Your merchant,' the Chief Minister confirmed. 'Read on.'

'It's been written in some haste, and not by a very practised hand,' I continued. 'But I think it says . . .' The words died in my throat as I read them.

'Your friend Handy gave it to my steward, on Two Jaguar – the day you visited the prison.'

'That was the day Shining Light was kidnapped – when his mother said he left the city.' I looked at the paper again. 'But that doesn't make sense – not if I read this correctly.'

My master had taken up the smoking-tube again and leaned back in his seat. I watched the lines on his face shift as the muscles under them relaxed, and for the first time in the years I had known him wondered how much pain he was in.

'I took it to mean this,' he said. '"This is my price for the rest of the sorcerers. Give me Yaotl, and they are yours." Do you agree?'

'Yes. But if he'd gone . . .'

'If he'd gone into exile, as his mother was saying, then I would have had to deliver you to his house, wouldn't I? Which I duly did, the next day. I assumed his mother would take charge of you in his absence. In the event Misty and his boy obviously tried to handle the thing themselves, and they made a mess of it, since you managed to escape.' He reached for the pipe again. 'I have had other messages. The one you found on the corpse out there' – a slight turn of his head indicated the general location of the canal – 'was one of them. But you think Misty – or Telpochtli, if that's who he really is – has the sorcerers, not Shining Light? That would mean the merchant was just carrying messages between me and Telpochtli. How amusing!' There was no laughter in his voice.

'I think their relationship is more complicated than that, my Lord. Shining Light and Telpochtli seem to have been lovers, and now Shining Light is Telpochtli's prisoner. He has the merchant and his merchandise, as well as your sorcerers.'

'So you said. So where does he live, this Telpochtli?'

'You don't know?'

'Of course not! What, you think the Chief Minister is going to be seen plucking at the hem of some small-time criminal's cloak?' In his agitation he waved the smoking-tube about, sending flecks of ash flying from its end. 'I have taken great care never to meet the man. It's bad enough that I have to entertain that boy of his on occasion.'

'But if you are to find the sorcerers . . .'

'I could simply do what Shining Light or Misty or Telpochtli or whoever has them asks me, and hand you over!'

There was a long silence. I wriggled nervously while the Chief Minister drew comfortably on his pipe. I wondered whether that meant the play-acting was now over, and the steward would be told to finish what he had set out to do on the morning of Four Vulture, by trussing me up like a deer and delivering me to Telpochtli.

Eventually he took the clay tube out of his mouth. 'Relax, Yaotl. If I wanted to exchange you for the sorcerers, would we be talking now? I would just have had Huitztic make the exchange, and that would be an end to it. But the truth is,' he went on, suddenly sounding older and wearier than ever, 'I'm sick of being made a fool of. All this talk of godlike strangers from the East – well, it seemed like the perfect opportunity. You know what I mean?'

'No, my Lord.' I thought I did, however: it was the tale of jealousy, vanity and greed that I had outlined to Handy and Lion only that morning.

'You heard some of it from the Emperor himself, I believe. Weren't you shown the box – the one that was washed up on the shore of the Divine Sea, with the marvellous cloth and the sword in it? Ever since I saw the things in that box I've been waiting for the men who made them to appear. Now they have, and who is going to be the man of the moment now, as my father was all those years ago? Montezuma? I don't think so. He's too preoccupied with omens and portents to be able to handle anything like this. All he can think of doing is consulting sorcerers over a silly fairy tale about some mythical ancestor of ours. If these strangers were to come to see him he'd run away – he'd find some cave to hide himself in. No, this was going to be my chance. I, Lord Feathered in Black, was going to be the man who made allies or slaves of these strangers and secured the things they brought with them, their weapons and goods, for the people! And who would have talked about Lord Tlacaelel then?'

I said nothing. I could understand his words but not the desire that lay behind them. It seemed to me not much of an ambition to be worth so many lives, simply to be a bigger man than your father.

My master toyed with the smoking-tube before putting it down for the last time.

'It's gone out. They always do, if you leave them,' he said regretfully, as he let it roll across the floor away from him. 'I know Montezuma thinks that I have the sorcerers, or that I know where they are. I know he told you to find them and bring them to him. You know why I can never allow that to happen?'

'Yes, my Lord. They could tell the Emperor that you instructed his major-domo to release them and hand them over to you. And you did that because you couldn't let Montezuma know you had consulted them yourself, about your plans to deal with the strangers on your own account.'

'I have to get those men back, dead or alive. If the only way to do that is to hand you over to the man who stole them from me, then that's what I'll do.' He let that hang in the air for a moment before going on: 'But he's laughing at me. I made a deal with Shining Light, to keep those men in a safe place until I could question them myself. Now I find that Telpochtli duped me and kidnapped Shining Light. He turned one of the sorcerers into a Bathed Slave for sacrifice and left another in the water outside my own house. So I don't just want the sorcerers back – I want this man killed.' My master's grim smile made his mouth look like just another line across his face. 'And as for you, Yaotl – if you don't want me to make a present of you to your enemy, you'd better help me think of a way of finding him!'

So my master wanted to shed still more blood. I might well have killed Telpochtli myself if I had the chance, but my sudden urge to be sick had nothing to do with the beating I had had or the tobacco I had smoked.

I forced myself to think.

'The only person who I know is in contact with him is the merchant's mother, Lily,' I said. 'She was hoping that if she could tell the boy, Nimble, enough about me, her son would be released . . .'

'He wasn't. She's still saying he's abroad.'

'Then she must still be talking to the boy. I thought that by going to see her I could offer myself as bait – I could get Telpochtli to come to me.'

'And it worked. He did!'

'Yes – nearly killing me in the process. Besides,' I added ruefully, 'thanks to your steward, I'd be even less able to resist him now.'

My master regarded me thoughtfully. 'You'll be over that in a few days. It's not as if you're going anywhere! But anyway, it wouldn't do to let you go on your own.' His chair creaked as he sat back, with his eyes closed and the fingers of one hand drumming thoughtfully on his knee.

I had to try to think faster than he could.

It was too much to hope he would let me go anywhere alone: he would assume that I intended to run away the first chance I got. The idea of repeating my attempt to lure Telpochtli out of hiding through Lily obviously appealed to him, but if he had his way I would have an escort of his own choosing – and in all likelihood neither Telpochtli nor I would survive the encounter.

I had to find a way of arranging the meeting so that old Black Feathers could not control the outcome, and I could have some chance of getting away.

'My Lord,' I said slowly, 'could the merchants be prevailed upon to hold a banquet?'

He opened his eyes and frowned. 'A banquet?'

'If you tell Lily and her father to give one, they will. You are always invited to the merchants' feasts. I would be in your retinue – and there would be enough of us to catch Telpochtli if he tried anything.' Not to mention, I thought privately, enough other people to enable me to hide in the crowd and make my own escape. It was not much of a plan, but it was all I could come up with.

'A banquet.' A dreamy look came into the Chief Minister's eyes. 'I like it. After all that family's put me through, I think a good meal is the least they can offer me!'

THIRTEEN SNAKE

1

'I have to wear this?'

'As long as you're part of h.s Lordship's retinue, yes,' the steward snarled. 'I don't know what you're complaining about. It's better than the rags you usually go about in.'

I might have pointed out that those rags were what the steward himself issued me with, but I saved my breath. I was still smarting from my formal admonishment, the tedious diatribe that recorded all my shortcomings as a slave and was meant to set me on the road to a Flowery Death. This was not a good day to answer the steward back, and so I contented myself with looking gloomily down at my skirt of rustling feathers and mumbling something about my master surely wanting me to look inconspicuous.

'Put your nose-plug in. You will look inconspicuous. This is a gathering of the rich and famous – the merchants and the chief warriors. If you walk around in a torn cloak and a soiled loincloth, you'll stick out like a Huaxtec's knob in a harem.'

As soon as he had stopped fussing over me I stumped off to find Handy.

During my brief absence the commoner seemed to have become a member of the household, running some of the errands that would otherwise have been mine. He had a stolid, reliable air that my master seemed to like. He was not

afraid of the steward: while I lay in my room, recovering
from my injuries and strictly forbidden from going anywhere, he had made a point of seeking me out, despite the
Prick's warning not to come near me. He had been anxious
to explain that he had had no idea the steward would come
for him the day he found me at his house.

'His Lordship had some message he wanted got to Shining
Light, and I'm the only one he trusts to carry them . . .'

'All right, what happened wasn't your fault,' I had said
absently. 'The messages were for Shining Light, then? How
did you get them to him?'

'I didn't give them to him in person. I left them at his
house.'

That was convenient, I had thought: it meant Lily was
still the only person who was in touch with her son, or his
kidnappers.

When I had asked Handy what had become of Ehecatl
and my brother, he had answered me with a grin. 'Don't
worry. Star took care of them.'

'What do you mean?'

'While the steward was occupied with you, she hid them
both in the same maize bin.'

That was when I had smiled, for the first time in what
had seemed like an age, at the image of Lion spitting husks
and oaths as he emerged from a dusty wooden bin, to the
sound of Star's helpless laughter.

My master had chosen Handy to accompany us to the
banquet. I had managed to persuade old Black Feathers that
a large armed guard would simply scare our quarry off,
besides upsetting the merchants; in any event, I had pointed
out, there would be enough warriors among the guests.

The commoner's costume was as ludicrous as mine,
although he was more stoical about it.

'He doesn't spare any expense, his Lordship, does he?' he said admiringly.

'What do you know? This is cheap stuff.'

That was unfair: our skirts might be only of heron feathers, our mantles of grackle feathers stitched onto rabbit's fur and the bands encircling our wrists and ankles of leather rather than ocelot skin, but the workmanship was flawless. I could hardly complain if my master, not about to be upstaged by his servants, kept the quetzal plumes and jade labret to himself.

Lord Feathered in Black's own outfit was resplendent. He had opted for a bright blue cape with a butterfly pattern, over a breechcloth with little butterflies done in gold at the ends. His arm- and calf-bands were gold, and in one of the armbands was set a turquoise. Jade ear- and nose-plugs set off his labret. The whole was topped by a headdress of red spoonbill feathers, with long, soft, blue-green quetzal plumes flaring from it, shimmering in the sunlight as he stepped into the canoe behind us.

As we settled ourselves in our master's canoe, he drew a heavy cape around him, to protect his finery and ward off the night's cold.

'Pochtlan,' he said to the boatman.

Thirteen Snake was not the most propitious day for a feast, but it was not bad: the auguries told us it would probably not rain, none of the diners was likely to choke on a turkey bone and the honeyed mushrooms ought to make the guests mellow rather than pugnacious. Certainly, I thought as the boatman poled us slowly through the city, the gods were playing their part: the whitewashed walls on either side of us glowed warmly in the setting sun, while above them only the frailest wisps of cloud clung to the mountain tops. It was a beautiful evening.

Old Black Feathers was in a chatty mood. 'This will be a good night. I haven't looked forward to a party so much in years. I might even dance.'

I hoped not. I was carrying the gilded drum device that he would wear on his back if he did dance, and the image of this glittering and flashing behind him as he stumbled arthritically through the steps filled me with horror. I suspected, though, that when the time came and the mushrooms had begun their work he was more likely to retire inside the house with a cup of chocolate, to swap visions with the other old men.

'Who will be there, my Lord?' asked Handy.

'Oh, everyone. All the chief merchants, of course, the Governor of Tlatelolco, his deputy, and a lot of the high officials – including your brother, Yaotl. They always make a point of inviting the Guardian of the Waterfront.'

I wondered whether my master had any idea how deeply Lion hated him. 'Everyone always makes a point of inviting my brother everywhere. He probably hasn't paid for a meal since he was appointed to his rank, unless he was giving a banquet himself.' I turned to Handy. 'Look, all this means is that Lily and Kindly are desperate to repair the damage Shining Light's done to their family name, not to mention their parish. When the Chief Minister politely suggested holding a feast, even at three days' notice, they weren't in a position to argue. They've probably lavished their last wealth on it, and the place will still be full of people who are ready to kill them. If you want my advice, don't eat anything, and drink all the chocolate you can hold to keep yourself alert.'

My master smiled benignly. Either he approved of my advice or he really was looking forward to the evening.

*

'A shield flower, my Lord. A stick flower, my Lord.'

'Thank you,' the Chief Minister replied graciously, as well he might since the man offering the gifts was no servant but, as was customary at a feast, a seasoned warrior. Holding his tobacco bowl delicately by its rim, my master passed it back to Handy before taking the flowers. The vast yellow sunflower he held in his left hand, like a shield, while the spray of frangipani was known as the 'stick flower' because it was taken in the right like a weapon.

'Lovely,' he murmured, sniffing contentedly at the frangipani as he joined the throng in the courtyard.

The veterans ignored Handy and me, looking straight through us at their next honoured guests as we hastened in our master's footsteps.

Lily had filled her house with a scintillating crowd. Gold, jade and amber lip-plugs flashed as their wearers turned to speak to new arrivals. Red, yellow, blue and above all green feathers nodded in time to words spoken in muted, well-bred voices. Capes of every colour – blue here, tawny there, carmine there – billowed against each other. These were the great of Tlatelolco, and not a few of Tenochtitlan's finest as well: merchants, able for once to show off their wealth, and warriors, here to remind the merchants that they could take that wealth off them whenever they chose.

Barely forty years had passed since the ancestors of those warriors had stormed into the the northern part of Mexico's island, driving Tlatelolco's last king off the top of his tallest pyramid and installing a military governor in his place. That governor's successor was here among the guests tonight. To watch him chatting genially to the chief merchants, it was hard to see him as a symbol of their formal subjection to Montezuma, but the signs of it were there if you cared to look. The merchants had all dressed down in subtle ways, so

as not to upstage him. So their quetzal feathers were from
the wing rather than the tail, their labrets of plain gold rather
than amber or jade, and their cloaks, although made of
cotton, bore simple flower designs instead of serpent masks,
shells, butterflies or eagles. And Lily would have ordered
the servers – again, veterans chosen for their prowess rather
than their daintiness, although they bore their baskets of
tamales and bowls of source gracefully enough – to be particularly attentive to the Governor, his deputy and the other
dignitaries.

Ostensibly, Handy and I were there to keep an eye on
these servers as they patrolled the edges of the crowd, in
case our master was tempted by some titbit. I was more
interested in the guests, though. It was easier to look at their
feet than their faces, and my eyes roamed the freshly strewn
earth on the floor in the hope of seeing, among the calloused, sandalled feet of the merchants and the warriors
and their cloaks' embroidered borders, a more delicate
ankle, the hem of a skirt or the tasselled fringe of a woman's
mantle.

In fact there were several women among the guests. Some
were merchants' wives, accompanying their husbands or
standing in for them, and some were there in their own
right, as directors of the marketplace. Whenever I furtively
raised my glance from their feet to their faces, however, I was
disappointed. There was no sign of Lily among them.

I had tried to plan what I would say to her if we met, but
the words would not come. From my master's point of view
it scarcely mattered: if she saw me here then, hopefully, she
would tell Nimble and then Telpochtli would come after
me, and that was all his Lordship wanted. But what did I
want?

I imagined myself accusing her of letting my enemy into

her house to try to kill me, reproaching her for betraying me, demanding to know whether the night we had spent together had meant anything or nothing. I pictured the hurt in her eyes, her head turned quickly away to hide it, the silver streaks in her hair catching the light.

Then I pictured her looking at me blankly, curling her lip in indifference or amused contempt, or laughing out loud.

'You're a fool, Yaotl,' I told myself.

'You've got that bloody right,' rasped a voice I knew very well indeed. 'Come here!'

A hand like an alligator's jaws clamped itself on my arm. 'Now you can stand still for a moment. I'm tired of wandering around after you.'

'Hello, brother,' I sighed. 'I didn't recognize you dressed up like that.'

Lion was his old self again. His cloak was brand new, the cloth still a little stiff and dyed a yellow even brighter than the sunflower in his left hand. His freshly trimmed hair was bound up immaculately and a splendid plug of green stone shaped like an eagle and set in gold jutted from his lower lip. His expression was ferocious.

'Don't try to be funny. What are you doing here?'

'You'll have to let go of my arm,' I pointed out. 'It doesn't belong to either of us.'

After a brief glance at my master, Lion did as I suggested. 'I assume you're here under orders? Still looking for your master's precious sorcerers?'

'Of course.'

My brother snorted derisively. 'What does old Black Feathers expect to learn from this lot? No one ever says anything useful at parties like this. I don't know why anyone bothers with them – they always make me want to throw up!'

His vehemence surprised me, but it was easy to forget that for all his status as a great warrior Lion had been born in the same room as I had, and unlike me he had not been schooled alongside nobles in the Priest House. Lion's home, as the midwife would have told him the day he was born, was on the battlefield, not in some merchant's courtyard making small talk about the price of cacao and how hard it was to get a cook who knew anything about armadillos.

'Well,' I said, 'it looks as if your hosts agree with you, since neither Kindly nor Lily seems to be here.'

'He'll be preparing for the sacrifice,' Lion reminded me. 'Either that, or he's already too drunk to care. As for her, someone told me she'd been taken ill and had retired to the women's rooms. Maybe she heard you were coming!'

'You still haven't told me what you're doing here.'

'I heard old Black Feathers would be here.' The way he spat the name out left me in no doubt about his feelings. 'I've a score to settle with that bastard, after what he made me and my men do in Coyoacan.'

I looked at him in alarm. 'You're never planning to . . .'

'I just want to keep my eye on him, that's all. If it was your master who got those sorcerers out of the prison and then lost them, then I want to be there when he finds them again. I want to make sure at least one of them gets back to Montezuma alive, to tell him exactly what his Chief Minister's been up to!'

I groaned. 'Oh, no, Lion, don't . . .'

'So, Yaotl, you're going to have to make your mind up, aren't you? Are you with me and the Emperor – or your master?'

I was spared the need to answer by a disturbance in the crowd around us. I turned quickly, half expecting to see Lily emerging into the courtyard to greet her guests, but it was only a server, bearing a bowl of steaming chocolate. Others followed him, carrying gourds and gourd rests and stirring sticks, and suddenly the air was filled with the smell of chocolate and nutmeg and an appreciative silence.

After the chocolate came the sacrifices.

The most important guest at the feast was one who never made a personal appearance. Huitzilopochtli the war-god must still have his flowers and tobacco, however, presented by his host on the altars at Huitznahuac, Yopico, Tlamatzinco and Pochtlan. The whole party had to go in procession from one parish to another, stopping at each of the small pyramids to watch Kindly mount the steps with his arms full of the god's fragrant gifts. I wondered how the old man would fare, but he seemed to take the long-accustomed ritual in his stride, holding his head erect as he hobbled up the pyramids' sides and conversing briefly with the priests before laying his offerings in the Eagle Vessel.

The fifth place where flowers and tobacco were offered was back at the house in Pochtlan, in front of the huge ground drum that had been set up in the middle of the courtyard in preparation for the dancing.

Most of the guests had seen and heard the ceremony many times, and they carried on their conversations in the room behind us, leaving Handy and me with an uninterrupted view.

'No sign of the lady, yet,' I said under my breath to Handy.

'Do you suppose she's done a runner?' he asked.

'She's meant to be in there.' I nodded across the deserted courtyard towards where I knew the women's rooms were. I was still trying to think of a way to sneak in there when the whistling began.

The shrill sound came from the musicians and the professional dancers, who put their fingers to their lips to summon the host. Then someone said, 'The master, Our Lord, has spoken,' and suddenly there, in the courtyard, were Kindly, looking not at all out of breath after climbing four pyramids in quick succession, and the black-robed, black-faced figure of the offering priest.

The priest bore a smoking incense ladle and Kindly had a live quail. As they approached the ground drum the ladle was carefully set down, next to the flowers and the still-smoking tobacco tubes, and the quail handed from one man to the other. Swiftly the priest pulled the bird's head off and threw its still flapping body to the ground.

Both men bent over it, intent on its death throes.

'It mustn't go north,' I whispered. 'East, south or west are all right, but north is an omen of evil.'

It seemed a long time before the two men in the courtyard stood up. They were between us and the offering, and there was nothing to see but a thin trickle of blood in the dust between their feet.

I knew what the priest was going to say before he opened his mouth. I knew it from the way his fists were clenched and the old man seemed to shrink before my eyes.

'There will be a death among your household.'

I let out a long, silent breath.

'North?' mumbled Handy.

'North,' I whispered, wondering whose death the little bird had prophesied in its last spasms.

Now the priest took his incense ladle. He turned towards the east and lifted it four times, and then he did the same for each of the other three directions, west, south and north in turn, before turning back towards the house to cast the burning copal resin into the hearth.

Kindly was left alone in his courtyard, silently contemplating the tiny corpse at his feet.

The warriors danced.

As night fell, to the mournful sound of conch-shell trumpets from the tops of the pyramids, the Food of the Gods was served: little mushrooms coated in honey to disguise their bitter taste. After that, there would be no other food till morning, and no need for any, although the chocolate would continue being whisked and poured.

The Governor came first into the courtyard, followed by his deputy, the other dignitaries including my master and my brother, the mighty warriors – Shorn Ones and Otomies – and last of all the veterans, the masters of youth, the eagle and the ocelot warriors. As the musicians struck up their song and the dancers shuffled into their places, some already had a detached, faraway look that showed the mushrooms were taking effect.

Fuelled by chocolate and mushrooms, most of the dancers would keep going all night. In their own minds, each one would be a proud, graceful, sinuous youth dancing on air to music made by gods. None would see himself staggering drunkenly about, hear himself giggling inanely or notice that none of his neighbours seemed to be following the same tune as he was. I was relieved when my master fell out before the dancing began, to retire indoors to the comfort of a reed mat and whatever magical dreams the gods sent his way.

The merchants did not dance. They sat at the edges of the courtyard, looking on and conversing quietly among themselves. Around them were spread the presents they would give out later, to any of their guests still capable of recognizing them: still more flowers and smoking-tubes, feathers,

paper garlands, turquoise mosaics and cloth treated with
mica to make it shine.

It occurred to me that, if I ran away now, probably
nobody would miss me before the morning. But where
would I go? I had asked myself this question before and
failed to find an answer. There was nowhere I could think of
making a home other than Mexico, and nowhere in Mexico
would be safe for long once my master woke up and found
I had deserted him a second time. And those two images of
Lily's face, the one shocked and hurt by my words, the other
indifferent, still haunted me, and would go on doing so until
I found out which was real.

Besides, with the merchants lining its perimeter and the
dancers gyrating in its centre, there was no straight way
across the courtyard to the street. It was going to be difficult
enough finding my way to the women's rooms. I had to slip
through whatever gaps I could find, trying to blend into the
background as well as my bizarre costume would allow, and
hoping that Kindly, at least, would not see me walking right
in front of him.

Half blind as he was, he probably would not have recognized me if one of the dancers had not wandered into
my path, forcing me to step quickly aside and put my foot
in the middle of the neatly ordered display in front of
him.

'I'm sorry. Excuse me,' I blurted unthinkingly.

'Hello, Yaotl,' the familiar old cracked voice responded.
He had recognized my voice and I had no choice but to
return his greeting.

'Kindly. You're not drinking tonight, then?'

Twilight gave his filmy eyes a pale gleam.

'At my own banquet?' He sounded shocked. 'How could
I? Besides, I have to sacrifice to Yacatecuhtli at midnight –

need a clear head for that. And before you ask, I'm not on the mushrooms either. Bloody things give me the runs.'

So he and I were probably the only completely sober people in the house.

'If you were looking for my daughter,' he went on, 'I shouldn't bother. She won't see you.'

I looked towards the women's rooms. They were dark, but who might be stirring in there? 'I'd rather like her to tell me that herself.'

'A man going into the women's rooms, uninvited? In the middle of a feast? And a slave, to boot? Unheard of!' He did not raise his voice, but there was an edge to it that told me I would get no closer to Lily before I was stopped. I remembered the burly warriors who had been recruited as servers for the evening. Part of the reason they were there was to break up any mushroom-induced fights among the guests, and any of them would have been more than equal to the task of subduing one scrawny slave.

His tone softened a little as he asked: 'Why did you come here, Yaotl?'

'To ask your daughter to help us find Misty,' I said, and then added, 'And to ask her why she helped him when he tried to kill me.'

'And would you believe her if she said she did not?'

'I don't know. I think that's why I have to ask.'

His answer seemed to come from a long way away. 'No one in this house bears you any ill will.'

I glanced down at him again, but he was not looking at me any more.

'Please don't try to see my daughter.' His eyes were fixed on her doorway. 'It would only distress her further, and there is nothing she can tell you – believe me.' He looked up again and smiled weakly. 'Besides, she's still in semi-mourning. Do you know she can only wash her hair once every eighty days until Shining Light returns? She won't want to be seen by anybody right now!'

'All right.' I turned to go. 'I'm sorry about your sacrifice,' I added over my shoulder, as an afterthought.

The old man's dry, cackling laugh surprised me. 'My family is having a bad run, isn't it? It probably means nothing . . . Oh, Yaotl, don't sulk! Look, I have a present for you.'

'Save it,' I said dismissively, with a look that took in all the riches spread around him. 'I'm a slave, remember? You need this to buy off your friends, the warriors.'

'No I don't! This stuff is a token. They expect us to lay it out here just to show we haven't forgotten who's in charge. When the warriors really want something from us, they ask for it in advance and we give it in private. Look – you should take something. The rest of them will just pillage it otherwise, and when they get it home they'll have no idea where it came from or why they took it. So why not? These feathers, now – they're my family's particular speciality. Why not take a bunch?'

Against my will I found myself accepting the bundle of long red feathers that he pressed into my hand.

'They're very soft.' I felt I had to say something about them. 'What are they, red spoonbill?'

'No, scarlet macaw.' He grinned up at me, as proud as a small boy who had just caught a frog. 'They're good, though, aren't they? Where do you think they came from?'

'I don't know.' I wanted to give the feathers back, but the moment for doing that had passed as quickly as it had come. 'The far South – Xoconochco, maybe?'

Kindly chuckled. 'Nearly. That was where we got the idea, but we grow them ourselves.'

I had a wild vision of a family sustaining itself on feathers sprouting from its members' own rumps, until I realized what it was Kindly had meant.

'Really?' I was fascinated in spite of myself. 'You mean you keep the birds here? How come I never saw or heard them?' Plenty of people kept finches, little twittering creatures that were quite at home hanging from the sides of houses in wicker cages. Parrots, I thought, must be a different matter. It would be hard to keep a parrot without the whole parish knowing about it.

'They went the same way as the rest of the merchandise,' he said bitterly. 'So where they are now, only the gods and my grandson's boyfriend know. But it was useful having them close at hand: it meant we could pluck a flight or a tail feather whenever the feather-workers needed one, and we saved ourselves all the effort of catching the birds and then packing the feathers and sending them home.'

I examined the bunch of feathers in my hand. In the twilight their rich, dark red reminded me of dried blood. 'I thought the only person in the city who kept these birds was Montezuma.'

'Oh, I expect he has a houseful. And good luck to him! They're almost more trouble than they're worth. Of course, having live birds to pluck feathers from is a good idea, and apart from the fact that they eat their cages they're not hard to keep, but . . .' His talk dissolved into a rueful chuckle.

'The noise?' I offered.

'It's worse than noise,' he confided. 'They talk!'

I had an odd sensation in the pit of my stomach. 'Talk?'

'Why, yes. You can train them to talk, but . . . Hey! Where are you going?'

I ran, darting this way and that to avoid the hurtling bodies of the dancers, looking for my brother.

2

I stared into the jostling, swirling crowd, but in the gathering gloom there was no way of telling the dancers apart. I took a deep breath and yelled at the top of my voice, to be heard above the drums, the flutes, the conch-shell trumpets and the stamping feet.

'Lion!'

None of the dancers even missed a beat. I was torn between relief and frustration. None of the assembled warriors seemed to have heard me, but where was my brother when I needed him?

I took another breath, but it caught in my throat as a man fell out of the crowd.

At first he did not seem to know which way was up, but in the few seconds he took to reach my side he had recovered enough to walk in a straight line and stand upright without swaying much.

'What?' Lion demanded, as I led the way indoors, out of the way of the gyrating bodies in the courtyard. We found ourselves in the same room as the Chief Minister, but, judging by the way his chin was bouncing on his chest, his mind was somewhere else. There had obviously been enough mushrooms left over for Handy too, since his head was moving in vague circles and he was dribbling.

'I've found the sorcerers.'

'That's more like it! Let's pick them up and get out of here. Where are they?'

'On a boat! Telpochtli and his son must be holding them there. The sorcerers trained a bird to call for help, though, and let it go . . .'

My brother stared at me suspiciously. Beads of sweat glistened on his brow and his breathing was shallow, but otherwise he seemed in command of himself. 'Have you been at the mushrooms?'

'No! Look, you remember what that offering of Shining Light's said, before he died, about a big boat? Everyone thought it was a prophecy – something to do with those pyramids on canoes the Emperor told us about – but it wasn't! He was just trying to tell us where he and the others had been held. He wanted to tell my master, because he knew old Black Feathers was looking for them, and he thought he would save them from Telpochtli. I'm so stupid, I didn't realize it until just now, when Shining Light's grandfather told me his family breeds birds. Big birds with red tail feathers – birds that can be trained to talk, Lion! And I saw one on the lake, that day I was kidnapped by Telpochtli and Nimble!' I groaned as I realized where I had seen signs of the bird, or others like it, since then: displayed among the stakes at the ball court, right in front of where Nimble and I had been sitting, and on the pitch at Tlatelolco market where Telpochtli had accosted me: the pitch belonging to Shining Light's family. 'The sorcerers must have been coaching the birds and they managed to let them go, or they got away, while Telpochtli and his boy were out abducting me. And it was the boat they were being held on, the big boat, that I came up under when I fell out of Telpochtli's canoe, only I didn't realize it at the time: I must have swum further under the water than I thought. That's where Telpochtli's warehouse is. It's not a big roomy place in the merchant's parish. It's in some sort of narrow, confined space where you'd have to use a knife if you wanted to kill someone because there's no room to wield a sword. It's a shelter on the deck of a boat, out on the lake!'

'If you can tell me where the boat is,' said a low voice that was like cold water trickling down my spine, 'I will owe you more than my life.'

Lion whirled as if he were still dancing. I turned around slowly.

Lily stood facing us in the doorway. Her eyes shone in the torchlight. I noted from the heavy rabbit's-fur mantle drawn tightly across her shoulders that she had been out, and not hiding in the women's rooms after all.

My tongue seemed to have turned into a lump of wood. All evening I had been seeking this confrontation and now it had come I could not get the words out. In the end I managed to say 'Lily' in a voice so thick the name was barely intelligible.

Lion recognized it, though. 'Lily? You're Shining Light's mother? Yaotl here reckons your son's boyfriend's holding a lot of sorcerers prisoner on his boat!'

My brother was not known for his delicacy of manner. Another woman – another man, for the matter of that – might have gone into hysterics. Lily just looked at me levelly. 'He's not my son's . . . Yaotl, you said that to me once, but you were wrong. Shining Light wouldn't be interested in Misty – not in that way, anyway. Whatever that man's hold is over my son, it's not that. He . . .' She caught her breath before going on. 'Shining Light likes them younger – he's more likely to have wanted the boy. I think Shining Light may have done the father's bidding for the sake of the son, at least in the beginning. I don't know. I've never met Misty.'

'Nor has anyone else, except me,' I said drily. I felt a

sudden rush of self-pity. 'Telpochtli doesn't go near anyone else − you, my master, Kindly − he sends the boy to see everyone else, but I've met him three times − and each time he's done his best to kill me!'

'Is he still holding your son hostage?' my brother asked.

Lily hid her face in her hands and stood for a few heart-beats with her shoulders heaving silently. Then she took a deep breath and looked at us both, blinking rapidly.

'I told the boy what you told me, Yaotl − about the girl in the marketplace. He said . . . he said it wouldn't be enough.'

'Go on,' I said grimly.

'That was the evening of the day you told me about the girl. He said I would have to . . . that his father would come to the house the next day, and . . .'

'And you had to tell the slave to let him in. You let that bastard in to attack me! I nearly died! Constant did die!'

'Do you think I don't know that?' she cried. 'The boy didn't tell me he meant you any harm. He just said there was something he had to know. My son's life was at stake!'

'So was mine!'

'Yaotl,' my brother warned me, in his best imitation of a soothing voice.

'And where were you?' I yelled. 'Couldn't bear to watch, is that it?'

She seemed to flinch, as if I had slapped her, before screaming back: 'Where do you think? I was trying to find my son! The boy told me to go back to the ball court in the morning, and I'd find him there, only' − her voice suddenly turned into a long, descending wail − 'he wasn't there!'

I wondered why that was. Perhaps my would-be assassin, piqued by his failure, had managed, in his flight from her house to the ball court, to overtake Shining Light's mother, and had got her son back on board his boat, hoping the young merchant might still be useful if he wanted to make another attempt on my life. It was more likely that Telpochtli had never intended to honour the bargain Lily had made for her son's freedom, and she had set out that morning on a fool's errand. As much as I resented what she had done I felt a twinge of pity.

'Lily,' I began gently, but Lion interrupted me.

'Before you two wake the Chief Minister up, let me see if I've got this straight. You're saying we have to look for a boat – a big one?'

'That's right,' I replied.

'Where do we start, then?'

'It was in a cove on the western side of the city,' I said, 'but that was days ago. They may have moved it since then.'

'So it could be anywhere on the lake? On any of the lakes?' Lily's voice was low with disappointment. Telpochtli had chosen his hiding place well: finding one craft among the many thousands plying the vast complex of lakes around the city could be almost impossible.

'What does this boat look like?' Lion asked me.

'I don't know. I scarcely saw it – I was busy being kidnapped at the time, remember.' I thought for a moment. 'If it's being used as a warehouse, it must be unusually big – like one of those seagoing craft the Mayans have, carved from a whole trunk, or even several lashed together. And that means it won't move very far or very fast – especially if it's just Telpochtli and his boy handling it. I don't think there's anyone else working with them.' I glanced at Lily, who did not demur.

My brother gave her a shrewd look. 'Madam,' he asked, his tone carefully polite, 'did you report to the boy this evening?'

'Sir – of course I did!' she snapped back defiantly. 'I had

to tell him Yaotl was here.' She caught my expression. 'Oh, don't worry – he won't come here tonight. There are too many people about.' So much for my plan to lure Telpochtli out of hiding, I thought.

'You must have had a pre-arranged meeting place.'

'Yes. On the Tlacopan causeway, at the nearer end. He's there regularly, at dusk, in case I need to report anything. I have to get there before they pull the bridges up, though.'

Lion and I looked at each other, the same calculations running through both our heads. If Telpochtli and Nimble lived on the boat – and how else could they guard their hostages? – then the boy must return to it every night. But if he needed the bridges open, that meant he had to cross the causeway. So the boat could only be moored on the western side of the lake, opposite the city, not far from the mainland end of the causeway.

'What do you do if you're late?' I asked.

'I don't see him at all that evening. I'd have to wait until the following night, unless we've arranged something else, like the ball court.'

'So he has to be on the other side of the causeway by nightfall.'

'There are lots of little inlets and places you could hide a boat on the edge of the lake,' Lion pointed out. 'How would we know where to look, especially if he keeps moving about?'

'But he won't move the boat every day,' I said, 'and I don't think Nimble would want to go blundering around there after dark. There can't be that many places close enough to the causeway where you could hide a boat that big.'

'We need a boatman to tell us where to look,' Lion observed. 'Where are we going to find one at this time of night?'

I stared at him. 'What do you mean, "at this time of

night"? No one's going anywhere now. Send a squad of warriors first thing in the morning.'

'No time,' said my brother. 'We've got to get to those sorcerers before your master does.'

'We have to go now,' said Lily quietly.

I stared at them both.

The woman rounded on me. 'Didn't you hear about the prophecy this evening? Someone in my household is going to die! And my son is on that boat! We have to go now!'

'But you can't go!' I protested. 'This is men's work – warriors' work!'

'My son is on that boat,' she repeated. She turned on her heel and walked away. 'You can do what you like. I'm going to find a boatman!'

'Come on,' Lion said as he set off after her.

I had taken one step towards the doorway when a familiar voice stopped us all in our tracks.

'Not so fast! Just where do you think you're going?'

Lord Feathered in Black was sitting up. He had obviously been awake for some time, and was now bright and alert. I could only admire the way the old man could handle his mushrooms: his eyes were rolling slightly but the set of his mouth was as firm as ever.

Lily glared defiantly at him. Lion and I looked at each other the way two small boys might if they were caught stealing squashes.

'So my sorcerers are on a boat, are they?' my master gloated as he rose, a little unsteadily, from his seat. 'Let's go and pick them up, then!'

We made a strange party, all looking for the same things – a boatman and a boat, to take us to where the sorcerers were – but at odds over what we would do if we found them. We worked our way along the landing stage outside Lily's house in a wary silence, while the noises of the banquet faded behind us and the water lapped loudly in the space under our feet.

Finding a boatman turned out to be as easy as finding a boat. Some of Lily's guests, including my master, had sent their canoes home, but others had left theirs tied up against the landing stage. Many of their crews had been left as well, to wait with their charges until their masters were ready for them some time after daybreak. Most had curled up and gone to sleep in the bottom of their boats, but we eventually found one awake.

He sat gazing up at the stars, as well he might. It was a clear winter's night and the sky was ablaze. He seemed oblivious to our approach until he had my master standing next to him.

'We need this boat,' Lord Feathered in Black told him bluntly.

The man almost fell in. He was still recovering himself as the rest of us gathered around my master, holding onto the jetty with one hand as he tried to stop the canoe swaying under him.

'What do you mean, you need the boat? You can't have it, it isn't yours! Who do you think you are, the Emperor?'

'Almost,' said his Lordship drily. 'Handy, bring that torch over here.'

Handy was approximately sober. Before we had left the house Lion and I had poured four cups full of strong honeyed chocolate down his throat. My brother had suggested tipping a fifth over his head, but there had been no need. At least he was capable of speech and had not stumbled into the canal, and the torch we had borrowed swayed only a little as he held it over the Chief Minister's headdress.

The boatman made an inarticulate noise.

'If this boat belongs to my cousin, the Emperor,' my master went on pleasantly, 'then I will apologize to him personally in the morning. If it doesn't, then it's mine!'

'But it's the middle of the night!' the poor man protested. 'You can't go anywhere in the dark!'

'Nonsense! The merchants travel by night all the time!'

The boatman went quiet. At night a woman's voice heard out of doors was as likely as not to be a portent. She might be the goddess Cihuacoatl, or the soul of a dead mother returned to Earth to haunt the streets and bring sickness to men, or one of those hideous hunchbacked dwarfs that would accost a man visiting the latrines after dark to tell him he was about to die. Lily was none of these, but the boatman did not know that.

The next voice he heard was Lion's. 'If you won't do it for the Chief Minister,' he growled, 'then you can do it for me. I'm the Guardian of the Waterfront. Either you do what you're told or I'll cut your legs off!'

The man slumped miserably in the bottom of his boat. 'All right. Tell me where you want to go, but you'll need another boat – this is a one-man job.'

'Fine.' My master lurched into the canoe and installed himself in the bow. 'Lily can come with us, she doesn't weigh much. Bring the torch.'

'We'd better get in the next boat,' I said, as Handy gave the woman the torch.

'It's empty,' protested Lion. I raced along the line of moored canoes until I found one with a boatman in it, but the man was fast asleep and snoring resoundingly.

'Hurry up!' cried my master, as Lily settled herself in his boat. His boatman, probably eager to put some distance between himself and my brother, pushed off from the jetty immediately.

I ran back to join Handy and Lion.

'They're getting away!' My brother's tone was anguished. 'We'll never rouse another boatman in time to catch them up.'

'Then we'll have to do without', I said. 'We'll take this one. Handy, you can paddle a canoe, can't you?'

Once we had cleared the last of the canals and reached the open water of the lake we turned left, following the glint of torchlight in front of us until the Chief Minister, Lily and their boatman reached the causeway. There they stopped.

As we drew alongside it became plain that something had got them excited. We could hear raised voices and see the boatman's paddle waving uncertainly in the air as he tried to make his point.

'What's up?' Lion called out.

Lily answered. 'This man thinks he knows the boat we're looking for!'

'If it's the boat with the birds,' the boatman replied, 'then everyone on the water knows it. Anyone could have told you, if you'd asked, and they'd have told you to give it a wide berth, too! I'm not going anywhere near it. There's no telling what would happen!'

'I can tell you exactly what will happen if you don't go on,' my master snapped. 'What are you afraid of, anyway?'

In a low voice, the man said: 'Sorcery.'

'Aha!' cried his Lordship triumphantly. 'We've found them!'

'What do you mean by sorcery?' I asked.

'There are sorcerers on that boat. You can tell, because they can change themselves into birds and fly away. I haven't seen it myself, but I know people who have. And why isn't it moored near the city, instead of tucked away in a creek by

itself? And strange sounds have been heard from it – horrible sounds, like men screaming.'

Lily sat impassively, holding the torch up unwaveringly as
she listened.

'How do you know the birds are sorcerers?' I asked.
'How do you know they aren't just birds?'

'They talk,' the boatman said in a hushed voice.

3

The surface of the lake was like polished obsidian, the stars' reflections, broken by ripples, as enigmatic as the shadows that would rise and fall in an obsidian mirror.

There were no voices or footsteps on the causeway and no paddles except ours broke the water around us.

The light from Lily's torch fell on the raised side of the causeway, throwing into relief the stones set into the wall. Since we had caught up with his Lordship's party, his boatman had been less eager than ever and Handy had no difficulty keeping up with him.

'You're on the wrong side of the causeway, for a start,' the boatman had pointed out sulkily.

'That's all right,' my master had responded blithely. 'The bridges are all raised at night. We'll pass through at the last one. We'd better cut across the lake and head straight for your creek after that. I've no intention of explaining myself to the warriors in the guard post at the end of the causeway.'

'Suppose we find Telpochtli's boat,' I had said, thinking it was high time somebody asked an obvious question, 'what do you propose to do then?'

'We'll make him come quietly, or we'll kill him. The boy too.'

'No!' My cry of protest had burst out of me before I had time to think about it. To the five shocked faces that turned towards me, I had explained: 'You can't just murder the lad out of hand. You don't know what he's done – maybe he couldn't help it, maybe his father forced him into it!' I had turned to my brother for support. 'The sorcerers – what about the sorcerers?'

The torchlight had thrown Lion's face into sharp relief, casting deep shadows that made it look like a bare skull and about as easy to read. His eyes had glittered like jewels in the flickering light as he looked from my master to me. 'We'll take the sorcerers – the ones that are left – and put them back where they belong: in prison. That's right – isn't it, my Lord? Those were Montezuma's orders.'

There had been a long, uncomfortable silence then, before my master had finally pronounced: 'It all depends on what we find when we get there. I will decide then!'

'And my son?'

Lily had still been holding the torch steady in the Chief Minister's canoe. Her hand had trembled slightly, shaking loose a few embers that had spiralled slowly into the water.

'It all depends,' my master had repeated gruffly.

Now Lion, Handy and I sat in silence as we watched the causeway slide by and waited for a dark interval to appear, revealing the last bridge and the place where we were to cross to the southern side.

Handy said: 'I still don't understand what Shining Light's doing on that boat. I thought he was on a trading venture. I saw him leave. He had a canoe full of provisions. It was One Reed, remember, and you thought it was a funny day to be off on a long journey.'

'I suppose the provisions were for Telpochtli, the boy and the sorcerers,' I said.

'Which means,' my brother pointed out, 'that whenever the merchant and his boyfriend – or his boyfriend's father, whatever – had their falling out, it must have been after that, mustn't it? Shining Light would hardly have delivered himself up as a hostage, complete with his own food supply.'

'So what did they have a row about?' Handy asked.

I hesitated while I tried to imagine what might have been going through the merchant's mind. 'I suppose Shining Light was going to lie low for a while, to keep out of the way of the merchants – not to mention the Chief Minister! He told his mother to pretend he'd gone on a trading venture. Maybe that's why you were asked to deliver his message to my master, Handy – so that you could attest to the fact that he was off somewhere with a boat full of provisions, as if he was going on a long journey. In fact he wasn't, but he needed somewhere to hide. The obvious place was Telpochtli's boat. Maybe being cooped up with that vicious young man for a few days was enough to convince Telpochtli and Nimble that he was more useful as a hostage than a guest. Then again . . .'

Then again, I realized, what I had just said was nonsense. Lily had told me that Shining Light had not known where Misty's warehouse was. If that was the truth, then Shining Light could not have delivered himself to Misty – or Telpochtli – willingly or otherwise, because he would not have known where to find him.

If that was the truth.

Lily had no reason to lie to me about that; nor had her father, who had told the same story, accounting for the bare room in their house. But suppose Shining Light had lied to both of them?

As soon as that thought occurred to me, the fabric of the story I had woven together out of the past few days' events began to unravel. Things that I had seen and heard and all but forgotten about came to mind, and each was like a loose thread pulled away from the cloth until there was nothing left of it but the truth.

And I had seen the truth myself, only that evening, without recognizing it. I had even told Lion and Lily about it, without knowing what I was saying.

'We've got it all wrong,' I started to say, but Lion interrupted me.

'Whatever they fell out over, you can ask them both about it soon. Here's the bridge!'

The Chief Minister's boat coasted through the gap in the causeway and then, just as we turned to follow it, it vanished. There was a faint hissing sound as Lily doused the torch in the water of the lake, and then there was nothing to see by but the stars and the water's own eerie phosphorescence.

Trailing his paddle in the water, Handy brought us to a halt next to the other craft.

'It's a creek, a little bit south of Chapultepec.' Although this was still a long pull away by canoe, my master's boatman had taken to whispering. 'When we reach the aqueduct we're almost there. The boat you're looking for is moored in its mouth, a fair distance from the shore.'

'That makes sense,' my brother muttered, 'if he doesn't want the sorcerers slipping overboard and swimming for it. We'll have to get into the creek mouth as quietly as possible and try to get between him and the shore. If Telpochtli or anyone else tries to escape that way we should catch them.'

Lord Feathered in Black silently prodded his boatman with his foot, and the man slowly took up his paddle and dipped it in the water.

'If there's a boat in there, I can't see it,' Lion whispered.

We lay in the bows of the canoe, staring into the tangled darkness that marked the edge of the lake. We dared not stand up, in case our quarry caught sight of us outlined against the stars.

'Are we sure this is the right place?' Handy asked.

'He seems to think so.' I looked over my shoulder at the dark, quiet water behind us, where I assumed my master's boat still floated. 'Our reluctant boatman was happy enough about finding the aqueduct.' The man had uttered a cry of delight, quickly stifled, when the long, low stone structure had emerged out of the darkness, as though he had surprised himself with his own skill. It had taken a long time to get that far, paddling cautiously through the gloom. The final leg of the journey, following the shore line down to the creek mouth where our quarry was supposedly waiting, had been all too short.

'Let's go anyway. I'm tired of waiting.' I spoke through teeth clenched to stop them chattering. I had told myself it was a cold night, although it must have been colder for Handy, because after we had passed Chapultepec he had taken his breechcloth off and wrapped it around his paddle to muffle it.

'If we keep to the middle of the channel,' Handy suggested, 'we ought to find them.' He thrust his paddle into the water and began to push the canoe forward.

A faint splash from behind us told me that the other canoe was on the move as well, but its boatman had not troubled to muffle his paddle, and we could hear its progress clearly as it forged ahead, steering a course wide of our own and much closer to the bank. A fleck of foam, gleaming white in the starlight, showed where the paddle blade dug into the water, tearing its surface and throwing it up as he sped past us.

'What's he doing?' Handy muttered. 'He's far too close to the bank! He's going to run aground if he's not careful!'

'Not to mention the noise he's making,' Lion said.

I suddenly realized what the man was up to. 'He wants to run aground! He's trying to escape!' I was already standing up, making our canoe rock as I strained to see where the other boat was going.

Across the water came a crash and the sound of splintering wood.

The brief silence that followed ended with the beat of heavy wings as some large bird, perhaps a heron, started from its roosting place and took flight across the lake.

'They've hit!' Handy observed.

'Quiet!' I snapped. Had I imagined it, or had there been another sound? Even as I struggled to identify it, however, it was obliterated by curses and recriminations from the direction of the wrecked canoe.

'Old Black Feathers is not happy,' remarked my brother.

'Nor is the lady,' added Handy.

It struck me that the merchants must bring their women up differently from the rest of us, because I was sure my mother had never known some of the words Lily was using. I wondered if she had learned them in the marketplace. I could not hear the boatman's voice at all. I supposed he had made good his escape, leaping overboard as soon as he knew the crash was imminent.

'Well, that's that,' declared Lion. 'Everyone on this side of the lake will know we're here now. We might as well forget it.' He scrambled to his feet to join me in standing unsteadily in the centre of the canoe. 'If Telpochtli was ever here, he'll be on the move. He can hardly have missed that lot . . .'

'Well, shut up, then!'

As Lion lapsed into shocked silence I looked hurriedly around. 'If he's moving, we should be able to hear him!' I explained. 'That's if my master and Lily will be quiet . . . Will you be quiet?' My last words were shouted to be heard over the commotion on the bank.

There was a momentary pause before my master's incredulous voice came back to me, reduced to little more than an outraged croak. 'What did you say?'

'Listen!'

Everybody listened.

'What was that?' asked Handy.

Simultaneously he, Lion and I turned around.

'Splashing,' Lion suggested. 'Is it someone swimming?'

Suddenly we were talking in whispers again. The three of us kept as still as we could with the canoe swaying beneath us, while we peered into the gloom around us, and even the voices from my master's stranded canoe were stilled.

'I can't see . . .' I began.

'What's that?' Handy seized my forearm and tugged it towards where he wanted me to look. 'Did you see?'

Lion joined in. 'Yes! Yes! I see!'

Then I saw it too: a flash of white, like spray driven from the surface of the lake. I saw it again, but the second time there was something else with it: a pale flicker of movement, the sort a bare arm might make, frantically wielding a paddle.

Raising my eyes a little, I saw a dark mass lying in the water, just in front of us and not much more than a spearcast away.

From behind me came the sound of maguey fibre ripping as Handy tore the breechcloth from the blade of his paddle.

'Come on, everybody paddle!' Lion had thrown himself into the bottom of the canoe and was striking the water urgently with his hands, and before I had time to reflect on how pointless this was I was doing it too, drenching myself in clouds of icy spray as I tried my pathetic best to add to our speed.

In no time my arms ached, the feathers of my ludicrous costume were plastered to my thighs and despite my exertions I was trembling with cold. My hands and feet were going numb and yet the strange, dark boat ahead of us seemed to get no nearer. My head began to spin and I closed my eyes for a moment to clear it.

When I opened them again, the boat was on top of us.

It was the largest craft I had seen. It must, as I had guessed, have been carved out of a whole tree, and a tall one at that. It had been decked over and a shelter the size of a small house stood on the deck, with a number of shapeless bundles scattered around it. I barely had the time to take all this in before we ran into it with a force that jammed my face into the bows of the canoe.

Out of the darkness, and over the ringing in my ears, I heard someone mumble thickly: 'We've hit!'

All around me were noise and movement: angry male voices and running feet. The canoe seemed to be swaying, although as soon as I tried extracting myself from the narrow space I had been tossed into I realized it was because my head was spinning from the blow it had taken in the collision. The thick mumbling voice had been my own.

I got to my knees, bringing my head level with the side of the canoe just as a sandalled foot landed on it. A moment later the foot took off again, and the canoe gave a sickening lurch as my brother launched himself into the air, screaming like an injured jaguar. As I tried to stand, with Lion's war cry echoing off the trees at the lake's edge, Handy shoved me aside. I heard the slap of his bare foot as he planted it where my brother's had been and then he too hurled himself across the gap between the boats.

'Wait!' It came out as an unintelligible gasp. What were they using for weapons?

Lion and Handy scrambled over the big boat's side. They stood for a moment near one end of the vessel before running towards the shelter in its middle.

By the time I saw the danger it was too late to avert it.

He had been crouching at the far end of the boat, keeping low to avoid being knocked overboard in the collision. To get to him, Lion and Handy would have to dodge around the shelter. Their foe had plenty of time, and took it, unfolding himself from the deck and standing up in lazy slow motion. The blades of his sword glittered faintly in the starlight as he raised it above his head.

With a triumphant cry, Lion leapt towards him, outpacing Handy.

Then the boy struck.

Nimble had been lying by the shelter, indistinguishable from any of the shapeless objects lying around him. As Handy passed him he leapt to his feet, with his paddle in both hands, and swung it at the unsuspecting commoner's head. I heard a soft thump and Handy toppled into the water with a loud splash.

My brother's reaction was eerily fast. He seemed to spin in midair as he turned to face the new threat behind him. Nimble had the paddle raised again. Lion leapt high in the air as he went for the boy, hoping to avoid the improvised weapon, or catch it at the top of its arc before there was any force behind it.

Nimble took a step backwards. He flipped the paddle over and thrust the end of its pole into my brother's stomach.

Lion flew into the pole with his full weight behind him, folded up around it with a loud grunt, and collapsed.

A horrible silence followed.

I stood, leaning heavily on the side of the canoe as I moved cautiously forward. Luminous shapes danced before my eyes in time to the thumping pain in my head. I stared at the strange boat.

Our canoe and the big craft were not quite touching, although they were still close enough that I could have scrambled across the gap between them. There was a sluggish feel to the way the canoe was moving that puzzled me until I noticed that my toes were under water. The impact had split the canoe's timber and it was slowly sinking.

The boy dropped his paddle with a clatter. The man at the other end of the boat lowered his sword and looked across the water at me. He was too far away in the darkness for me to see his face, but by now I did not need to.

I hailed him grimly.

'Shining Light!'

4

This time the merchant did not trouble to disguise his voice. I knew it at once, although it now bore little trace of the affable young man I had first met at the Festival of the Raising of Banners.

'Yaotl! Is that you?'

I did not know what to do. The urge to plunge into the lake was strong, even though I did not know how far away the shore was, but my brother was on the boat in front of me, at his enemy's mercy, and I could not bring myself to abandon him.

'I think you'd better talk to me, Yaotl! I need someone to tell me who I've got here – before I start flaying him. He might have trouble telling me himself, after I've cut his face off!'

He was standing over Lion's body. I did not know whether my brother was conscious or even alive. I was surprised to find that I cared. I might not have done until a few days before, when I had learned that his shame at what happened at Coyoacan equalled mine at being expelled from the Priest House.

Besides, I told myself, if anything happened to him I would only have to explain it to my mother.

'All right!' I told myself the water was too cold to jump into anyway. 'I wouldn't touch him, if I were you. He's not just some commoner who won't be missed.'

'I thought so! The Guardian of the Waterfront!'

'The Guardian of the Waterfront?' Nimble's voice was hushed with amazement. 'You mean, Yaotl's brother?'

'Who else? My mother told you they were at the banquet together!' My anger at the woman revived for telling him so much, for letting this go so far – and for letting herself be so cruelly duped. 'I am having a good night, aren't I? Fancy me bagging the Guardian of the Waterfront himself! The Emperor should give me jewelled sandals and a jade labret for this, don't you think, Nimble?' He laughed, but there was no humour in it, and the boy did not join in.

'What do you want?' I demanded.

'Isn't that obvious? What we want is you! Now get on this boat, before I start skinning your precious brother alive!'

I could probably have got away: the shore could not be that distant, and even if my enemy followed me, there was every chance I could evade him in the darkness. But then, I thought, where would I go? With neither my master nor the Emperor satisfied, the sorcerers unrecovered and the man who had taken them still at large, my brother's body turned into another grisly message to the Chief Minister and Handy probably drowned – who in the entire city would I have left to turn to?

'I'm coming,' I called. 'Just don't touch him, do you hear me?'

I scrambled across the gap between the boats and stood up in the big vessel's stern. Shining Light and Nimble were near the shelter, and I kept as far away from them both as I could.

Neither of them made any effort to move towards me. Several shapeless bundles lay at Shining Light's feet: with a chill I felt even over the cold of the night I realized that they were human bodies and my brother's was among them.

A commotion had started up on the shore. Voices, one of them my master's, called through the darkness, and someone was thrashing about in the undergrowth.

'What have you done with my brother?'

Shining Light looked down, as if noticing one of the heaps at his feet for the first time. I heard a thump as he kicked it casually, and Lion's voice letting out an involuntary groan. 'He seems to be still alive.'

When he stepped over Lion's body I noticed the glint of starlight on obsidian and realized that he was still holding his sword.

'I don't care about your brother. We only have to settle with you, now, and then we can go.'

Then the boy spoke up. He had not moved, and the young merchant had stepped in front of him. 'Shining Light, wait . . .'

'Wait?' Shining Light snapped, barely glancing over his shoulder. 'Wait? What for? You heard enough from Lily, didn't you? What's to wait for? We've no time!'

As he advanced, brandishing the sword in both hands, I tried to recall the warrior training I had had at the Priest House. I remembered how the instructors had coached us in mock fights with cudgels, and sometimes with real weapons that drew real blood. Slash, don't chop. Go for the legs, the arms. Avoid the belly, where a wound may be mortal: we want captives, not corpses. Seize your man by the hair and make him submit . . .

But I had no weapon and this fight was not going to be by the rules.

I stepped backwards.

'Settle with me? I don't understand. What do we have to settle?'

The volume of noise from the shore suddenly increased.

People were crashing and splashing through the reeds as though they were hunting an animal. The man hunting me halted for a moment, as though distracted by the sound, although he kept looking at me.

'You know who I am.'

'Yes, though you had us all fooled for a while. Even when I realized Misty didn't exist, it took me a while to work out it was you. I thought you were my old rival, Telpochtli.'

The young merchant laughed. 'You thought I was Telpochtli? That's funny! I thought my disguise was good, but not that good!'

'I thought you must be Telpochtli, and Nimble must be Telpochtli's son. I couldn't think who else would hate me so much they'd kill to get their hands on me. But then I realized there were all sorts of reasons why you couldn't be anyone else but who you are . . . Why, though, Shining Light? What's this all for?'

The sword's blades glittered as he turned the weapon over in his hands. I longed for him to take his eyes off me, just for an instant. 'It really is funny you thought I was Telpochtli,' he said thoughtfully. 'He died, you know: the Tarascans sacrificed him. Shall I tell you the story?'

'Go on.'

He wanted to draw this out, I realized, to savour his triumph for as long as possible. If I could keep him talking I might get a chance to go for the sword. Or perhaps I could appeal to the boy for help. He hovered uncertainly behind the other man's shoulder, looking as if he wanted to say something but could not find the words.

'There was this girl, Maize Flower – remember her, Yaotl? She, her lover and her unborn child had to leave the city in a hurry. You know why. If they'd stayed, they'd have been killed. They couldn't even stay in the valley. They tried, but there was nowhere safe – nowhere where anybody was prepared to risk making the Aztecs angry by harbouring refugees. So they tried to get out over the mountains. And that's where the girl died. She died in a cave, in childbirth.'

From the shore a furious shout drifted across the water.

Shining Light turned his head towards the sound.

I threw myself forward, crouching to get under the blades of the sword, but my wet feet skidded on the deck and sent me sprawling in front of him.

I lay there, helpless, hearing the weapon whistle as it swung through the air towards me, imagining how the blades would feel as they sliced through skin and flesh and bit deep into my shoulder or my back.

'No!'

Something deflected the sword, turning it over at the last instant so that its flat side slammed between my shoulder blades, knocking the breath out of me and driving my head into the deck so hard that my nose broke.

I heard a heavy blow and a curse just above me. Feet seemed to shuffle and dance on the deck around me. The boy had intervened again.

'No!' he cried. 'No, you mustn't! Don't you realize, he's my . . .'

'Shut up!' the merchant screamed. 'I don't care! I don't want to hear it! Shut up! Shut up!'

The weapon's wooden shaft swept through the air. I managed to twist my head around just in time to see the boy step back. He was too slow: the flat of the sword caught him in the chest and sent him reeling, to trip on one of the bodies on the deck and fall back against the shelter in a sobbing heap.

Shining Light let out a brutal scream. With the sword still raised, he whirled around to face me again. 'Now see what you made me do! I'm going to kill you for that! I'm going to cut your liver out!'

'What for?' I gasped. I was not playing for time now: I wanted to know. 'Why do you hate me so much?'

'Don't you know? Then you'd better listen. Somehow the child lived. Telpochtli had to leave him with some villagers who'd just lost their own boy. He bought him back again, years later, after he'd made a little money, and took him to live with him in Tzintzuntzan.'

Tzintzuntzan was the Tarascan capital. So Kindly had been right about where the bronze knife had come from.

'Of course, Telpochtli had a Flowery Death, eventually. The Tarascans tolerated him for a while, but as an Aztec, settled among our enemies, he was always living on borrowed time.'

'What about the boy?'

'Ah yes, the boy. Maize Flower's son.'

I lay still while he began stroking the back of my neck with the blade of his sword.

'The boy managed to flee. He made his way back to Tenochtitlan. He'd grown into a fine lad by then, strong – built like a ball-player – and handsome, but he was a foreigner with no money. What do you suppose he did for a living, in a city full of procurers and perverts? All he had with him when he came here was a bronze knife he kept as a memento. A pity I couldn't get that back for him, after Constant died.'

Slivers of obsidian pricked the back of my neck, forcing me to press my forehead against the deck until it hurt. I wished I could see the boy, whose sobs had given way to a childish whimpering. If only he would stir himself, I thought, and creep up on his lover with that paddle in his hands.

'So I was right about Nimble,' I said. 'He was Maize Flower's child, after all. And you and he . . .'

'I found him in the marketplace. He was desperate by then. I bought him off his pimp with some of the goods my old witch of a mother thought I was gambling away. She never knew what a good thing I was making out of idiots who thought I would give them better odds than they'd get at the ball court!

'We're good together, Nimble and I. Oh, not just in the way you think. We're a team. I invented Misty because I couldn't go on taking illegal bets in my own name, and then Nimble became Misty's son, and his messenger. He was good at it. He's quick, resourceful, level headed – but, oh, Yaotl! He's so much more than that – he could have been so much more still, if you hadn't blighted his life before it even began!'

'But I didn't . . .'

He raised his voice to call out over his shoulder without taking his eyes off me. 'Why don't you tell Yaotl what happened when your mother died, Nimble?'

For a moment all I could here was the youth's rapid, hoarse breathing. Then his voice came in gasps, as if each word was a struggle to utter. 'It was . . . it was what Telpochtli told me – it was the last thing he told me.' He paused. 'Maize Flower had a fever after I was born. She babbled, nonsense most of the time. But the name she kept saying, over and over again, was yours. Always "Yaotl". Never "Telpochtli". It was your name . . . always your name . . .'

As the boy dried up, the merchant carried on. 'His mother saved her last breath for you, you see, Yaotl. For you, even though you'd abandoned her and left her and Nimble to their fate. And you'd forgotten all about them!'

'I'm sorry.' It was all I could think of.

'If you'd cared,' the boy said dully, 'she might have lived, if she'd thought you cared. She might have fought for her life.'

I experimented with getting up, taking my weight on my palms, only to collapse again as the blades sliced into the back of my neck.

'And what do you want from me now, Nimble?' I asked as calmly as I could. 'Revenge, is that it?'

This was so unfair, I thought. It was not as if I had forced them to leave the city. Would it really have helped if I had gone into exile in place of Telpochtli? How was I to know the silly girl had loved me?

Shining Light interrupted the boy's reply. 'Revenge? For what you did to his mother and to him – for being sold twice, and driven from city to city, and turned into a whore! Wouldn't you want vengeance for that?'

He bent down so that his breath stirred my hair.

'Wouldn't you want revenge?'

Did the youth really want me dead for the sake of what I had said to his mother all those years ago? I forced myself to remember what it had led to: Maize Flower, delirious and dying in a freezing cave, Telpochtli dead and barbarians chewing on his dismembered corpse, Nimble's own squalid life. Had it turned him into a killer?

How many times over did I owe him my life?

'I might want revenge,' I gasped, 'and so might you, but Nimble doesn't! He just wants to talk to me, Shining Light! He wants to know who his father is – me or Telpochtli! That's it, isn't it, lad?'

I felt giddy. It may have been the blood I was losing from the cuts on my neck, or relief that the boy, at least, did not want me dead. Or it may have been the effort it took to voice the suspicion I had kept at bay for so many years: that Maize Flower's child may have been mine after all.

As if from a long way off, I heard Nimble speak. 'Father . . .'

Shining Light howled. 'Don't call him that!' Suddenly the blades stopped pricking my neck as he raised the sword. 'You're mine, don't you get it? This piece of shit is nothing to us. Nothing! And now he's dead!'

'But aren't you listening?' I cried desperately. 'Nimble doesn't want you to do this!'

'Shining Light, please!' the boy pleaded.

'Nimble.' It came out as a long, regretful sigh. 'You're so young. You haven't learned to hate yet, that's all. But I have. You taught me!

'I've heard your tale so many times, and heard you weep as you told it, and listened to you still weeping long into the night afterwards when you thought I was asleep. And I've burned with anger and wanted to flay your father alive for the pain he's caused you. And all you wanted to do was talk to him! Even though I could see it wouldn't do any good, I went along with it – I promised to help you find out the truth. I kept my promise, too – remember when I went to see Yaotl at my own house? But talking doesn't lead anywhere, love. It just hurts and confuses.

'So don't worry about Yaotl, Nimble. You'll get over his death in no time – I'll see to that!'

'Shining Light!'

In my brother's mouth the name sounded like an obscenity.

Lion was on his feet, leaning against the shelter. He lurched forward, seemingly oblivious to the boy just a couple of paces from him as he gave all his attention to the merchant. His voice was thick with pain and contempt.

'They'll burn you alive, you pervert. You're disgusting. You're like those little worms that fall out of our arses. You make me puke. You can't live cleanly and you can't even make money honestly.' Lion was trying to goad Shining Light into making the first move. 'Your sort don't even fight like men!' My brother truly resented being hit with a paddle.

I could not move. I could not see the sword or tell whether it was still poised to lop off my head or anything else. I could see only my brother, still mouthing insults as he staggered towards us and sank to his knees.

'It's no wonder you have to hide on the lake, surrounded by scum. You'd never be allowed in the city.' He was visibly weakening, toppling forward until his hands slapped the wood under him while his voice became a breathless croak. 'The women would sweep a piece of filth like you off the streets before morning . . . Yaotl! Look out!'

Lion shouted the last words.

In an instant he was on one knee and then on his feet. He had slipped his cloak off and held it in both hands, and as he leapt forward he hurled it over Shining Light's sword arm.

I threw myself to one side.

The cloak missed, but as he darted out of its way Shining Light slipped and toppled over me. Obsidian blades buried themselves in the deck beside me with a sound of splintering wood.

Roaring furiously, Shining Light tore the weapon free and jumped up to face my brother. Lion charged him with just his bare hands. The sword became a blur as it sliced the air between them. It carved flesh from both my brother's arms, but the blow was mistimed: Lion was too low and too fast and his wounds were shallow. He did not groan or cry out, but as the sword reached the end of its arc, before

Shining Light had time to react, he straightened up and delivered a kick to the other man's stomach that sent him sprawling onto his back, gasping for breath.

'Got you!' Lion cried joyously as he threw himself on his foe, hands clutching at his hair and twisting it brutally. 'You're mine now! My beloved son!'

'Lion!' I hauled myself to my feet. 'You're not on a battlefield now! Just fucking *kill* the bastard!'

I was too late. Shining Light writhed, twisted, slithered like a live fish out of my brother's grasp and jerked himself free to the sound of his own hair tearing. He ran towards the shelter, screaming for Nimble.

Shining Light still had the sword. As he scrambled away it flailed wildly behind him, missing Lion's face by a finger's breadth. My brother, thrown off balance, took a moment to get after him, and by the time he did, the merchant was on his feet again and facing us.

The boy stood by him, holding the paddle in both hands.

'What now?' I asked.

'The merchant's mine,' said my brother. 'You take the boy. When I say go . . .'

'Wait a moment! They're still armed!'

'Come on, Yaotl! Do what he says!' roared Shining Light. 'Let's finish this now!'

'Stop this!'

Nimble's cry was not loud. It was something between a sob and a muffled scream, a noise of distress and desperation that made the rest of us, all three, pause for an uncertain instant, staring at each other as though we had all seen something so momentous it dwarfed our quarrels.

'I didn't want this,' the boy gasped. 'I didn't ask you to kill those men. I only wanted to talk to Yaotl, to find out how it was.'

'I got you out of the marketplace,' said Shining Light.

'You didn't get me out of the city! You made me run your errands for you, you made me stay on the boat, you wouldn't let me go and see him, you wouldn't . . .'

'He'd have taken you away!' the merchant shouted. 'I'd have lost you! Didn't you want what we had – wasn't that enough?'

Suddenly I saw how it had been with Shining Light: the years of smothering and pampering by Lily, the urge to be free and what had resulted: the lies and the bizarre parody of a household he and the boy had built, here on the lake. Nimble had depended on him utterly, but there had always been a nagging doubt, the fear that someone would rival him for the lad's affections.

When it happened, it made no difference if the rival was the boy's father.

'Put the sword down, Shining Light,' I said gently. 'I'm not the one you should be afraid of.'

His head darted left and right, taking in the boy, my brother and me, before alighting for the last time on Nimble's upturned, troubled face.

'I've lost you, then,' he said desolately.

Nimble stared at the deck. The paddle slipped from his fingers and clattered onto the planks by his feet. 'It can't be like this,' he mumbled.

Shining Light did not speak again. He just raised the sword high over his head and charged.

He ignored my brother. He came for me, his mouth open in a scream of rage and his weapon poised to split my skull. I had no time to move or defend myself. It was Nimble who reacted, throwing himself forward and crashing into Shining Light from behind, knocking him down just as the blades began to fall.

Lion jumped in from the side, hurling himself at the merchant as he stumbled under the youth's attack. My brother made sure of the sword this time, snatching the wooden handle with both hands and twisting it as violently as he had earlier twisted his enemy's hair.

There was the briefest struggle before Shining Light relinquished the weapon. He did not want it. He wanted me. As my brother reeled backwards, caught off guard by the ease with which he had won his prize, Shining Light charged me again, leaving Nimble behind him and slamming his forehead into my freshly broken nose.

I shrieked in pain. With Shining Light's weight upon me I fell with a crash that jarred my backbone. The man's hands were around my throat, throttling me, jerking my head up and down and slamming it against the wood. I felt my feet kicking spasmodically and my hands clutching empty air.

In my brother's hands the sword seemed to move so slowly. As it descended, I saw starlight glance off every sliver of obsidian, from the base to the tip. I saw the last blade flash and go dark like a fire being doused, and heard bone splitting as my brother sank the weapon into Shining Light's skull.

5

Even dead, Shining Light kept up his assault, his head butting me violently as my brother tugged at the sword buried in his skull, before dropping onto my shoulder as if from exhaustion when Lion abandoned the weapon.

My brother turned on Nimble, ready to fight him with his bare hands.

The youth had not moved, and the paddle still lay where he had dropped it. He stared passively at Lion through pale, unblinking eyes.

I could hear my brother's breathing, heavy and rough from the struggle with Shining Light. He was poised in a feline crouch, ready to break Nimble's neck the moment the lad took a step forward, but Nimble just stood there, waiting for him, saying nothing and acting as if he did not really care what Lion did.

Dead men are heavy. I had to fight to get the corpse off my chest, shaking my head to get the blood out of my eyes as I rolled it away from me and stood up next to my brother. My head swam with the pain from my twice-broken nose.

Lion gave me an uncertain glance.

'What now?' he muttered tensely.

I looked at Nimble. 'How's it going to be, then, lad?' I asked quietly.

He said nothing. He kicked listlessly at the paddle, sending it sliding towards me across the spreading slick of blood. I left it.

'Where are the sorcerers?' Lion asked.

Nimble spoke for the first time since his lover had died. 'Here,' he said shortly.

'Here? But . . .'

I looked around me at the shapeless bundles lying on the deck. We were surrounded by corpses. It was the aftermath of a massacre.

My brother turned a full circle as he took in the scene, his head snapping from left to right as he counted the bodies. 'This isn't all of them?' He gave a despairing groan. 'Who did this? When?'

'He did.'

I dropped to my knees beside one of the huddled bodies. I pushed it with the palm of my hand and it turned over, showing flat, pale eyes and white teeth to the stars. It was cold, but not stiff: that had already worn off.

'He's been dead for days,' I said, looking up at Nimble. 'And the others?'

'After you got away from him at his house, Shining Light went mad. He came straight back to the boat and killed them all with the sword.'

'And what were you doing?' snapped my brother.

'Talking to his mother – I was at the ball court, trying to tell Lily her son wouldn't be coming home yet. I didn't know what he was doing. When I got back here he was . . . they were lying here, all around him, and he was sitting in the middle, grinning and covered with blood.' Suddenly his voice broke. 'I swear I didn't want any of this to happen! I only wanted to know . . . I only wanted to know about my father, but once Shining Light started this I couldn't stop it!'

I stood and faced the weeping youth. 'I don't understand why you had to go through all this just to talk to me. You could have seen me at my master's house at any time.'

'Shining Light said I mustn't. You might have told your master, or anyone, and then people would have known about us. If we talked to you, he said, we had to have you in our power. And besides, he — Shining Light — he was enjoying himself! I didn't see it until it was too late, but he enjoyed making a fool of your master. He thought it was funny, when he had the idea of making him send you to watch that peasant die at the Festival of the Raising of Banners, so you'd be implicated in what happened.'

'So Kindly was right,' I said, half to myself. 'He thought his grandson and Misty had dreamed it all up as a joke. Couldn't you have stopped it?'

'I didn't know he was going to do it — I thought at the time he was joking. It wasn't until he saw me afterwards, and made me go to your master and tell him what had happened, that I realized what he'd done.' Nimble groaned, a tormented sound. 'He hurt those men, the sorcerers. He tortured them to make them tell him what they'd told the Emperor, even though they obviously had nothing to tell — you could tell they weren't real sorcerers at all, just peasants who knew a few conjuring tricks. But Shining Light didn't really care — he just wanted to hear them scream.'

'He was your lover,' I said.

'He saved me! He bought me out of the marketplace. He didn't make me go back there! He was kind. Do you know what it's like, never knowing kindness, never being loved for your own sake?' He looked me straight in the eye then. 'I'd no father or mother. I'd been bought and sold so many times, I'd lost count. So much money has been paid for me, but before Shining Light no one ever treated me as if I was worth so much as a cocoa bean.'

'What do you mean, you had no father?' my brother asked harshly. 'What about Telpochtli?'

'Telpochtli wasn't my father.'

'You can't know that!' I cried.

'Yes I can – he and Maize Flower never made love. He wanted to – but he wasn't like you. He couldn't: his vows to the gods stopped him, and he'd mutilated himself too much, offering blood. I know, I saw what he did. They just used to talk, and hold each other. That's all some men want, some of the time,' he added, as one who knew.

'In the end you were the only one she'd give herself to, Yaotl. I'm your son.'

To hear it said was to hear and see so much misery: a woman I barely recalled, dying with my name on her lips; the child we had made, abandoned among savages when his only friend and protector was killed and eaten in the name of foreign gods; the young man passed from one pair of rough filthy hands to another; the mother who could not stop loving her only child, though she knew he was a monster; the madman tormented by a kind of jealousy I could scarcely begin to understand. I put my hands over my ears, then over my eyes, as if they could shut them all out.

I barely heard my brother asking why Telpochtli had treated Nimble as his own.

'For my mother's sake. He was devoted to her. He made a promise, to return me to my father – he made me promise, too.'

And all that misery to be laid at my feet. I could see now why Maize Flower had been wrong, and why the gods were stronger than us, after all. They could see the ends of things. If I had known what it would lead to, I would not have left her. I might have died, but I would not have felt like this.

'Nimble,' I heard myself say huskily, 'I'm sorry.'

'So am I.'

In my arms he was not the muscular youth I had seen on the boat and at the ball court. He was a child, trembling and weeping for everything we had both lost.

'You'll both be more than sorry in a moment,' my brother growled. 'Look over there.'

In the darkness it was hard to see what he was looking at, until a pale flash of spray showed where a paddle had been dipped in the water.

Whoever was wielding the paddle was no boatman, judging by the lack of any rhythm to the splashes. The curses that reached us faintly across the water might have come out of any canoe on the lake, but the voice uttering them was not male.

'Your master and Lily,' said Nimble. 'And she's paddling.'

'Their boatman must have escaped,' my brother said, 'and good luck to him! But even at that pace they'll be here soon.' He looked speculatively at Nimble and then at me. 'So what are we going to do? I have to get you back to Montezuma.'

'You can't!' I cried. 'Montezuma would kill him! He was holding his sorcerers prisoner, remember? And if Montezuma didn't kill him then old Black Feathers would.'

'But . . .'

'And besides, he's your nephew! Remember what Mother said?'

My brother opened his mouth to reply and then shut it again. That was unanswerable. An Aztec would raise his brother's children as his own, if his brother died. His nephew was his own flesh and blood.

He looked across the water again.

'I don't know what to do,' he confessed. 'If we get Nimble back to the Emperor, it will be the end of old Black Feathers, won't it? On the other hand . . .'

'On the other hand, how are you going to do it? Our canoe's sunk and my master's got the only boat – unless you're planning to paddle this enormous thing all the way back to the city!'

'I've got a canoe,' said Nimble. 'It's the one we took you in, when we abducted you.'

My brother stepped over to the side of the boat opposite where we had crashed into it. He looked down into the water for a long moment.

'Take it, then,' he said shortly.

Nimble looked helplessly at me. 'But . . .'

'Yaotl's right,' snapped Lion. 'If you're found, you'll be killed. Get in this canoe and paddle for dear life!'

'I don't want to leave you!' cried the boy.

'I know, son.' I had to force the words out past an obstruction in my throat. 'It's the only way – go on!'

Nimble hesitated. He reached out and touched my arm, and then he did the same to Lion. My brother flinched and said nothing.

The young man gave Shining Light's body one last, lingering glance, and what passed through his mind at that moment I could not begin to guess.

Then he was gone.

'They've stopped,' Lion observed.

The splashing had ceased. I could just make out the vague shapes of Lily and my master in their boat, apparently drifting.

'Can't hear what they're saying . . . What's that?'

To the voices drifting across the lake from the canoe a third had been added. It seemed to come from near by, from the surface of the lake itself. Following it with my eyes I saw, silhouetted against the starlit ripples, a dark round shape: someone's head.

'It's Handy! Lily's stopped to pick him up!'

'I bet your master's happy about that,' Lion said sardonically, 'but it gives us a breathing space. What do we tell them when they get here?'

I thought quickly. 'My master will want to send men out looking for Nimble. They won't begin until the morning, of course, so he'll have a good start on them, but it will be better if we can slow them down by making them think they're looking for two men instead of one. So we tell them this: after knocking Handy in the water, the boy bested you and broke my nose with his paddle. Then Telpochtli killed Shining Light with the sword and they got clean away.'

'You think your master will believe that?'

'Why shouldn't he? The sorcerers are dead. He'll be happy with that – they can't implicate him now, so as far as the Emperor is concerned he's safe. Montezuma won't be pleased, but he'll get the sorcerers back – and a dead sorcerer is much less frightening than a live one, especially a live one who's gone missing. And besides,' I added ruefully, 'I don't want to be the one to have to tell Lily what happened to her boy – do you? Let her go on thinking Telpochtli was here, after all. We can tell her her son tried to do something – he fought, he had a Flowery Death, whatever.'

'It beats me how you knew who he really was. I still thought we were after Telpochtli.'

'So did I, until tonight. But when Handy reminded me about seeing Shining Light in his canoe, I realized that the story of his being held hostage didn't add up.'

'How do you mean?'

'I just remembered what I'd said to Lily earlier – you know, about how nobody had ever set eyes on Misty? Not even my master, who had regular dealings with him. All we knew about him was that he took bets – but never in person, always through the boy – and had some sort of mysterious hold over Shining Light which led to the merchant's moving all his family's stock into his secret warehouse. That never really made sense – but once I thought the warehouse might really be Shining Light's own and he and Telpochtli were the same man I could see there was no mystery at all.

'Then there were other things. My master was amazed when I told him Telpochtli had his sorcerers – because he thought Shining Light had them! We convinced ourselves Shining Light must be acting as Telpochtli's go-between, but in fact my master had been right all along, and the messages he thought were from Shining Light – well, they really were from the merchant.'

I was talking to myself, reproaching myself aloud with all the reasons why I should have worked out the truth days ago. 'I saw Shining Light – in disguise, of course – at the marketplace, on the day I was attacked. I thought it was a coincidence, but it wasn't – he was looking at his own family's feathers, only I didn't realize that until Kindly told me about them at the banquet. Then there's the fact that he killed Constant. It wasn't because the servant was in his way. He could just have pushed him aside, but Constant was the one member of Shining Light's household who had seen him up close in his disguise. Shining Light knew he was probably too short-sighted to see through it, but he wanted to make sure.' I sighed. 'His grandfather told me what he was like. He thought he and Misty had a lot in common. It didn't occur to us that they had everything in common!'

'So you worked out that Shining Light faked his own kidnapping? That's amazing. Mind you,' Lion added, in what for him was a thoughtful tone, 'you were bound to find out who he was eventually – he'd have wanted you to know before he killed you. It's strange – even I never hated you that much!'

'Hate? I don't know, Lion. He might have said it was love. His mother told me once he had so much love in him. Maybe he had too much love for Nimble, maybe that was his trouble.'

My brother gave a noncommittal grunt. 'I'm not sure that's the word I'd use for it.'

The splashing had resumed, in a firm, steady rhythm that told us Handy had taken over the paddle. We both looked at the approaching canoe and its occupants: the sturdy commoner, the vile old man scowling in the stern, and between them the pale face of the woman. She was too far away for me to see her expression, but I could imagine it: the tight-lipped, impassive, distant look she had worn when we had first met.

'He's going to get away with it, isn't he?' My brother had eyes only for my master, and his voice was full of venom.

I did not reply. I was not much interested in the Chief Minister; tomorrow would be a good time to worry about him. It was the woman I was looking at, her pale features exaggerated and made angular by the night's deep shadows, as the boat brought her closer to us. What was going through her mind?

We had each lost a son. Was it worse, I wondered, to bring your child up, nurture him, love him for his faults and virtues and see him dead at your feet, or to find a child you had never known you had, only to lose him again that same night?

I barely noticed the thump as the canoe came to rest against the great boat's side. Handy scrambled aboard with a rope, and he had to greet me twice before I answered him.

All I could see or hear then was my son, out there somewhere, running for his life.

Yaotl's adventures are continued in

SHADOW OF
THE LORDS

Don't miss the enthralling sequel to
DEMON OF THE AIR

To be published by Simon & Schuster
In February 2005

ONE DEATH

1

'Listen!' my brother cried. Mamiztli – 'the Mountain Lion' – was staring across the lake towards the island and city of Mexico. 'Yaotl, what was that noise?'

'Daybreak', I said shortly.

For the first time in an eventful night, I noticed that the water surrounding us was no longer black. The lake's surface had caught the deep blue of an early morning sky. It was going to be a crisp winter's day, hailed by a yellow-white radiance spreading through the thin haze that veiled the eastern horizon. Mist blanketed the mountains surrounding the valley, and swirled around the countless temples in front of them, softening their harsh, angular forms.

Birds twittered and flapped among the sedges at the water's edge, but the sound my brother had drawn my attention to had come from one of the temples, and as we gazed towards its source it came again, drifting lazily towards us over the still water: the call of a trumpet, hailing the dawn.

Another followed it, and soon the air around us was alive with them, both from the city itself and the many little towns behind us on the lake's western shore, until it felt as if the boat we stood on was the only place on Earth where priests were not blowing lustily into conch-shells. It was strange to hear them from a distance, over the water. Perhaps that was why my brother had not recognized their sound. It felt as if they were calling to us alone, instead of proclaiming to the World at large their relief and delight that the Sun had come up one more time, and that today at least he would not desert his people.

For us, every morning was a struggle whose outcome could never be known in advance. Every time the Sun rose, he re-enacted the birth of our War-God, Huitzilopochtli, and his terrible battle with his half-sister, the Moon Goddess Coyolxauhqui, and his half-brothers, the Stars. Like the War-God, the Sun always won, but we could never escape the thought that he might not, and that we owed every day to the favour of the gods.

I shivered, and it was not from the chill of the early morning air. After such a night as had just passed, I could well believe that nothing, not even the Sun's rising in the morning, was certain. I had come out expecting to face an old enemy and found instead my own child, a son I had never known I had, and then watched him slip away and vanish, as fugitive as a fiery spirit on the lake.

As the last of the trumpet calls died away I felt an urge to do something that, in the days when I had been a priest, I had done out of habit: to offer the gods my blood, the nourishment the Sun needed for his day's journey.

Finding a sharp edge was easy. There were several slivers of obsidian scattered around my feet. They had been struck off blades set into the wooden shaft of a sword, at the moment when it had been driven into a man's skull. A weeping woman crouched over his prone body. I stepped delicately around her, avoiding the corpse and the other things – some of them human, none of them alive – that were scattered around it. I stooped to pick up one of the hard, glittering shards with one scrawny hand while the other reached up to my temple to tug a mass of long, tangled hair out of the way. Then I quickly cut into one of my ear-lobes.

With no bowl or paper to collect the blood, I let the warm fluid run down my hollow cheek and the side of my bony jaw, staining and matting the grey-streaked hair that lay over them. I stood and looked towards the city and the glowing sky beyond it and offered up a wordless prayer, remembering how it had once been every morning, the smell of incense and the vain fluttering of the quails we had sacrificed and our voices appealing to the Sun to do his work.

The woman's brittle voice shattered my reverie.

'Haven't you spilled enough blood for one night?'

The woman's name was Oceloxochitl, which meant Tiger Lily. The dead man was her son, a young merchant named Ocotl – the word for a pine torch or, as we thought of it, a Shining Light. A more vicious, treacherous, murderous youth would have been hard to find, although you would not have known it from the way his mother wept over his body, cradling it and shaking it as if to try to wake him up again, while his blood soaked her skirt, blouse and mantle and trickled along her bare arms.

'I didn't kill him, Lily,' I said. 'I told you how it was.' I appealed to my brother. 'Lion, you were here too.'

Lion's name normally suited him. He was a big, muscular man, every inch a warrior, but this morning he looked anything but fierce. He avoided my eyes, fixing his own on the city taking shape in the mist. He scowled. He hated lies and told them badly.

'It all happened like you said, Yaotl,' he said mechanically. 'What do you want me to say? Momaimati here . . .'

'Don't involve me,' growled the fourth person on the boat, a stolid commoner whose name meant One Skilled with His Hands or, in other words, 'Handy'. 'I didn't see anything.'

Which was true, if unhelpful. I looked desperately down at the bereaved mother, wondering what I could say to her now. The anguished face she turned up towards me had had twenty years' worth of lines etched on it in a single night. I had seen it looking very different once, very close and flushed with passion, black hair with its intriguing silver strands flowing from it like a spray of feathers from a fan as I pressed her down on a sleeping-mat. A lot had happened to us both since then, but I could not help wishing for something – some word of comfort, if not from me then from anyone else – that could make a start at smoothing away those lines. I watched as her hand strayed automatically towards the young man's blood-matted hair, before drawing back sharply as it brushed the blades set into the sword's flat shaft. My own fingers twitched in sympathy. I was about to lean forward, to reach out to her, even though I knew I would almost certainly be rebuffed, when another voice made me freeze.

It was the voice of an ancient man, hoarse with exhaustion and strain, but still clear and powerful. My master, Lord Feathered in Black, had not attempted to climb out of the canoe he had arrived in, and was still reclining in its stern, looking up at us as his craft bobbed gently beside the much larger boat I stood on.

'In case you've all forgotten,' he snarled, 'the man and the boy who did all this are still out there.' His glance swept over the carnage on the bigger craft. 'I want them alive and conscious. They're not getting away with what they've done, do you hear? I'll make an example of them. As soon as we get back to the city I'm sending warriors out here to start searching. Handy and Yaotl, you're to wait here, with the boat, until they arrive.'

Handy was a retainer of my master's – not a slave, but a common man who hired himself out by the day. I had no thought for his position now, though. All I could see was what my master was telling me to do. Then I imagined myself in the midst of his hunting party, and pictured its quarry, seeing the terrified, stricken face of a young man whose real identity the Chief Minister could never have guessed at.

'My Lord! I can't! You can't ask me . . .'

For a moment my master was speechless.

'"Can't"?' He was shrill with indignation. 'What do you mean, "can't"? Who are you to tell me what I can and can't do, slave?'

At that sharp reminder of what I was, I recollected myself, feeling like a man running blindly towards a cliff-edge who realizes only just in time what is in front of him.

'I . . . I am sorry, my Lord. I didn't mean to be impertinent. It's just that . . .'

I could not tell him. It would have meant death for me as well, to admit to Lord Feathered In Black, the Cihuacoatl, the Chief Minister, Chief Priest and Chief Justice of the Aztecs, the second-most powerful man in the World, that the boy he blamed for killing Shining Light, and for so many other things besides, was my own son.

I had lied about the night's events, both to Lily, to save her from the truth, and to my master, to save my own skin.

The big boat I was standing on had belonged to Lily's son, Shining Light – the same young man whose corpse she was weeping brokenly over now. He had been a merchant, a

member of the class of long-distance traders known as
Pochteca, who earned their fortunes and renown through
long, often hazardous journeys into distant lands. Shining
Light had found an easier path to riches, however.
Unknown to the rest of his family, he had hoarded their
wealth on this boat and used it to finance an illegal gambling
operation, taking secret bets on the sacred Ball Game.

Deceiving and stealing from his own mother and grandfather had not been Shining Light's only crime. He had
depraved tastes, particularly when it came to boys. Once, in
one of the marketplaces, he had picked up a rootless but
resourceful young man, an orphan named Quimatini, or
'Nimble'. Nimble had no place in Aztec society. He had
sprung from a brief, illicit liaison I had had with a pleasure-
girl. He had been brought up among the Tarascans, beyond
the Mountains to the West, and had drifted back into
Mexico as a youth. Shining Light had adopted him, in his
own perverted fashion, and the lad had posed as his lover's
son while he ran errands and collected bets from his customers.

One of those customers had been my own master, Lord
Feathered in Black. Shining Light had double-crossed him,
though. Many others were caught up in his treachery, and
some of them lay on the boat around us, murdered. My son
had been his unwitting accomplice.

Lord Feathered in Black had finally caught up with
Shining Light and Nimble on the night that had just passed;
but he had not learned the truth about either who they
were or what they had done. My master, my brother,
Shining Light's mother Lily, the commoner Handy and I had
gone in search of them, setting out across the lake in two
canoes. As it happened, the canoe with my master and Lily
in it had been deliberately run ashore by its boatman, who

had panicked and run away, and only Lion and I had confronted the pair. We were the only ones to learn that the man who had betrayed my master was indeed Lily's child, and that the young man he had in his thrall – who was in the end virtually his prisoner – was my own son.

My brother had had to kill Shining Light. We had set Nimble free, and when my master, Lily and Handy finally reached us, we had lied to them. We had let them think Lily's son had been held captive by the man he had pretended to be, and killed by him, and that that man and Nimble had escaped.

They appeared to have believed us; but even so, old Black Feathers was not going to let the matter drop. Nimble and his lover had seen and heard things that could imperil his life if the Emperor learned of them. Moreover, he had been duped. My master's was not a forgiving nature. He wanted revenge.

I was babbling, saying anything that came into my head if I thought it might help persuade Lord Feathered in Black to relent.

'I might let you down. I'm weak, my Lord. I've lost blood, the precious water of life. I might not be able to guide a search party . . .'

My master laughed out loud.

It was a strange noise, a prolonged hoarse cackle, ending in a series of harsh dry coughs. Then he cleared his throat and his ancient face settled into a grin.

'Oh, don't you worry yourself about that, Yaotl. So you might let me down – so what? It'll be so much the worse for you!' He threw a significant glance across the water towards the nearest of the temples. 'Right now you're probably worth more as a sacrifice to the gods than as a slave!'

My heart sank at this further brutal reminder of my position.

'You find the boy and his father,' my master went on relentlessly, 'and no excuses! If you don't, it'll be the worse for you!'

My master had no idea that he was telling me to deliver up my own child, but I knew that if he had known it would have made no difference.

Then Handy spoke up.

'My Lord, I am sorry, but you can't send Yaotl after Telpochtli and the boy.'

I stared at him. Terror made my stomach churn. I wondered what he had really seen and heard. He had been knocked into the water early in the fight with Shining Light, before Lion and I had found out who he and Nimble really were. Surely, I told myself, Handy could not know?

Then the commoner spoke again and, realizing what he meant, it was as much as I could do not to laugh out loud from sheer relief.

'Have you forgotten what day it is?' he went on wretchedly.

Out of the corner of my eye I saw my master's face, the taut muscles and bulging eyes seeming to collapse inward as his expression changed from fury to comical bemusement.

'Yaotl is a slave,' the commoner reminded him. 'He's sacred to Tezcatlipoca. My Lord, this is Tezcatlipoca's name-day. You can't give Yaotl orders today, it would offend the god. We're in the middle of the lake – what if he stirs up a storm?'

I saw my brother start at that, and then squint suspiciously at the sky. He had always been more god-fearing than I was. 'He's right, my Lord.' He looked down at my master, whose eyes had now closed in an expression of resigned exasperation.

'After all, you're in a little open canoe. It wouldn't do to take the risk – not on a day like One Death.'

Of all the gods there was none we Aztecs feared more than Tezcatlipoca. The Mocker, we called him, the Enemy on Both Hands, He Whose Slaves We Are. All those titles suited his character – untrustworthy, whimsical and dangerous. You could feel his influence whenever your affairs depended on chance. The merchant who set out on a long trip with his canoe richly laden with trade goods and ended up on a mountainside with vultures picking at his bones was a victim of Tezcatlipoca's caprice. So was the Lord who sat down in his reserved seat in the front tier overlooking the Ball-Court, with his stake laid out before him, only to watch helplessly while a small rubber ball flew and bounced from one player's hip to another's and reduced him to penury.

I had been no less a victim of the Lord of the Here and Now. Despite being the son of a commoner, from a poor family of farmers and paper-makers from one of the meaner parishes at the southern end of Tenochtitlan, I had found myself among the privileged few allowed to train for the priesthood; but I had ended up as a slave.

For a little boy, who just happened to have been born on an auspicious day, to be thrust into the care of the sinister, black-robed, bloodstained masters of the school we called the House of Tears had hardly felt as if a god were smiling upon him. Twenty years later, though, the man the boy grew into was to feel Tezcatlipoca's malice even more keenly, when for a minor and meaningless offence he was thrown out of the Priest House and trampled into the mud at the lake's edge by the men who had been his friends and colleagues.

My expulsion from the priesthood was only the start of my misfortunes. To the misery of knowing what I had lost –

not just my status as a priest, recognizable at once by my long hair and black face-paint, but also the daily round of penances and observances that had given my life its meaning – was added the ignominy of being picked up and taken home by my family. They had tolerated me, but never let me forget how I had let them down: how I had thrown away a chance my brothers and sisters had never had, not to mention whatever it had cost my father to secure my admittance to the House of Tears.

I had sought refuge from their taunts and reproaches inside a drinking-gourd. I hoped the sour taste of sacred wine would take away the bitterness of my loss. Instead it doubled my humiliation, getting me arrested for the crime of public drunkenness.

I ought to have died then. For priests and nobles, the penalty for being found drunk without lawful excuse was to be cudgelled to death. In some ways the alternative was worse. My life was spared, but all my hair was shaved off, in the plaza in front of the Emperor's palace, before a laughing, jeering crowd. How he wore his hair mattered to an Aztec, whether he had it piled up on his head like a pillar of stone to show he was a successful warrior or left it unkempt, bloody and matted as the mark of a priest. Having your head shaved was like being told you were nobody. It was what we did to a war-captive before sacrificing him, as a sign that, whatever he may have done in life, now he was just a corpse.

I had endured it only because I had known I was going to get blind drunk the moment I was set free.

I had paid for my next gourd full of sacred wine, and many more after that, by selling myself into slavery.

Slavery was not all bad. An Aztec could sell himself to cover his debts or provide for his family when times were hard or, as in my case, to keep himself in drink for a little longer. The deal had to be struck openly, in the market, before four witnesses. Then the law allowed the slave his freedom during the time it took to run through the money he was given, before he had to surrender himself to his master and do his bidding.

After that, his master owned his time but not his life. A slave's property was his own, not his master's. His master had no rights over his family or his children. A slave could not be ill-treated or killed or even sold without good reason — although once he had given his master cause to get rid of him he might well find himself being bought by the priests as a cheap sacrifice.

There were worse fates than slavery that could befall a man, so long as he had no self-respect. A slave could not glorify and enrich himself by going to war and dragging home captives, or pay his debt to his city by giving his labour to some great public work, as it was not his to give. In the eyes of my people, I counted for nothing more than an extension of the Chief Minister's right arm.